MIRRORED
LIFE

MIRRORED LIFE

ANITA BUNKLEY

KENSINGTON PUBLISHING CORP.

http://www.kensingtonbooks.com

DAFINA BOOKS are published by

Kensington Publishing Corp.
850 Third Avenue
New York, NY 10022

All Kensington titles, imprints and distributed lines are available at special quantity discounts for bulk purchases for sales promotion, premiums, fund-raising, educational or institutional use.

Special book excerpts or customized printings can also be created to fit specific needs. For details, write or phone the office of the Kensington Special Sales Manager: Kensington Publishing Corp., 850 Third Avenue, New York, NY 10022, Attn. Special Sales Department. Phone: 1-800-221-2647.

Dafina Books and the Dafina logo Reg. U.S. Pat. & TM Off.

ISBN 0-7582-0078-1

First Hardcover Printing: November 2002
First Trade Paperback Printing: November 2003
10 9 8 7 6 5 4 3 2 1

Printed in the United States of America

With love and gratitude to my husband, Crawford.

$\mathcal{P}rologue$

Bonham County, 1984
Mallard, Texas

The two men dressed in black frightened Sara Jane. Sitting beneath the kitchen table she squeezed her Barbie doll in a tight fist and watched the men's polished black shoes move briskly across the blue carpet, crushing the week-old newspapers scattered on the floor. When the men reached the sofa where her father was sitting, Sara Jane's gaze immediately shifted from their shiny shoes to her father's dirty work boots, caked with bloody sawdust from the floor of his butcher shop, planted squarely on the worn wool carpet as if they actually belonged there.

How dare he wear his dirty work shoes in the house? she fretted, recalling with clarity the many times her mother had reprimanded him for not removing his boots before coming inside. It was one of the few requests that her mother had made of her father that he actually heeded without grumbling under his breath.

But Momma would not say anything to her father today, or ever again for that matter.

Sara Jane pressed her forehead against one of the cool, chrome table legs and studied the shoes of the two men, who began speaking to her father in muted whispers too faint for her to understand. Her father's grunt of a response told the men what she already knew: he was upset and did not want to talk.

When the men turned away from the sofa and headed into the hallway at the back of the house, Sara Jane shut her eyes, praying that the shadows in the passageway would swallow the men, take them away, and return things to the way they had been before her mother got sick.

This morning, Sara Jane had awakened before daybreak and crept into the hallway to listen at her mother's door. Easing it open, she'd found her mother wide awake, her dark brown eyes focused on the ceiling. Her face had been filled with an emptiness that frightened Sara Jane. She'd tiptoed to her mother's bedside, relieved that her father was asleep on the sofa in the living room, and eased down on the white cotton quilt covering her mother's small body. Her mother had glanced over at Sara Jane and smiled, her eyes brightening for a moment.

The clock on her mother's dresser had softly ticked away the hours, accompanied by the occasional bark of a dog behind a fence or the sound of a passing car that always interrupted the quiet of a sleeping neighborhood. Sara Jane had remained at her mother's side, watching the rise and fall of the quilt on her mother's chest, loosely holding her soft, brown hand until sunlight had touched the lace curtains and pushed the shadows from the room. When the gentle movement of the coverlet had grown still and her mother's eyes fluttered shut, Sara Jane had gripped her mother's still-warm fingers and hung on until her father had come in and pulled her away. He'd told her to go sit on the floor under the kitchen table and stay there while he made a phone call. Soon after, the strange men had arrived.

They're taking Momma away, she realized, scooting forward as she craned her neck as far out from under the table as she dared. The bedroom door slammed shut with a sharp crack, sending a mood of finality over the house. The men approached her, carrying a canvas stretcher. Sara Jane rose higher on her knees, trying to see her mother one last time before they took her away. To see if her thick black hair was still spread out about her face like heavy rope that had come undone. To see if her gentle smile remained. To see her small, brown body in her blue and white nightgown. She had to stop the men from doing this awful thing, but she bumped her head on the underside of the table and quickly sat back down, hugging her doll to her chest, one hand over her mouth to keep from crying out.

Slumping back on her heels, she squinted at the beam of late-morning sunlight coming into the room through the still-open door. It cut into the faded carpet like spilled water on a dusty road, puddling in a corner to turn the dull white walls bright yellow. The sight reminded Sara Jane of the rays of light that shined through the stained glass windows at the Mallard Baptist Church, and it gave her a sense of safety that made her feel as if she were sitting in the pew beside her mother once more. Reaching out, Sara Jane wiggled her fingers in the shaft of light, made a fist, and tried to capture the warmth of the memory.

What happens now? she wondered. Would the men put her mother in a big wooden box with a flower and a Bible wedged between her hands and let people file past, looking down, whispering behind their hands? Sara Jane knew what they'd say: *What in the world is Buster Talbot going to do with a daughter to raise alone?* That's what they would say.

Violet Talbot's last words, which had been whispered to Sara Jane between fits of coughing, echoed in her mind. *Be a good girl, mind your father, and study hard in school.*

It was not going to be as easy to do as mother asked. How could she mind a father who rarely spoke to her except to reprimand her for doing something that made him mad? And going to school was not much fun. Facing classmates in cast-off dresses, skirts, and shoes given to her by the churchwomen or purchased at the secondhand store made her feel ashamed. In a small town like Mallard, everybody knew everything, and hand-me-downs were easily recognized.

When the men carrying the sheet-covered stretcher stepped into the living room, Sara Jane decided she could not wait any longer. Defying her father's order to stay put, she jumped up and grabbed the coattail of the man closest to her, balling her tiny fist around the fabric and yanking hard.

"Don't take her away," she said, looking up into dark eyes that suddenly seemed familiar; somber, patient eyes that made Sara Jane feel less empty and small. It was Mr. Porter, she realized, the man her mother called Deacon, the one who wore white gloves and passed the gold plate at church so the people could put their money into it. Deacon smiled a lot and shook everybody's hand. Surely, he'd listen to her.

"Please, don't take Momma," Sara Jane begged.

Mr. Porter signaled for his companion to set the sheet-draped stretcher down, then bent over, his kind eyes narrowing as he drew in a slow, easy breath that made the whiskers on his top lip quiver. "Now, Sara Jane Talbot," he started, casting a quick glance back at her father, who had not moved from the sofa since the men entered the house. "You 'bout eight years old, aren't you?"

"Seven," she corrected, her voice lowered to a whisper.

Mr. Porter rested one hand on top of Sara Jane's head, then swept his fingers along the single twist of braided hair that hung down her back. "All right, then. You're a big girl now." Cupping his fingers beneath her chin, he tilted her round face up and gazed down into her frightened brown eyes, which were quickly filling with tears. "You're big enough to understand what has happened. This man here," he gestured to the other man, "is from Monroe Funeral Home and he's taking your momma to prepare her to meet her maker. He'll do a fine job of it, too. So, you gotta take care of yourself now, and your daddy, too."

"I don't want to take care of Daddy. I want Momma back."

"Your momma's gone to be with the Lord. You gonna be fine, I'm sure." He patted her shoulder, straightened up, and untangled her hand from his coat. Nodding to the other man, he lifted his end of the stretcher and together, they walked out the door.

Sara Jane swung around and frowned at her father, challenging him to get up and say something to stop this horrible thing from happening. But Buster Talbot simply nodded his agreement with what Mr. Porter said, his face as dark and still as the black water that filled the old well behind their house.

Sara Jane bit down on her bottom lip, testing her father's unreadable face, daring him to stop her, then pushed against the torn screen door and went outside. She didn't care if he gave her the worst whipping of her life, if his belt buckle left star-shaped bruises on every part of her body, if he made her sit under the kitchen table for the rest of her life. She was not going to let her mother out of her sight.

On the porch, she watched Mr. Porter and the man from the funeral home slide the stretcher into the back of a big, black car that looked like a station wagon. In a panic, she leaned over the porch railing and squinted up the street, as if looking for help. She scanned the narrow strip of aging asphalt that cut through her neighborhood, crossed the railroad tracks, and continued on toward the outskirts of town. The only person out and about on Pierce Street this morning was Old Mr. Fellnos, gray-haired and bent, walking his slow-moving dog.

She turned her face in the other direction—toward town, to the point where the neat, single-story frame houses that made up her neighborhood ended and the business section began. In the distance, the square windows of the Rayisco Energy Building on Main Street caught and reflected the morning sunlight. Sitting in the heart of the ten-block stretch of offices and retail shops that made up the commercial heart of Mallard, the twenty-one story building was the town's tallest. Sara Jane often rode the elevator to the top, to look out over the rooftops of houses and buildings of her small hometown and trace the path of Interstate 35—the freeway that snaked its way southward through the rural countryside toward Dallas, until it disappeared.

At this end of Pierce Street, the narrow steeple of the Mallard Baptist Church peeped out from beneath its leafy cover of maples and oaks. As she looked at it, Sara Jane knew she'd never go inside again: Her father did not go to church and her mother was now gone. She would never again feel her mother's cool hand holding hers. Never sit impatiently between her mother's knees while having her hair combed and braided. Never hear her mother's voice singing hymns or those strange, yet beautiful, songs she used to sing while washing dishes, weeding the garden, or shelling peas on the back porch. Her mother's voice filled Sara Jane's head, and though she did not know the words to the tunes that were etched deeply inside her heart, she knew she'd never forget them.

The sound of the station wagon's engine turning over startled her. She tensed, her heart sinking. Mr. Porter drove away in a burst of acceleration, leaving her feeling as limp and beat down as the sun-scorched pansies lining the edge of her yard. The big, black car turned left at the corner of Pierce and Ash, then disappeared in a cloud of smoky-white exhaust. Swiping at the tears that wet her cheeks, she turned at the sound of a screen door slamming and looked across the street. Her neighbor, Joyce Ann Keller, who was wearing tight, white shorts and a skimpy halter top that barely hid the swell of her pubescent breasts, had come out of her house and was standing in her yard, staring hard at Sara Jane.

"Hey, Sara Jane," Joyce Ann finally called out, tilting her head to one side, as if trying to determine what to say next.

"Hey," Sara Jane replied, blinking, lowering her chin.

"You cryin'?" Joyce Ann asked, poking out her lower lip as she scrutinized her neighbor.

"No," Sara Jane lied. "I ain't cryin'."

"Good. No need to be a crybaby, you hear?"

Two years older than Sara Jane, Joyce Ann had told Sara Jane many times that she should never let people see her cry. Never. Not even if she got a whipping, if her stomach was hurting real bad, or if the teacher reprimanded her in school. Joyce Ann bragged that she had stopped crying three years ago on the night her mother left her at her grandmother's house and disappeared down the road in the middle of the night. What use was there in crying over things you couldn't change?

Sara Jane liked Joyce Ann well enough, and was glad to have her for a friend, even though she was kind of afraid of her. Not her, so much as her family. Joyce Ann lived with her granny and two uncles, who were always at home when other people were at work. The two men wore dirty, tight jeans and big tee shirts and carried hunting rifles everywhere they went, often firing the guns during the middle of the day while target practicing in the backyard. They liked to thunder up and down Pierce Street in their beat up pick-up truck, and cause a lot of racket, annoying the neighbors. And old Granny wasn't much better. Joyce Ann told Sara Jane that Granny had to be watched like a hawk whenever she went grocery shopping because she'd fill her pocketbook with apples, cheese, packages of donuts, or even cans of soup if she thought no one was looking.

Sheriff Goens pulled his black-and-white patrol car into Joyce Ann's front yard quite often, because of some trouble or other, and when that happened, everyone on the block would come out to watch, crowding the edges of the Keller's yard, gawking and whispering to each other. Sara Jane's father called the Kellers "nothing but trouble," which was probably true, but even so, Sara Jane thought Joyce Ann was wise, smart, and tough. Much braver than Sara Jane would ever be.

"Your momma's dead, isn't she?" Joyce Ann stated in her familiar no-nonsense way.

"Yes," Sara Jane whispered, her voice thick with grief.

"And those men took her away?" Joyce Ann pressed, stretching her long, brown legs over the low hedge at the end of her yard. She stopped at the curb and began kicking at the mound of brown dirt accumulated there, using the toes of her bare feet.

"Yes," Sara Jane managed with a sigh, eyeing her nine-year-old neighbor's exposed midriff, ashy legs, and hair that had been haphazardly pulled back into a bushy ponytail. She wondered how the girl had managed to get past her grandmother looking like that. Sara Jane's mother would never have let her go outside looking as if she'd just jumped out of bed.

"Well, folks die all the time, Sara Jane. You'll get over it."

Sara Jane sucked in a short breath, hurt by that remark. Who was Joyce Ann Keller to tell her how to feel? But instead of taking issue with her neighbor's advice, she nodded, unable to speak.

"You know, my momma's dead, too," Joyce Ann went on. "And you never see me crying."

"That's not true, Joyce Ann. You don't know she's really dead," Sara Jane countered.

"She don't write. Don't call. Might as well be dead."

"But she might come back. It's not the same. Not the same at all."

"Well, to me it is," Joyce Ann decided, waving her hand, as if through with talking about her absent mother. She crossed the street and entered Sara Jane's yard, quickly changing the subject. "I'm goin' up to the Stop & Shop and get a Coke. You wanna come or you gonna stand there and whimper all day?" Joyce Ann folded her arms over her bare stomach, waiting, daring Sara Jane to step off the porch and defy her father.

Quickly, Sara Jane shook her head, no, then backed away, afraid that her father might have already heard her talking to Joyce Ann. She'd tested his patience enough for one day. Better not say any more.

Six months ago when Buster Talbot had first seen Joyce Ann standing in her grandmother's yard, he had gone across the street, exchanged a few curt words with Granny, then stomped back home, forbidding Sara Jane to associate with her new neighbor, refusing to say more than, "That child is gonna turn out to be just like her mother. Trouble. You stay away from her." Even Violet Talbot had nodded in rare agreement with her husband, making Sara Jane think that Joyce Ann Keller must be a very dangerous person. But quickly, Sara Jane disregarded her father's warning, and began walking home from school with her new friend almost every afternoon, usually stopping by the Stop & Shop for a Coke or a Frito pie, looking through magazines talking about nothing in particular. She liked Joyce Ann, who made Sara Jane feel older, wiser, and as if she belonged.

"Come on. You're thirsty, ain't you?" Joyce Ann said. "I got money, see?" She dug into the pocket of her skintight shorts, pulled out two crumpled dollar bills, and held them up.

Though tempted to accept the invitation, Sara Jane stepped back. *Trash is what Daddy calls Joyce Ann,* she recalled, watching as her neighbor waved the dollar bills back and forth. *Motherless, welfare trash, he said. But I don't have a momma now, either. Am I trash, too?* she wondered.

"No. I can't go. Gotta stay here," she replied, wishing she could do anything other than go back inside the empty, silent house.

"Okay. Suit yourself," Joyce Ann said, smiling as she squirmed around to resettle her shorts on her small, round hips. "I'll use your money to buy me a hot dog."

"Who you talking to, Sara Jane?" Buster Talbot's voice boomed through the screen.

Whirling around, Sara Jane swallowed, pressed both lips together, and stared at the door.

"Didn't I tell you not to talk to that gal? You git on back inside, Sara Jane." He came out and gave his daughter a hard look. "And you, Joyce Ann! You git on home, and don't be comin' over here botherin' Sara Jane no more. You a troublemaker, just like your uncles and your momma. I saw it in your momma when she was your age, and I can see it in you from where I stand. My Sara Jane's not fooling around with the likes of you." He held the screen door open, his eyes locked on Joyce Ann, as if he was about to rush down the steps and thrash the girl, who turned and fled up the street without looking back. Scowling, Buster fingered his star-shaped buckle on his belt.

Sara Jane gripped her Barbie doll so hard she felt its tiny neck snap beneath her fingers. A hollow sensation rushed through her and cemented her feet to the porch. If only she had minded him and not gotten out from under the kitchen table without permission! If only she hadn't spoken to Joyce Ann. If only her mother were still alive.

The thought of living with her father's simmering rage and silent, punishing moods without protection from her mother trapped Sara Jane's breath in her chest. There would be no way to escape the sting of his belt or the cut of the buckle, now. Bursting into tears, she ran inside, wishing she could tear off up the road and go after Joyce Ann, grab her by the hand, and keep on walking forever.

Chapter One

They better not leave without me, Sara Jane worried, checking the time on her red Swatch watch—9:45. It had taken forever for her father to leave the house, and she hoped Joyce Ann and Precious were still waiting for her at the Dairy Queen.

After Joyce Ann Keller, Precious Trent was Sara Jane's next best friend. Shortly after Sara Jane's mother died, Edna Trent, accompanied by her daughter, Precious, had fulfilled her charitable duty as wife of the local pastor by calling on the widower Talbot and Sara Jane, bringing them food, clothing, books—things she believed the grieving family might need or appreciate in the absence of a woman in the home. During those visits, Edna Trent had never encouraged her daughter to be more than polite to Sara Jane, and Precious had obliged, remaining aloof and distant toward Sara Jane—until they entered high school. Then her attitude suddenly changed.

A rebellious Precious evolved from a holier-than-thou honor roll student into an outspoken girl who liked dancing, partying, smoking and hanging out with people of her own choosing, instead of the round of devotions, Bible study, and community service that her parents urged her to do. Precious' grades fell; she began sneaking out of the house after curfew, spending time with friends her parents did not approve of, started smoking and dressing entirely in black. This change in behavior had shocked her teachers, disappointed her mother, and infuriated her father, who openly prayed for Precious' salvation in church.

Now, Sara Jane tugged at the front of her black sweater, pulling it down over her stomach. Last year it had fit perfectly, but now it was tight under her arms and rode up above her waistline, irritating Sara Jane. She knew she had been gaining a few pounds over the last few years, but hadn't wanted to face it. When her mother died, her father, who did not know a skillet from a saucepan, had left her to her own devices, letting her eat whatever and whenever she wanted. A diet of McDonald's, Fast-Fry Chicken, Dairy Queen, and Burger Barn specials were catching up with her. She hated to admit it, but most of her meals came in a white paper bag.

Sara Jane sighed in resignation, accepting the fact that she'd never be as slim or petite as her friend Precious, but at fifteen, she had to admit she was much too heavy for her five-foot-six-inch frame.

Stopping at the railroad tracks, she glanced along the dark metal rails and saw the single, bright light of the 9:45 in the distance. Right on time, as always. Quickly, she bolted across the tracks, leaving her side of Mallard, which was populated with small one-story, wood-frame houses, and entered the brightly lit commercial area of town. The train rumbled past, vibrating the ground. Sara Jane folded her arms across her stomach and continued on, thoughts of her mother suddenly coming to her, thoughts about the only train ride they had taken together—to attend a funeral, whose, Sara Jane could not remember. During the trip, her mother had sat close to her, whispering, pointing out sights along the road. The memory was a rare, happy one, a recollection that Sara Jane cherished, because shortly after their return, her mother had fallen ill and never traveled far from home again.

The passing train evolved into a faint thumping sound that echoed back to Sara Jane and stayed with her until she arrived at the Dairy Queen where she saw Precious in the parking lot, smoking a cigarette, pacing back and forth. Fair-skinned, tiny, and dressed totally in black, she placed one hand on her hip, tilted her head to the side, and waited for Sara Jane to cross the asphalt lot.

"What's up?" Sara Jane asked, entering the light from the street lamps illuminating the parking lot.

"Nothin' much," Precious said, tossing her lit cigarette to the pavement. She crushed it under her Nike-clad foot, then shoved both hands into the pockets of her tight jeans. "I was gettin' ready to cut out, girl." She hunched her shoulders against the evening air and turned up the collar of her black leather jacket. "Shit, it's cold out here."

"Yeah," Sara Jane mumbled. "And it's not even October yet." She glanced around. In addition to Joyce Ann's dented blue Honda, there was a souped-up low-rider belonging to Tommy Alvarez and Marcella Jacobs' new Buick parked in the lot.

"Joyce Ann inside?" Sara Jane asked.

"Yeah. I came out to watch for you."

"Sorry I'm late, but you know I'm grounded. Had to wait for my father to leave before I could get out. Let's hope he stays at Pop's 'til it closes." Sara Jane moved past Precious and reached for the door, but before she could touch it, Precious grabbed her by the arm and guided her beneath the dark overhang on the side of the building.

"Be prepared," Precious warned.

"For what?"

"Joyce Ann. She's in a nasty mood. That's why I had to come out here. She's inside talking crazy. Ready to fight."

"Fight who?"

"Marcella Jacobs."

"Why?"

" 'Cause Marcella says her Dairy Queen is now a nonsmoking zone, and Joyce Ann can't smoke in there no more. I told Joyce Ann to come on out here with me, but she said she ain't moving. Told Marcella can't nobody make her leave until she's ready."

"Oh, Lord."

"Yeah, girl. I ain't fighting with her. Not tonight. She bought a six-pack over at Bates' with that fake ID of hers. Drank most of it already."

"Damn. Jim Bates knows Joyce Ann ain't but seventeen."

"Yeah, but he's related by marriage to her grandmomma."

"Whew!" Sara Jane sighed. "She's been pulling some crazy shit lately."

"Right, and I don't need the hassle." Precious walked away from Sara Jane, head lowered, eyes downcast. She circled the street lamp and studied the ground, her small shadow spreading like a black spot of oil that had been spilled onto the asphalt. "You know, I've got a bad feeling, Sara Jane. It's fun hanging out with you guys, especially since Joyce Ann got that raggedy Honda. You know, cruising and drinking a few beers, driving around is fun, but I ain't looking to get in real trouble. Joyce Ann's got something else on her mind. Tonight she was downright mean."

Sara Jane nodded. "Yeah, I've noticed."

Precious exhaled, clearly relieved to hear that Sara Jane was worried, too.

"Joyce Ann's pressing her luck," Sara Jane went on, thinking about the incident last Tuesday night.

She had been sitting with Joyce Ann, their backs against the hedges at the edge of her yard, when Joyce Ann had suddenly started crying. Embarrassed to see her friend's tough-girl image crumbling, Sara Jane had been confused and timidly put her arm around Joyce Ann's shoulder, hoping to comfort her. But Joyce Ann had jerked away, then slapped at Sara Jane, yelling at her to go away and leave her alone. Sara Jane refused to leave. Finally, Joyce Ann confessed what was wrong: her mother had really died. A mugger on a dark street in some city far away had killed her, and because Joyce Ann's grandmother could not afford a funeral, Joyce Ann didn't even know what had happened to her poor mother's body. She made Sara Jane promise never to tell a soul about it, especially the part about seeing her cry.

"Maybe her grandmother is on her case about her grades," Sara Jane hedged, not about to betray Joyce Ann's trust. "She did fail algebra for the second time."

"Yeah," Precious conceded. "Come on. Let's go inside. It's too damn cold to stay out here any longer."

Inside the brightly lit store, Sara Jane waved at Joyce Ann, who was wearing a blue denim jacket with a matching denim cap pulled low on her forehead over her shoulder-length braids. She was sitting with her back to the smudged, mirrored wall at the rear of the room.

"What's up?" Joyce Ann tossed out, squinting as she flicked her lighter and lit a slim, filter-tipped cigarette.

"Not much," Sara Jane replied, plopping down in the booth with her friend.

Joyce Ann shook the green and white pack of Newports at Sara Jane, who grinned, took one and stuck it to her lips, then leaned across the table for a light.

"Thanks," Sara Jane said, inhaling deeply, ignoring the warning glance Precious threw at her. If Joyce Ann could smoke in the Dairy Queen, she could, too. But as she nonchalantly blew a ragged smoke ring into the air, she saw Marcella Jacobs approaching from the corner of her eye.

The following Friday night, Sara Jane found herself, once again, at the Mallard Dairy Queen, but this time she was sitting inside Joyce Ann's car and not in one of the red vinyl booths. The street lamps created a wash of yellow light that hung like a halo over the lone car parked in front of the strip shopping center, and as Sara Jane waited for Joyce Ann and Precious to come out, she gingerly touched her right earlobe.

Damn, it hurts, she thought, tracing her index finger over the third piercing in her ear. It was swollen, hot, and sore. Frowning, she pulled her hair back over her ear, praying the puncture would heal soon. If the infection got any worse, she'd have to go to the doctor, and he would tell her father, who would have a fit. There was no money to pay for a doctor, let alone a prescription for an antibiotic, and Sara Jane didn't want to hear her father's "I told you not to mess up your ears with all those holes," again. She'd just have to use hydrogen peroxide a while longer.

Shifting in her seat, Sara Jane put her face close to the window and scanned the interior of the store. What was taking so long to get a few cones and a sundae? She eyed the clock on the dashboard. Midnight. An hour past her curfew.

Last Friday night she had taken the same chance but had come home to find her father sitting in his recliner, leather belt in his hand, waiting. He had slapped the belt against his leg, called her a disrespectful liar, and had ordered her into her room. He threw the phone against the wall and raised his arm, belt in hand. Sara Jane had snatched the belt from him, daring him to hit her, and when he glared and left, she had collapsed in relief. He would never hit her again, she knew, and the shift of power between them had alarmed her as much as it had frightened him, leaving both of them unsure of what would happen next.

After Violet Talbot's funeral, Sara Jane had stopped talking to her father, torturing him with her silent presence. The more she withdrew, the moodier he became, often yanking off his belt to threaten her simply for what he called "her damned accusing stare." And as time passed, they had grown even more estranged until now they were simply sharing space under the same roof, barely communicating, like two prisoners doing time. When and how would it end? Sara Jane wondered, unable to visualize her future.

Buster Talbot was a big man with muscled arms and hands strengthened by twenty years of handling frozen carcasses of pork and beef, and he could be as mean as a recently branded bull when he was angry, crossed, or drunk. But tonight, Sara Jane didn't fear him. She was tired of tiptoeing around his moods, of listening to his lectures about staying away from Joyce Ann Keller, of his reprimands for mentioning her mother's name.

The flickering taillights of a slow-moving car pulled Sara Jane's thoughts from her father. She watched as the car passed the barbershop; Alfreda's Cafe; the Exxon gas station; and the Mallard Motel, which sat dark and small beneath a canopy of huge live oaks. The car came to a halt at the intersection of Main and Thornton, despite the fact that the stoplight had been out of service since the big storm that tore down from Oklahoma three weeks ago. Tonight, the light swayed dark and sightless over the street, like a head silenced by a hangman.

A dead traffic light didn't matter much to the folks in Mallard, who knew where to stop out of habit. No one sped through town anyway, preferring to drive real slow so they could wave at their neighbors, crane their necks to see who was going into or coming out of whose house, and pull over to chat on the side of the street. Sometimes fast-moving motorists coming off of Interstate 35 violated Mallard's business district's forty-five-miles-per-hour speed limit, but old Sheriff Goens, who was pushing ninety, was rarely around to witness the infraction, let alone write up a ticket.

The car turned a corner and disappeared. Sara Jane rolled down the passenger side window and resumed her vigil. Inside the store, stiff cardboard cutouts of strawberry sundaes, chocolate cones, and frothy banana splits swayed in the breeze from the whirling ceiling fans. All of the tufted red booths were empty and no one was sitting at the long counter that ran the length of the store.

Where the devil are they? Sara Jane wondered, hoping Marcella Jacobs wasn't giving them a lot of mouth. Last Friday the prim and proper manager had put all three of them out of the store before they could order anything to eat because Joyce Ann and Sara Jane had dared to light up and pollute her air. The fast-talking redhead had been furious. Her son, Bruno (six feet six and as wide as the commercial freezer in the back of the store), had escorted the girls out of the store and watched them until they drove away.

Joyce Ann better not do anything stupid, Sara Jane prayed, finally catching a glimpse of her friends as they made their way toward the front of the store. Marcella was walking in front of them and she looked stiff and angry—really pissed off. Her white powdered face was as tight as the skirt of her DQ uniform and when she got to the cash register, she stalked around the counter, her lips turned down in defiance. She put her hands on her hips, as if daring Joyce Ann to say something.

The old goat's still mad about last week, Sara Jane thought, grinning as she pressed her chest against the doorframe and propped her arms in the open window. She was tempted to get out and go inside so she could hear what was going down, but knew better than to go against Joyce Ann's order to stay in the car and wait. Getting out would make Joyce Ann mad, and Sara Jane didn't want to spoil the evening by doing anything to anger Joyce Ann, who had been downright civil to her all week.

The fragility of their bond kept Sara Jane on edge, but she needed Joyce Ann's friendship too much to jeopardize the relationship. Their friendship had been forged at a time when Sara Jane had been lost, lonely, and desperate for someone to talk to. Joyce Ann had been in a bad place, too, though she'd been too proud to admit it. Now, she was dealing with the fact that her mother was really dead, and her tough-girl act was threatening to dissolve. For years Joyce Ann had bragged that she didn't need anyone—not a mother or a father to make it—she could take care of herself. And now that she was totally alone, the reality had hit her hard. And for Sara Jane, having a friend her father disapproved of was an easy way to get back at him for the remote way he treated her.

Inside the Dairy Queen, Joyce Ann was slowly backing up, taking long steps to put space between herself and the cluttered countertop. Sara Jane frowned, puzzled, then gasped when Marcella screamed.

Joyce Ann screamed something back.

Precious cautiously edged toward the door, giving the angry women wide berth.

Sara Jane yanked on the door handle, jumped out, and raced across the street. She *had* to see what was going down. Joyce Ann and Marcella were cussing each other out. It was one of those crazy confrontations that they'd laugh about for weeks, like the time they rolled Mr. Seager's yard with toilet paper because he shouted at them when they cut across his perfect lawn on their way to school. Sara Jane grinned her excitement. Joyce Ann sure was putting Marcella in her place.

She put one hand on the door, ready to enter, then stopped, her grin dissolving into surprise when Joyce Ann yanked something small and black from the pocket of her blue denim jacket. Sara Jane flinched, then squinted, horrified. It was a gun, and Joyce Ann was pointing it at Marcella. It was the gun Joyce Ann had bragged about being able to get because she knew the combination of the safe where her uncle kept it. Sara Jane had seen it once: the day they skipped class and went to Joyce Ann's room to drink beer and play video games on her new TV. She had refused Joyce Ann's invitation to touch the gun, and had not liked the casual way her friend had handled it.

Sara Jane watched, terrified, as Joyce Ann waved the gun in front of Marcella, who suddenly turned and tried to run. But Joyce Ann stopped her, shoved the gun up under Marcella's flabby chin, and prodding her flesh with the snub-nosed revolver, forced the frightened woman to open the cash drawer and stuff the contents into a white paper bag.

Sara Jane felt every muscle in her body become as rigid as the cardboard cutouts of frothy desserts that were mounted on the counter. She silently counted to ten, forcing her heartbeat to slow, willing her hands to stop shaking, more amazed than frightened by what she was witnessing.

Should I break and run? Get back in the car? Go in and try to stop this? Confused, she began jumping up and down, making whimpering sounds, frantic over what to do. She glanced up and down the street. No one was around! This was unbelievable! Joyce Ann was actually robbing the Dairy Queen.

It would not have surprised her if Joyce Ann and Precious had trashed the store, thrown paper napkins around, smeared whipped cream on the windows, or scrawled nasty messages in bright red lipstick on the ladies room mirror; stuff they had done before. But this was *armed robbery*. Serious shit. And here she was standing on the sidewalk, watching. Waiting for the robbers to come out.

Chapter Two

A thrill of nervous energy shot through Sara Jane and riveted her to the sidewalk. She was not about to turn tail and run out on the most excitement she had ever experienced during her fifteen years of life. She could envision the headlines of the Mallard Mirror, the weekly that was thrown on everybody's lawn: LOCAL TEEN ROBS MALLARD DAIRY QUEEN. Maybe they'd put Joyce Ann's picture in the paper, too, Sara Jane thought, just as a Marcella cried out and raced toward the back of the store. Joyce Ann's arm shot up and the gun went off—two times—the loud *pop pop* ripping the eerie silence. To Sara Jane it sounded like the firecrackers the kids in the neighborhood set off on the Fourth of July.

She slapped a hand over her mouth, horrified. What in the world was Joyce Ann doing? She was only supposed to scare Marcella, make her sorry for being so nasty. Not kill her!

God, this is goin' down hard. Sara Jane groaned, unable to take her eyes off the scene that was playing out inside the store. Joyce Ann, still holding the gun, reached over the counter, grabbed another stiff paper bag, then shrieked at Precious to hold it open while she stuffed more money into it.

The terror that gripped Sara Jane started deep in her stomach, flashed quickly into her head, and made her dizzy. The three Bud Lights she had gulped while cruising away the dull Friday night churned her stomach, threatening to rush up and spill out onto the sidewalk. She drew in a long breath. She had to get a grip, do something to help her friends.

Whirling around, she raced back to the car, jumped into the front seat, slid behind the steering wheel and groped for the ignition, her fingers shaking so badly she had to sweep them along the steering column twice before she closed in on the heart-shaped key ring.

Oh, God. Her luck had finally run out. She should have known, sooner or later, that breaking curfew, skipping class, drinking beer, stealing those bras from Wal-Mart, all of this craziness would catch up with her. But she never dreamed she'd be involved in armed robbery! Frantically, she turned the key, tensing when the engine came alive and the car began to idle.

At fifteen, she had a Texas learner's permit, but had never driven a stick shift in her life. Too late to worry about that now, she told herself, pressing down on the clutch as she pushed the gear shift around until it ground its way into first. Sara Jane gripped the wheel, poised for action: the first real action in her dull, uneventful life.

When the front passenger door burst open and Joyce Ann flung herself down onto the seat, the car rocked back and forth, tilting so far to the left Sara Jane feared it might flip over.

"Drive!" Joyce Ann ordered, slamming the car door. Bending double, she put her head between her knees and shoved the money-filled bags under the seat.

Sara Jane froze.

"What's wrong with you? Sara Jane! Get the hell out of here!"

"Where to?" Sara Jane screamed, lifting her foot off the clutch as the car lurched away from the curb, unaware that she was leaving Precious behind.

"Who the hell cares?" Joyce Ann cursed. "Just get the fuck outta here. Fast."

The sound of a ringing alarm burst from the Dairy Queen, filling the street and Sara Jane's head. She jerked the gearshift into second and stepped on the gas.

"Stop. Wait for Precious," Joyce Ann shouted, reaching around to open the back door for the girl who was running alongside the car.

Sara Jane slammed on the brakes, forgetting to push in the clutch, and the Honda shuddered and died.

"Damn!" Precious said, diving into the backseat, screaming. "What the fuck you guys doing? Leavin' me hangin' out here. Shit. This ain't funny. I think Marcella's dead." Precious slumped to the floor, shoved her head between her raised knees, and started crying, her wails ricocheting off roof of the car.

"Shut up, Precious," Joyce Ann ordered, looking into the backseat. "Marcella ain't dead. This little ol' twenty-two can't do more than put a little hole in somebody. I aimed for her legs. She'll be all right."

Sara Jane got the car restarted. Concentrating, she stepped on the clutch, pressed the accelerator down hard, and sped off, shocking herself with the sound of screaming tires, which did not drown out the sobs coming from Precious or the boom of Joyce Ann's triumphant laughter as she jostled around in the front seat.

"You weak-ass divas didn't think I'd do it, did you?" Joyce Ann shouted.

Sara Jane and Precious were silent.

"I told you Marcella was gonna pay for the sorry way she treated us. I ain't sure," Joyce Ann went on, "but I'd bet there's a thousand dollars in those bags. Not bad, huh? Shit. I guess that bitch won't mess with us anymore. Huh?" Joyce Ann got up on her knees, looked over the back of her seat, and stared down at the huddled shape on the floor. "Girl, get up from there. Ain't nobody following us. We're home free."

Slowly, Precious inched her head off her knees, her body off the floor, and scooted into a corner of the backseat, pulling her feet up under her hips. "Nobody's comin'?" she whimpered, glancing out the back window.

"Naw," Joyce Ann replied. "You see anybody 'round here? Sheriff Goens ain't even in town. Heard he went over to Corsicana to bury his brother. Whew! Ninety-six, he was. Them Goens live forever."

Sara Jane chewed on her lip as she sped down Main Street, thinking Joyce Ann had better be right. She could not get caught. Marcella could tell the cops that Precious and Joyce Ann were in her store, but Sara Jane Talbot was not in there. Her daddy might actually beat her to death rather than let her go to jail. She glanced nervously into her rearview mirror as she turned onto Pierce Street and flew past her house, moving so fast she could not tell if any lights were on or not. *If he's sitting there holding that belt, waiting for me to come home, he's got a hell of a long wait,* she decided. After what happened tonight, she might never be able to go home again.

At the four-way stop at Pierce and Ash, Sara Jane screeched to a halt, throwing Joyce Ann against the dashboard, then sat there, breathing hard, looking from left to right.

"Which way? Joyce Ann! I'm coming up on 35. Which way?" Though nervous, she was suddenly charged with a great sense of energy, and driving fast made her feel liberated, powerful, and in control—for the first time in her life.

"South!" Joyce Ann decided. "Let's go to Big D and have us some fun."

With a sharp jerk, Sara Jane swung the wheel to the right and burst onto the feeder road, entering the sparse flow of late-night traffic on the interstate at eighty miles per hour.

"All right!" she yelled, relieved to see the stretch of smooth, well-lit highway unwinding in front of her, the dim lights of Mallard receding in the mirror. She had made it out of town without getting caught, and as far as she was concerned would make it to Dallas, too, where they could hang out for a long time without anyone knowing they were there.

"You're doing great, Sara Jane," Joyce Ann remarked, popping open a can of beer, which she pulled from the six-pack on the floor. She took a long gulp, then belched. "Damn, girl. I didn't even know you could drive a stick shift."

"I can't," Sara Jane laughed, loving the way the lines in the road rolled past in an unbroken ribbon of yellow. She felt brave, proud of herself for having had enough presence of mind to get behind the wheel and take charge. If only she could feel this way at home, when her father started in on her for some infraction of his ever-changing rules. Or at school when the teachers singled her out and made her feel dumb because she did not understand the question. As long as Sara Jane could remember, someone was always embarrassing her, reprimanding her for speaking her mind, scolding her for not doing better, or berating her for no good reason, making her feel as if she were nothing. The only people who had ever made Sara Jane Talbot feel alive, strong, and smart were Joyce Ann Keller and Precious Trent.

A tractor-trailer thundered past, creating a whoosh of air in its wake, but Sara Jane didn't panic. She held the car steady, like a seasoned driver, even adjusting the rearview mirror with one hand while she managed to stay in her lane.

A green metal road sign slipped past. DALLAS 56 MILES. Sara Jane relaxed and settled in for the drive. She was doing just fine. What she wanted to do was drive past Dallas, completely out of Texas, and on to some place far away. Maybe California so she could put a great deal of distance between herself and her run-down house in Mallard, a father who lived for his next drink, and a school where she had never fit in. Maybe she could find a place where no one would look at her in pity or make her feel as if she did not belong.

The tires hummed and the Honda ate up the miles. Joyce Ann rocked to the music blaring from the tape while Precious sniffled miserably into her hands. Joyce Ann ripped off the blue baseball cap she had pulled down over her mass of thick braids, jammed another cassette into the tape player, then turned the volume up and began singing. Sara Jane joined in, nodding her head to the beat, driving so fast she couldn't feel her foot on the accelerator. When she swung around an eighteen-wheeler and cut in front of a moving van, she did not feel her hands on the steering wheel, numbed by the thrill of her own reckless adventure, infused with the sensation of being beyond her father's reach at last.

What *would* he do when he found out what happened at the Dairy Queen? she wondered. Sara Jane wasn't stupid. She was in deep shit and there was no turning back, so she might as well play the scene out to the finish—like Ali McGraw had done with Steve McQueen in the movie *The Getaway*.

Well, I won't miss Mallard or anybody in it, Sara Jane thought. *My father ought to be grateful that I've simplified his life by leaving. Now, he won't have me around to remind him of Momma. He can devote all of his attention to his drinking buddies at Pop's and the bottle of bourbon on the kitchen table.*

"All right!" Joyce Ann called out, startling Sara Jane back to the moment. "Only thirty-six miles to Big D!"

Sara Jane released the steering wheel long enough to slap palms with Joyce Ann in a loud high-five, clearing her mind of Mallard, her father, and the loneliness that had moved into her heart the day her mother died. From this moment on she would lead an exciting, glamorous, fast-paced life filled with adventure and beautiful people. It would happen for her. It simply had to.

Inside the dark car, Sara Jane hummed under her breath, comforted by the sound of the wheels spinning against the hard, flat road, the music coming from the tape player, and the sense of security that came from being alone with her two friends. This was the kind of peace she had never felt, this sense of acceptance and respect and power.

But, fifteen miles north of Dallas, red and blue lights suddenly flashed into her rearview mirror, forcing Sara Jane to face the reality of the mess she was in.

"Shit! The cops!" Joyce Ann spat out. Leaning down, she shoved her empty beer can under the seat, then pulled out the bags of money. "Here! You take it, Sara Jane." She thrust the bags into Sara Jane's lap. "Put it under your seat. You ain't but fifteen. They won't do nothing but call your daddy to come get you. I'll be eighteen next month, and I can't do that kind of time."

"Are you crazy? No!" Sara Jane flailed her hands at Joyce Ann as she tried to shove the money back and hold the steering wheel steady. One of the bags ripped open and a rain of crumpled bills scattered to the floor. "What's wrong with you?" Sara Jane screamed. "I didn't have anything to do with this robbery." The fact that Joyce Ann wanted her to take the blame hurt Sara Jane more than the prospect of going to jail. How could she turn on her like this? Wasn't she her friend? Furious, she shifted into second gear and began to slow down.

But Joyce Ann whipped out her gun and pressed it against Sara Jane's right shoulder. "Don't you dare stop this car!" she yelled, grasping at the money on the floor with her free hand, trying to stuff the bills back under the seat. "Keep driving, you weak-ass bitch. You wanted everybody to think you were so tough. You been hanging around me, trying to be like me since the day we met, and now that I need you, you wimp out. Well, you ain't about shit. If you were a friend, you'd listen to me and hold the cash. You won't do any jail time! I know about these things!"

"Shut up," Precious yelled. "Shut the fuck up. This is *your* mess, Joyce Ann. You ain't nobody's friend."

"We Kellers know how to be tough," Joyce Ann tossed back. "If you can't take the heat, Miss Priss, you should have stayed home with your preacher daddy instead of acting like you were so ready to hang." She pressed the gun harder against Sara Jane's side. "Drive! We can outrun 'em. I am not going to jail!"

Without argument, Sara Jane shifted into third, pressed down on the gas pedal and forced the Honda back up to full speed, moving so fast the road became a dark tunnel with no one in it but her. She focused on the blurry yellow lines, the wedge of light created by her headlights, the feel of her nails cutting into the hard vinyl surface of the steering wheel.

"Oh, God, they're on top of us. We can't get away!" Precious yelled, jerking around to look out the back window. Three additional squad cars had joined in the chase, and all of them were rapidly closing in.

"You've got to pull over, Sara Jane," Precious screamed. "Put that gun away, Joyce Ann. If they see it, they'll start shooting at us."

"I don't think so," Joyce Ann snapped.

Suddenly, the prospect of being riddled with bullets, her body parts splashed all over Interstate 35 hit Sara Jane, who knew her short-lived thrill was over. She shifted the car into second and began to slow down. "Okay, okay! I'm stopping," Sara Jane shouted, sagging in relief.

"Oh, no you're not. It's not so easy, " Joyce Ann snarled, furious that Sara Jane dared give up. She removed the gun from Sara Jane's side, jammed it into her belt, then stretched her left foot over the console and smashed it down hard on top of Sara Jane's, flattening the gas pedal, propelling the car forward like a racecar on the track.

"Stop it, Joyce Ann. Let Sara Jane stop the car," Precious pleaded, groping over the front seat to grab a handful of Joyce Ann's braided hair and yank hard. "Get your big-ass foot off the gas and let Sara Jane stop the car. It's over."

But Joyce Ann refused to budge, forcing the car to zoom to the left side of the road, where it crashed into the cement divider, flipped over, righted itself, then spun away.

"Oh, shit!" Sara Jane shrieked, letting go of the wheel to put her hands over her eyes. She waited for a crash, an explosion, a fire. "Oh, God, what's happening?" she moaned, hunching down as the car slid across all four lanes, scraped the median on the opposite side of the road, then jolted to a stop. Sara Jane's head slammed against the dash. The smell of hot rubber and blood rushed into her nose, forcing her to tears.

Tugging at her seat belt, she struggled to get free. "I gotta get out. Let me out! I can't breathe."

"Damn!" Joyce Ann growled, raising her head. "You really trashed my car."

"You shut the fuck up," Precious shouted, reaching over to ease Sara Jane's head around toward her. "Girl . . . you're bleeding. Your head is busted open!"

Sara Jane raised herself up with arms so weak and trembling they felt numb. She peered into the rearview mirror, more horrified by the flood of spinning lights in the street and the crowd of police cars behind her than the blood that was running down her chin. She touched her bleeding lip, then ran a finger over her front teeth, realizing one of them was cracked in half. Wincing, she sank down, prepared to face the consequences of this terrible, humiliating experience.

The officer tapped on the window. A surge of fear shot through her, bringing a bitter taste into her mouth. *What happens now?* she wondered. *Will he handcuff me? Haul me off to jail? Lock me up where no one will ever find me?*

The fear that gripped Sara Jane as she rolled down the window and stared into the officer's unreadable face wasn't the kind of fear she had felt when brashly handing a forged note to the principal, or while sneaking in after curfew, praying her father was not at home. It was the kind of paralyzing fear she had felt when her mother drew her last breath, sank down into her pillow, and closed her eyes forever. At that moment Sara Jane had been unable to think, talk, or feel. She had only been seven years old then, but now, eight years later, she felt it again: the terror of being absolutely alone.

Chapter Three

Warden Andrews, the man who ran the Cave—as the women incarcerated at Gatesview Correctional Facility for Women (GCFW) called the three-story brick building where they were housed—motioned for Sara Jane to sit down. He was a solid, imposing man, with flecks of gray in his wiry, brown hair and a pallid complexion. In the stark, white light beaming down from the mesh-covered fluorescent lamps in the ceiling, he resembled a giant cement block with a jumble of wires sticking out of his head. He had the bulky appearance of a retired pugilist, but none of the rough-guy character. In fact Warden Andrews was an even-tempered man who controlled the prison with razor-sharp zeal, walking its maze of cement floors, inspecting the cubicles behind the iron bars, and making himself known to everyone inside its dark gray walls. He took a great deal of interest in his inmates, as well as pride in the fact that, once released, few who did time under his watch ever returned to the Cave.

Today, he folded his arms on top of his desk and cleared his throat. "You've done well, Sara Jane. Stayed out of trouble, followed the rules and got yourself out early. We could have held you here for a while, until you turned twenty-one, but the Board of Juvenile Pardons and Paroles feels the five years you have been here are enough to teach you about staying out of trouble."

"Yes, they have," Sara Jane quickly agreed, eyes wide with expectation and relief.

"You have been officially released," the warden stated without any display of emotion. He pulled several sheets of paper from a folder on his desk. "This is your certificate of discharge. Read it. Then sign this form to collect any personal belongings that were taken from you on the day of your arrest." He leaned back in his chair and waited.

Sara Jane's hands shook as she accepted the document issued by the Texas Department of Criminal Justice. *This nightmare is almost over,* she thought. She'd done the time, kept out of trouble, and now she was on her way out. She skimmed the lines on the documents, took the pen the warden handed to her, and signed the form.

"Thank you," the warden said, taking the papers from her.

Sara Jane went limp, her shoulders curving forward in relief as she drew in a deep breath, wrinkling her nose at the familiar smells of Pine Sol and humanity that clung to the walls, oozed from the floors, and lingered in every corner of the crowded, outdated facility.

Running a hand over her closely cropped brown hair, she studied the paper in her hand, the significance of the moment sinking in. Yes, doing time had changed her, mentally, emotionally, and physically. When she entered prison she'd been rebellious, overweight, and consumed with anger at her mother for dying, at her father for withdrawing emotionally when she needed him most, and at herself for not fitting in. Now, at twenty, she was thirty pounds slimmer, a great deal wiser, and much less concerned with winning anyone's approval. Five years was a long time to hold on to anger, so she had let it go. But she could never forget the fact that Joyce Ann had tried to make her take the fall and even lied in court when she told the judge that Sara Jane had been involved in planning the Dairy Queen robbery. *Why?* she still wondered. *Why did Joyce Ann turn against me?*

"And here is your State of Texas Cosmetology License, Sara Jane," Warden Andrews said, interrupting her thoughts. "I hope you use it to make sure I never see your face in here again."

Sara Jane gingerly took the document, both amazed and proud to see her name above the title, Licensed Cosmetologist, typed in faint small letters on the certificate. In her mind's eye she could envision the permit framed and hanging at her workstation, and the prospect of being out in the world earning money, doing work that she enjoyed, was as exciting as it was frightening.

"Sara Jane," the warden continued. "You have a good shot at turning yourself around. Do it. If you don't take advantage of what you've learned in here, you will be back. It's your choice. You're free, think about what that really means."

Slipping down in the green vinyl chair, she rubbed her thumb and index fingers together, thinking about the loneliness, humiliation, anger, and depression she had endured. The price she had paid for that ill-fated joy ride with her friends had been too high to ever think of messing up again. Doing time had taught her how to rein in her temper, control her impulsiveness, and steer clear of anything that smelled remotely of trouble.

Tears pricked Sara Jane's eyes, and she took another deep breath, holding it tight in her lungs until the threat of breaking down eased. She thought about Precious—frail, little Precious—already released to her parents' custody. Pastor Trent had hired a top-notch lawyer to get his daughter's sentence reduced after she had been injured in an assault by three women on her cellblock. The attack had damaged Precious' spine, leaving her disabled and confined to a wheelchair, making her dependent on her parents once more.

What a waste, Sara Jane thought, remembering how animated and energetic Precious had been. Their youthful rebellion had certainly left its mark. However, Joyce Ann, convicted of first degree manslaughter, had seventeen more years to serve.

I will walk out of here dry-eyed and clear-headed, Sara Jane silently vowed, sucking back her fright. *I've shed enough tears over this sorry chapter in my life. I've got to start over, move on.*

When the warden launched into his standard prerelease pep talk, which he must have given hundreds of times, Sara Jane nodded absently, barely listening to what he was saying. Yes, she would keep away from known felons, drugs, alcohol, and firearms. Yes, she would avoid any situation that might be connected to criminal activity. She would find a job as soon as possible and get on with her life.

"Remember, you are not a bad person, Sara Jane," Warden Andrews said. "You made bad decisions. If you've learned anything from your mistakes, I hope you have learned that you *can* change. Become a new person when you leave here. Do something useful with the rest of your life, and put the past behind you."

An unexpected sense of gratitude came to Sara Jane, and for a moment she was unable to reply. Warden Andrews seemed to genuinely care about what happened to her and expected her to make it on the outside. His tone and his message were suddenly very comforting.

"Thank you, Warden. I won't let you down," she finally managed. "Things are going to be a whole lot different now. I promise, you'll never lay eyes on my face again."

"I hope not," the warden stated, closing her folder. "Do you plan to return to Mallard?"

Sliding her palms along the arms of the chair, she examined her freshly clipped nails. "I'm going home to tell my father good-bye, then I think I'll leave Mallard for good."

"Where do you plan to live?"

"I don't know," she whispered. She had not thought that far ahead, but knew it would be impossible to create the life she envisioned for herself if she returned to Mallard. That chapter of her life was finished and there was nothing for her at home.

Her father had come to the jail on the second night of her arrest, but only to tell her he'd predicted all along that she would get herself in just such a mess. He had refused to pay for an attorney, leaving her fate to a court-appointed lawyer. A good lawyer might have gotten her off on probation. A loving father would have tried to make that happen for his daughter, but Buster Talbot had done nothing, and after her sentencing, he had only phoned one time. They had had little to say to each other, and after a strained attempt to communicate, she had hung up the phone. It had been her final contact with him.

Staring out the window, she looked into the empty exercise yard where water from last night's rainstorm had collected in pools on the grassy areas. She thought of all the days she had spent out there, walking in circles, thinking about the close-knit community of Mallard and how impossible it would be to go back after what she had done.

Now, she wondered if her father even knew she was being released today. Precious had written to her a few months ago that she had seen him in the drug store, but he had not spoken to her when she greeted him. He had pushed past her in a huff, as if in a hurry to get someplace.

"There's a voluntary halfway house in Dallas that might be a good place for a girl like you," the warden was saying as he reached into a drawer and took out a single sheet of paper. "It's called Havensway. It's small. You can come and go as you please, and it's a place to stay while you get your bearings." He scribbled a few lines on the bottom of the page and handed it to Sara Jane. "Nina Richards, the director, can be very helpful during this transition. Why don't you check to see if she has a vacancy?"

Sara Jane nodded, took the paper, and glanced down at the words of reference the warden had jotted on the page. "Thank you."

"Well, good luck," the warden said, extending a hand.

Sara Jane shook it, held it for a moment, then said good-bye. As she walked away from the warden's office, she was startled by her reluctance to leave the smelly, crowded place that had been her home for five years. Would it be difficult to adjust to life without the routine and order that had shaped her days and nights for so long? Had living under the watchful eye of guards, counselors, block captains, and supervisors stripped away her confidence? But the freedom she had craved for five long years was finally here and she could not be afraid.

But she was tired. Tired of wondering how her life might have turned out if her mother had lived. Tired of imagining how different her childhood might have been with a loving, attentive father. And tired of wondering where she might be today if she had never defied her father and befriended Joyce Ann Keller on the day her mother died.

The bus driver put down her clipboard and assessed her passengers in a visual sweep that indicated she had made this run many times before.

"Once this bus pulls out of Gatesview, no standing up or walking around. Make sure you can see me and I can see you in the rearview mirror at all times. No talking. No smoking. No trouble. Got it?" She let her eyes drift slowly over her charges, as if memorizing each face, then sat down, released the brake, and pulled the doors shut in a thud.

The air conditioner whirred, giving off a blast of cold air that made Sara Jane shiver, even though it was a humid day in mid-July, creating a sheen of white vapor on the bus windows. Clearing a circle with her thumb, she kept her eyes on the third window from the left on the second floor—her home for five long years—until the fenced complex of Gatesview faded in the distance.

The bus zoomed along, its bright headlights penetrating the early morning mist that curled in gray wisps above the slick, black asphalt. It passed cornfields, ranch-style houses with curtains in the windows, and long stretches of thick, green pines that crowded both sides of the road. Winding westward, the bus moved like an earthworm burrowing its way through tall, wet grass.

Settling back in her seat, Sara Jane tugged at the short sleeves of her flimsy white tee shirt with the GCFW logo on the front, hating the fact that she was starting her new life wearing state-issued clothing. She looked around, envious of the women who were dressed in new sweatshirts, blouses, and sporty pullovers, given to them by mothers, fathers, husbands, boyfriends, sisters, or even caring members of a church. No one had come to visit Sara Jane Talbot, carrying a shopping bag filled with new clothes, makeup, or shoes. No one had come to the visitors' room to talk with her, hold her hand, wish her good luck today. No one, save Warden Andrews, had cared what happened next, but she'd be damned if she would feel sorry for herself. At least she was free and had earned a ticket to stay out of trouble and get on with her life.

Sara Jane's classes in cosmetology had excited and challenged her in a way high school never had. At Mallard High she used to watch the clock, count down the minutes, and pray for the dismissal bell to ring. At the Cave, she had actually looked forward to classes, eager to learn new techniques, willing to prove to herself and her instructor that she could do the work. And now that she had the credentials, she wanted to work hard at learning the business and focus on owning her own beauty salon.

Reaching into the brown duffel bag provided by the prison, she pulled out a mirror and examined her face. She was thinner, and that was good, but her light brown complexion was dull and her short prison haircut did nothing to flatter her appearance. She'd let her hair grow out, she decided. Maybe add some streaks, and get to work on bringing life back to her complexion. With some decent makeup, new clothes, and a new attitude, she'd be fine.

Sara Jane put the mirror back into her bag, removed a coffee-stained, dog-eared copy of *Black Hair Today*, and flipped the pages until she came to a two-page spread featuring a sleek chrome and glass salon that had just opened in Denver: *The Diva's Den*. Gleaming with shiny Lucite counters, marble floors, and crystal chandeliers hanging above each station, it was not like any salon Sara Jane had ever seen. The owner, Carmela Strong, was a striking woman with dark brown skin and eyes that sparkled with pride. Sara Jane felt as if the woman was looking straight at her, challenging her to take the first step into the world of beauty and illusion she wanted so much to be a part of.

I will have it one day, she vowed, tilting back her head, closing her eyes. For all of the hardship and sorrow she had suffered in her young life, she had to admit that her stint behind bars may have been the best thing that ever happened to her; a blessing that had set her on a path that would finally get her out of Mallard, out of poverty, and away from a father who did not understand her need for independence and respect. Never again would she allow herself to feel rejected, impoverished, or humiliated. Never.

Sara Jane pulled her arms through her flimsy tee shirt and wrapped them around her body, vowing to throw the shirt and everything she owned with the Gatesview Correctional Facility for Women logo on it into the trash as soon as she could. Her days of wearing cheap tee shirts and faded jeans were over.

Chapter Four

No place in the world smelled like Mallard on a Thursday in July, when trash cans lined both sides of the street and roses bloomed in every front yard. The town smelled like soggy paper bags, rose perfume, and freshly cut grass, and Sara Jane had to admit, it smelled like home.

She dodged a sweaty little boy on a skateboard who zoomed past, and instead of yelling at him for forcing her off the sidewalk, as she once would have done, she just shook her head and continued on.

Leaving the bus station, heading toward her house, she noticed that little had changed. The Rayisco Building still anchored the business district to the center of town, and cars crowded the limited parking spaces along Main Street. The sign outside the Pizza Hut was still missing two letters, and even the peeling paint on the two-story house that was really a second-hand store, still hung on in desperation.

She headed directly into the resale shop and quickly scanned the racks in the ladies' section, settling on a nearly new blue linen blouse for three-ninety-nine, a pair of beige khakis for five dollars, and a pair of tan leather loafers for six. She also bought a small Samsonite suitcase for four dollars, leaving her thirty-one dollars and one cent from the fifty dollars given to her by the Prison Release Fund on her departure.

After making her purchases, she went into the dressing room, put on her new shoes and clothing, and tossed her state-issued tee shirt, jeans, and tennis shoes into the trash can.

On her way out of the store, she passed a woman holding a little girl by the hand. She nodded politely to the woman in a neighborly, Mallard way, then continued on. But half a block away, she stopped on the sidewalk, turned around, went back to the resale shop, and looked into the window. The woman had deposited the little girl on a chair and was standing in front of a rack of clothing facing the window.

That's Mrs. Rhodes, Sara Jane confirmed. *The guidance counselor at Mallard High, and she did not recognize me.* Turning away, Sara Jane shook her head, recalling the numerous conversations, consultations, and unhappy sessions she had had with the woman while in school. *Good,* Sara Jane thought, continuing on. *The Dairy Queen robbery and Marcella Jacob's murder are probably still hot topics in Mallard and the last thing I want to do is explain my role in that mess.* She pulled back her shoulders and hurried on toward Pierce Street, to the wood-frame bungalow sitting beneath a shady pin oak.

The house might have been called pretty at one time—if not pretty, at least neat and serviceable—like the other well-built, but small houses on her street. Now, it looked sad and empty, as if whoever lived there had stopped paying any attention to the place. Forlorn and neglected, it waited in dreary silence, a chain-link fence now separating it from the street.

Sara Jane studied the uneven places in the wooden porch, the screen door, and the thin coat of white paint her father, she supposed, had slathered over a scrawl of bold, black graffiti. When she was living at home, no one would have dared do that to her house. She was friends with Joyce Ann Keller, whose uncles were feared in the neighborhood.

The rush of memories that came over her as she ascended the steps sent her mind reeling back to the night when she sped past the house on her way to the interstate. Joyce Ann screaming. Precious crying. The car lurching every time she changed gears. It seemed so long ago.

She placed the Samsonite suitcase on the porch, then opened her duffel bag and took out a manila envelope with the letters GCFW stamped on it. She shook the contents into her hand. A heart on a chain, two plastic hair clips, four tarnished silver earrings, and a key fell out. In the bright sunlight, she stared at the items that had been locked away during her incarceration at the Cave. The necklace had turned brown with rust, one of the hair clips was cracked, and the earrings were missing their backs. She placed the key in her mouth while she dumped the other items back into her bag, and with her shaking fingers, stuck the key in the lock. *I'm twenty years old. Not a little girl. He can't order me around and scare me anymore.*

The key turned easily and the door opened quietly. She stepped inside and stood in the entry, gripping the doorknob, assessing the room.

What she saw was her insurance against ever giving up on her dream of making something of her life. It was the fuel she needed to leave Mallard, her past, and her father forever.

The television was on, the shades were drawn, and the house smelled like the inside of a closet that had been shut for months. Sara Jane closed the door, went to the TV and turned it off. Her father must be at work, she decided, because he always left the television on when he left, convinced that the sound of voices inside the house would deter potential burglars, though Sara Jane could never understand why he thought a burglar would target their home. Everyone in Mallard knew that Buster Talbot did not own anything of value.

The empty welcome had a hollow familiarity that made her sad, bringing back the feelings she had felt during days and nights alone in the house. She glanced into the kitchen. A bottle of bourbon was sitting on the kitchen table and the sink was full of dirty dishes. She wondered how long it had been since anyone other than her father had been inside the house.

At her father's bedroom, she knocked out of respect, and waited a few seconds before touching the doorknob. It felt cool against her fingers, and turning it, she eased the door open. As she had hoped, no one was there.

Sara Jane entered the room, thinking, remembering, suddenly missing her mother's calm presence. She touched the carved leaves that decorated the walnut headboard of the bed where her mother died, ran a finger over the old cotton quilt, then went to the tall chest of drawers to stare at the faded pen and ink drawing of a wildflower that had always hung there. Set in a simple wooden frame, it had been on the wall above the chest for as long as she could remember, and she smiled to see, in the corner of the drawing, her mother's childlike signature: *Violet Talbot*. Sara Jane could remember her mother sitting at the kitchen table, drawing pictures like this one in a grade-school notebook. She had always leaned very close to the paper, concentrating on every line and curve, never talking, totally engrossed in her work. Sara Jane recalled that her mother had never sketched while her father was at home and had never framed any but this one, a delicate sketch of a plant with spiked leaves, a slender stalk topped with tiny star-shaped flowers with a tough, barklike bulb at the base. The sketch was yellow and brittle with age.

Impulsively, Sara Jane removed the picture from the wall, leaving a clean, white spot where it had hung and sat down in the wicker chair beside the bed to study it. She began rocking back and forth, looking at the drawing, imagining her mother sitting at the kitchen table while she drew it, stealing a moment of pleasure from her never-ending chores.

The other drawings must still be here, Sara Jane thought, getting up to open the closet. Inside she found a box of papers and books, and sitting on the floor, she began rummaging around, opening old folders, envelopes, and boxes until she pulled the frayed school notebook from beneath a stack of old Ebony magazines.

Sara Jane slowly turned the pages, amazed at the exquisite details of the various plants and flowers. Her eyes began to water. Death had come to Violet Talbot on a hot summer day like this, softening the furrow between her brows, replacing the grimace of pain that had wrinkled her smooth red-brown skin with a peaceful expression. Her long, black hair, which she had always worn braided and coiled at the back of her head had been loose and soft that day, spread out over her pillow. Her mother had had what her friends would have called "good hair" back then, nearly straight and fine, not at all like Sara Jane's which was mouse brown and coarse. Sara Jane would never forget that morning when Mr. Porter had taken her mother away, when even in death, she had been beautiful, her youth restored at the end.

If only she had lived long enough for me to really know her, Sara Jane thought, realizing that her childhood memories of Violet Talbot were quickly fading away. She knew her mother had been a quiet woman, devoted to her family, and preferred to stay to herself. Sara Jane could not remember neighbors dropping by, and other than church suppers and Sunday services, Violet had done little socializing. She also knew her mother had married a man her family hadn't approved of and the marriage had cut her off from relatives in Oklahoma. She had given birth to Sara Jane, her only child, at the age of thirty, and had learned to accept her husband's sullen, stormy nature, accepting the fact that he talked very little, drank too much, and kept her isolated from her family. Life with Buster Talbot must have been a routine of getting by, making ends meet, and meals eaten in silence, but Sara Jane could not recall her mother ever complaining, not even at the end.

If only he had taken her to a hospital. He should have insisted, if not for himself, for my sake. But he let Momma die. When she was too sick and in too much pain to talk, he should have seen how desperately she wanted to live. But he gave up. Sara Jane could still remember the words of Dr. Lewis when he told her father that treatment that might stall the growth of his wife's tumor was available at the hospital in Denton. But Buster had simply shaken his head, no. He'd treat her as best he could. Strange white men would never cut on his wife. Then he sat down in the very chair Sara Jane was sitting in now, to rock in silence and wait for the end.

The screen door slammed. Startled, Sara Jane jumped up from the floor, dropping the framed pen and ink drawing, shattering bits of glass all over the floor. Quickly, she bent down to clean it up just as a shadow fell across the open doorway. Sara Jane raised her head, coming face to face with Buster Talbot's suspicious, bloodshot eyes.

Without speaking, she calmly tossed the broken picture frame and glass into the wastebasket, then stuck the drawing between the pages of the notebook, having already decided she was taking it with her. Holding the notebook to her chest, she watched her father, who did not seem happy to see her digging around in his bedroom closet.

He hasn't changed that much, she noticed. A little fleshier, a little grayer, and a little slower to move, but otherwise he looked the same.

"What's this about?" He wiped both hands on the front of his bloodstained butcher's apron and frowned, pulling the ruddy brown skin of his forehead into three deep lines.

She tapped the notebook with her palm. "I'd like to have these drawings. They were mother's," she said, doubting he had ever known they existed.

He shrugged. "If that's what you want."

"It is." She didn't know what else to say.

Buster took a step closer. "Pop Smith called me on the job. Said he saw you walking down Main Street. What you doin' here?"

"You didn't get a letter from the warden? I assumed you, as my next of kin, had been notified about my release." She sat again and resumed rocking back and forth, determined not to allow the encounter, which she had both anticipated and dreaded, shake her. A part of her was angry, a part of her was sad, but mostly she was filled with an empty restlessness that made her want to bolt the room, run out of the house, and get on the first bus headed out of town.

"I didn't get no letter."

"Well, it doesn't matter. I'm out."

"So I see," Buster Talbot grunted, then groped his way into the room where his wife had died thirteen years earlier. Standing in front of the chest of drawers where his wife had kept her things, he squinted down at Sara Jane. "Well I hope you learned a lesson or two about the kinds of friends to choose from now on."

She pressed her spine into the hard frame of the chair, pulling courage from the stiff wicker flush against her back. "I did," she admitted. "I learned an awful lot in prison."

"Well, Sara Jane, now that you done finally learned how to listen to your father, you come crawling home." Buster pushed thick brown fingers into the tufts of hair at the sides of his head, giving her a look that, in the past, would have made Sara Jane tremble. "Maybe now you see why I laid the belt on your butt when you were sassing me and running wild. I tried to teach you, but no, you had to go and get yourself arrested and thrown in prison before you learned."

Sara Jane knew he was gearing up for a full-blown argument, and she was not about to be baited. He was glad to have someone to bully again. Lifting her chin, she pinned him with a stare that forced him back two steps.

"I haven't come home," she corrected firmly. "I've come for my things." She got up then, and moving closer, let him see that she was going to hold her ground. Nothing could erase the mistakes of her past, but he had not won and she would not be a part of his future. Breathing hard, she looked defiantly at him. "I'll never live here again."

"Where you gonna live?" Buster Talbot stuttered. "Huh? How you gonna manage?"

"Don't worry, I can take care of myself now." Pushing past him, Sara Jane crossed the hall and entered her old bedroom. Everything remained pretty much as it had been the night she slipped out to meet Precious and Joyce Ann at the Dairy Queen. A thick layer of dust covered every surface, but many of her things were still in there, even her old blue terry-cloth robe with the spray of Texas bluebonnets on the back, which was lying in a corner, covered with dust. He had probably not set foot inside her room since the day she left.

Buster stood in the doorway, watching.

"Surely, you don't care what happens to me, do you?" Sara Jane said, opening a drawer to take out a sweater and two belts she thought might be useful. She tossed them on the bed. "Aren't you glad I won't be around to get in your way, give you more worry? You don't have to pretend that you care or worry about neighbors calling the police because I yelled too loud while you beat the crap out of me. Aren't you glad I'm all grown up now, Dad?" She reached behind the bed to raise the water-stained window shade. It flapped loudly when it sprang up, letting a bolt of sunlight into the room.

Now she could see him more clearly and the sight brought on a flood of memories she had worked very hard to forget. How many times had he come raging into this very room, blind with drink, to punish her for playing her radio too loud, for staying on the phone too long, for wearing lipstick and eye shadow to school? She opened a drawer, took out a photo of her mother that had been taken on the front porch, and holding it facing her father, calmly said, "She loved me. Momma loved me just as I was, but you couldn't. And she's gone because you let her die."

Buster Talbot quietly studied his daughter.

Sara Jane stuck the photo into her bag.

"Well, well. That's what you think? You're talking real smart, Sara Jane," Buster finally replied. "Guess time sitting around in jail yakking with other troublemakers done rubbed off on you. Better watch your mouth, girl. I'm still your daddy, and this is my house."

Sara Jane stiffened, the familiar phrase taking her back to the times had he said that to her, over and over, to the slap, slap, slap of his belt. "I'm still your daddy," he used to tell her. "This is my house! You do as I say." Overcome with emotion, she sat down on the edge of the bed, determined to maintain control. She did not want to say anything she could not live with once she walked away. Enough angry words had passed between them. What use was there in adding more?

"Yeah, Dad. It's your house," she agreed, clasping her hands in her lap. "And I won't interfere. I plan to leave as fast as I can." Getting up she continued packing, finding a pair of flat shoes, a denim jacket studded with rhinestones that had turned dark with age, a red blouse and matching skirt, and a loose fitting shirtdress she estimated might be useful. She had thirty-one dollars and one cent to her name, and she'd have to make do with whatever she could lay her hands on. For now.

"Ah, well, I suspect you'll get in trouble again soon enough," Buster taunted, hiking up his pants. "You'll be running with a wild bunch again. You're just as hardheaded and sassy as ever."

Sara Jane crammed her finds into the Samsonite suitcase, including the notebook of her mother's sketches, then left the room, her father close behind. At the front door she stopped to give the place a final look, knowing she would never be back. Her anger had dissolved into pity, and as she watched her father pick up the bottle of bourbon off the kitchen table, turn his back to her, and pour a large splash of whiskey into a coffee mug, she wanted to cry.

He drained it quickly, then asked without facing her, "Where you going?"

"Dallas," Sara Jane replied, shouldering the brown duffel bag, gripping the Samsonite suitcase. "I've got to catch the bus."

Buster turned then, and with one hand on the kitchen table and the other beneath his bristly chin, stared glumly at his daughter. "You made it real hard for me to raise you, but I did the best I could. Wasn't easy without your mother."

Sara Jane swallowed her disappointment. Why hadn't he spoken to her like this when she was living here, trying to get his attention, unable to understand why he didn't talk to her? But would she have listened? she wondered, her bitterness toward her father moving further from the surface.

"Maybe it wasn't easy," she admitted, "but I wish you had tried harder. And I wish I could forget all the pain we caused each other, but I can't. And that's why I've got to go."

Chapter Five

Light seeping through the slits in the mini-blind created smoky yellow stripes on the carpet. Hearing footsteps outside on the walkway, Precious Trent rolled her wheelchair to the window, separated the slats, and looked into the street, absently twirling a strand of hair between her fingers as she tried to see who was approaching her house.

Why, it's Sara Jane Talbot! she realized, impressed by her friend's svelte new appearance. She let the mini-blind slats snap back into place and stuck both hands into the pockets of her pink terry-cloth robe, thinking. Inviting Sara Jane in would violate her parole, but Precious knew she was not about to turn away the only person she really wanted to see, the only person who might understand what she was feeling now.

Quickly, Precious wheeled to the full-length mirror hanging on the back of her closet door, smoothed her hair away from her face and hurriedly banded it into a short ponytail. Then, she straightened the collar of her robe, tightened the belt, and took a deep breath, not very happy with the image in the mirror. She'd always taken pride in her appearance, been careful about what she ate, and worried about gaining weight, but confinement to a wheelchair had taken its toll and she'd put on too many extra pounds. Now she felt like she was looking at a stranger.

Upon her release from the hospital after the attack, Precious' doctor had started her on a tough regime of physical therapy in an attempt to help her regain some use of her legs. She'd begun her treatment with great enthusiasm, but after a few months with little progress, she'd become discouraged and abandoned the grueling routine. Her return to Mallard had been bittersweet, though she was grateful for the early release her father had arranged by dipping into his retirement fund to pay for a top-notch attorney.

At first, she had been sullen and resentful about returning to her old room, embarrassed to be living at home like a child again. She snapped at her parents and avoided the members of the church who dropped by to visit, refusing to believe that any of them actually prayed for her salvation, loved her, or had forgiven her adolescent transgressions. When former classmates came by to see her, she'd engage in polite small talk, strategically avoiding any reference to her plans now that she was back in Mallard. The lopsided conversations were uncomfortable and embarrassing, instilling a sense of guilt and failure in Precious, who resented her parents' fussing over her and their attempts to make her believe that life would simply return to the way it had been before the "incident" changed everything.

What she needed was someone to talk to who could relate to the loneliness that gripped her, the regret that filled her, and her need to create an independent life on the outside. Because of the conditions of her release, she had not called Sara Jane, but now she needed to talk to her friend and was willing to take the chance.

Precious unlocked the door and pulled it open as soon as the doorbell chimed.

"Hello, Precious," Sara Jane said, shifting her duffel bag onto her other shoulder.

"God! Sara Jane, it's good to see you," Precious said, smiling.

"You, too," Sara Jane said quietly, stepping into the entryway. "It's over and I'm finally out."

"When I saw you coming up the walk, I was so glad, but I couldn't believe it. You're here!" Precious extended her arms, and Sara Jane leaned down to hug her friend hard, breaking her promise to Warden Andrews to stay away from convicted felons. She laughed, then stepped back. "Girl, I couldn't leave Mallard without telling you good-bye."

Precious checked out the bags Sara Jane had set down in the hallway, then nodded. "Where're you going?"

"A halfway house in Dallas called Havensway. Warden Andrews recommended it. Just until I get a job and my own place."

"That'll work," Precious said, wheeling toward the kitchen. With her back to Sara Jane, she continued talking. "Hell, it's great to see you, girl. Come on in. Nobody's here. We can talk for a few minutes."

"I was hoping you'd be alone. Been a long time since we talked without a guard staring us down."

"Yeah, crazy Reggy's gone." Precious glanced over her shoulder, burst into laughter, and waved a hand as Sara Jane, laughing too, followed her into the kitchen.

"Right," Sara Jane agreed, "along with all those other crazies. Whew! What a nightmare." Sara Jane sat down at the table, then assumed a more serious tone. "How are you doing? Really?"

Precious sighed, her shoulders slumping forward. "Well, some days are better than others, that's for sure. Today, as you can see, I'm being lazy." She groped at the collar of her robe and pulled it closer to her neck, sensing Sara Jane's surprise at the way she looked. "Girl, some days I don't even bother to get dressed," she tried to laugh it off. "What for? I don't have a job to go to, you know?"

"What do you do all day?" Sara Jane wanted to know.

"Oh, I work on some church records for my dad, do some of the mail, make calls. Things like that."

"From here?"

"Yeah. I don't like to go out too much. And I really don't need the whispers and stares, you know? So, I stay around here, thank you very much. My computer is great company." Precious wheeled to the counter, picked up two mugs and set them on the table, giving Sara Jane a nod of approval. "You look good, girl. All thin. Like a model or something." She nodded again, more slowly. "Boy, things have changed, haven't they?"

"Yes, they have," Sara Jane replied. "You know, after your accident, I never got to talk to you. I wanted to call, but knew I couldn't. I'm just sorry it happened to you, Precious. . . ."

"Instead of Joyce Ann?" Precious interrupted, trying to make a joke.

"No," Sara Jane went on. "That's not what I meant. I'm sorry about . . . about everything."

"About the robbery?" Precious finished. "That we let Joyce Ann fool us into thinking she was our friend? That Marcella Jacobs is dead? That we got caught? That I'm in a wheelchair now?" Precious shook her head. "Sara Jane." Her voice fell to a whisper. "There's too damn much to be sorry about to even begin, so let's not go there, okay?" She studied her hands, trying to keep her mind from wheeling back over the past five years, as it would if she didn't force her thoughts into another direction.

"Okay," Sara Jane replied. "I know we were all in it together, but for you to be here . . . like this."

"Well, where else should I be?" Precious whispered. "Isn't this what I deserve?"

In the silence that followed, she wanted to tell Sara Jane how mis-

erable she was, how fragile and vulnerable she felt, but knew she had
to keep the conversation light, too afraid of going into that dark,
painful place where she hid her fear and guilt. Swiveling her chair, she
reached for a plate of coffeecake. "Hope you didn't get so used to
prison food you can't eat my momma's pecan rolls." She set the rolls
on the table, smiling.

"Girl, don't even start," Sara Jane said, pretending to gag. "I will
never eat oatmeal, hamburger, or Jell-O again. Never."

"You got that right," Precious nodded as she picked up the
coffeepot and began to fill the two mugs.

"When did you get out?"

"This morning."

"What about Joyce Ann?"

"Still there. In and out of trouble. Got sent to isolation, last I heard."

"Not surprised," Precious said, her tone hardened. "She's got real
problems. But, if she wants to spend the rest of her life behind bars,
that's her call. Thank the Lord we made it out."

"Right. But I feel kinda sorry for Joyce Ann," Sara Jane admitted.
"Her mother dumped her on that grandmother of hers, who was not
all there, if you know what I mean."

"Um-hum." Precious agreed.

"Nobody had respect for her family, so I think she just decided to
live up to her uncles' hell-raisin' reputation by showing off. She didn't
have a chance to be much more than what she turned out to be."

"That's true, " Precious agreed.

Sara Jane continued. "When my mother died, Joyce Ann came
across the street to tell me that she never cried, and I was so happy that
she wanted to be my friend. She acted proud, but she was sad, too, now
that I think about it. Just another unhappy little girl who was struggling to handle her own pain, and the only way she could manage was
to adopt a hard-hearted attitude." Sara Jane took a sip of her coffee.
"Yeah. Joyce Ann didn't know how to care about anyone but herself."

"Too true," Precious said. "But, let's get off that subject, please."
She took another bite of her roll, then placed it on the small, white
china dish on the table. "So, it's Dallas, huh?" She had to change the
subject before bursting into tears, keenly aware that she'd caused most
of her own troubles by acting out—hanging out with Joyce Ann and
Sara Jane to feel connected while breaking free of her parents' tight,
yet loving control. For that, she had paid a very high price. "Dallas is
as good a place as any to start over. Nobody will know you there."

"Exactly," Sara Jane replied. "I can't live here in Mallard."

"Yeah. Now, you can become somebody new . . . forget about this place and everything that's happened." A tremor broke her voice, and she reached for Sara Jane's hand, blinking away a sudden rush of tears. "I'm jealous, girl. I wish I were you."

"But you have parents who care, a real home," Sara Jane began, taking Precious' hand.

Precious lowered her chin in deference to that remark. "Sure, my family and the church folks say they've forgiven me, but I feel so useless, like a burden to everyone."

"But you're not," Sara Jane comforted, giving Precious' fingers a light squeeze. "Hold on. Try to stay positive, Precious. It's hard, I know, but it's only been a short time."

"I'll never get used to this!" Precious slammed a fist against the side of her wheelchair, then held onto the big round tire.

"You can't imagine how hard it is to do everything! Simple things take forever and some things, I've given up trying to fool with, so I have to depend on people to do so much for me. I hate it, Sara Jane. I hate it."

"You've got to hang in there, Precious. You'll adjust. Give it time. Things will get better. Look at me. I can walk, but I don't have anyone who cares what happens to me."

"Your father—" Precious began, sniffing back her tears.

"Forget about him," Sara Jane cut Precious off. "As far as he's concerned, I could still be at Gatesview. There's too much damage between us to ever repair. I'm better off on my own."

"Probably so," Precious agreed. "I guess I shouldn't be complaining, but I hate this town, this wheelchair, this house."

"You could leave," Sara Jane suggested. "If you want to come live with me when I get my own place, we'd manage, somehow."

Averting her eyes, Precious sighed, then spoke in a whisper. "It's not that simple. I can't leave here, Sara Jane. This is the only place I can live now." Looking up, she fixed Sara Jane with a look that was filled with yearning, yet begged for understanding. "Things should never have turned out like this."

"No," Sara Jane replied softly. "They shouldn't have."

"But they did," Precious continued. "And it's God's punishment for the lies I told and the things I did that were wrong. I hurt my mother, disappointed my father . . . myself. And think about poor Marcella Jacobs. Her family. Not right. None of it was right."

"No, it wasn't . . . but we were young, stupid. Having too much fun."

"And look what it cost us."

Sara Jane bit her lip. "I know. I know. Now, we've got to move on.

Precious, please hang in there. Don't let this get you down so bad you forget everything great you've got going on."

Glancing out the kitchen window, Precious murmured, rather unconvincingly, "Sure."

"I'd better go," Sara Jane started, standing up. She held onto the edge of the table as she assessed her friend. "You take care. I probably won't contact you again. Don't want to cause any trouble." She went into the hallway, followed by Precious and picked up her bags. Turning, she said, "I hate leaving you here like this."

"Girl, go on. Don't worry about me." Precious pulled back her shoulders and lifted her chin. "I'll be fine, but there's nothing here for you anyway, Sara Jane."

"No," she replied, "there isn't."

"So start over in Dallas. Disappear. Lose yourself in the world. Think of it, Sara Jane. Other than the people who live in Mallard and the Texas Prison system, who knows that you exist?"

"Or cares what happens to me?"

"I care," Precious replied, touching Sara Jane's arm.

"I know you do." Sara Jane covered Precious' hand with hers and stood silent for a moment.

"Will you let me know where you are, so I can find you, at least?" Precious asked. "Never know when I might need my homegirl, or you might need me."

"I'd better not promise anything, Precious. I just can't say what will happen to me." Then Sara Jane opened the door and left.

When the door had closed, Precious covered her face with both hands and gave in to her own disappointment, crying until she had released the tension of seeing Sara Jane again. Sara Jane was free while she was desperate to escape and overburdened with guilt. She had been hateful, selfish, and reckless with her life, and had to be punished for disrespecting God.

Pushing back a strand of brittle brown hair that slipped from her ponytail band, Precious wheeled around, placing her back to the door Sara Jane had just closed. If only she had realized how dangerous a game she had been playing, how dangerous her friendship with Joyce Ann would turn out to be, she would be leaving Mallard, too.

Precious rolled into her bedroom, opened the bottom drawer of her dresser, and took out a white envelope. Inside were fifty-two white pills she had squirreled away from the many sleeping pill and painkiller prescriptions her doctors had written for her. She had enough pills to go to sleep forever, if she decided the burden was too great and her courage too small. She had contemplated suicide several

times, but had never had the guts to act—not because she was afraid
to die, but because she feared she had angered God enough. Her involvement in Marcella Jacob's death had been a terrible sin. God
might forgive a youthful mistake, but He would never forgive her for
taking her own life. And Precious never wanted to sin again.

On the bus to Dallas, Sara Jane was consumed by a hollow fear that
resembled the fear she had experienced when the policeman had
tapped on her window after the car wreck, when the judge had pro-
nounced her sentence, when the door to her cell had swung shut with
a loud clank, leaving her in the dark. Everything familiar had vanished in an instant, leaving her facing a vast, black hole that threatened to pull her in. Now, even Precious, her final tie to her hometown
and her less-than-happy childhood had been taken away from her.
She felt restless and unsure.

To distract her thoughts, she unzipped her duffel bag to get a magazine to read, but reached for her mother's sketchbook instead, and
the drawing that had been framed. For the first time, she noticed faint
pencil writing on the back of it, and curious, held the single page
under the overhead light to read:

*Spanish Bayonet—peel the bulb, rub on stains. Crush and beat in water to
wash skin or clothes. Heals broken skin. Makes hair soft.*

Sara Jane turned the paper over and studied the pen and ink drawing more closely. "Spanish bayonet," she whispered, intrigued. The
writing was clearly a recipe for some kind of medicine or soap, perhaps the kind her mother had used on her as a child. Sara Jane began
leafing through the notebook, checking the backs of each page, and
found a recipe for some kind of ointment, remedy, cure, soap, cream or
tea on the back of each one. Sara Jane smiled, feeling a deep connection to her mother, curious about the information as well as her
mother's purpose in creating the book. She stuck the notebook back
into her bag and closed her eyes, anxious to get to Dallas.

Sara Jane waited until everyone had gotten off, then smoothed the
wrinkles from her new blouse and grabbed her two bags. She stepped
into the noisy station and merged with the crush of people moving
through the busy terminal.

There were panhandlers and street people, young couples with
arms locked around each other, businessmen with briefcases kissing
women good-bye. There were groups of children giggling with their
heads close together, elderly couples standing in line waiting to buy
tickets: The crush of humanity concentrated on going someplace for
some reason.

She headed toward the exit doors, no one paying any attention to her, the sharp sense of isolation frighteningly pleasant. An announcement boomed from the loud speakers above her head, but Sara Jane paid no attention.

No one's looking for me, that's for sure, she thought, as she went over to a newsstand and purchased a map of the city. Gripping the straps of her brown duffel bag and the handle of her one piece of luggage, she stepped through the automatic door and emerged into the scorching afternoon.

The heat and humidity of Dallas was as annoying as the gridlocked traffic that welcomed her. She squinted up at the tall skyscrapers, feeling small and unimportant, then took in a long, deep breath. It was an absolutely wonderful feeling, a deliciously liberating sensation not to have anyone to answer to.

It would be so easy to disappear, she realized, Warden Andrews's words returning to her mind. *Become a new person when you leave here,* he had advised. And even Precious had told her, *In Dallas you can become somebody new, Sara Jane.*

The possibilities simmered in her mind, growing more plausible with each step she took into the outside world. She knew that people often used nicknames, shortened versions of their real names, or simply chose to call themselves a name that they liked. Politicians, movie stars, writers, recording artists did it. Why couldn't an ex-con who wanted a clean slate adopt a new name to go with a new life?

She crossed the street when the light turned green, then stopped under an awning to get the brochure describing Havensway that Warden Andrews had given her from her bag. Then she checked the map, and discovered that the street she wanted was only about eight blocks away. She'd walk and conserve her funds.

Heading east on Texas Avenue, Sara Jane read signs and made up names, trying out different combinations, thinking of the exotic names of salon owners and hairstylists she'd read about in beauty magazines: Raveen, Tamar, Destry, Queen, names that made a statement, created an illusion, and left an indelible impression. Yes, that's what she'd go for—a name that made a statement, if she changed her name.

The late afternoon sun was brutal, but Sara Jane kept walking. Perspiration created dark spots under her arms and stained the front of her new linen blouse, but she continued on with purpose, not at all concerned. The suitcase grew heavier with each step and her second-hand loafers, which had felt great in the store, began to pinch her toes, so she stopped to sit down on a wrought iron chair outside an outdoor cafe.

A waiter approached and she shyly asked for a glass of water, which he produced with a smile and no charge. While sipping the water, Sara Jane eased off her left shoe, wiggled her aching toes, then glanced into the window of a lingerie boutique across the street. It was filled with mannequins wearing red and black peignoirs in a variety of styles. The sign in the window read: ALL SERENA LINGERIE BY ST. JAMES NOW 50% OFF.

Sara Jane shoved her foot back into her shoe, drained the paper cup of water, and hurried across the street. Standing in front of the sign she read it again, then scrutinized her dim reflection. She was thin, almost too thin for her height, but her high, slightly rounded cheekbones gave her face a softness that kept her from looking gaunt. Her lips were slightly pouty; bow-shaped on top and full on the bottom, and her teeth would have been perfect except for the one with the chip in the front. Her hair needed help— but that would come soon enough, when it grew longer and she had something to work with. Her light brown skin was smooth, though dry, despite the humidity that pressed over the city, and her posture could use some attention. Overall, she was neither pleased nor disappointed with her reflection, just anxious to pull this person together that would become her new self.

"Serena," Sara Jane whispered, reading the sign. "Serena St. James." She nodded, thinking, then murmured the name again. "Serena St. James." Examining her reflection, she smiled. The name had flair, sophistication, class. Yes, Serena St. James sounded much better than Sara Jane Talbot, who in her mind was already dead.

Chapter Six

A t exactly twelve o'clock, three short buzzes sounded on the call system, forcing Joyce Ann Keller off her bunk. She went to the bars at the front of her cell and waited for her door to swing open. When it did, she stepped quickly into the corridor and fell into line.

The dining hall was stifling hot and reeked of disinfectant. Stainless steel tables and chairs gleamed under bright fluorescent lights anchored in the ceiling, and the dull brown tile on the floor was cracked and worn, battered by the thousands of inmates who had marched along the serving lines and up and down the aisles.

Joyce Ann picked up a tray and held it up to the server, who dumped a spoonful of spaghetti onto it.

"Can't you do better?" she complained, holding her tray steady until the server slapped down another serving of red meat sauce and pasta.

"All right," she said, moving down the line, where she added a bowl of Jell-O and two pieces of bread to her tray.

Overcrowding at Gatesview had forced the inmates to eat lunch in three half-hour shifts between eleven and one, with Cell Block D assigned to the noon shift, followed by thirty minutes in the recreation yard, weather permitting. Now, Joyce Ann sat at the table where she always ate, her elbows close to her sides, her head bent, her mind on the news she had just heard, not on the meal she was about to eat.

Sara Jane Talbot had been released yesterday. First Precious, now Sara Jane. And here she was still inside: eating mess-hall food, wearing GCFW clothes, fighting to survive.

She hunched down in an appearance of concentrating on her food, but the only thing on Joyce Ann Keller's mind was getting out of Gatesview. The years that loomed ahead frightened her, yet she refused to let it show. The long stretch of time that lay ahead was like a dark tunnel filled with boredom, altercations, rage, and the recurring nightmare that always left her in a panic.

In the dream, she was sitting in the prison visitors' room waiting for her mother to arrive, but when the guard announced her visitor, it was always a blood-covered Marcella Jacobs who walked in, not the mother she so desperately longed for and missed. The dream would jolt Joyce Ann awake and bring tears to her eyes, which she quickly wiped away with her rough cotton sheet.

Before her incarceration, Joyce Ann thought of herself as tough, smart, and strong enough to survive any situation. Cutting school with Sara Jane, stealing bras and purses from Wal-Mart, buying beer with a fake ID, and even taking her uncle's gun, had been easy and fun. She'd never planned on killing Marcela, or ever doing hard time, for that matter. The situation in the Dairy Queen had spun out of control. Why hadn't Sara Jane helped her out? If she had taken the fall that night, everyone's sentence would probably have been shorter; Precious might not be paralyzed and Joyce Ann might be free, too.

Joyce Ann let her shoulders droop, a coil of exhaustion tightening. Sara Jane and Precious were starting new lives on the outside while she remained inside, bossed around by guards. How in the world would she ever survive seventeen more years in this place without breaking up?

A tap on her shoulder jerked her from her thoughts. She looked up at Reggy, the toughest guard on her cell block, frowning down at her. She held the guard's cold stare with steady eyes for several long seconds.

"Head guard wants to see you."

"Now?" Joyce Ann asked.

"Yeah, now. Get off your butt and come on."

An hour later, Joyce Ann was back in her cell, a dark scowl on her face. She was so angry, the vein that ran from her left temple, over her cheek, and down to her muscled neck was standing out like a piece of purple cord. When she entered prison, Joyce Ann had been a big-boned girl with thick braided hair and enough height to command respect. Now, her head was shaved and her height had become imposing because of the way she had bulked up from lifting weights. Her upper arms and shoulders strained against the fabric of her white, state-issued tee shirt defining the extent of her strength.

Impulsively, Joyce Ann began hurling questions at Lili, not waiting for her cellmate's answer before she asked another.

"That new one, next door. What's her name? Where's she from? How long she been here, anyway?"

"Her name's Myra," Lili replied. "Been here a few weeks."

"Myra, huh? She's got nerve. Trying to start trouble for me."

Lili shrugged and walked away from bars at the front of the cell she shared with Joyce Ann, then flopped down on her bunk, watching her cellmate closely.

Joyce Ann, who hadn't expected a reply, continued clenching and unclenching her fist as she thought about what had happened. "She wrote a bunch of crazy shit about me in a letter and sent it to the warden."

"Yeah? The bitch! What'd she say?" Lili was excited.

"Said I'm smuggling all kinds of shit in here. She better watch her back or she ain't gonna have a hand to write with."

"I know that's right," Lili tossed back, nodding, agreeing with Joyce Ann. She scooted across her bed and pressed her hips against the wall. "So, what happened?"

Joyce Ann knew better than to admit that the letter Myra had written to the warden had contained the truth: She *was* the ring leader in a smuggling operation that could get anything—illegal or legal—into the hands of the women at Gatesview. Joyce Ann was proud of her negotiating skills, and loved the sense of power that came from striking a deal and successfully arranging a compromising situation to use when she needed leverage. Bribery, theft, verbal abuse, physical intimidation—she used them all to get what she wanted. And what Joyce Ann wanted most were respect and attention, which she received from the inmates who feared her and the power she wielded. They came to her for favors, protection, or contraband, providing a rush that kept Joyce Ann pumped up. To her it was fun, ordering people around and she had Reggy, a guard on Cell Block D, to help ensure that things went smoothly.

Joyce Ann knew what made her happy, and it had nothing to do with material things. After all, how many cigarettes could she smoke? How many candy bars could she eat? How many radios could she listen to at one time? And she did not use drugs at all. No, it was respect she demanded in return for her services, and at Gatesview they gave it to her, which was more than she could say for Sara Jane Talbot, Precious Trent, or anyone living in Mallard.

"Anything might go down, now," Joyce Ann said to Lili, fixing her with a frigid stare. "And you better not say nothing to her, either."

"Why would I speak to that skinny thang?" Lili began. "Kinda scary looking, if you ask me."

"Yeah," Joyce Ann muttered. "And she's gonna look a lot worse." Joyce Ann lay down on her cot, turned her face toward the wall that separated her cell from Myra's and began tapping her fist against it. "She'll be sorry. She'll be sorry," Joyce Ann said, thumping the concrete bricks. When her knuckles began to bleed, she turned onto her back and lay very still, staring at the ceiling.

It wasn't Myra's face that filled Joyce Ann's mind as she lay there thinking. Nor was it the letter that Myra had written that made her want to scream. It was the news that Sara Jane Talbot had been released that still upset her. She had trusted Sara Jane to watch her back, act like a true friend, but she had let Joyce Ann down. As long as Joyce Ann could remember, the yokels in Mallard had vilified her uncles, her grandmother, and even her mother. In their opinion, the Kellers were trash—troublemakers and hell-raisers, not worthy of respect. So, why not live up to my family's reputation? she had vowed long ago.

Stealing the gun had been easy. The small .22 had felt good in her hand, initiating an immediate feeling of invulnerability. Joyce Ann hadn't planned on killing Marcella Jacobs but she had planned on firing the gun. She wanted to know what it felt like to hold a gun that had just gone off, to see if smoke really came out of the barrel, to witness the reaction on Precious' face when the rounds exploded in the firing chamber. But when she had discharged the gun at the floor, Marcella had run right into the path of the bullet. If old Sheriff Goens hadn't taken so long to get there, Marcella might not have bled to death on the Dairy Queen floor.

It was a good thing Precious had been inside, too, Joyce Ann thought. Having an accomplice had deflected enough of the blame from Joyce Ann to prevent a charge of first-degree murder.

And Sara Jane Talbot. So naive and stupid. Driving the car, as Joyce Ann had predicted. If only Sara Jane had held on to the money and kept her big mouth shut at the trial, all three of them might have come out of the mess in better shape. But Sara Jane had always been weak.

Why hadn't Reggy been able to stop Myra's letter from getting through to Warden Andrews? Joyce Ann began to wonder, realizing there was no one she could absolutely trust. When the shit had hit the fan during the robbery, even Sara Jane had wimped out. Joyce Ann would never forgive her.

Now, Joyce Ann picked up a magazine from the floor and began to tear out the pages, crushing them, one by one, into paper bullets, which she hurled at Lili.

"Little Miss Tell-All has got to pay for every fuckin' word she wrote about me," Joyce Ann said, thinking, *just like Marcella had to pay for kicking me out of her chickenshit Dairy Queen, and Sara Jane Talbot will pay for not doing like I told her.*

As soon as the lights-out buzzer sounded, night fell quickly in Cell Block D, and except for the dim yellow globes at each end of the long corridors, which allowed the guards to watch the shadowed movements within the barred cubicles, it was dark. The noise in the prison began to fade, shifting from loud yells across the corridors and blasting radio music to low singing, muted arguments, and the sounds of lovers coupling in the shadows—sounds that could be easily ignored or difficult to bear, depending on the situation.

Reggy's pulling her shift by now, Joyce Ann thought, turning onto her side to listen for the guard's footsteps as she made her rounds. Joyce Ann curled her fingers around the small glass jar of bleach she had managed to slip out of the laundry room two days ago. She had known it would come in handy precisely when she needed it.

Early in her incarceration at the Cave, Joyce Ann had been accosted and had retaliated swiftly, putting everyone on notice that she was not a pushover, making sure no one dared speak up about what they had seen, heard, or thought they knew. Her reputation as a tough chick not to be messed with spread quickly.

Now, Joyce Ann slipped out of her bunk, eased onto the floor, and scooted toward the front of her cell. She placed her left temple against the wall that separated her cell from Myra's and studied the glass jar in her hand while she listened for a movement next door. She had to do this. If not, word would get around that she had turned soft, that she'd let Myra get over on her. All of her life, it seemed, she'd had to fight to hold her own, to prove she would not be bullied. Prison was no different.

"Psst," Joyce Ann hissed, shutting her mind to any thoughts of backing off.

"What you want?" Myra hissed back.

"Be quiet! Just come over here. I got something important to tell you."

"Forget it."

"Better come listen. You ain't been here long enough to ignore me."

After a moment of silence, Myra got out of her lower berth and appeared on the floor near the bars. She leaned forward to try to see Joyce Ann. "What you want?"

Joyce Ann did not answer, but swiftly poked her right arm through the bars, flicked her wrist, and splashed the contents of the glass jar back into Myra's cell.

"Damn you," Myra screamed, her outburst initiating an eruption of catcalls and yells and loud voices from others on the block who joined in. The noise brought two guards running to see what had happened.

Quickly, Joyce Ann smashed the glass jar on the floor, picked up a long shard of glass and stabbed it deep into her mattress, then threw the rest of the broken bottle into Myra's cell.

"What's going on here?" Reggy shouted, shining a light into Myra's cell, then Joyce Ann's.

"She attacked me!" Joyce Ann replied, now standing, hands on her hips.

"That's a lie," Myra protested, poking one hand through the bars as she tried to hit Joyce Ann.

"She's the liar!" Joyce Ann snapped. "I was sitting here minding my own business when I see her hand, coming at me. Just like she's doing now. See? I slapped it back, and the shit she was trying to throw on me broke and splashed all over the place. Look. The damn bottle's broke all over her floor. Ain't no glass over here!"

"Shut up. Both of you. Stand up Myra. Joyce Ann, turn around. You're both on your way out."

The handcuffs pinched Joyce Ann's wrists and the chains around her ankles made her hobble, but she proudly worked her way past the curious inmates, staring straight ahead. When she arrived at the six-by-six cell, she stared at the electronic door, knowing she was facing at least forty-eight hours in isolation. She'd have forty-eight hours to cool off, to prove she had learned a lesson and would not make any more trouble, and if she worked it right, she might be in a much better position than she was right now.

The guard punched in a code, led Joyce Ann inside, and then pushed a button to lock down the cell.

Could be worse, Joyce Ann thought. It was small, but the corridor was quiet, and no one would bother her. She needed some solitude. So far, things had gone as she'd hoped. *No reason to rush,* she decided, sitting down on the bunk to concentrate on the next phase of her plan.

Chapter Seven

Nina Richards, a recovering alcoholic, had changed her life by divorcing her multimillionaire husband and abandoning her luxurious lifestyle to dedicate her energy to helping troubled women. When the fair-skinned, red-haired woman moved into a rundown Victorian in a predominantly black neighborhood, the residents eyed her with skepticism and wondered why she had come into their area.

They soon learned that Nina Richards' goal was to open a house that would provide a bridge for women whose lives on the fringes of society had left them helpless and vulnerable, trapped outside the mainstream independence they deserved. She renovated the house, landscaped the grounds, and put up a sign: HAVENSWAY—A PLACE TO HELP WOMEN OVERCOME THE OBSTACLES THAT HAVE SIDETRACKED THEIR LIVES.

After eight years of operating her halfway house, Nina became well known in the Dallas area as the woman to whom rebellious teenagers, runaways, ex-cons, and abused or displaced women could turn for support and a safe place to live while they struggled to turn their lives around.

Nina unselfishly used her flush divorce settlement to staff and maintain the fifteen-room mansion, and was more than an absentee landlord–benefactor who assuaged her conscious by writing checks and making phone calls to raise funds for her charity cases.

She purchased a car for the center and willingly let the residents use it to take their driver's license tests, go to work, visit their children, and keep appointments related to their rehabilitation. She accompanied the women to banks to help them open accounts, found lawyers who were willing to donate their time, and assisted them in solving their legal problems. If a client needed clothes, Nina took her shopping and offered advice on how best to dress for a job interview. And, since most of the residents did not have medical insurance, she made arrangements with several local clinics for treatment, picked up the tab, and called on her extensive list of contacts in the medical field to donate their services for conditions too serious for the clinic to handle.

For Sara Jane, and all of the women at Havensway, Nina Richards was their fairy godmother, counselor, sister, and friend.

Soon after Sara Jane settled into her room on the third floor of Havensway, Nina went to work on her newest resident, arranging for Sara Jane to have her chipped front tooth repaired, get her driver's license, and purchase appropriate clothing for job interviews.

Infused with hope, Sara Jane immediately approached the most popular and successful African-American hair salons, but had no luck. The owners wanted a beautician with references and more experience using the newest techniques and products designed especially for black women.

She soon discovered that the personnel heads of the chain establishments in department stores and malls would accept her applications and interview her, but no callbacks ever came. Her lack of experience and her cosmetology license issued by the Texas Department of Corrections were obviously working against her. Who wanted to take a chance on an ex-con when so many qualified girls with clean records were available?

As the weeks passed, Sara Jane grew discouraged, but refused to give up. Her goal was to become a successful hairstylist, with her own salon, elevating herself to financial independence. Accepting a minimum wage job as a waitress, a fast-food server, or a hotel maid would mean trudging through life, moving from one low-paying job to another, and that was not what Sara Jane envisioned for her future. She had overcome the loss of her mother, an unhappy childhood with a nonsupportive father, and prison. She was strong, and would keep looking until the job she wanted came around.

A month after her arrival, Sara Jane was sitting on the edge of her bed, toweling her freshly shampooed hair, thinking about the next day's interview at another personnel agency. The hot shower had helped wash away some of the day's disappointment, but still she was unsettled. While drying her hair, she rehearsed answers to the standard interview questions she knew would be put to her, trying to sound as upbeat, confident, and worthy of employment as possible. As she finger-combed her short hair, which was rapidly growing out of its prison cut, she thought about adopting a new look, realizing her hair would soon be long enough to curl again with a curling iron. Maybe a makeover would boost her spirits.

Everything changes, she murmured, hoping for a break very soon.

Havensway was fine, and Nina Richards had been wonderful, but Sara Jane wanted to be on her own, to live the independence she craved. She opened the top drawer of her dresser, took out a nightgown and pulled it on, but before closing the drawer, she decided to look at her mother's book of sketches, which she kept between several folds of clothing.

Sara Jane went to the chair next to the bed, and opened the book. The drawings seemed to strengthen her desire not to give up. Her mother's life had not been easy, either, and she owed it to her mother's memory not to run away, but to stay and make the best of her situation.

"I'm trying, Momma," Sara Jane whispered to Violet Talbot. "I won't let you down. A break is coming, I just know it." Thinking, she turned over the sketch from the wall of her mother's room and reread the words on the back.

"Spanish Bayonet." Was this a recipe for soap or lotion? Could it be both? And would it, as well as the other recipes in the sketch book, do any good? She got up, went to her mirror, and leaned closer, examining her face. She had to admit that with makeup her skin looked to be in great condition and from a distance her light tan complexion appeared to be smooth and soft. But up close, she saw that the skin on her forehead was dry and flaky, there were tiny dark patches on her cheeks, and the area along her jaw was a shade darker than the rest of her face: the effects of poor skin care and prison life. Might her mother's recipes help? she wondered, scrutinizing her profile, thinking that perhaps, her mother had sent her an answer.

The next day, the thought was still with her, intriguing Sara Jane so much that she skipped the interview with the personnel agency and went to the downtown library and began her research. Using the computer at the library, it didn't take long to find more information about Spanish bayonet, as well as the other plants sketched in the book. They were all plants called amoles, indigenous to the Southwest, and various Indian tribes had used them for hundreds of years to make potions, remedies, and soaps. Digging deeper, Sara Jane went to websites devoted to natural soap-making and cosmetics, but found nothing referring to Spanish bayonet. Intrigued by the information, and more curious than ever about her mother's legacy, she wondered how her mother had come by these recipes, which must have been very important for her to document and label so carefully. What exactly did this book, the only tangible connection to her mother, mean?

Leaving the library, Sara Jane went to a health food store, a nursery, and a florist but got very little information about the plant. The florist was unable to name the plant when shown the sketch, and had no knowledge of its use. The clerk at the health food store shook her head, puzzled. She had never heard of it.

As Sara Jane headed back to Havensway, her resolve to continue the search increased. The significance of the rare plant had captivated her imagination, compelling her to discover exactly how it and her mother were connected.

After another week of searching, she finally found a job—at the Eastside Barber College on the south side of Dallas, doing five-dollar haircuts nine hours a day, six days a week. The pay was not great and the hours were long, but the experience, as well as the variety of clients that came through the doors, provided Sara Jane with an excellent opportunity to perfect her skills. She cut all kinds of hair—men's, women's, curly, straight, black, white, Asian—and was lucky enough to be guided by a kind instructor who willingly passed on his tips on customer relations and how to get bigger tips. Sara Jane finally began to feel as if her goal of personal and financial independence might be coming within reach. And on her one day off, she continued her search for a source for Spanish Bayonet.

Her lucky break came while surfing the Internet on the library computer. She discovered a wholesale nursery run by Seminole Indians in Palm Beach, Florida. Her communication with the nursery confirmed that the plant could be used for making soap and other lotions. They even provided a basic recipe.

Sara Jane immediately ordered a box of the strange black root, and one night, alone in the kitchen at Havensway, she launched her experiment, measuring, adjusting, and incorporating the ingredients exactly as her mother had written them down until a frothy soap appeared in the bowl. Carefully, she spread the thick concoction in the bottom of a plastic tub and took it to her room. Three days later, she cut the solidified mixture into small squares and began using it on her face, body, and hair, watching for results. After only one week, her skin was no longer dry, her hair was softer, and she looked generally better—vibrant and alive.

Over the next three weeks, she used her homemade soap religiously, and the results were so evident that Nina Richards asked Sara Jane if she were taking special vitamins, and if so, what kind? Not ready to divulge her secret, Serena attributed her improved looks and attitude on having finally found a job.

Two months passed. Sara Jane persevered, and the results inspired her to take more dramatic steps, starting with her mouse-brown hair that had grown long enough to style. She texturized it with a mild relaxer and brought it to life with bronze highlights that emphasized the glow of her skin. With a makeup kit she purchased at a local beauty supply, she began experimenting with color, creating contours with foundation and blush to alter the shape of her face. She played up the shape of her full lips with a ruby shade of liner and gloss, drew emphasis to her eyes with new shadows and color, and deepened the hollows beneath her strong cheekbones with several layers of blush. And when the other women at Havensway saw the new and improved Sara Jane, they wanted to know what she had done, and would she show them how. They crowded into her room requesting makeovers and information.

Sara Jane was happy to oblige, providing each one a small square of her special soap, stressing the importance of abandoning all other cosmetics and soaps they had been using. In time she became very adept at improving, not only a woman's appearance, but her attitude, demeanor, and self-confidence. Nina Richards was very impressed.

After three months at Havensway, on October tenth, Sara Jane turned twenty-one. She celebrated with the women who lived there, eating chocolate cake and vanilla ice cream, but when she went to bed that night, she was not happy. The job at Eastside Barber College was not paying her enough to fully support herself in an apartment, where she'd have to buy groceries, pay utilities, and mostly likely take on a car note. What she was making at Eastside was spending money. She wanted and needed more.

Sara Jane struggled to stay positive. More drastic measures than simply redoing her physical appearance would have to take place if she was going to make it. Realizing how powerful Nina Richards was, and how easily the woman could make things happen—things that seemed impossible—Sara Jane went to see Nina in her room late one night, ready to ask for the help she believed would solve her problems.

"I want to change my name," she blurted out, watching Nina carefully.

Nina pushed a stray curl of her unruly red hair off her forehead, folded the newspaper she had been reading, and gave Sara Jane her full attention. "Change your name? That's a pretty drastic decision. What's brought this on, Sara Jane?"

"I want to start over. Completely over, with a new name and none of the baggage from my past that is always going to get in the way."

"But you're doing fine."

"I'm working, yes, but what kind of future do I have stuck at a barber college?"

Nina lowered her chin and studied Sara Jane, much like a mother about to scold a child. "Don't worry so much. You'll have the future you want. Be patient. It's—"

"Going to take time," Sara Jane interrupted. "I know all of that," she went on, in a hurry to say what was on her mind before Nina made her change. "I've thought about it a lot. You are the only person I've met since leaving Gatesview who knows about my past, knows where I came from, why I left, and why I cannot go back. And I want to keep it like that. If I erase who and what I used to be, I can truly start living, become the person I know I can be. Please, will you help me?"

Nina reached out and took Sara Jane's hand. "You are a lovely young woman with great ambitions." She smiled, leaning closer. "If only I had felt as strongly about what I wanted from life at your age, I might have avoided a great deal of pain and not wasted so much time. I envy you, Sara Jane."

Sara Jane's sharp gaze connected with Nina's and she held the older woman's attention for a moment. Then she lowered her eyes and focused on their clasped hands, with Nina's white fingers, warm and strong, firmly planted on top of her slim brown hand. They were very different, yet Sara Jane felt that Nina understood her so much more than anyone in her life ever had.

"Will you help me?" Sara Jane asked again.

Nina removed her hand from Sara Jane's, leaned back in her chair, and let out a soft sigh. "Of course, I will," she replied. "Give me a few days to see what I can arrange."

Three days later Nina informed Sara Jane that she had located an attorney who was willing to work with her, if that's really what Sara Jane truly wanted to do.

Three weeks and two court appearances later, Sara Jane Talbot legally became Serena St. James. The attorney had been able to persuade the judge that Sara Jane deserved a chance to start over with a clean slate. And even though her juvenile court records would be sealed, a new identity would ensure that the dark specter of her past would not rise up unexpectedly and destroy what she would have built with her new identity.

She was able to change her driver's license and cosmetology license into her new name, and she got a new Social Security card, but retained her original number. She quit her job at the barber college and moved on to the cosmetics counter at Ultimate Beauty, as a sales representative demonstrating a line of water-based makeup in the store. Her pay was not much better than at the barber college but she earned a fifteen percent commission on each bottle of foundation, package of blush, tube of lipstick or mascara she sold. At first, she did very well, but as the novelty of the new line wore off, most people coming in only wanted to sit for the free makeover session and not buy anything new, leaving the store with beautiful faces, but no products in their hands.

Sara Jane was good at pitching the product and closing sales, but had not been enthusiastic enough about the product to rack up the numbers Ultimate Beauty expected. After forty-five days on the job, her boss gently released her, handing her a check for one hundred sixteen dollars and a bag of assorted cosmetic samples.

During the holiday season she worked in retail sales at Lord & Taylor, determined to learn all she could about merchandising, management, and how to run a store, fueled by a heady sense of anticipation. Serena felt that something good was going to happen, and when it came to her it would erase all anxiety from her life.

Lying in her bed after an exhausting day, she gazed out the window at the pitch black night and thought about the day when she would walk into her own salon and greet elegant dark-skinned women sitting on tiny golden chairs, stylishly dressed, anxiously waiting for Serena to make them beautiful. She would have an entire line of cosmetics based on her mother's formulas on the shelves of her exclusive salon. The images were so strong and recurring that Serena knew they would never go away. Time, patience, and faith could make them real.

During this time, Nina Richards watched Serena closely, struck by her talent, impressed by her spirit, and moved by her determination to do more than just survive. Rarely had she witnessed, among the many women who passed through Havensway, the passion that Serena displayed. Nina made up her mind to push Serena out on her own. It was time she left Havensway.

Nina called on her patron and good friend Giani Pilugi, who owned one of the most exclusive salons in the city and had helped her out by hiring women from Havensway to give them a start. She told Giani about Serena St. James, and he said he could take Serena on as a laundry maid and let her work in the shampoo area, but he couldn't do much more. If her goal was to become a stylist for black women, he didn't have a black clientele on which to get experience or anyone to supervise her training. But if Serena worked out at Upscale, he would provide her with a good recommendation that ought to open doors for her in other salons, wherever she wanted to work in the future. That was all he could offer.

When Nina told Serena about Giani's offer, Serena jumped at the chance to work at Upscale, the salon where local celebrities, socialites, and visiting dignitaries went to be pampered and made beautiful.

Six days a week, Serena left the halfway house before sunrise to get to work by seven and rarely returned before dark. She became more of a loner than ever, no longer eating with the other women in the huge airy kitchen where family-style meals were served on a fairly rigid schedule. That did not bother her. She was far too busy working to worry about meals or making friends; she was focused on learning how to run a salon. This intense focus stayed with her while she swept the floors at Upscale, replenished towels, and shampooed an occasional client. It rode home with her on the bus during the two-hour trip across town from North Dallas back to Havensway in the heart of the city. It followed her into her simply furnished room and clung to her exhausted soul until she fell asleep.

Yet, she walked to the bus stop in a long-legged stride, her head held high, her slim jaw thrust forward, as if daring anyone to get in her way. Her glossy hair, which had grown out once she began using the Spanish bayonet shampoo, was now a blunt cut bob that hugged her cheeks and emphasized her sculpted cheekbones and slightly up-turned nose. Serena's luminous tawny eyes glowed like those of a female tiger on the hunt, flitting over the people on the bus, the strangers on the street, the customers at the salon as she watched, assessing, and calculating everything around her. If she wasn't at Upscale working, she was in the bookstore leafing though *Beauty Industry Update, Black Hair Today,* or *Cosmetology Highlights,* or in the library on the computer researching her cosmetics project. This vouluntary isolation infused Serena with great strength and kept her going when she was almost too tired to continue. This restless determination propelled her into each day and kept the promise she had made to Warden Andrews uppermost in her thoughts: she would make something of herself and never return to prison.

That conversation came back to her often, and she remembered how his words had made her feel, the way he had looked at her when he'd said, "I do not want to see you back here again." Serena never wanted to walk those dull gray corridors or smell the fear and anger of inmates again.

Chapter Eight

Serena learned much about the beauty business during the twelve months that followed. Grateful for the opportunity to work for Giani Pilugi, an internationally known stylist, she keenly observed how he created an atmosphere of luxury and calm that attracted celebrities, socialites, and career women from Dallas and around the world. She watched as he handled difficult clients, flattered delicate egos, and juggled the hordes of sales reps who descended on his salon everyday, hyping a wide variety of shampoos, conditioners, hair-sprays and styling tools.

As Serena went about her business, retrieving wet towels from the backs of chairs, sweeping floors, stocking cabinets, and polishing the sleek marble countertops that lined the walls, her eyes darted from station to station absorbing the details of the smoothly running opera-tion. Her ears took in comments that she filed away for reference, and she appreciated the opportunities Giani gave her to be a part of his profitable venture, by trusting her to place product orders, assist at the front desk, and cover his phone when he was out.

The majority of the staff had welcomed Serena to the salon, and re-mained friendly, though aloof. Only Alexis Bonat, the senior stylist and her supervisor seemed less than happy about working with Serena, tolerating the assignment only because Giani had asked her to.

A former protégé of Giani's, Alexis had overprocessed limp, brown hair, a rail-thin body, a wire-taut temperament, and a propensity to lash out at anyone who ruffled her edgy veneer, using treacherous language to remind them exactly how important her presence was to the continued success of the salon. Her appointment book was always full and her reputation for using bold, sophisticated color, in both hair and makeup, kept her celebrity clients coming back and Upscale's profile high. Alexis had been at the ritzy, exclusive salon for seven years, had won every top award in the cosmetology industry, and was clearly jealous of the interest her boss showed in Serena, his charity case.

On a busy Saturday morning in early December, soft classical music seeped from the speakers in the damask-covered walls, barely audible above the whirr of blow dryers, the chatter of clients, and the constant ringing of phones.

Serena grabbed a soggy Egyptian towel from the hook outside Alexis's station, stuffed it into her rolling linen cart, and then entered the stylist's cubicle to set out fresh towels. When she turned to leave, Alexis stopped her, a tall black can of aerosol spray held high, pointed at Serena.

"I told you to fold the towels so that the monograms are facing out." Sniffing in annoyance, she glared at Serena, her pale blue eyes glinting as she tapped the hair spray can on the back of her client's chair, waiting.

Without comment, Serena adjusted the folds of the three thick towels so that the gray satin "U" on each one was prominently displayed. During the year she had been at Upscale, Alexis had never told her to place the towels on her station that way. But she wasn't surprised. Once a week, it seemed, the bossy stylist came up with another quirky rule or demand that Serena had never heard of: *Put the white towels on top of the gray ones, separate the combs from the brushes by color, place the styling gels to the left, then the right, hair spray cans on the table, under it, sweep hair from beneath my client's chair within minutes of it touching the floor, leave it until I am finished with the client.* Serena never knew what to expect, but she refused to let Alexis get to her.

"God, what a day. Trying to manage the help and concentrate on my clients is impossible," Alexis muttered, dismissing Serena with a wave of her comb as she backcombed the puff of blonde hair beneath her hands. "Why Giani thinks he can save the world by hiring girls like her, is beyond me."

Outside of Alexis' mirrored cubicle, Serena gripped a dirty towel in one hand, her heart thundering beneath her gray Upscale smock. No matter how hard she tried, she never got a kind word from Alexis, who was still talking to her client, deliberately raising her voice to make sure Serena could hear what she said.

"Another one of those girls from Havensway, Gloria," Alexis said. "What can I say? " She sighed loudly, then added, "This one seems so secretive. Never talks about herself. No one knows where she's from or what she's done."

"Surely Giani checked her out," the woman in Alexis' cubicle replied.

"I guess so," Alexis assured her client. "You know, that halfway house has become Giani's pet charity. We've had four other girls from that place over the past six months, and not one stayed around long enough to learn how to do the job right. Runaways, recovering addicts, street people, you know? All they want is enough cash to get back to whatever they were doing before they came here, but don't want to work for it."

"Well, Giani ought to simply write a check instead of hiring them." Gloria added in a breathy tone. "That's the easy thing to do." Lowering her voice, she went on. "It can be dangerous getting too involved with people who live in shelters and halfway houses . . . on the fringes, if you know what I mean."

"Exactly," Alexis confirmed.

Serena squeezed her eyes shut, bit down hard on the inside of her lip, and counted to ten, her chest growing tight with resentment. Alexis calling her lazy! Implying she was dangerous! Instilling fear in the clients! Serena was infuriated. Well, she hadn't let the guards, the butch-divas, or the isolation of prison break her, and wasn't about to let a skinny, self-absorbed hairdresser ruin her best chance of starting over. She'd been at Upscale nearly a year, the amount of time she had promised Nina she'd stay if Giani hired her. When the time came to leave, it would be her decision and she planned on taking a positive recommendation from Giani with her, whether Alexis Bonat liked it or not. Serena knew that bitching, crying, grumbling, and complaining were counterproductive and she had long ago stopped feeling sorry for herself.

Moving among the mirrored cubicles, Serena continued to collect the towels, thinking about the frayed scraps of cotton that had hung in her bathroom at home, the stiff gray squares of institutional toweling given to the inmates at Gatesview. So much in her life had changed, and so quickly.

This may not be what I expected, she thought, stopping to assess her surroundings. *But I'm free and I'm learning the beauty business in the most elegant salon imaginable.* Her eyes traveled over the reception area and the busy stations where all of the staff were completely absorbed in their work.

This morning, two well-known socialites and a local television celebrity were sitting on delicate gold wicker chairs in the reception area, calmly waiting for Giani to arrive. Giani had bragged to Serena that his furniture had been especially designed and crafted for

Upscale by Rene Leanchi, a furniture maker in Rome who flew to Dallas twice a year to inspect, repair, and replace his exclusive chairs and tables. Black and white floor tiles gleamed like polished pieces of onyx and pearl, designed for Giani by artisans in Mexico. Cream-colored silk Roman shades covered the wide front windows, so sheer and light they were nearly invisible, and an expanse of green-tinted glass created the back wall, separating the salon from a lush tropical atrium where clients could sit among blooming oleanders and palms while they sipped imported champagne, waited for their nails to dry, and chatted about themselves.

Throughout this dreamlike montage of Roman columns, French impressionist art, and Italian furniture, were the most beautiful people Serena had ever seen. All of the stylists were thin, fine-boned, and as required by Giani, dressed in expensive gray slacks and white shirts beneath their Upscale smocks. Among the customers were brunettes, blondes, redheads and those with touches of gray at the temples, their hair coiffed in bouffant puffs, long silky waves, punk-rock spikes, jaunty flips, and wraps that hugged their perfectly shaped heads. And everyone in the salon was white—except Serena St. James.

At nine-fifteen, Giani swept through the door and made his standard grand entrance, pausing to make sure his busy, trusted staff knew he had arrived. He was a short man, with dark curly hair, a round face, and keen eyes that immediately took in the morning's activity as he moved briskly from station to station, nodding his approval, hugging a client, making suggestions, and tossing out compliments. Though he was small in stature, his presence in the salon created an instant ripple of excitement and expectation, making each of his stylists stand a little taller, work a bit faster, and his clients engage in more animated conversation.

Giani Pilugi had shrewdly built his client base by providing the rich and famous a safe, comfortable haven away from the public rabble who routinely gushed and stared at them whenever they were out. At Upscale, the unstated motto was: Here you can bare your real face, expose your dark roots, show your cracked nails, relax among your own kind, and be assured that Giani has your best interest at heart. This dedication to cloistered pampering had paid off handsomely for him in many, many ways.

After blowing a kiss at Maria, the receptionist at the front desk, he shrugged off his black leather jacket, tossed it casually over his arm, and entered his Romanesque studio. A few minutes later, he emerged and motioned for a woman who was in the waiting area to come back. He met her at the entrance to his private styling area, draped her in an orange and black tiger-striped smock, then holding her hand, led her to the shampoo area. There he paused, searched the salon for a moment, and then zeroed in on Serena. He smiled and crooked his index finger, signaling for her to come over.

Serena set down the can of coffee and the filter she had been preparing to use to make a fresh pot of coffee, and went to see how she could help.

"Well, Serena," Giani started, "I need your help today. Everyone is swamped. So, put that dreadful laundry cart away and help me out. Let's see what you can do with this." He ran his hands through the woman's silky black hair. "Patricia needs a deep conditioner and a Fine-Shine Rinse to bring out those highlights Alexis put in last week. They are looking a little dull already, and we can't have that, can we?"

Patricia smiled, then sat down at one of the shampoo bowls. "I'd like it a little lighter around my face, too," she added, fingering a few strands of hair that had cascaded over one eye. "I'm leaving this afternoon for New York."

"Plan to stay through next week and spend Thanksgiving with those grandchildren?" Giani bantered, showing his customary attention to his clientele.

"Yes, I certainly am. So, think we can do the highlights today?" she asked.

Giani tilted his head toward Serena, one eyebrow raised. "Sure. I think we can handle it. Don't you, Serena?"

Surprised and pleased that he would trust her with a delicate highlighting job, Serena quickly nodded. "No problem. I'd be happy to do it."

"Okay," Giani replied, handing Patricia over to Serena, telling her, "It's time you got your hands into more than towels and capes around here."

"Wait a minute. I'd prefer Janice to do my client!" Alexis called out over the clatter of her curling iron hitting the floor.

A frown came to Giani's smooth olive face and silence settled over the other stylists, who interrupted their work to focus on the upcoming exchange.

Alexis stood with her hands on her slim hips for a moment, then stepped over the hot iron on the floor and hurried to the shampoo area. "Thanks, Giani, but I'll take care of this. Janice always handles Patricia's hair for me." She nodded at a smock-clad girl who interrupted the shampoo she was giving an elderly woman to look over her shoulder at Alexis.

Serena froze, aware that every eye in the salon was on her.

"But Alexis, my dear," Giani firmly replied, gesturing for Patricia to remain seated, "Janice is busy and Serena is free. It's fine. I'm sure she can handle a few highlights."

"Not on Patricia. Sorry." Alexis crooked her finger at the woman, indicating that she get up.

But Patricia scooted to the edge of the chair and glanced from Giani to Alexis. "It's okay, Alexis. I'm kind of in a hurry this morning and Janice is busy. I don't mind if this young lady takes care of me. Really."

"You see?" Giani said, lifting his hands, palms up, in a gesture of surrender. "Just calm down, Alexis, and let me handle this."

"Don't do this to me, Giani," Alexis said through clenched teeth. "Patricia Wilson is *my* client. I decide who works on her."

The remark made Giani step back and eye Alexis before he replied. "Oh? I beg to differ, Alexis," he coolly tossed back. "Anyone who walks through that front door is a client of Upscale . . . and I . . . Giani Pilugi, am the owner. You'd be wise not to forget that."

"We'd better talk in your office," Alexis challenged, tossing a frigid look at Serena before stalking toward the back of the salon.

"I agree," Giani said, rolling his eyes, as if he had been through similar scenes before. "Carry on," he told Serena, who nodded and began gathering her supplies.

She was startled by this uncharacteristic power play carried out in front of everyone. Clearly, Giani enjoyed his near-celebrity status—which he went to great pains to cultivate, but rarely threw it around this way.

Please God, don't let me mess up, Serena prayed as she hurried to the back room to get a clean smock. Putting it on, she said a silent prayer of thanks for this chance to prove herself to be more than a shampoo girl, drawing courage from the fact that Giani was firmly on her side. Suddenly, she no longer felt like an outsider doing time, waiting to escape. This might be exactly where she belonged.

Chapter Nine

Serena gazed out the bus window at the early morning frost that covered the tops of cars and slicked the sidewalks. December had started off rainy and cool, and now, six days before Christmas, the weather was downright nasty. A few newspaper vendors and shopkeepers, anxious to get a jump-start on holiday sales, were already out and about on the cold, frigid streets. At the corner of Park and Llano, Serena stepped off the bus and pulled up the collar of her heavy trench coat with zip-in lining just as a passing taxi barreled down the street, swerved into the gutter and churned up a spray of icy slush. She jumped out of the way, into a muddy puddle of water, soaking her feet. She glanced down at her shoes, the loafers she had bought in Mallard on the day of her release from prison, and frowned. She did have several new pairs of shoes in her wardrobe now, but did not want to ruin them in such bad weather, so she'd opted for the second-hand loafers today since her black leather boots were in the shoe repair for new heels. If the salon was not too busy, she'd slip out at noon and pick them up because she'd really need them tomorrow. The weatherman had predicted freezing rain again, and the ride in was going to be just as long, cold, and wet.

Giani had a very strict dress code for his staff, and though he didn't pay Serena much more than minimum wage, with her salary and tips she had managed to improve her wardrobe beyond the basics he absolutely required: two pair of gray wool slacks, four white tailored shirts, and three red and gray Upscale smocks at seventy-two-fifty each. The clothing had to be dry cleaned, not laundered, and the cost of keeping her Upscale image intact put a strain on her closely managed budget, so she rarely bought anything frivolous. Her frugal lifestyle had allowed her to save enough money to lease that studio apartment she had her eye on, purchase basic furniture, and buy a car by the first of the year, when she planned to leave Havensway and move out on her own.

Living at the halfway house for the past seventeen months had been a godsend, giving her time to adjust to the demands of working everyday and learning how to budget her money. She had never realized how much it would take to manage on her own on the outside and Nina Richard's support had made it all possible.

Now, Serena hurried across the street, digging into her purse for her keys. Giani had asked her to open the shop, turn up the heat, and put on the coffee before the rest of the staff arrived. Serena didn't mind filling in for Maria, the receptionist who was on maternity leave, even though it meant she had to roll out of bed before five A.M. and take two different busses to get to the salon by seven.

With Christmas approaching, Serena expected the salon to be crowded, the stylists heavily booked, and the clients busy chattering about what they planned to buy for this person or that, what they'd wear to which party, and what kind of champagne or caviar they planned to serve at their dinner parties.

Every day Serena listened impassively to the swirl of conversation about holiday plans, painfully aware that she had only one gift to buy—for Nina—and had no family to visit, no dinner parties to attend or plan, though the five women staying at Havensway during the holidays had decorated a small tree and placed it in the big bay window. The Coalition for Women's Reform was coming to the halfway house on Christmas Day to serve a turkey dinner, but Serena had little appetite for such a meal. In fact, she would be glad when Christmas was over with and gone because it brought on too many painful memories; memories of her father drinking the day away while she stayed out of his way, retreating to her bedroom with her magazines and books.

In Mallard, and other towns near the Texas–Oklahoma border, it was not uncommon to have snowstorms in December, and on one cold Christmas Eve when she was twelve years old, and the snow had been swirling in great circles for hours, she had proudly prepared a turkey dinner for her father, but he had passed out before she could set it on the table. Defying his orders to stay away from the Kellers, she'd crossed the street to Joyce Ann's house, where she sat around and ate Granny's dry fruitcake and pretended to have a good time. When they got bored, the two had sneaked up to the windows of the Mallard Baptist Church to look in during Christmas Eve service. There, Precious Trent, dressed in red velvet and shiny black patent leather boots had been singing a solo while her mother accompanied her on the piano. Joyce Ann had laughed gruffly, criticizing Precious' brave attempt to entertain the congregation, but now Serena remembered thinking that Precious sounded like an angel, and had hoped her voice might be going up to Heaven where her mother sat looking down.

She had wanted to go inside, sit down, and join in, but when she had looked at the women in their pretty holiday dresses, the children in their festive red, green, and gold costumes, and the men in their stern black suits and crisp white shirts, she had realized that she did not belong in there, not in patched blue jeans and the fuzzy cable knit sweater that had come from a box of used clothing the church women had left on her front porch. Standing at that window, she had wished she were anyone other than Buster Talbot's daughter, especially when Precious' mother had looked up from the keyboard and seen her with Joyce Ann. Mrs. Trent had frowned sharply, shaken her head in reproach, and shooed the girls away with one hand, never skipping a note.

Now, Serena took a deep breath, stuck the key into the shiny brass lock, and opened the door to Upscale, feeling as if she had never left the place. She flipped on the lights in the waiting area, plugged in the silver Christmas tree in the foyer, and watched as the tree began to rotate on its gleaming metal stand while Christmas carols came from the tiny cassette player inside its base. The small blue and white lights strung on its branches twinkled like flecks of sparkling diamond dust, and Serena gently touched one of the red glitter balls tied in gold thread and adjusted it so that it hung straight. When she looked down at the stacks of gaily-wrapped packages beneath the tree, she had to stifle a surge of self-pity. The Secret Santa exchange. Of course, her name had not been included. Well, she had never heard of such a thing. The rules set by the stylist stated that gifts had to be at least fifty dollars in value and Serena could not imagine such a thing. Spending more than ten dollars on a coworker was enough, she thought, but then, she had never known people like this before, either.

Heading to the break room to make coffee, Serena shrugged. It still amazed her, how intensely passionate the people who came to Upscale were about their possessions, their friends, and their busy social lives. Well, she had more important things on her mind, like getting away during her lunch break to pick up her boots from the shoe shop and putting down her deposit on her own apartment.

Once the coffee was perking and the stylists' stations had been checked for supplies, Serena began to feel excited about starting another day. She did love the salon atmosphere and, since her run-in with Alexis over Patricia, had settled into a strained, but workable truce with the temperamental stylist.

A rapping sound on the front door brought her to the reception area, puzzled. The employees parked in the rear and came in through the back entrance. Who would be at the salon door at 6:59?

Through the heavy, beveled glass she could make out the shadow of a woman in a coat. *Must be one of the regulars without an appointment hoping to squeeze onto the books,* Serena thought, considering her options.

When Giani had handed her the keys to the salon, he had cautioned her not to answer the door or let strangers inside the salon before another staff member arrived. There had been a few robberies in the area, but mainly convenience stores and banks. Serena hesitated. A robber wouldn't knock. A stranger in trouble would go to a convenience store to use the phone. The weather was so bad it might be a client waiting to get in. Perhaps it was the wealthy Mrs. Rittingon, or the fancy lady who wore fringed shirts and owned a big ranch near Waco and drove 194 miles round trip to have Giani do her hair. Serena would catch hell if she left a valuable customer like that out in the cold, especially when it was obvious that someone was inside the salon.

Rubbing the back of her neck, Serena stepped closer to the door.

"Who's there?" she called, feeling foolish, but needing to be cautious.

"It's Trudy Jenkins, from Song City, across the street. The music shop, you know?"

Yes, Serena thought. Song City. Many of Upscale's clients bought tapes and CDs there. Serena had never been in the shop but knew that rock stars, jazz musicians, and singers appeared at Song City when on tour, signing autographs while in town. Alexis had had her picture taken with Bruce Springsteen at Song City when he signed covers there two years ago.

"Just a minute," Serena shouted, thinking the poor woman must have gotten herself locked out or was in some kind of emergency. Giani would want her to help out a neighbor, wouldn't he?

Serena turned the deadbolt lever and quickly opened the door, relieved to see Trudy Jenkins, a beautiful African-American woman, standing there. She had heavy brown braids that were held back from her face with a bright piece of green and yellow Kente cloth, beautiful ebony skin on which her makeup had been perfectly applied, and a white mohair muffler thrown over her shoulders and pulled up to her chin.

"Hello. I'm Trudy Jenkins and I am so glad I saw you opening up."
She extended a gloved hand, shivering.

Serena shook it, smiling. "No problem. Come in. What can I do for
you?"

"I need a favor," Trudy said, stepping inside. She shut the door,
then launched into her request. "Can you do a friend of mine today?"
Her words came out so rapidly Serena hardly understood what she
said.

"An appointment? Well, we're real busy, but I'll check and see who
might be able to," Serena said going around the counter to open the
big appointment book.

Trudy leaned across the counter, shaking her head. "Not someone.
You. I want *you* to do a friend of mine . . . well, not a friend exactly, but
a very special lady who needs her hair done today. Please, please tell
me you can do it."

Serena laughed, "Me? Oh, no. I couldn't." She shook her head at
Trudy, who had leaned so far over the counter Serena could smell her
expensive perfume and more closely examine her flawless ebony skin.

Trudy slumped back, one hand on her hip. "Why not? That is what
you do over here, isn't it? Hair?"

"Well . . . yes," Serena began, as "Silent Night" started up on the
musical tree. "I'm sure we can work something out. But I don't . . ."
Then Serena stopped, sensing the woman's near-panic.

"Diana Devreux is coming to Song City at noon," Trudy rushed to
explain. "*The* Diana Devreux. Can you imagine the crowd? The press?
It's going to be awesome."

"My God! Really? Diana Devreux is your friend?" Serena was impressed. Trudy was talking about one of the greatest R&B singers in
the country. Maybe the world.

"Yes, and I need your help," Trudy stated. "You see, Diana's chauffeur and I went to high school together. That's my connection. See, my
homeboy, Craig, and I grew up in Tennessee together and he's Diana's
chauffeur. He called me last night to tell me he persuaded Diana to
come out to my store today, but only for one hour to sign autographs.
And . . . only if I have a hairdresser on site to do Diana's hair before
the television reporters arrive. Kahi, Diana's regular stylist, checked
out."

"Checked out?"

"Yeah, she quit. Flew back to Los Angeles last night because of
some family mess." Trudy lowered her voice to a whisper. "Divorce
court, I think. Anyway, Diana had a wild concert last night at the

Arena. Sold out. Sweated out her 'do. Needs major repair, understand?"

Serena nodded, holding her breath. Was this for real? she wondered.

"Now," Trudy continued, leaning forward to lock eyes with Serena, preparing to enter serious negotiations. "I don't know a thing about you . . . ah . . . what's your name?"

"Serena St. James." How easily her new name rolled off her tongue.

"Uh, okay, Serena. You work at Upscale. So, you must be licensed and you've got to be good. You are qualified to do hair, right?"

"Yes."

"Okay. I've seen you coming and going over here for weeks." She smiled slyly and put one hand to the side of her mouth. "I gotta say, you're the first black stylist Upscale has ever had. You go, girl."

"But, it's not like that," Serena began, uneasy about the way Trudy was rushing ahead.

But Trudy cut her off. "Honey, if Giani's smug-ass self brought you into his fancy-schmancy salon, you've gotta be good. So, I told my friend, Craig—Diana's chauffeur—yes, I could get a stylist over to the shop for her, and when I mentioned Giani Pilugi's salon, he said fine. Diana had heard of Giani and knows he works with celebrities, temperamental divas, all that. But I'm sure you already know that. Anyway, Diana won't let a white person touch that famous hair. You know how she wears it all loose and wild. Natural, she calls it, but I always thought it was a weave. Whatever. Can you do it? Please say you can, 'cause she won't come out to my store unless I promise I will have somebody from Upscale over there at eleven. Please, sister. You've got to help me out."

Exhausted from just listening to Trudy's frantic plea, Serena drew in a long breath, gathering her wits as well as her courage. She hated to tell Trudy that, unfortunately, she was a maid/shampoo girl who occasionally did special clients, but who could not possibly accept such an assignment without Giani's permission.

A noise at the back door interrupted the conversation, trapping Serena's confession in her throat. She swung around to see that Alexis had let herself in with her key and was heading toward the front of the salon, her pale blue eyes narrowed into slits.

"What's going on?" Alexis wanted to know, pulling off her short fur jacket as she walked toward the two women.

Serena bit her lip, calculating the risk she was about to take, the opportunity she could not pass up. Trudy wanted her to style Diana Devreux! The beautiful, three-time Grammy winner who rarely made personal appearances in places like Song City in Dallas, Texas. Serena had read about, dreamed over, and studied the famous entertainer's hair in numerous issues of *Black Hair Today*, and knew precisely which products and techniques the diva used to twist her locks into that wild, fine, chestnut-colored mane that floated in a cloud of ringlets around her tiny oval face. One of Diana's trademarks was the way she flipped and tossed and teased her hair while belting out a song.

This was exactly the moment Serena had been searching for among the tangle of strangers, confusion, opportunity and disappointment that had overwhelmed her since her arrival in Dallas. Alexis Bonat was not going to ruin this, that much she knew. But how in the world would she ever get away from the salon on one of the busiest days of the year?

"Trudy," Serena said quickly, grabbing a piece of paper and a pen from the reception desk. "Don't worry about a thing. Write your phone number down for me. I'll call you within the hour."

Placing a hand on Serena's arm in relief, Trudy took the paper and scribbled down her number, then pulled open the door. "Eleven o'-clock sharp, sister. And don't mess up on me, you hear?"

"I won't," Serena promised, ushering Trudy outside before Alexis could intervene.

Chapter Ten

Craig Alexander stepped out of the shower, wrapped a towel around his waist, then snapped on his thin, gold Cartier watch. It was six-fifteen in the morning and all he wanted to do was go back to bed and sleep for a few more hours. But he was too restless and too unsettled to even try.

The heavy hotel drapes were pulled tightly shut and it was as dark inside the luxury suite as it was outside, but the light from the adjoining bathroom created a soft glow that allowed him to maneuver about the room without awakening Diana.

He stood at the foot of the bed and watched as Diana Devreux slept, absorbed in the sight of her smooth brown body entangled in a swirl of white satin sheets. In sleep, she resembled a piece of polished bronze, a slumbering statue of Venus that might come to life at any moment and suck him back under her spell.

The soft curve of her back, the roundedness of her hips, and the way she had pulled her shapely legs up against her flat stomach both stirred and bothered Craig. He let his gaze travel over her honey-colored breasts, remembering how her now-soft nipples had tasted hard and sweet between his lips, how she'd arched her back and pressed her sweat-sheened flesh against his less than an hour ago. And her face, that flawless oval set with huge brown eyes had soft thick lashes resting on her cheeks and a ropey tangle of auburn curls hugging the sides of her neck. Even in sleep, with no makeup, no designer clothes, and no fabulous jewelry to support her famous diva image, Diana Devreux looked far, far younger than her forty-three years. Craig was ashamed that simply looking at her had made him grow hard again, and had made him want her so fiercely he had to hold his breath and count to ten to will his erection away.

Like a father covering a sleeping child, he gently tucked the satin sheet around Diana's nakedness, then began searching for his pants, which he finally found buried under Diana's red sequined dress on the chair beside the door.

Her concert last night had been one of the longest and most exhausting of the One and Only tour so far, even though the turnout had been low. Diana had been very upset when, at seven o'clock the Dallas Arena had been only half-filled, and had threatened not to go on. But the die-hard Diana fans had hooted and stomped and clapped until their diva had finally walked out at nine o'clock and given those who had shown up more than their money's worth, singing nonstop for nearly two hours. And the appreciation shown by the less than sell-out house had ignited Diana's energy, making her prance and joke and sing her heart out, even allowing three middle-aged women in the front row to come onto the stage to groove and dance and sing along with her, something she rarely did. Even the young men who had thrown *their* underwear at her feet, had been rewarded with air-blown kisses, and personally autographed CDs when they appeared backstage after the concert. Diana Devreux's fans in Dallas had demonstrated their love for her, but what she needed were ticket sales.

Craig hoped she'd do better in New York, where a packed house was the only definition of success. As her driver and bodyguard it was his job to move her safely from one place to another, guard her while she was on stage or interacting with the public, and keep the press in line. She enjoyed giving interviews and went to great lengths to be accessible to the media, giving them enough access to keep them from calling her aloof. Seldom did a situation get out of control, but if it did, it was up to Craig to extricate her immediately, whisking her on her way.

At three A.M. this morning Craig had finally pulled Diana away from a boisterous after-party thrown for her by a local television mogul. When the revelers had begun tossing their clothes into the aquamarine pool to stand naked on the three-tiered fountains and sing, and the smell of marijuana had become stronger than the aroma of shrimp sizzling on the grill he had yanked her out.

Back in her suite, Diana had been too hyped-up to consider going to sleep and had asked Craig to stay a while, relax with a glass of wine and discuss logistics for the next and final stop on the tour—New York City. He should have known better than to accept her invitation, but he'd been wired, too, and very aware of how much she needed company to come down from the high of the evening.

Now, disappointment began to close in, and he was angry at himself for being so weak. But he always had a hard time resisting Diana. He worked for her, and whatever she asked him to do, he did, whether it was to go out for a gallon of Rocky Road ice cream at four A.M., change hotels because she did not like the room service, or have sex with her in the middle of the night instead of retiring safely to his room.

He shook the wrinkles from his slacks and was about to put them on, when he glanced over at Diana and saw her watching him.

"What are you doing?" Diana's muffled voice was husky with sleep.

Staring, he wondered if she had been awake all along, enjoying the idea of him looking at her. A smile came to his lips as he watched her stretch her legs and fluff out her hair before sitting up on one elbow to wait for his answer.

"Going to get the paper, read the review." He turned as if to leave.

"Don't you dare desert me," she breathed, twirling a lock of hair. "That's not nice, sneaking out of bed like that."

"I didn't sneak out and I'm not deserting you," he said, thinking she sounded genuinely hurt. This was not the first time he had slipped out of her bed, showered and left before she had awakened, and he had not thought it mattered if he were there in the morning or not. He came closer, curious about her mood. "Thought I'd get some breakfast, too, while I was downstairs. Let you get some sleep."

"That so? Well, you could have waited for me." Her voice was soft, yet slightly accusing.

Despite having just awakened, she looked beautiful. She was rich and spoiled, used to getting whatever she wanted, and Craig knew he had to set some boundaries or she would suffocate him. What had begun as occasional, no-strings-attached sex had been slowly edging toward a full-blown relationship and he was getting nervous. "Go back to sleep, Diana. Enjoy the break. You don't have rehearsals today or a concert tonight."

"You're right. I don't have a thing to do except that favor for your friend who owns that record store."

Craig flinched, feeling trapped.

Diana eased one arm from beneath the satin sheet and grasped the bottom edge of the towel Craig had wrapped around his naked torso. She tugged it hard. "Besides, I'm not sleepy." She gave the towel another hard yank, and laughed when it fell away.

Craig felt his stomach muscles tighten when he looked down and saw the obvious indication of his eagerness to please. Diana's fingers grazed his inner thigh. He caught the gleam of anticipation in her eyes, watched the way she pouted her lips, and knew his condition excited her. He stood like a soldier awaiting orders, groaning silently when she took his swollen erection in her hand and squeezed him gently, urgently, as if giving him a massage. He tried to pull back. She refused to let go, and holding him firmly, let him know she was in control. Craig thought he was going to burst.

God, how can I make her see that I will not be her lap dog, ready to jump at her every command if this is the way I react? he worried, loving the fire that raced in his veins while hating the shame that swam in his mind. He put his hand atop hers and gently pried her fingers away. "Diana. Please. Not now." He picked up his towel and started to wrap it around his waist.

"And why not now?" she wanted to know, sitting fully up. She managed to grasp the edge of the towel again and flung it across the room. Leaning back against the headboard, she folded her arms beneath her pointed naked breasts and smiled.

Craig groaned and closed his eyes, wishing he *had* an answer to give her, wishing he had some unshakeable reason to resist this delicious temptation. But there was none, save his own tormented conscience, and she knew it.

At twenty-nine he had slept with dozens of women and had even been serious enough about one or two to put rings on their fingers. But working for Diana Devreux meant staying on the road, working odd hours, and meeting tons of gorgeous women. He did not try to establish anything approaching a normal relationship. The women he met on the road were willing to settle for phone calls from hotel rooms, late dinners after the show, quick, though satisfying sex, and abrupt goodbyes with promises to stay in touch, which he never kept. Such relationships were part of the deal, but they often left him empty and frustrated. He had stopped looking for true love a long time ago.

Great sex with the famous Diana Devreux was all he needed. He thought.

Craig slipped down on his knees beside the bed and took Diana's face in his hands. He studied her huge, baby-doll eyes, then placed his lips over hers. They were still warm and soft from sleep. She smelled like the pink roses and white orchids that filled huge vases throughout the suite, and he breathed her scent deep into his lungs, allowing himself to enjoy the flicker of her tongue, the bite of her small fingernails on his buttocks, the thunderous pounding inside his head. Bending forward, he gathered her to him, urging her so close she tumbled from the bed and fell onto the floor in a tangle of soft sheets, silky skin, and bouncy auburn curls.

Craig lay down atop Diana, pressed his face into her shoulder, then gently parted her legs and touched the fluff of matching curls that were rubbing against his stomach.

"Give it to me," she whispered, running her tongue along his neck. "Stop acting as if you don't want me. That's not very nice, you know?"

Craig placed both hands on either side of Diana's head and pushed himself up so he could see her face. "I never said I didn't want you," he corrected. "I said, not now."

Diana stroked his back with the tips of her little fingers, making delicate circles along his spine. "I see you've changed your mind," she murmured, locking her legs around his waist.

"Yeah," he whispered, entering her, letting her in like a drug that he craved and could not do without. "I guess I did." Then he claimed her with a calm, insistent urgency that made her cry out long before he had satisfied himself.

Chapter Eleven

Serena studied Trudy's retreating figure as she slowly shut the door, unsure about how much she ought to tell Alexis, who was tapping her dark red fingernails impatiently against the reception counter. The smell of damp winter air mixed with the pungent scent of fresh evergreens and holly that filled two silver bowls on a three-tiered etagere stacked with an assortment of perfumes, shampoos, lotions, and creams.

Alexis walked over to Serena. "That was the woman who runs Song City, wasn't it?"

"Yes. Her name is Trudy Jenkins."

"What'd she give you her phone number for? She want an appointment?"

"No," Serena replied evenly, adjusting the placement of a rose-shaped bottle of hand cream atop the stack of jars, not about to divulge more than she had to.

"Just as well. We don't have anyone on staff who can do her kind of hair," Alexis replied.

Serena knew a twist of the truth was necessary now. "She wanted to see me. I've been looking for an early cassette by Aretha Franklin, and she came to tell me she located it."

"Oh," Alexis said, shrugging her shoulders as she pushed past Serena and leaned over the book to scan the day's appointments. "God, we're going to be busy today," she muttered. "Giani put in an order for a temp to work the front desk, so you will work the back today."

"Fine," Serena said, dreading the thought of turning Trudy down.

As soon as Alexis left the reception area and returned to her cubicle, Serena smoothed out the crumpled piece of paper Trudy had thrust at her and studied the phone number, still in shock. What should she do? Be upfront about the situation and tell Giani what Trudy wanted her to do? Lie to him, say she was ill, then leave and go over to Song City and do Diana's hair? But someone from the salon would surely find out about it, or see her over there. Then she'd get fired, and where would that leave her? No, she had to be honest and ask Giani for permission to do Diana Devreux's hair. But if he agreed, what would she use? The styling products and tools she needed were not in stock at Upscale.

Serena sank down on the gray velvet banquette behind the reception desk, her chin in one hand, thinking, desperate to come up with a plan before she approached her boss. This opportunity was greater than anything she had ever dared to imagine might come her way, and she could not let it pass. During many lonely nights at Havensway she had lain awake, mentally discussing her hopes and dreams with her mother, never imagining her luck would change with the arrival of a woman wearing braids and Kente cloth who ran a record store. It was a sign, she was sure, that her life was on the right path, that big things were going to happen. Somehow, she had to direct the outcome of this situation so that it would work in her favor. But how?

Giani controlled her time, her talent, and her future, with the power to challenge, stifle, or nurture her ambitions. What would he do this time? she worried, trying to imagine what her mother would advise if she had been there to help. Serena could almost hear her mother whispering in her ear, "You're a good girl, Sara Jane. Be truthful, trust your instincts, and everything will work out fine."

The phone rang, startling Serena from her thoughts. The temp who was to fill in for Maria had not arrived yet, so she picked up the phone, hoping she would not get stuck manning the front for long. Looking around the shop, she saw that all four of the shampoo girls had come in. Thank God. That part of the salon was covered for the day.

"Upscale. How can I help you?" Serena tried to sound cheery and professional, but her mind remained on her dilemma.

"Serena?" It was Giani on the line.

"Yes, Mr. Pilugi. This is Serena." She felt her heart pounding against her ribs as she waited to see what he wanted. How could she tell him that she wanted to leave the salon at eleven, the busiest time, to style a superstar's hair? And if he denied her request, she'd have to find a way to get around him.

"Serena," Giani began. "I'm stuck at home waiting for a call from Masters in New York and I don't have his product list here with me. Are you at the front desk?"

"Yes, Mr. Pilugi. What can I do for you?"

"Please, go into my office, look in the black lacquer tray on the corner of my desk and you'll see the Masters product line order form right on top. I want you to fax it to me. Okay?"

"Yes."

"Fine. My fax number here is 214-555-7890. I'll hold until it comes through."

"Yes, sir," Serena replied.

"Oh, and I won't be in the salon until about two. Call Mary Whitten and reschedule her for three o'clock."

"Yes, Mr. Pilugi," she said, pressing the red button to put him on hold.

In his office she found the Masters product list, placed it in the proper position on the fax machine, and punched in his fax number, her mind spinning. Giani wasn't coming in until two. She had to call Trudy right away. And if she planned to be upfront and honest, she'd have to tell Giani everything right now.

As the cream-colored paper slid through the machine, she groped for leverage, for some payoff for Giani. He was a businessman, a savvy entrepreneur, and he would need a valid reason to grant Serena's request.

By the time the form had been faxed, she knew exactly what to say, and after confirming his receipt of the order form, she boldly slid into his green leather Italian chair, spun around, and put her back to the door. Bending low, she launched into Trudy Jenkins' dilemma, swiveling nervously as she waited for his reply.

"That is ridiculous!" he burst out, barely giving her time to finish. "Why doesn't Trudy Jenkins call Antoinette at Hair Heaven or Thomas at the Beauty Boutique? They are the best black hairdressers in Dallas. Besides, I couldn't possibly spare you, even if you had the experience and credentials to touch the head of someone as famous as Diana Devreux. I'm sorry, Serena but there is no way I'd let an inexperienced stylist like you take on a job so important and . . . delicate."

"But I have done hair like hers. In . . . class," she hedged, unable to bring herself to say "in prison," though Giani knew where she had been trained. "There was this girl, Nancy, and she had hair just like Diana Devreux. I used to practice on her and copy Diana's hairstyle. Everyone in our class started calling Nancy Miss D. because she was a dead ringer when I was finished with her. I can do Ms. Devreux's hair, Mr. Pilugi. I know I can."

Giani laughed under his breath, a dismissive chuckle that let Serena know how absurd he found her reasoning. "Serena. Listen to me. You have never worked with a superstar, never been involved with a high-powered celebrity. I have. And let me tell you, it can be a horror. I know how temperamental, choosey, eccentric, and downright mean they can be. Diana Devreux's hair is her trademark. It is most likely insured for at least a million dollars. No way would I open myself up for a lawsuit from that woman. As wonderful as this bizarre request may sound to you . . . and I understand your excitement . . . this entire scenario is a nightmare just waiting to happen. I can't afford to take a chance on sending someone like you out on a job as important as this. Who are you? What can you do?"

"I'm Serena St James," she said, drawing power from the sound of her new identity. "And apparently Trudy Jenkins thinks I am good enough to do Diana's hair simply because I work at Upscale."

Giani sighed in exasperation. "I assume she doesn't know your main job at Upscale is to shampoo clients, does she?"

"No."

"Precisely. You've misrepresented yourself."

"So what? I'm a licensed cosmetologist, according to the state of Texas, and if you would give me more opportunities to show you what I am capable of doing, you might believe me when I tell you I can do this!"

The silence that followed terrified Serena. She slapped a hand over her mouth and held her breath, eyes wide. Her tone had been rude, her voice too loud, her anger too close to the surface. What if Giani fired her? Spread the word that she was a risk, so that no one else would touch her? But it was true. He had never, in all the time she'd been in his employ, taken much interest her talent, only using her to fill in when the other stylists were swamped. What he wanted most was a cleaning woman and a back-up person to keep his fancy salon running. Serena trembled with indignation, though in the back of her mind she worried that he might have a point. It might be a lawsuit waiting to happen, but it also might be the opportunity she had been praying for. All she needed was a break.

During her classes at Gatesview, her instructors had singled her out, calling her the most promising student in the class, and she had worked hard, learning how to assess hair types, determine which products to use, which styles would flatter the model's features. Even now, she studied her old textbooks, devoured industry magazines, and had paid the fifty-dollar dues to the National Hairstylists Association of America. True, she did not have experience, like Antoinette or Thomas or other African-American beauticians who worked with black hair on a daily basis. That did not mean she was incompetent or

would automatically fail. What a coup it would be for her to successfully create the illusion of Diana Devreux!

"You stay at the salon today, Serena," Giani ordered. "Do as I say
and forget this nonsense."

Resentment shot through Serena, igniting every nerve in her body.
His paternal admonishment threw her back to the ugly times when
she had been at the mercy of her father . . . her teachers . . . the guards
at the Cave . . . people who manipulated her with their power. She
could hear their voices in her head: *Listen to me! Do as I say! Forget
about what you want. What you want does not matter. Your opinion has no
value.*

The voices had to stop, and only Serena could make them go away.
Risking her tenuous security at Upscale was the only answer.

"Mr. Pilugi," she began. "Can you afford the negative press that
you and Upscale might receive if I were to tell Diana's friend that my
boss ordered me not to do her hair? Diana Devreux is an international
star, as you know. The press might get wind of this . . . they could in-
terpret your refusal to mean that the snobbish Giani Pilugi refused to
allow his staff to touch Diana's hair while she was in Dallas because
she is black. That's what the reporters might say."

"Don't threaten me, and don't be overly dramatic, Serena."

"Maybe you don't need a black clientele to be successful, and that
is your prerogative, but you do need a reputation as a decent human
being, not a person who would insult a three-time Grammy winner by
refusing to let your staff do her hair. Think about the positives, Mr.
Pilugi. If Diana is satisfied, I am sure she will spread the word about
you and your generous spirit."

The hum of the silent line was terrifying. Serena pressed the phone
so hard to the side of her head that the plastic mouthpiece cut into her
flesh. Giani Pilugi was not a stupid man, and had not gained a reputation as one of the High Princes of the beauty industry by playing it
safe. She had heard him tell stories of his early life as a day laborer in
the shipping yards near Boston, working eighteen hours a day, living
in a fishing shack, eating fish for every meal until a man looking for an
assistant in his barber shop in Boston took him on. Walking away from
the docks, Giani had gone with the man to Boston and eventually became a barber, too. Within three years he had his own barber shop, but
realizing that women spent far more money than men on their hair, he
closed his barber shop, took a train to New York and entered cosmetology school. There, he found his niche and concentrated on developing
his flair for handling female tresses as well as a keen understanding of
what women wanted. It did not take long for him to establish a repu-

tation as one of the most sought-after stylists in the city. But when competition for the kind of wealthy, celebrity clients he served became fierce and his overhead in Manhattan soared beyond reason, Giani took a risk and left, settling on Dallas, where money flowed like oil and big hair ruled. It had been a shrewd, calculated move on his part, but it had paid off handsomely.

Serena knew Giani was a risk-taker who recognized opportunity when it came his way. Couldn't he see she had made a valid case? Couldn't he take a chance on her?

Unable to hold back a hint of a smile, she thought: *Sara Jane Talbot, you no-name, ex-convict from Mallard, Texas . . . you're holding the cards now. Giani Pilugi has to defend his hard-won reputation.*

"Well, I understand where you are coming from, Serena," Giani muttered tersely, a bite of annoyance sharpening his words. "However, you forget one thing. At Upscale, I do not stock the tools nor the products necessary to style hair like Diana Devreux's, and I assure you I don't plan to buy them. So, even if I give you permission to fulfill this Trudy woman's request, what would you use?"

"Are you saying I can do it if I can get the products and supplies?" Serena jumped at this slim ray of hope.

"I didn't say that," he hedged. "But I certainly would not want as high profile a person as Diana Devreux to think I had intentionally snubbed her."

"I agree."

"If you are willing to spend your own money for the tools and products and can do this on your lunch hour, I guess it would be acceptable." He coughed, clearing his throat, buying time, Serena assumed, to think of more rules to lay down. "And for God's sake, keep your mouth shut about it. I do not need *any* publicity. Go on and do it, but you'd better do it right and get back to the salon as quickly as you can. The books are full—overflowing, to be exact, and you have a lot of work facing you."

After hanging up, Serena pressed the buttons on the phone with trembling fingers, dialing Song City. She had been in Giani's office much longer than she had anticipated. She could hear the salon coming to life: customers talking, phones ringing, hair dryers humming in unison, and she prayed the receptionist from the temp agency was out there, otherwise she might have to fill in out front. Alexis was probably watching the red lights on the extension phone on the wall outside her cubicle, wondering what she was doing.

Trudy came on the line immediately, confirming that the dressing room used by the visiting celebrities at Song City was outfitted like a minisalon, with a sink, a styling chair, makeup mirrors, and hair dryers; everything except the particular products the stars preferred.

"Don't worry about cost," Trudy told Serena. "Just go over to Dally's Beauty Supply in Fort Worth and get whatever you need. She uses that Triple D shampoo and fast-set conditioner. Just bring me your charge slip and I'll pay you back."

The sinking feeling that came over Serena started at her throat and rapidly worked its way down into her stomach. Go over to Fort Worth? That would take an hour each way, and she didn't have that kind of time. And how? The busses didn't run that far, plus she didn't have a MasterCard or Visa to charge this stuff. Feeling in over her head, she bluntly confessed to Trudy, "I don't have a car."

"What? Oh, shit, I forgot you ride the bus." Trudy cursed again. "Okay. Take a taxi. Get a receipt. I'll cover it, too."

"Uh . . . I don't have money for that . . . or a credit card to cover everything." Serena could feel her confidence slipping down to the floor. Her chest grew tight and her body tensed. She had a twenty-dollar bill in her wallet that was earmarked for the shoe repair bill on her boots, which she had planned to pick up on her lunch hour today. Obviously, that would have to wait.

Embarrassment burned her cheeks and brought on a flush of shame that dulled her initial excitement. Who was she trying to fool? She had no transportation, no financial resources, no experience. Nothing to bring to the table except a fierce determination to prove she could do this job.

How stupid could she be? Neither Trudy Jenkins nor Diana Devreux cared about her dreams. They needed a sister they could count on, not a broke wannabe with absolutely no control over anything. Tears surged to the brims of Serena's eyes and stayed there. She thought of slamming down the phone, disappearing from the whole humiliating mess, but she was too close to that shadowy dream to give up now.

"Damn, girl!" Trudy shot back. "No car? No credit cards! Where'd you come from? You been living in a cave?"

The phrase made Serena jump, and she almost said, *You got that right*, but lowered her voice and whispered, "No, I recently moved here and I've had to work a few things out."

"Jesus! I don't understand how a sister can expect to get ahead without decent transportation and at least one piece of plastic. I'd have thought Giani paid his hairdressers well enough for y'all to be driving BMWs and eating out every night."

"Maybe some, but not me," Serena lamely confessed. "But I do have a driver's license," she added, grateful for Nina's prodding insistence that she use her car to take the test.

"Thank the good Lord for that," Trudy grumbled. "Can you drive a stick?"

"Sure," Serena replied smoothly, unwilling to admit that the last and only time she had been behind the wheel of a car with a standard transmission was when she drove the getaway car during an armed robbery.

"Okay. Take my Celica. I'll call over to Dally's and clear it for you to charge everything you need on my credit card. How soon can you get going? Traffic over to Fort Worth is a bitch, and in this weather it will take all morning. I want you over there and back here as soon possible. Dally's is open right now."

"Fine." *If the temp from the employment agency is here to cover the front desk,* she worried silently.

Swiveling around in Giani's soft leather chair, she faced the door and was jolted alert by the inquisitive stare of Alexis Bonat and the sly smile that curved over her lips.

How long has she been standing there, listening? Serena wondered, gently replacing the phone into its cradle.

Chapter Twelve

Craig Alexander nudged the white stretch limousine up the winding drive toward the front door of Mansion on Turtle Creek and came to a stop next to the tubs of bright red hibiscus that flanked the hotel's gleaming wooden doors. He got out, circled the front of the long expensive car, opened the passenger side door, and then nodded at the uniformed doorman. The doorman tipped his hat, flung open the heavily carved doors, and lifted his chin in acknowledgment at Diana Devreux as she swept past him in a clatter of spiked heels and jangling silver bracelets.

The people standing around outside the hotel stared at the diminutive diva, who was wearing a tight red jumpsuit, a silver turban, and oversized sunglasses that covered nearly all of her famous face. She was carrying her glossy fur coat over her arm, despite the frigid temperature.

"Diana! Diana! Wait!" A man's voice shot out of a knot of people nearby.

Craig slammed the limo door as soon as Diana was safely inside, hurried around the back of the car, and got in behind the wheel. When he started the engine, preparing to pull away from the curb, he heard the man shout Diana's name again.

"Diana! I love you! Marry me. I love you!" the man was yelling.

Disgusted, Craig stepped on the gas and moved the heavy car into the center of the driveway, but he was watching the man in the rearview mirror, annoyed to see that he was racing after the limo. Craig sped up, anxious to get away, but a loud thump shook the limo and Craig had to stop. Looking back he saw that the overzealous fan had slammed his body against the passenger side of the car and had pressed his face flat against the darkened window.

"Shit," Craig cursed. He didn't need this kind of mess. Staged accidents and threats of lawsuits were always possibilities whenever Diana Devreux mixed with the public, and he ought to be used to stuff like this, but it still annoyed the hell out of him. Why people acted so crazy and irresponsible in the presence of a famous person was beyond him. It seemed as if all common sense flew out the window, taking all self-control when a celebrity became accessible.

Craig turned around to get Diana's reaction, but her sunglass-shaded eyes were focused on the darkened one-way window.

"Want me to check this situation?" he asked.

"No. I doubt he's hurt," Diana sharply tossed back. "Let's go."

Craig proceeded down the curved brick drive and into the traffic on the main street, then glanced into the mirror, surprised to see a smug smile on Diana's lips. Obviously, she wasn't that upset. But her moods were often difficult to predict.

Diana could be sweet and accommodating, or downright difficult. Few people in her entourage, which besides Craig, included her business manager, Vincent Ruby; three backup singers; and Kahi, Diana's stylist and personal assistant could be certain about what to expect. For twenty-three years Diana had worked hard in the music business, thriving on the attention and adoration of those who told her she was beautiful, talented, sexy, and smart. Her fans, her friends, her business associates, the columnists for the trades, and the talk show hosts also went out of their way to reassure Diana that, at age forty-three, she still had it going on.

But Craig sensed her insecurity, her desire to stop the clock that was fast ticking away her youth, as well as the erosion of her popularity. On this, her first tour in four years, ticket sales had been inconsistent and Vincent Ruby, her manager, was not happy.

Diana pulled her fur over her shoulders, scooted to the far side of the semicircular tufted seat, leaned her head back, and sighed. She was definitely not in the mood to be bothered with her fans today. "Jeez, what an idiot," she grumbled, shifting around on the soft leather cushions so she could focus on Craig's eyes in the rearview mirror. "Throwing himself into the side of a moving limo. How stupid. And I better not hear the word 'lawsuit.' Not today," she said, sinking down into the cocoon of her fur.

"I doubt it," Craig replied. "There were plenty of witnesses around."

Diana kicked off her red suede mules and tossed them to the floor. Craig raised himself high enough in his seat to see that she had pulled her shapely legs up to her knees, and with her chin on them was staring back at him. "Right," she said. "Good thing no reporters or cameras were around. I don't need any photos of a situation like that . . . or of me looking like this." She tugged her silver turban down over her ears and tucked a few stray curls of hair auburn beneath it.

"You look fine, Diana," Craig assured her, amused by her vanity. She never went out in public wearing anything like the turban and sunglasses she was wearing today unless she had something very important to do . . . or needed a shopping fix to settle her nerves. He swung into the early morning traffic, leaving the man standing in the hotel drive staring after them.

Craig concentrated on the thick morning traffic, aware that Diana must still be upset over the fact that Kahi, her stylist, had left last night, headed home to Los Angeles for an upcoming appearance in divorce court, leaving Diana stranded. Diana had been livid, accusing Kahi of abandoning her at a time when she needed her most. The tour had been rocky, her appearance was key to the success of this tour, and now, without Kahi to style her hair, do her makeup, consult on her wardrobe, and take care of the details that had to be handled, Diana would be lost.

Craig had been Diana Devreux's chauffeur for five years, and in that time he had learned how to deal with her moody, impulsive behavior, yet struggled with her penchant for demanding more from him than he truly wanted to give. But after all, she was the star and he worked for her.

"Where to?" he prompted, trying to get her mind off the unsettling incident.

"I don't care. Just drive. I'm so bored, Craig," she blurted out. "This is the longest damn tour. I'll be so glad to get home. I hate Texas. Houston, Austin, San Antonio, now Dallas. I feel like I've covered half the country and here I am, still in Texas."

"Well, you can relax today, and you're almost finished."

"Right. New York," she sighed, then added, "They love me there."

"Yep, the Big Apple, then it's home to Vegas," Craig agreed, nervous about the final concert. He had overheard her screaming at Vincent Ruby only yesterday about his inability to book her on *The David Letterman Show*, outraged that the talk show host would snub her like that.

"I've still got that New Year's Eve bash at the MGM, remember? So, it's not quite over," she corrected.

"Yeah, but that's different. At least, in Vegas, you'll be at home."

She pushed her sunglasses onto her forehead, then stared gloomily out the window. "I could kill Kahi for cutting out on me. Right before New York!" She pulled off the glasses and the silver turban, releasing a tumble of soft chestnut curls. "Your friend found someone qualified to do my hair, didn't she?" Diana combed her famous locks with her fingers.

"Sure did. A hairdresser from Upscale. Giani Pilugi's salon."

"Good. I've heard he's fabulous. A sister, right?"

"Absolutely. Don't worry, everything's gonna work out fine," Craig assured her, thankful that Trudy had come through for him.

Diana thoughtfully pressed her lips together, examined her long silver fingernails, then spoke to Craig without looking at him. "You know, Craig, signing autographs in a record store is not how I planned to spend my day."

Craig glanced back and saw her arched brow, aware that she was testing him. "Ah, Diana, it'll be good press. And I really did *need* you to come through for my friend. You know how it is. Trudy's my homegirl."

"I never had a homegirl . . . or homeboy I felt so compelled to impress," she tossed back sarcastically. "But since you *needed* me . . ." Her voice trailed off softly.

Craig felt an unexpected stir between his legs, totally understanding her inference. She was doing him a favor, keeping him from looking like a fool after promising Trudy he could get Diana to come to her store if she ever toured in Dallas. Now he would have to reciprocate, and he knew exactly what Diana wanted.

He swallowed dryly and willed himself to get control over his reaction. There certainly could be worse ways of returning favors than slipping into bed with a stunning, famous woman, even if she was fourteen years his senior.

"You'll like Trudy, she's fun," he began, easing the conversation away from what lay ahead and tried to focus on Trudy. What must she look like now? he wondered. He hadn't seen her in more than ten years. After high school they both had escaped small town life in Newton, Tennessee, to go their separate ways, with Trudy winding up in Dallas managing a record store, and Craig in Los Angeles, valet parking cars. One rainy afternoon he had snagged Diana Devreux's attention after delivering her car to her at a charity luncheon at the Beverly Hills Hotel. She had given him a look that he had quickly understood, then tipped him a twenty-dollar bill. He had boldly handed her his card with an invitation for her to call him if she ever needed a driver. He had never believed anything would come of it, but a month later she called and asked him to drive her to a nightclub in Malibu. He had driven her there, waited in the car while she partied until three in the morning, then drove her back to her hotel. The next day she called him again, and offered him the job of personal driver and part-time bodyguard.

Diana's permanent home was in Las Vegas, but she traveled extensively and had been looking for a permanent driver who would be willing to go on the road with her. She did not like using limo services in various cities or having strangers drive her around, so Craig had accepted her offer and had been with her ever since.

When Trudy Jenkins learned through mutual friends that Craig was working for the famous Diana Devreux, she had tracked him down and made him promise that if Diana ever came to Dallas he'd bring her to her record store. Bravely, he'd immediately replied, "No problem," and now he had to make good.

"She'll set you up real nice," he told Diana, confident that Trudy was still the organized, sensible girl he remembered. She never did anything less than first class.

"She'd better," Diana murmured, leaning up to place her arm against the back of Craig's neck. "This cowboy country is getting to me. I think I'm ready to ride out of here. Aren't you?"

Craig smiled, but knew better than to respond. She could infer the most seductive things without ever saying the words. He knew what she wanted and expected from him and maybe that was what attracted them to each other.

Craig settled back on the cushy leather seat and let Diana press her arm against his neck, allowed her to tease him with her soft, fluttering fingers. It drove him mad, but he loved it, and did not tell her to stop.

They had slept together for the first time two days after he had officially come on board as her chauffeur. She had telephoned him late one night, asked him to come over, and when he arrived, had boldly led him into her bed. He had not resisted, in fact he had welcomed the attention, allowing himself to be seduced by her playful sex, her youthful spirit, and her fantastic body, which she kept in great shape by working out and eating little more than lettuce and tomatoes for weeks at a time.

After a while, Craig had tried to avoid their intimate encounters, aware that he needed his job too much to fuck it up with this personal involvement with his boss. But somehow, Diana always managed to ease back under his skin, distracting him from his mission to pull away. At times she simply liked to lie in his arms without making any sexual demands and talk to him. After four marriages and several broken engagements, Diana admitted to having been burned by too many men to consider marriage again, and most men, she thought, dated her because of her fame and her money. Diana said she wanted nothing more than terrific sex now and then, a warm bed when she felt lonely, and an absence of pressure, judgment, or expectations about the future. Craig fit the bill perfectly.

This attitude was something Craig understood, too, because he did not trust himself to enter into a serious relationship either. When he was sixteen years old, he'd gotten his girlfriend pregnant. Her parents and his had formed an alliance, pressuring him to marry the girl. Though devastated, he had gone along with the plan and prepared himself to give up his freedom to take on the role of a teenage dad. But his girlfriend miscarried the day before the wedding, and he'd cried himself to sleep, so relieved to have his life back again. After that terrifying experience, he vowed two things: always wear protection and never consider marriage unless he was in love. So far, he had not broken either.

So, his relationship with Diana Devreux was exactly what they both needed. He didn't love her, and she realized that. She viewed him as a distraction, and it didn't bother Craig. She was an attractive, intelligent woman who did not ask for more than he could give. A full-blown affair was impossible, so they willingly settled into an unspoken arrangement based on trust and sexual need. Whenever he . . . or she . . . needed to feel the warmth of a nonjudgmental soul, they had one another to turn to.

Craig dated, and sometimes bedded, other women, while Diana maintained a stable of willing escorts to go out with and entertain at home. For weeks, even months at a time they would treat each other with cool politeness, respecting their roles of employer and employee. And on rare occasions, when they were out in public and Diana wanted to discourage a particularly aggressive fan or suitor, she might hold Craig's arm and give the impression that there was more between them than there really was. Craig let her do it. Why not? It was kind of fun to play at being a couple, shocking those who watched them. Afterward they would laugh about the rumors they had started and the gossip that inevitably turned up in the trade papers that followed the celebrities' every move.

Diana never pressured Craig to sleep with her, but made her wishes known in gentle, nonverbal ways that usually melted Craig's resistance. She might stand very close to him, touch him, watch him with those huge brown eyes, and he had to admit that he found Diana Devreux impossible to deny.

Now, tuning out the feathery stroke of Diana's fingers on his ear lobe, he prayed that Trudy, the girl he'd known all his life and had taken to his high school prom in Newton, would not let him down. Diana was doing him a great favor by going over to Song City to sign autographs, and he didn't want anything to go wrong.

"Take me to Neiman's, Craig." Diana decided, giving his ear a light squeeze before removing her hand. "I'm sure they can arrange a private room for me to look at a few special things."

"You got it," Craig answered, inwardly groaning. Her impromptu shopping sprees could take hours, and today was definitely not the day to get caught up in one of her madcap adventures in a store. He had to get her to Song City by noon, or his credibility would be shot.

Craig knew that Diana considered clothes good for one thing—to make a dynamite first impression—and once that mission had been accomplished they were basically useless. Wearing a piece of clothing once (maybe twice, if she had not been photographed in it) kept the custom-made closets in Diana's Las Vegas home as crammed as Filene's Basement. And she held on to every glittering evening gown, costume, dress, jacket, skirt, or pair of slacks she had ever bought.

For Diana Devreux, shopping was a form of entertainment that had only two rules: All clothing had to be in some combination of red, black, silver or gold (the only colors she wore), and anything she bought had to be delivered to her hotel room, home, jet, or yacht within two hours after selection. She never carried packages, a purse, or money. If the items could not be charged to Diana Devreux, Inc., and delivered to her immediately, she passed them up. Few salespeople balked at honoring her requests.

Raised by a hard-working single mother in a modest apartment on the East Side of Cleveland, Diana Devreux had grown up wanting everything, especially to be beautiful. An only child, she had hated the restraints her mother placed on her because of their tenuous financial situation, and dreamed of having more clothing than her mother could possibly afford, of spending more money than her mother could ever spare, and of receiving more adulation than she truly deserved. A minor role in her high school's production of *Carousel* brought Diana a great sense of joy, as well as relief from the tension between herself and her mother. Immediately, she knew that the spotlight was what she craved, and focused her energy into plotting how to stay there. While on stage, she could amass the affection, the attention, the money, and material things her mother was unable to give her. And she believed that costumes, lighting, and stage makeup were magical tools that could keep her beautiful forever.

Now, at age forty-three, three Grammy's and a long-standing reputation as one of the top selling R&B singers of all time, she had accomplished everything she had set out to do. All she had to do now was stay on top, and that meant staying young.

Chapter Thirteen

At ten-fifteen, Serena was finally heading west toward the I-20 Freeway, praying the traffic would give her a break because the weather certainly was not cooperating. The misty drizzle that had been falling all morning turned into a blinding downpour, forcing the traffic on the freeway into one long, slow-moving snake-of-a-line that crawled over the glistening asphalt toward Fort Worth. Hunched close to the steering wheel, Serena stared straight ahead, terrified.

She rarely drove Nina's car since accepting the job at Upscale, and this was the first time she had ever taken the freeway to Fort Worth, and the amazingly heavy traffic was daunting. Riding the bus suited Serena just fine. Only this opportunity to style Diana Devreux's hair could have forced her out on a mission like this.

The creeping pace, the unfamiliar landscape, and the splatter of raindrops that pummeled the car made her feel vulnerable, too far away from the predictable surroundings she had come to depend on to feel safe. The rhythmic sweep of the wiper blades as they slapped back and forth and the blurry red taillights blinking back at her increased the tension that had begun building the moment she got into Trudy's car.

How in the world would she ever find her exit in this storm? she worried, doubting she'd make it to the beauty supply and back to Dallas by eleven o'clock. Hopefully, the store manager had bagged and rung up the items Trudy had ordered, and all Serena would have to do was dash in, sign the charge slip, and leave. Every minute counted.

Serena fumbled with the knobs on the dash until she found the defroster and quickly dispensed the layer of mist that had begun to cloud the windows. Cool air drifted up from the vents, touched her cheeks, and eased her claustrophobic nervousness.

After fifteen more minutes of driving rain, the downpour finally slacked off, the traffic jam broke apart, and Serena sped up, trying to make up for lost time. When she saw exit 13A, the one Trudy had told her to take, her nervousness eased a little. She switched on her right-turn blinker, checked the side mirror, then headed down the exit ramp.

At the stoplight, she sank back in her seat, relieved to be off the slick freeway at last, and on a much less crowded side street. She picked up the notepaper with directions scribbled on it and tried to get her bearings. Right at the light, left on Richardson Drive, go down two lights, turn into the Avon Place shopping center. Dally's was next to the Fashion Barn. Glancing at the clock, she saw that it was ten-thirty-five and she tightened her grip on the steering wheel. She had to make it back on time.

Remembering that it was legal to turn right on red, Serena depressed the clutch, stepped on the accelerator, and moved smoothly into the intersection. From the corner of her eye, she saw a flash of white and immediately yanked the car toward the right, hoping to give the vehicle that was barreling down on her room to pass. But her maneuver failed. She plunged off the road and slipped into a water-filled drainage ditch, landing front end down, settling at a fairly sharp angle.

"What the devil?" Serena muttered, holding the steering wheel fast as she stared in fright into her mud-splashed windshield. The engine still whirred and the wheels were digging deeper into the soft mud. She could not do anything but sit there, stunned, more worried about the car and the inconvenience than frightened over what had just happened.

Quickly, she took stock of the situation: she was not hurt. The engine was still running, and other than being mired down in mud, the car did not seem to have been damaged. Jerking around, she peered out the back window, squinting into the rain-spotted glass, and saw that a long white limousine had pulled up behind her.

"Dammit," Serena cursed, twisting the key to silence the engine. "He saw me enter the intersection first and deliberately ran me off the road." She unbuckled her seat belt, opened the door and struggled to get out, though the angle of the car made it difficult.

"Are you hurt?" the man shouted, running up to the open door on the driver's side. He leaned over, peered inside, then asked. "Are you okay in there?"

Serena pushed herself up more forcefully until she managed to swing her feet to the ground, then glared at the stranger, furious. His official looking chauffeur's cap and jacket did not make her feel any better. Forgetting about her raincoat, she swung out of the lopsided vehicle, but pulled back when the man offered his hand.

"My name is Craig. Craig Alexander, and I am terribly sorry. Here, let me help you get out," he offered, reaching for Serena's arm.

"Don't bother, Mr. Alexander," she snapped, pulling back. "I can manage." Standing, without his assistance, she straightened her shoulders and lifted her chin. "And no, I'm not hurt," she told him. "Thank you very much for asking."

"Good," Craig replied, looking her up and down.

"Why'd you run me off the road? Are you crazy?"

"I swear I didn't see you," Craig started, stepping back, palms toward Serena in defense. "God, I'm sorry . . ."

"You should be," Serena shot back, placing one hand on the side of the car to keep her balance. Looking down, she saw that she was standing in a hole and her loafers were covered with brown muddy water. She wiped her free hand across her cheek, shaking her head. "This is just great. Now, what am I supposed to do?" Without waiting for an answer she sloshed around the rear of the car to check the damage, and was horrified to see that both front tires were submerged in the mud, their once-shiny hubcaps completely invisible. Only a tow truck could get her out of this.

The brief lull in the rainstorm vanished in a roll of thunder and a sharp crackle of lightening and the storm resumed with a furious downpour. Huge drops of rain smacked the pavement, splattered like broken eggs, and created puddles on the highway the size of silver dollars.

Serena was steaming mad, wishing she didn't feel so helpless. The man was cautiously watching her, as if he expected her to explode, but she was determined not to lash out. *Going crazy will not help,* she told herself, refusing to give in to her anger. She had to get to Dally's and back to Song City. This disastrous situation had to be resolved. Fast. Standing in the downpour with her jaw tight and her hands balled into angry fists, she glared at the man, hoping he felt her anger while she wanted to sink down into the mud and cry. Why had this happened to her?

I should have known this would never work, she mentally chastised herself. It was a sign that she was not supposed to be, even briefly, in the company of someone as famous as Diana Devreux. Was this her payback for misleading Trudy? For thinking she was qualified to touch a diva's hair? But now that she was in this mess her ass was on the line and she had to find a way out.

"Believe me," Craig begged, taking off his cap in a gesture of respect despite the heavy rain. "I didn't see you, and I'd never do anything like this on purpose." He took off his jacket and gingerly placed it over Serena's shoulders, holding it by the collar, as if afraid she might throw it off and try to hit him. But she grudgingly let him put it around her. "I was in a hurry. Wasn't paying attention."

"You're damn straight about that," she snapped, swallowing the anger that was crowding her throat. "I have important business to take care of this morning." she started. "You may enjoy driving like a bat out of hell, hurling yourself around town in a big fancy car, frightening innocent drivers off the road, but I am not impressed. Look what you've done!" The unexpected crack in her voice made her stop and gather her sense of perspective. She closed her eyes for a second, took a long breath, then went on. "What are you going to do about this?"

Pulling the man's jacket over her arms, she shivered, waiting for his answer. She wanted to cuss him out, really level him with a tongue-lashing he would never forget, but knew it would do no good. Besides, the man seemed truly sorry and she could tell that he was worried.

She watched him carefully, wondering who might be inside his limo. He was attractive, in an open, easy manner, and she calculated that he was probably in his late twenties. He had skin the color of graham crackers and dark brown hair that was cut very short. His deep brown eyes, set beneath thick, straight brows emphasized the smooth skin of his forehead and the soft curve of a jawline that was youthful and strong. His uniform shirt, now soaking wet and clinging to him, defined the shape of his well-toned upper arms and shoulders, while his hands, which were settled over the expensive-looking leather belt at his waist had short, neat nails and no rings on any fingers.

Serena blinked raindrops from her eyes, shoved wet hair from her face, and stepped a few feet closer to him. "I think I'd better call the police," she decided, focusing on a phone booth across the street, thinking it could be a set-up—one of those intentional accidents to lure her out of her car. *But that's not likely,* she thought. It was broad daylight and she was at one of the busiest intersections in Fort Worth, and the people who were driving by had begun to slow down to see what was going on, backing up traffic in the intersection. "This is not my car and I don't want any trouble."

"No," Craig said, "I'll call a tow truck on my car phone and take care of everything. There won't be any trouble. No police, please. I assure you I'm not a rapist, a pick-up artist, a con man, or a player. I'm just a hard-working brother who is very sorry to have inconvenienced a beautiful sister like you."

The easy flow of his words sounded convincing, and she wanted to believe him, but she also wanted more information. "If your name is Craig Alexander, why do you have DD monogrammed on your shirt?"

Craig glanced down at the pocket of his wet shirt, then took out his wallet and removed his chauffeur's driver's license. "See. There's my name. Right there, and here's my insurance card. Don't worry about anything. I work for Diana Devreux. I'm her chauffeur, and she'll take care of everything. No problem. I just hope you're not hurt."

"I'm . . . fine," Serena meekly admitted, her eyes widening as she assessed the limo, the brash, good-looking driver, and thought about what he had just told her. *He's got to be lying,* she thought. *Diana Devreux? The same woman whose hair I'm out here in the rain for?* "Are you for real?" she bluntly asked.

"Absolutely," he replied, tugging the front of his wet monogrammed shirt away from his muscled chest. "Diana Devreux likes to put her stamp of ownership on everything and everybody around her," he joked.

But Serena wasn't smiling. "So, you're saying she owns you?" She emphasized her point by skeptically looking him up and down, eyebrows raised.

"No, I just work for the lady. I assure you, I'm my own man."

"Then I guess you're going to have to fix this mess. And fast."

"All right. Get in the limo, out of the rain."

"Sure," Serena impulsively agreed, retrieving her coat and bag from Trudy's car. She'd take him up on his offer, if for no other reason than to see what the inside of the limo looked like. He had been honest about accepting responsibility for the accident, and *was* trying to be helpful.

But this man's a player, too, she thought when Craig put an arm around her shoulders and escorted her to the limo.

"Is *she* in there?" Serena asked, pointing at the darkened windows, hoping her introduction to the famous diva would not be under such humiliating circumstances.

"Oh, no," he chuckled. "Miz Devreux is shopping at Neiman's. She sent me out to find a place called Dally's Beauty supply to get some special hairspray she likes." Craig shrugged, rolling his eyes. "Her stylist quit yesterday and she's in a tizzy about her hair. I was headed into that shopping center over there when I ran you off the road. As I said . . . wasn't paying attention. I'll call a tow truck, then take you wherever you need to go."

"Fine," Serena replied, sliding onto the gray leather seat. She pulled Craig's jacket closer around her shoulders. It smelled sweet and musky and masculine, a mixture of scents that suddenly made her smile. And when she glanced back at Craig, who was about to shut the door, she saw that he was smiling, too.

It was eleven-fifteen when Craig finally pulled into the crowded parking lot of Song City. Serena was sitting in the backseat of the limo, a stack of parcels in her lap, a heavy crystal glass of club soda in one hand. Behind them, an AAA tow truck pulling Trudy's car slammed on the brakes and shuddered to a stop. Serena leaned forward, placed the glass in its special little holder, and reached for the door handle, tipping the heavy bags from her lap in her hurry to get out.

"Wait!" Craig stopped her. "Don't open that door!"

Serena froze, then slowly scanned the crowded parking lot and the frustrated security guard who was trying to control the entrance of fans into the tiny store. Apparently several people thought Diana Devreux was inside the limo because they turned and pointed at it, then started edging toward the car.

"I know you and Diana look nothing alike, but if you get out right now, you might get trampled." He motioned for Serena to stay put as he eased open the door and got out.

Watching him approach the guard, Serena held her breath. What a strange, confusing, yet wonderful situation. First, she's run off the road by Diana Devreux's chauffeur, and now she's sitting in the diva's limo, protected by this awesome brother who took care of everything with a few phone calls. *Not bad*, Serena thought, nodding her head. Things were definitely looking up.

Chapter Fourteen

Driving into Dallas, Serena and Craig had chatted about music, movies, Diana's tour, and the upcoming event at Song City. Serena had explained how Trudy had come to her at Upscale to ask her to style Diana's hair, and why she had been so eager to accept the assignment, even though it meant borrowing Trudy's car. Of course she did not tell him she was broke, was a maid and shampoo girl at Upscale, or that she'd never actually styled a celebrity client's hair during her tenure at the salon.

When Craig had asked her about her work, she had artfully revealed only necessary specifics, telling him she'd had lots of experience with temperamental types because of Upscale's clientele. This seemed to put him at ease, as he nodded, then visibly relaxed.

"Well," Craig had mused. "This is very interesting. You sound like the hottest thing going in the business in this city. Diana's going to love you."

Serena had closed her eyes, praying he'd be right.

Now, watching the guard as he tried to control the entrance of people who were clutching CDs, tapes, and photos of Diana, Serena became very nervous. She eased back in her seat, hiding her face from the curious ones who were certain their diva was inside. She wondered how movie stars and famous people could put up with such frightening masses of curious fans. Shaking her head, she began to pick up her packages from the limo floor.

Craig returned and got back in, sitting in the driver's seat. He turned around to look at Serena. "The place is jammed. Trudy came through, all right. This might turn out to be a pretty decent gig for Diana after all."

"I hope Ms. Devreux isn't mad. I was supposed to be here at eleven."

"Don't worry. She's still shopping at Neiman's. I'll pick her up at noon."

"Noon . . . but, Trudy said . . ." Serena started, worried about the delay, the crowd, the amount of time she would need to work on Diana's hair.

Craig tilted back his head, one eye nearly shut as he assessed the anxiety on Serena's face. "Calm down." He reached over and patted her hand. "Diana Devreux is never on time. She doesn't have to be. Other people do that. If you work for her you had better be punctual, or even better, early, so when she arrives late, it all comes together. That's why I asked Trudy to tell you to be here at eleven. Relax. Diana can't get here until I go pick her up, and if she's found some things she likes, she'll shop until I drag her out." He gazed evenly at Serena, then ran a finger over the back of her hand. "You seem like a real nice person, Serena."

She swallowed and glanced down, uncomfortable with his tone, his words, his touch. "I try to be," she answered.

"Well, I'm sure Diana's going to like you," he went on. "Just do your thing and go with the flow. In a flash it will all be over." He winked. "But I'll miss you when you're gone."

"Yeah. I'll bet," she said sarcastically, trying to act uninterested, yet stirred by the sincerity in his tone. *Stop it, Serena,* she cautioned herself. *This guy probably plays this same song with every girl in every city he visits, and you don't want to be his next conquest.*

"It's true," Craig whispered, lowering his eyes. "Our meeting was a really strange coincidence and I like you. I wish I could take you out to dinner. Make up for the stress I caused today. But, as I said, we're leaving tomorrow."

"Where to?" Serena asked, her heart pounding like a jackhammer hitting concrete.

"New York. Last stop."

Serena pulled her hand away from his and stuck it under the packages in her lap, wondering how to handle such a self-assured, flirtatious brother. No man had ever winked at her, stroked her hand, told her she was beautiful, let alone looked at her with such interest, and with such intriguing eyes—eyes that seemed intensely keen, drawing her in, forcing her to look away.

During the seventeen months since she had been out of prison, she had thought about meeting someone special, of a relationship with an attractive, attentive man like Craig, but never dreamed it would actually happen. And now that someone interesting had entered her life, he was not going to be around long enough for her to get to know him. Once Craig Alexander left Dallas, that was it. There'd be no way she'd ever see him again.

"Let me give you a bit of advice," Craig began, sounding very solemn. "Once you get inside the record store, get everything lined up and set to go. Everything. Shampoo, styling gel, all that Triple D stuff she uses, hot combs heated and ready. I know how Kahi, her former stylist, did things. I'm telling you, when Diana walks in, don't speak to her first. Please, don't do that. Just throw a cape around her shoulders and get busy. If you try to talk to her, she gets all upset and might walk out. Can't let that happen. Trust me. I know. I've been with her a long time."

"So, all I have to do is keep my mouth shut and work, right?" Serena asked.

"Yes. Unless she speaks to you. You'll know what to do. If she likes you it'll go great. If she doesn't . . . well, I can't promise what might happen."

"Gee, thanks," Serena muttered, now more nervous than ever. It was going to be a whole lot different than washing the hair of society matrons and local near-celebrities at Upscale.

"You know," Craig continued, "I thought you were joking when you told me you were on your way to Dally's to pick up supplies to do Diana's hair. Some coincidence how things work out, huh? Kahi leaving, me running into you."

"Oh, maybe not a coincidence," Serena replied, gaining on her nervousness. Craig was trying hard to make her feel comfortable and had been patient, honest, and polite from the first moment of their encounter. "Maybe it was destined. You know, set in motion a long time ago . . . from the moment you met Trudy Jenkins." Serena laughed to break the tension.

"That's deep," Craig tossed back, smiling. "Thanks for trusting me to help you."

"I'd still be standing in the rain waiting for a tow truck if I hadn't. I don't know what I would have done if anyone other than you had run me off the road." Nervous, she gathered the bags in her arms. "Sorry for overreacting."

"Apology accepted," he told her in a level voice that made Serena feel warm inside.

"Well," he said, glancing across the street at the gray-domed awning in front of Upscale. "Let's say we both came along at the right moment."

"I guess so," she murmured, loving the sound of his voice. She could sit and listen to him forever, but she had work to do. "I'd better get going," she said, not sure if she should open the door and get out or wait for Craig to do it for her.

"Yeah, it's late," Craig agreed, breaking eye contact with her as he turned away to get out. He opened the door for Serena, took the packages from her, then gently held her by the elbow as she stepped from the limo.

The curious onlookers outside the music store moved closer, but when they realized the woman with the chauffeur was not Diana Devreux, they resumed pressing against the rope that the guard had stretched across at the entrance to the store.

Serena stayed close by Craig's side, her trench coat covering her wet, wrinkled clothing. Good thing she had thought to put an Upscale smock into her bag before she left the salon this morning. Hopefully, Diana would not notice her soggy, misshapen loafers. Her feet were so wet and cold, she thought they might never warm up.

"You'll do fine," Craig whispered in her ear.

"I hope so," Serena whispered back, buoyed by his closeness, the warmth of his breath on her neck, the touch of his hand cupped under her elbow. She wanted to turn around, go back into the safe cocoon of the limo, and resume the conversation they had started. He had made her feel so normal, so special, she wanted to be alone with him again, so she could experience those good feelings all over.

As they approached the guarded door, she tried to focus on the job ahead instead of the confusing swirl of emotions that were sweeping through her. Meeting Craig had changed everything, making her realize that she was attractive and desirable, attributes she had not given enough thought to during this difficult time of transition. It was time for that to change.

"Here," Craig said, lifting the rope. He held it up for Serena to pass through. "See you when I come back?" he asked, handing her the bags over the ropes.

"Sure," Serena replied, backing away.

"And remember," Craig reminded her. "You are going to be fine, and Miz D is going to love you! Trust me." Grinning, he waved and left.

Serena hurried inside Song City, then turned to look at Craig through the smudged tinted window as he walked back to the limo, her eyes traveling over his straight back, down his long legs, and back up to his compact shoulders, already missing him. At the limo, he stood up in the open door and waved again. Serena waved back, then hurried off to find Trudy, her feet skimming over the floor.

"You will not believe what happened!" Serena started right in as soon as she saw Trudy, who was arranging a stack of Diana's CDs on a display in the wide center aisle.

Trudy lifted a hand in relieved welcome. "Girl, where've you been? I called over to Upscale and they said you left at nine-thirty."

"I did, but . . ."

"Later," Trudy cut her off. "Come on."

Serena followed Trudy up the back stairs, explaining about the accident, how Craig had taken care of her car, how he'd purchased the beauty supplies, and how apologetic he had been about running her off the road.

"Enough," Trudy interrupted Serena's rambling. "I get the picture. But the diva herself called here twenty minutes ago, looking for Craig and she sounded mad as hell."

"Oh?"

"Yeah, and don't act like you don't know what I'm talking about, Serena. Craig Alexander can be a slippery dude where women are concerned. I know him. Watch out, girlfriend, that's all I've got to say."

"But, I only said . . ." Serena stuttered.

"Yeah. And you don't have to tell me anymore. He's cool," Trudy remarked, now smiling. "I've known him a long time. He's gorgeous and loves to play the hero, so don't be too impressed, too fast. For now, at least. You've got work to do."

Serena hurried down the brightly lit corridor toward the star dressing room, barely listening to Trudy's advice. For the first time in months, maybe in years, she felt genuinely happy.

Chapter Fifteen

At five-feet-three, 104 pounds, Diana Devreux was diminutive, but when she burst into the dressing room at Song City, clad in skin-tight black leather pants, a red-fringed western style shirt, and intricately tooled cowboy boots with shiny silver heels, her star power lit up the room.

Serena drew in a sharp breath. Stunned by the diva's beauty, poise, and electrifying presence, she stared at Diana as the star breezed past her and headed toward the oversized poster of her latest CD cover, *One and Only*, which Trudy had hung next to the huge window overlooking the main part of the store downstairs.

"God, I love that cover!" Diana remarked to no one in particular. She stepped closer and scrutinized the airbrushed image of herself swathed in frothy black lace, lying on a zebra skin rug. Red roses were strewn strategically over private areas of her satin-doll body and she was holding a silver champagne flute in one hand. "That was a great shoot. Brian Chow is the best. From now on," she said, spinning around on a silver heel, setting the ropes of fringe on her shirtsleeves swinging, "he must do all of my covers."

"Good idea," Craig agreed, walking into the room. He pulled the door shut, then placed Diana's Gucci bag on the glass-topped coffee table in front of the dark blue suede couch at the far end of the dressing room. He smiled at Serena, then at Trudy, who started across the room.

"Hello, Craig," Trudy said, giving him a tight, friendly hug. Stepping back, she held onto his arm. "Looking good. Life in the fast lane must be treating you fine. Haven't changed a bit."

"It's all good," he tossed back, returning her hug. "Well, here she is," Craig bragged to Trudy, lifting a hand in Diana's direction. "As promised."

"So I see. Welcome to Song City, Miz Devreux," Trudy said, extending her hand. Diana sweetly ignored it. Flustered, Trudy let her hand drop, but pressed on, determined to play the grateful hostess. "I do appreciate you making time to stop by. My customers will be thrilled to meet you." Trudy paused, waiting for Diana to say something, but when the singer simply watched Trudy with wide, bemused eyes, she nervously pulled a small camera from the pocket of her jacket and held it up in front of her face. "Do you mind, Miz Devereux? Please? You and Craig?"

Remembering what Craig had told her about speaking to Diana, Serena braced herself. Surely Diana Devreux was not going to allow herself to be photographed before her hair was properly styled.

"Not at all," Diana said in a breathy voice, smiling over at Craig, who hurried to move closer to Diana, then casually draped an arm around her shoulders. Diana giggled, adopting a camera-perfect expression, her turban-wrapped head tilted back against Craig's chest. He was looking down at her, a tender expression on his face.

"All right!" Trudy remarked, snapping away.

Their evident intimacy surprised Serena, and she wondered just how close they might be. Could Trudy be right: Was Craig Alexander simply a player who got his kicks flattering women, even his boss?

After posing for several photos, Diana ducked from beneath Craig's arm and returned to the window, where she stood with her back to everyone and looked down into the crowded store below.

Serena lifted an eyebrow at Craig and mouthed the words. "What now?"

Craig pointed to his watch, then made a circular motion with his hand, urging Serena and Trudy to get busy.

"Uh, Miss Devreux," Trudy began, in a hesitant, yet respectful voice, "this is Serena St. James, your stylist this afternoon."

Diana spun around. She scrutinized Serena's red and gray Upscale smock with a critical air, then ran her stern gaze down to Serena's feet and back up to her face.

Serena warmed with embarrassment under her assessment, aware that shoes were stained and soaking wet from her ordeal in the rain, her hair was frizzed, and she must look like a refugee who'd just walked a hundred miles, not the professional stylist she had made herself out to be. Remembering Craig's advice not to speak first, she gathered her courage and waited.

"You're the stylist?" Diana remarked, walking closer to Serena, a finger to her cheek. "You appear far too . . . uh . . . young to be a . . . well. I mean . . . whose hair have you done? Aretha's? Patti's? Natalie's?" she wanted to know.

"Oh," Serena murmured, groping for an appropriate answer, not about to blow this gig before she got a chance to show Diana what she could do. "I am sorry, but it's my policy never to discuss my clients. As much as I'd *love* to reveal my favorites and tell you all about them, Giani would have my head if I did."

"Well, I can understand that," Diana said. "It's just that I've never heard of you . . . I didn't know Giani had a black stylist on his staff."

"Oh, I'm fairly new at the salon," Serena hedged. "But Giani knew you wanted a black stylist, so he insisted I slip out today, even though I am booked, and come over to take care of you." When Diana didn't say anything, Serena glanced at Trudy, silently pleading for some helpful interference.

"Ms. Devreux," Trudy jumped right in. "You have so many fans here in Dallas. I've sold two thousand copies of *One and Only* since its release last week."

"Really?" Diana perked up. She placed her tiny hands on her slim hips, and beamed at Craig. "Hear that? Isn't that good news?"

"Absolutely!" Craig agreed.

"A record number for my store," Trudy rushed on. "And you being here this afternoon is going to push *One and Only* to the best-seller of all time for my store. It is hot, hot, hot."

Nodding, Diana went to the styling chair and sat down, forgetting her cross-examination of Serena as she stretched out one of her heavily tooled boots and admired it. "So, folks in Dallas think it's hot?"

"You bet, and so many of your die-hard fans are downstairs now, waiting for you to sign their posters and CDs," Trudy continued, engaging Diana in conversation while Serena tossed a purple cape over the diva's petite form, the purple drape creating a tent from which Diana's oval face peeked out like a fragile china doll. "Many have been waiting since nine o'clock this morning. No concern for the rain, the cold weather. Plus, reporters from two radio stations and the ABC affiliate are supposed to be here, too."

"Really? Humm," Diana murmured thoughtfully, touching the tangled fluff of matted curls that fell to her shoulders when Serena carefully removed her silver turban. She squirmed playfully in her chair, clearly pleased to hear about the press that was coming out to see her.

"Well," she said, now addressing Serena. "Make me look great for the cameras."

"That's my plan," Serena replied, pumping the foot pedal to raise the chair, anxious to begin her work.

"My hair is almost as famous as I am," Diana said in a serious tone. "You do know how to make those long wavy curls and the . . ."

"Absolutely," Serena assured her. "I know exactly what you want."

"Of course. I'm sure you do," Diana replied in a kinder voice as she wriggled deeper into her chair. Pointing a multiringed index finger at Craig, she called out, "Craig, why don't you and Trudy go down and get everything set up? Leave Serena and me alone. Oh, and please put *One and Only* on the sound system so I can hear it up here."

"Sure thing," Craig tossed back, crooking a finger at Trudy. "Let's go calm the natives and let Serena work her magic. We've got some catching up to do, anyway."

Alone with Diana, Serena did not try to engage the star in conversation. Most celebrities preferred to be left alone, so unless a client was particularly chatty and initiated the conversation, Serena knew to keep mum and concentrate on her work. The pampering experience could be ruined by too much talk, and she was certain Diana Devreux lived to be pampered.

For the next forty-five minutes Serena worked steadily, transforming Diana's famous locks into a vision of chestnut-red curls that swept down from a striking zigzag part in the center of her head, falling in a cascade of soft twists around her face. Hoping to maintain the star's carefree, untamed style while stamping the creation with her own signature, Serena had come up with a look that was different, yet not too far from the diva's trademark 'do. Diana had to look sexy, but not cheap, trendy but not over-the-top, and as close to outrageous as she could venture without alienating her ultrasophisticated audience that loved her great sense of style. It was a challenge that Serena was determined to meet.

Diana, who had maintained a cool, but cooperative attitude during the session, did not utter a word until Serena gently pulled the last burnished curl down over the diva's left eye and handed her a mirror.

"Fabulous!" Diana breathed, seriously impressed. She twisted around in her chair, trying to see her hair from every possible direction, even holding the red plastic hand mirror above her head to study the surprisingly attractive zigzag part Serena had created across the crown of her head, from which an intricate weave of loosely coiled tendrils erupted. Tossing her shiny, multilength bob from side to side, she tested its ability to bounce and move with her rhythm, smiling as the coppery coils swung exactly as she wanted. "You really got this together, Serena. Kinda different. Kinda funky, but classy, too. I need pictures of this so I can show my next stylist how to do it."

Setting down the mirror, Diana got up and retrieved the Gucci bag Craig had left on the table for her and rummaged around inside it before pulling out a large square makeup case.

"You do makeup, too, don't you?"

"Of course," Serena replied without missing a beat. Surely she could touch-up Diana's near-perfect face. "It would be an honor to do your makeup."

Diana opened a jar of cold cream, snapped a tissue from the box on the dressing table and began removing her makeup. "Let's start from scratch, okay?"

"Sure," Serena said, watching as Diana toweled off every trace of foundation and powder. Once Diana's bare skin was exposed, Serena was surprised to see that her skin was not in very good shape. She had tiny dark spots on her left cheek, and just below her eye there were patches of dry flaky skin. It was clear that Diana was past her prime, but still a beautiful woman, and would have to take better care of her skin if she planned to hold back evidence of aging much longer. Immediately Serena thought of the Spanish bayonet soap she had made from her mother's recipe and how much it had helped clear up her skin. Perhaps, it would help Diana, too.

"Needs work, huh," Diana prompted, sensing Serena's thoughts.

"No. You have very beautiful skin."

"Maybe, but I'm not a teenager, anymore. I know that much."

"True, but would you really want to go back that far, even if you could?" Serena smiled empathetically, trying to ease Diana's obvious reluctance to discuss the status of her skin, as well as her age. Serena could tell Diana was both worried and annoyed by the fact that the aging process had forced itself into her life and was not going to go away. At forty-three, Diana Devreux had been riding the wave of fame in the music industry for almost two decades, but had barely changed her signature appearance since bursting on the scene when she opened for Earth, Wind and Fire at the Los Angeles Coliseum in 1981.

Diana laughed softly, then lifted her bare face to Serena, as if inviting a closer inspection. "Every spot and wrinkle on this face is hard-earned, honey. Paid for with hundreds of hours of rehearsals, recording sessions, concerts, and nights in airports and hotels. Life on the road is a bitch, and it takes a hell of a toll on the old body. Let me tell you, it ain't easy being Diana Devreux."

Serena nodded. "If you don't mind my suggesting, I can recommend something that would keep those flaky spots from erupting and brighten your complexion."

"Yeah? Tell me more."

"I developed a product, made from natural ingredients, that will eliminate those dark, flaky patches real fast."

"What is it? A miracle?"

Serena grinned. "No, not a miracle. It's a natural soap made of from an old-fashioned formula of my mother's. I use it."

Diana inspected Serena's face. "Your skin is like silk. I was jealous as soon as I saw you." She shrugged, arching a brow. "But how old are you? Twenty? "

"Twenty-one," Serena replied.

Diana laughed. "Big difference, huh?"

"Yes," Serena agreed, "but this soap can also be used as a mask if you lather it up, then let it dry on your face for about ten minutes. Pulls all that dead skin off, and leaves your skin very soft." She removed a plastic bag containing several small pale squares of the ivory-colored soap from her bag, and showed one to Diana. "Want to try it?"

"Humm. You think it would work on me?"

"I know it would help," Serena promised. "It's all natural. No chemicals." She held the bar under running water at the sink, then worked the bubbles into a creamy paste. "Here, smell it, feel it."

Diana sniffed the creamy foam, took a tiny bit on her finger, then smoothed it on the back of her hand. "Very silky. Great texture, not heavy at all. Nice. Umm . . . I like this. Okay. If it'll help me look young and beautiful, I'm game. Lay it on."

Serena got busy, thrilled to have the opportunity to rejuvenate the public face of Diana Devreux and update the diva's trademark image, which over the past twenty years had been seen on magazine covers, TV, and plastered on too many album, tape and CD covers to count. Serena dug in, determined to help Diana glow with a brighter, more sharp-edged brilliance than when she'd walked through the dressing room door only an hour ago.

Serena cleansed Diana's skin, made a mask of Spanish bayonet, and lathered it on Diana's face, leaving it to dry for ten minutes. When she rinsed it off, the results were clearly evident. Diana's skin was toned and firm, the flaky areas had disappeared, and the tiny dark brown spots were much less evident.

For Diana's makeup, Serena chose lighter, less dramatic colors and opened up the star's diminutive features with contour shading and highlights. Under Serena's touch, Diana's eyes grew larger, her cheekbones softened, and an impression of youthful maturity emerged that still celebrated the diva's experience. The fresh contemporary look Serena was aiming for would definitely serve Diana better in a business dominated by slim-hipped teenagers in halter tops, sequined jeans, and sneakers.

"God, I'll be glad when this tour is over," Diana grumbled under her breath as Serena applied her final touches.

Serena said nothing, concentrating on the sweep of rose-colored blush she was applying to Diana's now flawless cheekbones, glad the singer felt comfortable enough to talk to her so openly. Diana was not the demanding, temperamental ogre Serena had expected to deal with this afternoon, but simply a slightly insecure superstar whose stylist had not given her the creative attention she deserved.

Diana continued. "Living on the road, signing autographs, making rehearsals, dealing with agents, managers, and the public . . . it's getting tougher and tougher to do. Singing is the love of my life, but all the other stuff has to be done, too and sometimes it's hard to manage everything. Especially when my stylist abandons me in midtour! Aaah, don't get me wrong. I love the business and my fans, but sometimes I'd rather curl up with a good book in bed than gussy up and face the masses. Maybe it's getting close to my time to make an exit . . . you know?"

"I hope not," Serena replied. "You'd disappoint a lot of people."

"Honey, I've won a ton of awards, sung with the best of them, and performed in every major city in the world." She paused, sighed, fluffed her hair, and shrugged. "There comes a time when it's best to stop, walk away, and leave the public remembering you at your prime."

Serena uncapped a tube of soft plum lipstick and began to apply it as she spoke. "You look fabulous, and have many great years in the spotlight ahead of you, Ms. Devreux." Serena slowly recapped the tube, perplexed by this conversation that verged on a confession, chalking it up to an emotional reaction to her stylist's sudden departure. Serena hoped her work would make Diana feel better. She removed the purple plastic cape and stood back.

Diana scooted closer to the mirror, eagerly assessing her reflection. For several long seconds she held her lips in a tight plum-colored pucker and lifted her chin, eyes lowered into slits. She tilted her head from side to side, checking out Serena's work. "Humm . . . you certainly know your stuff. Took off a few years with this new 'do, and that magic formula of yours, didn't you?"

Serena went weak with relief. "I'm so glad you're pleased."

"Ever thought of producing, selling that stuff?" Diana went on, as she continued to inspect her face.

"Maybe one day," Serena hedged, thinking about the sketchbook filled with potential beauty enhancers, which she did not dare tell anyone about.

"What's stopping you?"

"Money, for one. Time to work it all out. And the guts to try and do it, I guess."

"Ah, yes. Money and time are, unfortunately, what stifles many women's dreams." She fluffed her hair again. "Well, Serena, don't get discouraged. You've got a lot going on. Hang in there, one day it will all come together." Then she gave the underside of her chin a firm pat with the back of her hand and began repacking her makeup case.

Serena quietly watched Diana. Everything had turned out exactly as she'd envisioned. Diana's new hairstyle, color palette, and intensive skin rejuvenation had made the star dazzle once again, as she should.

A knock on the door, followed by Craig's appreciative whistle when he saw the transformed Diana, prevented Serena from responding to the diva's compliments.

"Hey, that's some look," he told Diana. Turning to Serena, he spoke in a grateful tone. "Thanks. You really hooked her up, Serena. I've never seen her look so beautiful."

Diana swatted at Craig, as if she were angry. "What a thing to say! You *have* seen me look more beautiful and you know it."

Craig backed off, smiling. "Maybe, but Serena could have taught Kahi a trick or two."

"Yes, she could have," Diana remarked.

"Thank you," Serena murmured, taking in the possessive way Diana was looking at Craig and the uneasy way he was fiddling with the CD in his hand.

With a flip of her curls Diana got up and tugged on the legs of her tight leather pants. "I guess the crowd is getting rowdy, huh?"

"Why? You're only two hours late," Craig joked.

Diana took the CD from him, then turned to Serena. "Just for you." She scribbled her name across her airbrushed photo, then handed the plastic square to Serena. "Thanks again. You did great." Then she disappeared into the hallway, Craig close behind. He did not even tell Serena good-bye.

Serena stared at the closed door, feeling relieved and pleased, but somewhat dismissed and used. She studied the CD with Diana's illegible signature, realizing it was not even a personalized autograph. But what had she expected? A hundred-dollar tip? No one had ever discussed payment for her services, and Serena hadn't been brave enough to bring the subject up. It was her own fault if she felt used.

And Craig! He had left without as much as a see-you-later glance. What was it with him? she wondered. In the limo driving to Song City, he had been friendly, even flirtatious, and had acted as if he wanted to get to know her better. Now, he was wrapped so tight with Diana he acted as if no one else existed.

Teach her stylist a thing or two? I don't think so, Serena silently fumed, gathering her things. *Thanks for the compliment and the CD Miz D., but I wouldn't give my secrets to your stylist, or anyone else, for that matter. Obviously Kahi kept you trapped in a time warp and didn't have a clue about how to keep you looking current. If you really were so worried about the competition, you'd have fired Kahi long before she walked out on you.*

But of course, Serena could not say any of those things. She had to draw satisfaction from the fact that she had succeeded with her first real client. And what a client! The downside was that she could not tell anyone about what had happened to her today. No publicity, Giani had warned, and of course she'd keep her word if she wanted to keep her job, but it would have been nice to tell Nina, or the other women at Havensway, about her bizarre experience.

I can't even risk calling Precious, she realized, missing her only friend. *I'm Serena St. James, now. All of my connections to Mallard, Texas, and Sara Jane Talbot have been severed for good. It's got to stay that way.*

Serena went to the huge expanse of glass at the end of the room and gazed down into the main part of the store where fans had crowded around Diana. She watched Diana work her way toward the table draped in gold cloth that had been placed on a raised platform backed by a huge cardboard stand-up of her provocative CD cover. Craig was standing close by, poised to respond to Diana's every wish. Serena's shoulders slumped forward with her audible sigh, and she wished she didn't care where he was standing, how many times he touched her arm, or took her hand, or how extensive his responsibility was to Diana Devreux. It was obvious that Craig Alexander loved his job.

"Craig Alexander," she whispered watching the pandemonium below. For a few moments he had made her feel attractive, special, and appreciated. Memories of his easy banter, his sly, come-on smile, and the way his skin had warmed hers when he'd held onto her fingers were all she'd have once he left Dallas and moved on with Diana.

So, don't spoil it, she chastised herself, turning away.

Incarcerated at Gatesview at the age of fifteen, Serena had never had a real date or experienced anything remotely resembling love. She had never been kissed in a dark theater or the backseat of a car. Now, at twenty-one, she was still a virgin, and knew nothing about what men wanted, or what she should expect from them. She had a lot to learn about romance and men, and it would be nice to have a man like Craig teach her what she needed to know. But after today, she would never see Craig Alexander again.

When Serena turned around, she caught her reflection in one of the big dressing room mirrors. Her stint in the rain earlier in the day had destroyed her chin length bob, creating a fluffy brown wedge of soft hair that gleamed with a healthy glow, emphasized by the gold-blonde highlights that trailed around her face. Her heart-shaped visage was luminous, void of makeup, except for a hint of mascara and a clear bronze blush that accentuated the curve of her prominent cheekbones. Serena smiled at her reflection, pleased with what she saw. *Not so bad,* she decided, nodding at her image. *I'm no diva, but those sisters downstairs don't have much on me.*

She started toward the door, dismissing thoughts of Craig, romance, and love from her mind. Love. What was it all about, anyway? She'd loved her mother, but she'd died and left her all alone. Loving her father had been difficult because of his guilt-driven drinking and emotional abandonment. Even her youthful, misguided devotion to Joyce Ann Keller had turned against her, nearly destroying everything. And now Precious, the only person she could possibly call a friend, was off limits and no longer a part of her life. Loving had left scars on Serena's young heart, but she knew she'd gladly risk the pain of loving again if Craig Alexander came into her world.

Chapter Sixteen

Joyce Ann Keller used the tail of her sweat-soaked denim shirt to wipe perspiration out of her eyes. The pain in her back had radiated down into her legs, and she massaged the ridges of her spine, pressing her knuckles hard against the bones. She was so tired she could scream. Bending over, she picked up another load of dirty linen and plunged it into the massive washing machine, frowning into the swirl of water as she waited for the rotating agitator to pull the tangled sheets down into the tub.

The concrete floor was slick with sudsy water, the atmosphere was thick with steam, and the room stank of dirty clothes, bleach, and strong disinfectant. Every washer and dryer was running full tilt in a deafening cacophony of thumping, whirring, sloshing and knocking, and it was driving Joyce Ann's migraine headache to the point of making her ill. It had started yesterday morning and was still with her, the pain increasing by the minute.

She narrowed her eyes, rubbed her temples, then squinted over at the two guards who were in charge of the early morning crew. They were talking quietly while waiting for the wide overhead door at the back of the laundry area to roll up so the delivery trucks could come in.

Joyce Ann checked the time on the big round clock above the cage where a guard was waiting for the morning pick-up van, which arrived at five-thirty every day. Today was no exception, and Joyce Ann nodded in relief when the gray steel door started rolling up, the sight momentarily erasing the painful pounding inside her head.

For Joyce Ann, this work detail was brutally exhausting, but the suffering was going to pay off very soon, as had her self-initiated stint in solitude last year.

Her sentence in isolation had accomplished precisely what Joyce Ann had hoped: she'd gotten the warden's attention and after serving her time, had been watched like a test rat in a cage. With her every move monitored, written up, and reported on by the guards, the warden had been informed about how well she was using her time, how hard she now worked to control her temper, and how much better she got along with the other inmates on her cell block. Warden Andrews knew who she talked to and when, what she ate for breakfast, lunch, and dinner, and how well she slept. Joyce Ann had endured this invasive scrutiny without complaint and, in fact, had turned it to her advantage, becoming a model inmate in the eyes of those who controlled her life, going to great pains to demonstrate that she was cooperative, held no grudges, and was not a threat to anyone. The strategy had helped her learn how to be patient, subdued, and observant, giving everyone the impression that Joyce Ann had finally accepted Gatesview as her home and was resigned to doing her time.

And her progress had so impressed the warden he had approved her request for work duty in the prison laundry—exactly what Joyce Ann wanted. There, she followed the rules and refused to give the supervisors any reasons to distrust her.

The shard of glass she had shoved into her mattress over a year ago was now wedged inside the drain hole of one of the twin tubs behind her, where she could get at it when the time was right. When the last driver got out of his truck and handed the guard his pick-up orders, Joyce Ann knew today was the day.

She studied the driver standing off to one side while six inmates loaded the tubs of clean linen into his dark green van. Her intense gaze barreled down hard on the man, who must have felt her staring at him because he eventually glanced her way. She smiled slyly, then grinned even broader when he jerked back, recognizing her. And when their eyes met, she knew what was going to happen next.

The driver's name was Steve. Joyce Ann had first seen him four months ago when she'd been working the night shift and he had delivered a load of soiled linen to the graveyard shift so they could sort and prepare them for washing the next morning. Under the much less strenuous supervision of the guards on the night shift, Joyce Ann had chanced nodding at Steve, whose laid-back manner and small frame had caught her eye. When he'd gotten back into his truck, she had boldly approached him, smiling when he'd leaned out the window and made a low come-on remark under his breath.

She'd glanced around to see that the lone guard who had been standing on the far side of the truck, was now back in his cage, engrossed in sorting out the paperwork, not paying any attention to Steve, or to her. She had acted swiftly, slipping into the front seat of the truck with Steve to get down on her knees and give him what she knew he wanted, doing it so quickly he hardly knew what had happened. Then she had calmly slipped out and returned to work while he fumbled with his pants.

Now, Joyce Ann followed Steve's every move, calculating the time it took for him to get back into the cab of his truck, signal for the guard to open the door, and the door to slide down and clang back into place, sealing the laundry room off from the outside.

When the guards had resumed their routine and the inmates had returned to their workstations among the washers, dryers, and long folding tables positioned around the room, Joyce Ann eased over to the twin tubs and looked down into the drain. It was still there. Shiny and dark. She reached in and pulled out her ticket to freedom.

The next morning, at five-thirty-five, Joyce Ann saw Steve back his dark green van into the loading dock again. *Right on schedule*, she thought, calmly, picking up a bundle of stained towels and heading toward the twin soaking tubs. She casually dumped them in. Bending over the tub, she pretended to press the towels down as she eased her hand beneath the soiled linen, stuck her index finger into the drain, and slipped the slender shard of glass out of the hole. Palming it, she continued with her work, filling the tub with water and bleach, submerging the towels into the solution; routine tasks she performed everyday. But from the corner of her eye, she was monitoring the activities of the inmates assigned to loading Steve's van as they moved back and forth from the pallets to the truck, stacking his deliveries for the day.

"That's it," she heard the guard tell Steve.

And this is it for me, she thought, picking up a dry towel, which she draped over the hand holding the weapon. She walked over to the guard, who was outside of his wire cage signing off on Steve's work order.

"The last load's been sorted and put in the soak tubs," Joyce Ann told the guard, interrupting his discussion with Steve. "Need help here?"

The guard did not glance up, but Steve's eyes shifted to her, a smirk on his lips.

Joyce Ann's expression remained as blank and flat as a clean bed sheet.

The guard looked up at her, then glanced around, before nodding at Joyce Ann. "One more. Over there. That box goes, too. Get it on so he can get out of here."

Without comment, Joyce Ann went over to the pallet, picked up the last box, and put it on a gray metal dolly. Slowly she pushed it toward the van, calculating her timing until the guard had returned to his cage and begun sorting through his paperwork as he waited to press the buzzer and raise the overhead door. Quickly, she jammed the box into the van, and when the door rolled up, stepped closer to Steve, who grinned, then turned to open the driver side door.

Swiftly, Joyce Ann stuck the glass knife into his right side. She twisted it hard two times, frantically scanning the inside of the van. The keys were still in the ignition, just as she had hoped.

"What the fuck?" Steve shouted, struggling to shake her off. But Joyce Ann had wrapped her muscular left arm around his neck and pulled him flush against her chest. With a grunt, she dug the shard of glass deeper into Steve's intestines, just as the guard realized something was wrong. He bolted from his cage, leaving the wide door open, one hand on his gun.

"Hold it!" he shouted.

Steve sagged against Joyce Ann, blood gurgling from his mouth. She spun around, pushed Steve's body at the guard, sending both of them to the cement floor. In a flash, Joyce Ann jumped into the van, started it, and pressed down hard on the gas pedal, streaking from the building like a blast from a cannon.

Once outside, she felt light-headed and energized as she sped toward the padlocked gate on the chain-link fence that separated the back of the prison grounds from the road. At the fence, she rammed the metal barrier with such force that the lock broke, allowing her to burst through, then skid into the bushes on the other side of the road. Quickly, she regained control, stomped on the accelerator, and tore off down the narrow two-lane highway just as the wail of a siren burst from the prison yard.

Chapter Seventeen

Two blocks from Upscale, Serena stepped off the bus, bent her head, and hurried down the street, taking long strides on the icy sidewalk toward the salon. The temperature was near freezing and she shivered under her coat as she made her way to the salon. Half a block away from Upscale, she looked up and saw a white stretch limo, headlights on, parked in front. Hoping it might be Craig Alexander, and not one of Giani's impatient customers waiting for the salon to open, she slowed her pace, hoping to appear calm and unconcerned. But when Craig opened the door on the driver's side, stood up and waved at her, she broke into a grin and hurried over.

She had lain awake far into the night, thinking about Craig, recalling their conversations, reliving the few moments they had spent alone together, her restlessness fueled by the hope that their paths might cross again.

"Good morning," she said, warm air streaming in a cloud from her lips.

"Hello," Craig replied, coming around the front of the car to meet her on the sidewalk. "I remembered you said you ride the bus to work, so I parked here, hoping you might come this way."

"You guessed right," she replied lightly, astounded that she was looking, once again, at the face she had worked hard at memorizing only yesterday. *Has he come to ask for my phone number? Tell me he wants to stay in touch?* she hoped. After all, it was six-thirty in the morning and freezing outside. Why else would he be sitting in a limo waiting for her? "This is my regular route." Serena tucked her hands under her arms and hugged her body, more to control her nerves than to try and stay warm. "Didn't think I'd see you again."

"Well," he began. "I have to confess, it wasn't my idea to come."

Serena's eyes narrowed. "Oh?"

"Yeah, Diana asked me to find you."

So much for my romantic fantasy about him wanting my number, she thought, hoping Diana hadn't had some strange reaction to the Spanish bayonet soap. Giani had warned her about a lawsuit, hadn't he?

Craig opened the middle door of the limo, then stood back. "Get in," he invited in his easy, smooth voice.

Serena checked her watch, calculated that she had about seven minutes before she had to open the salon, then ducked into the luxurious, sweet-smelling car.

"Hello, Serena," Diana's silky voice came from the far end of the gray leather wraparound seat.

"Hello, Miss Devreux."

Diana, encased in glossy brown fur, was facing the front of the car. She settled back and waved her hand in a welcome gesture, making it clear that she wanted Serena to sit in the seat opposite her. "Please, relax," she said, picking up a small silver pot on the bar in the middle of the limo to pour more coffee into the demitasse cup in her hand. "Coffee?"

"No, thanks," Serena replied, unsettled by the fact that Craig had been waiting for her on Diana's orders, not because he wanted to see her.

Diana glanced up and caught Craig's eye in the rearview mirror, then nodded. "We'd better get going," she told him.

"Get going?" Serena remarked, surprised to feel the limo beginning to pull away from the curb. She couldn't go anywhere. She had to get to work. "Where are you going?"

"For a little ride. Relax."

"Uh, I can't go anywhere, Miss Devreux." Serena reached into her bag, pulled out the keys to the salon, then turned around to face the back of Craig's head. She jingled the keys in his ear to make her point. "I have a job. I need to go. Will you please stop this car? Giani will be furious if I'm late opening the salon." But Craig kept driving, acting as if she hadn't said a word. Serena jerked around and stared at Diana, and for a fleeting moment wondered if she was being kidnapped, then nearly laughed out loud. No one, not even Nina Richards, would pay as much as ten dollars in ransom to get her back.

"Oh, settle down. Serena. And you can forget about Giani," Diana said, pushing a button to raise the window that sealed the two of them from Craig. "You are nothing to that man but a charity case and there's no future for you at his salon beyond cleaning up after his messy clients, washing his dirty laundry, and accepting a rare opportunity to use your styling skills."

"You know about me?" Serena gasped, dreading what must be coming. Her scheme had backfired, and just as Giani had feared, she was going to be sued for embellishing her credentials, for impersonating an experienced stylist. Giani had predicted that this might happen. Serena tensed, waiting, fearing the worst.

"Oh, yes, my dear. I know *everything*," Diana assured Serena, tenting her gloved fingers in thought before taking another sip of coffee. She carefully balanced the delicate cup in the palm of one hand as she leaned closer to Serena. "You are really Sara Jane Talbot, age twenty-one. Born in Mallard, Texas. You served five years in prison on a charge of accessory to armed robbery and murder, and you have no family, except a father you detest. You own approximately four changes of clothing . . . mostly uniforms you wear at the salon, and you live in a halfway house where you have no close friends and you are enormously lonely."

"How did you find out?"

Diana laughed in a throaty, satisfied way. "Do you think I would have invited you into my limo if I hadn't checked out everything about you?" She studied Serena's shocked expression quietly, then said, "Don't worry. Your secrets are safe with me."

"Why did you bother to check me out?" Serena wanted to know, not happy to realize that Diana had managed to dig up, obviously overnight, the past she had gone to such lengths to bury. "Why do you care about who I am or who I used to be?"

"Because you are an enormously talented young lady."

"So?"

"So, you remind me of myself when I was even younger than you." Diana put down her cup and eased back the soft collar of her fur coat, allowing Serena to more clearly see her perfectly made-up face. "You saw me with no makeup yesterday, and then you recreated the image of Diana Devreux. Do you think I was born looking like this? Do you think my mother named me Diana Devreux?"

Serena shrugged, not chancing her voice to speak.

"I was born Barbara Green in Cleveland, Ohio, and I was a very plain and unattractive girl. My mother was an unwed teen who raised me with no help from my father, who had been a teenager, too, when he fathered me. I grew up dreaming of being someone other than who I was, and as soon as I got my first break singing with the Spirit Sisters, I reinvented myself, just like you have done. I changed my name, had plastic surgery, and buried my past. Any press that is written about me contains very little truth and lots of fabrication, details which I have faithfully embellished over the years to protect and enhance my career. Diana Devreux exists because I created her. Out of necessity, as is done all the time by people who either need to be somebody else, or don't like who they really are. Serena, I understand you . . . and I want to help you."

"How? Why?" Serena whispered, trying to comprehend exactly what Diana meant.

"By hiring you to be my personal stylist. Hair, makeup, everything. You have an unusual eye for structure and color, and a great sense of what it takes to create illusion. People pay a great deal of money for such talent."

Serena sat quietly, listening.

"I am forty-three years old," Diana went on. "I've been in the public spotlight since I was seventeen, and I am getting a tad weary of the same old Diana. As I told you yesterday, being a public personality can be draining. But you . . . your enthusiasm and fresh approach that updated my appearance and rejuvenated my look brought back a spark of confidence that I feared I had lost. I need you, Serena. Coming on board will be mutually beneficial."

Now, Serena sank back in her seat and rested her head on the soft cushions, taking her time to examine the fine age lines around Diana's huge brown eyes, the soft pad of flesh beneath her chin, the erosion of her once-firm jawline. Yes, she could understand why Diana would want to look fresher, younger, and less dated. But a total makeover would take time and a great deal of thought. Though tempted to say yes, Serena needed some answers before making such a commitment. Diana was shrewd, competitive, and focused. Serena would have to be careful.

"Did you tell Craig about me? My real name, my criminal past?" she wanted to know.

"No. Why does that matter?"

Serena hesitated before answering. Did she dare admit that it mattered because she was attracted to Craig? That she feared he might not give her a chance to get to know him better if he knew she had a record as a convicted felon? But, instead, she replied, "It matters because I am Serena St. James now and I would appreciate it if you did not share your knowledge of my former life with anyone. The fewer people who know about my mistakes, the better. I'm a different person, and I don't want to spend my life explaining my past."

Diana nodded. "You have my word. Your past is your business, not

Craig's or mine, and I promise no one will ever learn anything about you from me. I admire you for being strong enough to discard old baggage and start over."

The compliment should have pleased Serena, but instead, it frightened her, bringing home the fact that she'd have to be very diligent if she wanted to maintain and protect her new identity. "I don't feel very strong right now," Serena meekly admitted, ready to trust Diana.

"Well, you are. And, honey, so am I. It takes a lot of hard work for me to transport people from their everyday realities into my world of song, stories, and sentimental images. I go to great lengths to give my fans what they want, to be what they expect me to be. And you are doing exactly the same thing. You have what I need."

"And what is that?" Serena wanted to know, curious that the great Diana Devreux was being so honest and revealing in her comments.

"You have vision. An ability to create an image that only you can see in your mind, sense in your soul. It is an intuitive creativity that my former stylist, Kahi, did not possess. I predict that your talent could keep me visible and competitive in this crazy, cutthroat music business for a long time." She paused, flexed her fingers, then pressed her lips together in thought. "And quite possibly, you could make a fortune with that natural soap formula of your mother's, if you are willing to listen, learn, and take a few risks."

A shiver of anticipation coursed through Serena, pushing her to the edge of her seat. Taking the Spanish bayonet formula to commercial heights had always been in the back of her mind, and now, the possibility of bringing her mother's legacy to the marketplace was taking shape. "Do you really think it could be a viable cosmetic product?"

"Yes, but you'll need professional consultation, experimentation, and testing, to move it that far," Diana said, a gleam of excitement brightening her eyes. "But the possibilities are there, I am certain."

"I never thought I'd hear anyone say that, except me," Serena chuckled, then added, "I talk to my mother, you see."

Diana smiled. "What you did with my hair and makeup yesterday, under less than professional working conditions, was extraordinarily clever. You created that balance of sexiness and sophistication, youthful energy and wise maturity that Kahi could never quite manage to achieve. With practice, some guidance, and the right environment to work in, I guarantee you will go far."

"This is unbelievable," Serena murmured to herself, her mind whirling with the possibilities of what her future might be like, working for Diana Devreux. But just as quickly, her current situation came back to mind and she knew Alexis was probably grumbling, wondering where she was. "Where are you . . . we going? I've got to go to work. You know, think this over . . ."

"No time for that, Serena. You're coming to New York with me."

"Now?" Serena asked, worried.

"Yes. My next appearance is at Radio City Music Hall on December 22. And when I step onto that stage, I want the audience . . . and the world, to see the new Diana Devreux, created by you, Serena St. James. Song City was simply a rehearsal."

"And after New York?" Serena asked, startled that everything sounded too good, was moving too fast, and could fall apart just as quickly. "What then?'"

"You'll go with me to Las Vegas."

"Vegas?"

"Yes, that's where I live."

"Not Los Angeles?"

"No, I left that L.A. rat-race years ago for my slice of heaven in the desert. It's a great place . . . a refuge where I can have privacy and concentrate on my music. With your help I will prepare for the Vegas debut of my new image at my New Year's Eve gig at the MGM Grand. We're gonna have fun, Serena," Diana said lightly, reaching over to touch Serena on the arm, obviously pleased and excited about her plans. "Lighten up. Don't look so worried. It is going to be great!"

But Serena, concerned at how quickly and easily Diana had come to the conclusion that she would accept her offer, did not laugh. In fact, Serena wasn't sure she liked what was happening, even though it sounded exciting. She had to think this through. Diana talked fast, was very sure of herself, and acted as if she genuinely cared about Serena, but was she for real? Once they were on the road would Diana concern herself only with *her* future, abandoning Serena's dream? And how generous was she, really? Serena wondered, recalling the hurriedly autographed CD Diana had thrust at her yesterday with little more than a quick thank you. From her conversation with Craig, Serena had been led to believe that Diana could be difficult and very self-involved. Working for her might be tricky, to say the least. And what about salary? No mention of money had been made.

Serena brashly asked, "What's the pay to be your stylist?"

"I'll pay you what you're worth."

"And that is?"

"Only you can determine that, Serena"

Perplexed, Serena studied Diana's face, wanting desperately to trust her. But how could she run off to New York with this famous woman without as much as a handshake for a contract? No firm offer of salary? Desert Giani Pilugi and Nina Richards, the two people who had helped her most? No, she was crazy to even entertain the idea. And besides, why should such good fortune come to her? Serena worried, never having had many breaks in her life. Suddenly, she knew she was in way over her head and had to get out before ruining the little security she had managed to create.

"Thanks, Miss Devreux, but I have to think this over," she decided, swinging around to tap on the window to get Craig's attention.

"Craig, please, stop the car and let me out." Turning back to Diana she lowered her voice, trying to convey her urgency without sounding reproachful. "I am flattered by your confidence and your offer, but this is way too sudden. I need time. I need to tell Giani why I'm leaving. I'd need to go home and pack my things, anyway and tell Nina, the director of the house where I live, good-bye. She's been very kind and helpful to me. I can't just disappear."

"Why not? Sara Jane Talbot did," Diana smoothly replied.

The remark cut deep. Serena blinked, an image of the girl she used to be flickering through her mind: Overweight. Frightened. Insecure and desperate for attention. Clinging to Joyce Ann Keller because she was lonely. And who was she now? A much thinner and wiser young woman who wanted nothing more than to be a part of the world of beauty and illusion, a world she'd spent a long time dreaming about. What did she have to lose, really?

She extended her hand to Diana. "You're right. I'm in."

Diana shook it, smiling. "I am warning you, I'm determined to exploit your potential." She chuckled. "I guess I should thank Kahi for abandoning me, otherwise, I never would have met you, Serena St. James."

Serena tilted her head to the side and assessed Diana. "Why are you so certain I'm the one to replace Kahi? You don't really know me at all."

Diana made a tisk-tisk sound with her tongue. "Instinct, my dear. Learn to trust it. If you don't, you will never get what you want out of life." Diana pursed her red lips in satisfaction. "Now, on to New York and the beginning of our partnership."

"But I don't have my clothes, any of my things," Serena started, uneasy with the way Diana simply made decisions, then moved on. It was all so crazy! So wonderful and wild!

"You don't need a thing. We'll go shopping in New York. But if you want, I will call this Miss Richards and arrange for your things to be packed and shipped to my home in Vegas."

"Good," Serena replied. The only thing she wanted from her past was the sketchbook, which was stashed in the top drawer of the dresser in her room. Everything else was in the canvas bag at her side. Serena pulled the tote bag to her chest and wrapped her arms around it, drawing strength from the fact that, in a way, her mother was helping her leave this dreary life behind. She thought about her boots, still at the shoe repair shop, the soggy loafers on her feet, her spartan room at Havensway, and the unrelenting loneliness that had crowded her soul too long.

This is best, she thought, settling in with her decision. Not only would she be able to leave Texas and all that it reminded her of, but she'd be near Craig, and that thought made her relax.

As the limo swept through the streets, Diana's proposal slipped through Serena's mind like clear water tumbling downstream, bringing unexpected tears of relief to her eyes. If this offer of Diana Devreux's was the elusive "change" she had been longing for, dreaming of, whispering about to her mother in the dark, then going to New York would either be the most intelligent decision or the biggest mistake she would ever make.

No, Serena reminded herself, pulling in a deep calming breath as a smile curved her lips. *The biggest mistake of my life is already behind me, and I served my time for it.*

The private jet that Diana had chartered to take her small entourage to New York took off immediately after everyone had boarded. Besides Serena, Craig, and Diana, there were three backup singers, Tammy, Jon, and Freddy, who had worked with Diana for many years, and her manager, Vincent Ruby, a tall, lanky, man with a ruddy-brown complexion. He was wearing a rumpled tweed jacket over a collarless shirt, and round horn-rimmed glasses that had slipped down low on his nose. To Serena, he looked more like a distracted college professor than the shrewd businessman who guided Diana Devreux's career.

The three singers interrupted the card game they were playing long enough to greet Serena with a friendly hello. Vincent Ruby shook Serena's hand in a perfunctory, businesslike manner, slipped into a seat and motioned for Diana to sit beside him. Then he opened his briefcase, took out his cell phone and began pressing buttons as Diana bent over and whispered something into his ear. Serena took the empty seat next to Craig, who was two rows behind Diana and Vincent.

Takeoff was smooth, but as the small plane climbed into the sky, it encountered a great deal of turbulence. Serena gripped the arms of her seat, terrified by the bumpy jolting motion that was making her stomach churn. She noticed that no one else was bothered at all by the unsettling rolling motion.

All I need is to be sick all over myself, she worried, clenching her fingers into fists.

Craig calmly reached over and placed his hand over hers. "It'll smooth out soon," he promised.

"Are you sure?" Serena whispered, terrified that the plane was going to plunge directly into the ground. Even Craig's firm hand on hers did little to calm her anxiety.

"Once we climb above this bank of clouds, it'll be better. I promise," Craig reassured her, easing his fingers off hers.

Craig leaned back and turned his head to see Serena better. "Are you always this tense when you fly?"

"I've never flown before," Serena snapped, ashamed to admit how limited her life experiences had been.

"Never flown?" he repeated, eyebrows arched in disbelief.

"Never."

"Oh. That's interesting," he remarked, lifting a shoulder as he watched Serena's face. "You never had a reason to get on a plane?"

"No, I've never traveled outside of Texas," she confessed, steeling herself for another perfectly innocent question, which she'd have to answer very carefully.

"So, you were born in Dallas?" Craig wanted to know.

"Yes. That's right," she easily lied, knowing better than to mention Mallard, Texas. He might want to know where it was, what it was like, and how she had spent her time in such a small town. Saying she was from Dallas sounded much more anonymous and normal, a place he had heard of and knew something about. She focused on the door to the cockpit, praying for the awful rolling motion to stop, and for Craig's questions to end.

There were hundreds, probably thousands of things she had never done that would be considered routine experiences for most women her age. She had never stayed in a hotel, never ordered a meal in a fancy restaurant, never ridden in a taxi for that matter. From now on, she would have to choose her words very carefully, especially when talking to Craig.

Chapter Eighteen

Two black stretch limos were waiting at JFK for Diana's entourage. Moving quickly and in a manner that seemed practiced, Craig replaced the driver of the lead limo, helped Diana and Serena get settled inside, then slipped behind the wheel and pulled away, leaving the backup singers to follow in the second car with Vincent Ruby.

The airport was a crush of fast-walking people moving in a blur of black trench coats, with brown briefcases in one hand, cell phones in the other. There was a long line of private cars, taxis and limos vying for space at the curb. Serena leaned closer to the limo window, taking in the scene, enthralled with the new world she was entering.

"Something else, isn't it?" Diana remarked, wrapping her fur coat more tightly around her body as she scooted over to make room for Serena.

"It's amazing," Serena replied. "I can't believe I'm really in New York. So many people. Everywhere."

"Yep. And it never slows down." Diana closed her eyes and leaned back, as if she'd seen it all before. "It's exciting, fun . . . like no other place in the world, but New York can also be a cold, cruel place that can break a person who is not ready for it," she muttered, eyes still closed.

Serena did not reply. For Diana, a successful tour was all that mattered, and the pressure would be on Serena to make sure that happened; that New Yorkers attended a concert they would never forget, and Diana made an impression that proved she still had what it took to please and pull in the big crowds. Serena St. James would be her secret weapon.

After a fifty-minute crawl through snarled traffic, they arrived in Manhattan. Instantly, Diana perked up. Serena was not impressed by the slushy streets and crowded icy sidewalks that seemed to be filled with focused, harried, fast-walking people, but the holiday decorations were over the top, dazzling the city despite the crowds and the dismal weather. Every window, doorway, street lamp and tree contributed to the festive fairyland ambiance.

When Craig pulled up to the gold-plated facade of the Trump International Hotel, Diana asked him to unload the luggage, then drop her and Serena on Lexington Avenue to do some shopping. Their buying spree began at the cosmetic counter at Bloomingdale's, where Diana asked Serena to test, analyze, sample, then purchase nearly a thousand dollars worth of makeup, lotions, oils and brushes; whatever Serena said she might possibly need to help her work her magic. At Saks Fifth Avenue they hit nearly every department in the store and at Macy's in Herald Square Diana helped Serena pick out a new wardrobe, clearly enjoying a reason to spend money. Chattering to Serena as they continued on, Diana swept in and out of several trendy boutiques, rushing from rack to rack like a teenager on a scavenger hunt, picking out shirts, slacks, dresses, shoes, and even lingerie for her new stylist. And throughout the day, every sales clerk who timidly presented Diana with a bill received a casual wave of the diva's fingers and instructions to charge the purchases to Diana Devreux, Inc., then deliver them to her suite at the Trump International within two hours. Then she would hurry off, leaving the sales staff staring adoringly after her.

Diana's fame, wealth, and power impressed Serena. The aura of detachment that Diana carried made her seem totally unapproachable, but the fans who were brave enough to ask for her autograph received a gracious smile, her signature on whatever piece of paper they thrust at her, and a reminder about her upcoming concert. Diana was generous, impulsive, and demanding, yet never demeaning when she was involved in a transaction with sales staff. Quick to express her likes or dislikes, she also bestowed compliments when warranted. And for the store managers who fawned and fussed over her, trying to meet her expectations, she promised complimentary copies of her latest CD. In the limo, she even called the hotel and ordered flowers to be sent to a sales clerk who had been particularly helpful about arranging for immediate alterations on a suit she bought at DKNY.

What must it be like to be so loved and so secure? Serena wondered, sitting back wearily in the limo. Her first foray into Diana's world had been exhausting, and the amount of money Diana must have spent was staggering, her zeal for shopping dangerously obsessive.

As Craig expertly maneuvered through the gridlocked traffic, heading back to the hotel, Serena thought about the hard work, years of struggle, hours of rehearsal, tears, laughter, and pain that Diana must have endured during such a legendary career. Sure, things looked easy at first glance, but Serena now understood what Diana was worried about. Nothing had come without a price, and Diana Devreux had paid her dues. Serena sneaked a look at Diana's profile. It was still stunningly beautiful and vibrant, yet the sparkle of her youth had begun to dim, affected by long hours under lights in heavy stage makeup and too many late nights on planes, and in limos to count. She definitely deserved a chance to shine as long as possible.

Diana looked over and caught Serena studying her.

"Tired?" Diana asked.

"Not too much," Serena replied, embarrassed to have been caught assessing Diana's profile.

"Good," Diana said. "Because when we get back to the hotel, we've got a lot to do. The fun part is great, but it isn't always like this, you know." Diana turned toward the dark limo window and lost herself in watching the cityscape slip by.

Yes, Serena thought, *and now the pressure will be on me to produce the miracles you expect.* The immediacy of her commitment hit home, and Serena tried to remain calm, determined to prove Diana right.

Throughout the afternoon, Serena had tested a myriad of lipsticks, contours, blushes, eye shadows, foundations, and powders, so see what colors worked best on Diana, paying careful attention to the claims made by in-store makeup artists and product representatives about their cosmetic wonders. The volume of creams and gels available was as impressive as the claims: guaranteed to fade age spots overnight; brighten skin tone with one application; magically erase crow's feet; and tone sagging skin to a tight, youthful shine. And Diana had bought a ton of them, though Serena had tried to guide Diana in her choices, urging her to purchase one item over another, without avail.

Though it was only six o'clock when they finally swept up to the gold-plated facade of Trump International Hotel and Tower, it was getting dark. A doorman in a maroon uniform trimmed with gold braid hurried to open the door for Diana, who got out, breezed past the man, and entered the hotel lobby with Serena hurrying behind.

Inside, the pear-shaped concierge rushed over to Diana, making his pleasure at her arrival known to everyone within earshot.

"Welcome back to Trump International, Miss Devreux," he said, giving her a wide toothy smile. "Always good to see you. So glad to have you with us again."

"Thank you, Chester. Have my packages arrived?" she asked.

"Yes, Ms. Devreux, they just went up and your luggage is waiting in your room."

"Good," Diana said, then went on to inquire about the amenities she always requested, making sure the usual security arrangements were in place to ensure the absolute privacy she required.

"Yes, everything is set, and you have the same suite as last time, as you requested. And Miss St. James' room is one floor below yours, along with the rest of your party."

"Please change that for me, Chester," Diana replied. "I want Miss St. James on my floor. Across the hall since I assume it's free."

"Oh, yes, no one is on that floor but you, so I will arrange it right away." The concierge looked Serena over, as if calculating her importance to Diana Devreux's entourage, then flashed her a tight, accepting smile.

"Fine," Diana finished. "No calls, no maid service, no interruptions," Diana stated, then headed toward the bank of elevators on the other side of the lobby. "Serena," she said over her shoulder, "let's get busy."

Hurrying into the mirrored elevator with Diana, Serena wondered how Diana could keep going. She must have gotten up at dawn to have been at Upscale so early, and after the three-hour flight from Dallas, had shopped all afternoon. Now she wanted to work? Serena put the thought of resting in her room out of her mind. Obviously, Diana had other plans.

As the elevator rose, Serena inhaled the scent of rich wood paneling and eyed the gold veins in the marble trim inside the elevator wondering if Giani had called Havensway looking for her and what Nina would think when she learned what had happened. Leaving Dallas without telling Giani or Nina good-bye bothered Serena, but she had grasped an opportunity to move on with her life and didn't regret her actions.

For the next two days Serena worked with Diana nonstop, trying out different hairstyles, creating new ways to use makeup, drafting illusions to enhance Diana's beauty. She experimented with every facial cream, depilatory, rejuvenating gel and mask they had bought, then late in her room, working alone, she studied labels, compared ingredients, and educated herself on what went into the expensive cosmetics, beginning her journey to find the right combinations to enhance her mother's formulas.

Serena assessed Diana's wardrobe, discussing color, cut, fabric, and style, guiding her toward a new image. The work left Serena exhausted, tense, terrified, and happy. She had a vision of what the new Diana Devreux ought to look like: an illusion of glamorous, contemporary energy. Serena could not explain how it came to her or why, or even if it would work. All she knew was that a source deep inside her mind and heart was feeding this creative drive.

But Diana was not so easy to work with, bringing Serena to near-tears more than once with her sharp directives and adamant opinions. But Serena gritted her teeth and held in her feelings, until the end of the day, then she'd go to her room and shed her tears in privacy, thinking of Joyce Ann Keller every time it happened. Joyce Ann had taught Serena how to keep her chin up and maintain a strong facade even when she felt like crying, and for all the trouble her friendship with Joyce Ann had brought, Serena was grateful for that advice.

But the bright side of her new job always chased away her anxiety. Her room, across the hall from Diana's five room suite, had a pink marble bathroom, glittering crystal lamps, gilt-edged chandeliers, and blue satin throw pillows heaped on a matching quilted bedspread. The thick white terry-cloth towels stacked five deep on rows of glass shelves matched the equally luxurious bathrobe and slippers set out for her each night. The rich amenities were overwhelming, and the view of Central Park made Serena catch her breath every time she opened her drapes.

Two days ago she had been worried about retrieving her second-hand boots from the shoe repair shop. Now she had designer clothes and three pairs of soft, black Charles Jordan pumps in her closet, and a five-piece set of Gucci luggage stacked beside the door. A year ago, she had been sitting in a jail cell, worried about the bleak future that awaited her on the outside. Now she was sleeping in one of the finest hotels in the world, employed by a superstar who wanted to guide her career. How had such luck fallen her way? How long would it last?

The frenzy Diana Devreux had created at Song City was nothing compared to what happened the moment she stepped onto the stage to give the final concert of her *One and Only* tour. When the spotlight hit her beaded gown, which looked as if it had been stitched onto her Barbie-doll figure, Serena beamed with pride. The pale pink silk beaded dress and matching silk roses pinned in Diana's tousled hair created a vision of youth and magic. Her hair danced like a halo of spun brown sugar around her delicate face, her mass of fine curls catching and reflecting the multicolored stage lights with every seductive twist of her hips, shrug of her smooth bare shoulders, and dance step performed in four-inch platform heels. Serena had insisted Diana elevate herself on the massive stage, and tonight, the tiny diva was huge, demanding and receiving the undivided attention of everyone in the excited, pulsing crowd.

Serena nodded in satisfaction, pleased with her idea to dress Serena entirely in pale pink, and had shaded the area from the base of Diana's throat to her prominent collarbones in rose-tinted makeup, too. The star glowed. Not in the harsh gold tones she usually wore, but with a glow that bounced onto her face to create an illusion of youthful vigor. Serena's attempt to soften Diana's look was a success, greatly diminishing unflattering lighting angles, taking years off Diana's face and throat. Her trademark gold and silver, which had cast every fine line on Diana's beautiful, though middle-aged face in shadow, were gone and no one seemed to care.

The uproar when the spotlight hit Diana was deafening. She looked more fabulous than ever, better than she had in the early days of her career. The audience's response filled Serena with an exhilarating mix of excitement, awe, and satisfaction, and she knew Diana was loving this thunderous reception and outpouring of love. The applause when Diana launched into *Missing You,* her signature song that began and ended every concert, was so loud and long it shook the floor beneath Serena's feet. The fans wanted more, and refused to let their glamorous diva leave the stage as they sang along with her. Diana gave the audience what they wanted, belting out her throaty rendition of two more songs, singing nonstop for another fifteen minutes.

At the end, Serena stepped deeper into the wings backstage, to see the frenzied crowd. The mass of cheering, whistling, and clapping fans were on their feet, screaming at Diana, throwing flowers at her feet, yelling how gorgeous she looked, and when those who could not contain themselves rushed the stage and tried to touch Diana, the stoic policemen stationed around the orchestra pit had to force them back into their seats.

Finally, Diana gave her final bow and relinquished the spotlight for the fourth time. A stagehand handed her a bouquet of pink roses. Diana kissed him right on the lips, took the roses, and bowed, waved, then threw kisses at her fans, then hurried offstage and grabbed Serena by the shoulders.

"Thank you, thank you, thank you! You are a miracle!" Diana hugged Serena to her pink-beaded chest, then leaned back and pushed her wild hair off her perspiring neck, holding it up with one hand. "Yes! You are my magical, miracle angel. That's what you are. And I never plan to let you go! Did you hear the gasps when I walked out? The whistles? I felt so sexy, so ready to go, like I haven't felt in years."

Serena could only nod, her eyes beginning to water. This was exactly what she wanted to hear: Diana Devreux was happy. She, Serena St. James, had helped bring a happy ending to Diana's tour. This retooling of Diana's physical appearance marked the starting point in what she knew was going to be a grand adventure.

The party room at the Trump International was jam-packed. The after-party had not begun until midnight and now, at two-thirty, it was totally live. The crowd consisted of musicians, movie stars, stage actors, television entertainers, business associates, long-time friends, reporters, and even a gaggle of groupies who were so well known to Diana that she could call them by first name. The scenario was a dream come true, but strangely, the attention and praise, which made Serena happy, also made her anxious. *Wasn't this what she had envisioned success might be like?* she thought wishing her chest didn't tighten and a sinking feeling wouldn't sweep through her stomach every time Diana spoke about her. Smiling and nodding, Serena tried to hide her discomfort with the burgeoning fabrication of her new life, as well as the possessive hold she realized Diana now had on her.

From her seat at Diana's table at the edge of the lighted dance floor, Serena inspected the people: rich and beautiful and ever so full of themselves. The atmosphere intrigued her. The music pulsed. The champagne flowed, and the VIP guests drifted by in twos and threes to bestow air-kisses on Diana's cheeks and tell her how fabulous she had been tonight. Serena overheard the remarks attached to the words of congratulations as they were whispered into Diana's ear:

"Darling, what have you done?"

"You look fabulous."

"What happened to Kahi and who is your stylist now?"

"Please give me a name."

Diana's answer was a twitter of laughter, a glance at Serena, and a proud introduction, in which she greatly embellished Serena's background, credentials, and abilities to work miracles. Noticing Serena's discomfort with the pumped-up background of her new stylist, she finally eased close to Serena, lowering her voice. "I am so glad to have you with me, Serena. Relax. You look overwhelmed by all of this . . . the people, the glitz, the rushing around, the crowd. I know I plunged you into this pretty fast, but you've come through beautifully. And that is all that counts. Results!" She stopped talking to wave hello to a well-known New York TV anchor, who had just entered the room, then went on. "Go with the flow, okay? I know what you're thinking, but don't worry. When we get to Vegas things will slow down. Right now, I've got everything under control."

"I'm not worried," Serena replied, wishing it were true. The trendy people, the swirl of conversation, the heady atmosphere—it was so much more than she'd expected, but exactly what she wanted. She was Serena St. James, stylist to a superstar and she was going to play the role, just as Diana expected.

"Diana, I should be thanking you," Serena whispered back. "This is the most important and wonderful night of my life."

"Good. Now enjoy it," she ordered, giving Serena a quick hug before standing up to greet the reporter who drew her into a hug.

"A few words for *Entertainment News,* Miss Devreux?" he shouted over the din of conversation and music.

"Why, of course," Diana said, smiling. "Let's go where we can talk." Smiling, she glanced back at Serena. "I'm off. Enjoy yourself, but remember, we leave early for Vegas. You'd better get some sleep."

"Right," Serena replied, glad for an excuse to end the evening.

Diana lifted a finger, "Oh, and if you see Craig, tell him I won't need the car any more tonight."

"Sure," Serena replied, wondering if Craig had been in the audience at Diana's performance because she had not seen him. Probably a security thing, she thought, realizing that after he dropped her and Diana at the stage door before the concert, he had driven away and not been around all evening.

The waiter assigned to Diana's table appeared, paying close attention to the star's stylist's needs. He had been bringing canapes and champagne in a steady stream all evening, often removing plates and glasses so swiftly Serena could hardly finish one round of fancy hors d'oeuvres before another was placed before her. And every time the waiter had refilled Diana's champagne glass, he had automatically poured more in hers. Diana might drink the bubbly like water, tossing down glass after glass between air-kisses to people who dropped by the table, but Serena was not used to drinking alcohol. However, she had to appear sophisticated, so she tried to keep up, but worried about getting sick.

She looked around. The room was suddenly smoky and too warm. The music seemed loud and nonstop. And the swirl of conversation between the strangers who filled the room made her feel small and lost.

Diana had shown her off, bragged about her talent, and Serena had enjoyed the affair, but now it was definitely time to go. Her head was beginning to swim from too much champagne and cigarette smoke and her new five-inch heels were beginning to get to her.

Now Serena watched Diana, who was engaged in an animated interview with the reporter, talking with her hands. Serena eyed her perfect body, the haughty lift of her head, the way she tossed her mane of hair while talking. Standing in a quiet spot near the bar, Vincent Ruby, her manager, nodded and grinned, obviously pleased with the final concert and Diana's new look.

Deciding it was time to go, Serena discreetly edged away from the crowd and made her way to the bank of elevators, ready to turn in for the night. But at a table in the bar at the end of the mirrored hallway, she spotted Craig, dressed in a dark suit and a black turtleneck, instead of his chauffeur's uniform, sitting alone in an alcove that faced a wall of windows that provided a glittering view of the city.

Chapter Nineteen

Serena eased between two men who were smoking cigars, standing by the elevators, and went over to Craig, carefully studying his profile. She noticed that Craig was deep in thought, holding a glass, as he concentrated on the sparkling Manhattan skyline.

"Hello," she said, startling him.

He jerked around, then smiled, seemingly pleased. "Oh, hi." He nodded, put down his glass and motioned for her to sit down. "Partied out?"

"For me, yes." Serena sank into the deep red leather club chair next to his and crossed her legs. The slit in the skirt of her black velvet dress fell open, revealing a good portion of her thigh. Diana had snapped up the strapless creation as soon as she had seen it on a rack at Bloomingdale's yesterday, buying it for Serena without letting her try it on. Serena, never having worn a strapless dress in her life, had been worried that it might not fit, that it might make her look foolish, or that she'd have to walk around with her arms at her sides to hold up the top of her dress.

But, of course, Diana had judged it right. The dress fit Serena as if it had been custom made for her and the sensuous fabric hugged her bodice in a series of soft folds that emphasized her small waist and flared just enough to show off her curvaceous hips. The back was cut low, the side slit high, and the classic sheath created an overall impression of money, class, and style. Diana had even bought the jet earrings and necklace to go with it, as well as a tiny black sequined purse shaped like a shell. Serena loved the way she felt tonight: sexy, sophisticated, and beautiful.

She started to pull the opening in the skirt closed, but decided against it, deciding it was fine the way it was. Craig's eyes flickered briefly over her legs, then up to her face before he winked and said, "Very nice."

"What's so nice?" she teased, uncharacteristically flirtatious.

"The dress, the shoes, the jewelry, the hair. All of you," he said in a voice that was level and soft.

Serena ran a hand along her thigh, smoothing the velvet skirt. "Diana picked it out. She's got great taste."

"And the money to indulge it," Craig quickly added.

"Well, I never would have bought a dress like this, even if I could have afforded it."

"Why not?" Craig asked.

Serena inwardly flinched, wishing she hadn't voluntarily provided an opening for Craig to ask her that question. She'd have to be more careful. "Because money has always been very hard to come by, and spending it on fancy clothes has never been a priority."

Nodding, Craig said, "Well, you sure look good, and not at all like the half-drowned girl I rescued from the side of the road a few days ago."

Serena traced a fingernail over the shiny wooden tabletop, making small circles, thinking about his compliment. "Yes, only a few days ago." She lifted her eyes and caught his even gaze, holding it for a moment. "Seems like I've known you much longer than a few days."

"True. A lot has happened in a short time, but life with Diana is like that. Things are going to be very different for you from now on, and I doubt that money will be your biggest worry. You're in high cotton, Serena St. James." He laughed, lifting his glass in a salute. "Diana has a big heart, but she's careful with whom she shares it. She likes you, wants you to succeed, and that's great. But be careful. She's been known to take advantage, and will if you let her, so try not to let that happen, Serena. You're very talented. Young. Smart. You'd eventually make it big without her help, just maybe not so quickly." Craig took a sip of his drink, then signaled to the waiter, who hurried over.

Craig nodded to Serena. "What do you want?"

"Nothing, thanks. I think I overdid the champagne."

"I know what you mean." He turned back to the waiter. "I'll have a Perrier and lime, please." Focusing again on Serena he continued their conversation. "I saw Diana hug you offstage in the wings tonight. She's really pleased with this concert . . . and that's good."

"You saw us? Where were you? "

"In the control room," he said. "Great view from up there. I can see the audience, the pit, the wings. Check things out with little interference. And by the way, tell Diana the lighting tonight was superb."

Serena heard the depth of Craig's commitment to Diana Devreux in his words, and noticed that the firm set to his jaw and the touch of determination around his mouth evidenced how seriously he took his job. But how deeply were they connected? she wondered, deciding to venture into the subject. "You're much more than a chauffeur to Diana, aren't you?" Serena prompted, keeping her voice as even as possible, hoping she did not sound too interested in their relationship.

"I'm whatever she needs me to be," Craig quipped lightly, seeming unruffled by Serena's question. "And I try to be accommodating," he finished, lifting his chin slightly, as if waiting for the next question.

But Serena held her tongue, taking in his reaction, admiring the clear-cut lines of his face, dark against the light pine paneled wall behind him. She wanted to know exactly what "accommodating" meant, but didn't dare press the subject, silently admonishing herself for even wanting to know. Craig Alexander didn't owe her any kind of explanation about his place in Diana's world.

"Diana's totally changed my life, that's for sure," Serena changed the subject. "Three days ago no one could have made me believe that I'd be sitting in the Trump International Hotel in New York City, attending a party for Diana Devreux, let alone working for her."

"Yep. I understand. It took a while for me to get used to this job, too."

Serena grabbed the opening to press for more details about Craig. "How long have you worked for Diana?"

"Five years."

"So, you've gotten to know her well. Seen a lot, huh?"

"Yes, sometimes more than I'd like." Craig frowned, the tight skin of his smooth brown forehead wrinkling between his brows. He tossed back the last of his drink, then hunched over his empty glass, letting his remark settle in. "All of this may seem glamorous, Serena, but there is a price to pay. I hope you understand that." He shoved his glass aside and took her hand. "I'd hate to see you hurt . . . or disappointed because life, especially on the road, with a superstar is like a roller-coaster ride. Some days you're up, other days you're at the bottom of the curve . . . and when you're not sure where you are . . . hang in. It will change, that's one thing I guarantee. Remember that, okay?"

Serena wondered how many ups and downs he'd lived through, how they had affected him, and what lay ahead for her. No matter what it was, she felt ready, and with Craig to help her navigate this fast-paced, unknown world, she'd give Diana her all. She squeezed Craig's hand, then ran her thumb over his strong fingers, and looked up. "Thanks," she murmured, letting go.

"Sure. Anytime," he replied, then cleared his throat and sat back.

Under his quiet gaze, Serena was acutely aware of his interest in her, his attempt to be as honest and helpful as he could. But she was also very aware of the noisy group at the table next to theirs and the lateness of the hour.

"Enjoy the party?" he asked, breaking her concentration as he jerked his head toward the party room.

"Oh, yes. It was great, but I'm exhausted. The past two days are coming down on me. Staying up all night is not what I usually do."

"Not so glamorous a life, huh?"

"Oh, no. It's glamorous, all right," Serena corrected. "I'm not complaining about that. Just tired, that's all."

Craig turned in his seat, looking back toward the room where the music still rocked and the celebratory conversation was sprinkled with the clink of champagne glasses clicking together. He checked the time on his Cartier watch. "Better see if Diana needs the car."

"Oh, she asked me to tell you she won't need you—" Serena said, then stopped and clarified, "I mean, the car, tonight."

"That's good," Craig murmured, twirling the melting ice in his empty glass. He set it down, threw a twenty on the table, then bent his head closer to Serena's. "Let's get out of here."

"Go out?" Serena checked her watch. "It's a little after three."

"So?" He replied nonchalantly. "New York never shuts down."

Though she wanted to say yes, she hesitated, afraid that things were moving too fast, that this new world could easily suck her into making less than sound decisions. Did she dare go out on the town at three in the morning, when Diana had told her to get some sleep? That they were getting an early start in the morning? As much as she wanted to be with Craig, she had better exercise caution, get a handle on this fast-paced lifestyle she'd so eagerly jumped into. Meeting Craig, accepting Diana's offer, flying to New York, the marathon work to make Diana over—all of it seemed blended into a blurry montage of limos, airplanes, boutiques, strangers, and impulsive decisions. Nothing was normal, anymore. Maybe she'd better pull back.

"No, I think I'd better call it a night."

Craig frowned. "And spoil my only night off in New York?"

Now, Serena laughed aloud, her fatigue momentarily fading.

"What's so funny?" he wanted to know.

"You," she said.

"What about me?"

"Your *night* off? It's already morning!"

His eyes brightened with anticipation. "Precisely why you need to go out with me . . . so I can help you get into the groove of working for Diana Devreux . . . where the days are long, the nights are longer, and most of the time they are very mixed up. Goes with the territory, so get used to it."

Aware that he wanted to test her, give her a survival lesson in her new job, Serena squared her shoulders and accepted his challenge. "Okay. Where do you want to go?"

"All right," Craig agreed, his look of anticipation switching to excitement. "Wherever you want. In this city, there are hundreds of places I could take you, and from what you've told me, you have a lot to see." He took her hand again, turning serious. "I'd like to make your first visit to the Big Apple one you'll never forget."

Tensing under his touch, she said softly, "But it already is."

"I'll bet I can top everything you've seen and done, so far," he taunted, clearly enjoying the challenge.

"I'll bet you can," Serena replied, pleased that he wanted to continue spending time with her. Alone. A few moments ago all she had wanted to do was go to her room, take a hot shower, and fall into that deep fluffy king-sized bed and sleep forever. Now, her thoughts were centered on Craig Alexander and she'd willingly go wherever he wanted to, as long as they were together.

The Golden Trumpet Cafe, located in the basement of an ancient brownstone on 155th Street, had been the home of a wealthy financier during 1940s. The owner had enjoyed inviting jazz musicians to come in and play for him and his guests after the other clubs closed. When they finished he'd serve breakfast to many of the famous musicians of the era. Now they still came to eat and play at the Golden Trumpet, which was packed from six in the evening until nine in the morning, with long lines of people waiting to eat breakfast and hear some of the best music in the city. Some nights the blues seeped out of the doors and windows of the fabled structure, while most mornings, it was country-western music or Caribbean sambas that entertained those dining at the small round tables.

Craig hated for the night to end, but knew, when the sky began to lighten above the tall skyscrapers, that it was time to get Serena back to the hotel. They had explored the city from Midtown to the Upper West Side and up to Harlem, then over the Brooklyn Bridge. They had gone window shopping on Madison Avenue, gazed down on the empty skating rink at Rockefeller Center, and had visited the Empire State Building where Serena had insisted on getting out of the limo to stand on steps so he could snap her picture with the disposable camera he had bought for six dollars in an all-night store in Harlem. And now, as they waited for their eggs, bacon and pancakes, he began to feel the impact of having spent the past four hours in the company of a most mysterious, attractive woman. He was intrigued with Serena St. James, a young woman who was extremely reluctant to talk about her past, and though he wanted to respect her privacy, he also wanted to know more about her.

From the moment he met her, looking at her through that rain-spotted window, he had sensed she was different: innocent, yet worldly, but unlike any of the women he met on the road. He suspected there was more to Serena than showed on the surface, and it intrigued the hell out of him. She was open, interested, and curious about the world, and he felt privileged to be her guide and confidant.

The bustle of the big city excited her, the colorful mix of nationalities intrigued her, and she inspected every one of the tacky tourist souvenirs she found in the vendors' stalls with great care. Her interest in everything made him also want to smell, taste, and experience things he had taken for granted. Yet, she paid exceptionally close attention to her surroundings, observing the people more closely than he ever did, as if trying to read their thoughts, assess them, or fix memories in her mind to bring out later and think about.

Once the waiter had placed their breakfasts on the table and left, Craig cautiously ventured forward, hoping to learn a little more about Serena St. James.

"You'd better write those postcards to your friends tonight and mail them in the morning, so they'll be postmarked, New York," he advised.

Serena buttered a piece of toast as she calmly replied, "Oh, I'm not sending them to anyone, I bought them for myself."

"Not even to one friend?" he asked tentatively, testing her desire to tell him more. She had told him that her mother died when she was seven and her father died while she was in high school, and since then she'd been on her own, working her way into the beauty business by moving from one salon to another until Giani Pilugi at Upscale hired her.

"No," she replied. "I don't have any close friends."

"Too bad," Craig said.

"Don't worry," Serena said. "I've always been a loner. My life has been pretty ordinary. Uneventful, really, until your friend Trudy came looking for me."

Craig thought about the differences between them, realizing how chaotic and unsettled his life had been since the day he arrived in Los

Angeles. They were opposites in so many ways, but it didn't matter. For the first time in years, he was spending time with a woman who didn't play games or make crazy demands, who wanted to have fun and simply do her job and enjoy life. She was almost too good to be true.

Serena spread a dab of strawberry jam on a triangle of toast. "This place is so lively and . . . awake!" She stuffed the toast into her mouth. "Does anyone ever sleep?"

"Hey. This is nothing. Wait 'til you see Vegas. Now that's a city where the lights absolutely never go out."

Serena set down her knife. "I hope Diana isn't worried. Maybe I should have left a message that I was going out."

A warning signal flashed into Craig's head, to hear Serena's worry, and he flinched to realize how quickly she had fallen under Diana's control.

"You worry too much, Serena. Here's my last piece of advice for the evening. Let Diana know you have a life, otherwise you will be miserable. She likes control . . . over everything and everyone in her little world. She knows you need her. But remember she needs you even more. Respect her, but establish the rules up front and keep your personal life your own." As he said the words he wished he had had the guts to do the same, and wondered what Diana would say when he told her he had spent the evening with Serena. She'd be annoyed, but so what? He was not going to let Serena St. James get away.

Inside the limo, Luther Vandross crooned on the CD player and Serena inched closer to Craig. By the time they entered the parking garage adjacent to the hotel, she had pressed her leg so tightly against his, he could think of nothing else. Craig nosed the limo into the dim parking space assigned to his car, turned off the engine, then slipped his arm around Serena's waist.

She sighed low in her throat and let her head fall back against his shoulder, closing her eyes.

Craig stroked Serena's hair from her face, then studied her features in the soft yellow glow that was coming from the overhead lights spaced throughout the parking garage. Her full, smooth lips were curved into a tender smile of satisfaction. Her black velvet dress, cut low in the front created a stark contrast to the bronze sheen of skin that rose and fell as she breathed. The soft shadows playing over the highlights in her hair, drew him closer, and he eased his lips over one ear, inhaling the perfume she had dabbed on her neck.

It was nearly dawn, and the garage was quiet, with every space filled. Even the guards, who routinely buzzed around in their tiny white golf carts, were nowhere in sight. Craig sank back, relieved that Serena hadn't insisted on getting out of the limo as soon as he parked. He didn't want this evening to end, and apparently, thank God, she didn't either.

"I'm so glad you're here," he murmured, taking in the slightly floral scent she was wearing. Her perfume reminded him of the small pink flowers that he used to pick in the spring in the Tennessee mountains. He remembered how his mother used to smile her thanks when he handed them to her, and how she'd take down the blue glass jar that was always in her kitchen window and arrange the flowers with great care. He had felt so proud then, and he'd liked the idea of making the most important woman in his life smile. And that's exactly how he wanted to make Serena feel: happy and proud, because, from the little he had learned about her, she had not experienced much happiness in her life.

Craig closed his eyes for a moment, surprised at the direction his thoughts had taken. No woman had ever turned his mind back to pleasant memories of his childhood, especially not while he had been pressed close to her like this, inside of a dark parked car. What was going on? What was it about Serena that made him want so badly to please her?

"I'm glad I'm here too . . . glad I took Diana up on her offer," Serena replied, stretching out her legs, allowing her body to fit against the length of Craig's from his shoulder to his knee. "Did you know Diana was going to ask me to work for her when you approached me outside the salon?"

"Yep. It was my idea." The confession brought him a sense of pride, yet he felt slightly embarrassed. He had known from his first encounter with Serena that he wanted to see her again, and after the fantastic job she had done on Diana at Song City, convincing his boss to approach Serena had been easy.

"Oh? Your idea?" Serena remarked, shifting to look into his face. "For real? Care to explain?"

In the softly illuminated interior of the car she had become a mix of soft shadows, sensuous warmth, and delicious smells that were thick with promise. Craig was too aware of her breath on his neck. Too aware of how it feathered his skin and made him want to kiss her, made his desire swell in his groin. It would be so easy to pull her to him and take his chances, but he knew better than to rush things. He could wait. Serena had to make the first move, give him a signal, show him the passion he knew was simmering beneath her innocent, cool facade.

"Explain? Well . . . you looked hungry, " he said, adjusting his arm so that it rested only inches below her breast.

"Hungry?"

"Not for food," he clarified, "but for anything other than what you were doing. That probably sounds crazy, but my first impression of you was that you were trying to get away from something that you were worried about."

"You did run me into a ditch."

"Not that," he studied the way her now-tousled hair was cascading over one eye, giving her a very sexy appearance. He brushed back a few strands, then went on. "Make sense?"

Serena nodded. "Perfect."

The sound of cars slipping over the dark street below filled the limo as her reply hung between them.

"So, my discontent with my current situation was that obvious?" Serena remarked.

"Umm-hum," Craig agreed. "And when I realized you were more angry with yourself than me, and so worried about Trudy's car, I knew something else was going on."

"Are you always so perceptive?"

He laughed. "No. I'm not. But when you were talking about your job at Upscale, you didn't seem that enthusiastic, and after Diana fell in love with what you did for her . . . well, that was all I needed to hear. She had to have you. So I found you. The rest is history, so they say . . ." his voice trailing off, rough with emotion.

"And I had been praying I might see you again," Serena confessed, nuzzling the tip of his nose with hers. "But kidnapping me? That was a bit much."

"I swear I didn't know Diana planned to do that," he defended. "All she told me was to find you and ask you to get in the car so she could talk to you about helping her out. I thought she meant temporarily, until she talked Kahi into coming back."

"So why didn't you stop the limo when I banged on the window and shook my keys?"

"Because I take my orders exclusively from Diana Devreux," he joked, ducking when Serena swatted playfully at him.

"That's a mean thing to say!"

"I know," Craig chuckled, grabbing her hand, brushing her fingers over his lips. "Now, if Diana had told me to stop, I would have. But she didn't. So, here you are." He pressed the back of her hand to his cheek. "I couldn't let you get away. Something about you hit me the moment I saw you. Serena, you are so different from all of the women I've met. You don't now how refreshing it is to finally meet someone who is not out to get a foothold on me in order to get close to Diana. The music industry is a race filled with all kinds of rats, and some of them can be quite beautiful and cunning."

Serena lowered her lashes, looking down into her lap.

Craig's breath caught in his throat as he watched her. The light from the overhead lamps had created tiny gold flecks scattered all over her body and the effect was ethereal, almost angelic, and he struggled to control his urge to take her face between his hands and kiss her hard on the lips.

"I didn't want to lose track of you either," she replied huskily, now turning her face up to his.

When Serena placed her lips to his, Craig reached up and touched the side of her face, then ran his index finger along her jaw, deepening the kiss until he felt her begin to respond. When she parted her lips, he tasted her, entwining his tongue with hers, knowing she wanted him to explore her, savor her, ignite her with the intensity he was struggling to hold in check.

Craig's heart thumped with the beat of the music filling the limo, reverberating in his chest like the sound of the tires outside the garage that were bumping over the slick wet street. He slipped his hand along her leg, enjoying the feel of soft black velvet against his palm, searching for the revealing slit he knew was there. When his fingertips met her flesh, he tensed for a moment, waiting to see if she would pull away. She didn't.

He eased his hand beneath the velvet fabric, slid it between her dark warm thighs, and made his way past her thigh high stockings to the moist lacy silk of her panties.

"Craig," Serena moaned, caressing him.

He froze, unwilling to do anything she did not want. He started to pull his hand away, but she reached down and took it.

"Don't stop," she said, pressing her head into his neck as she pressed his hand into her flesh. "Please, don't stop."

He bent his body fully over hers and eased her legs apart with one hand. It was easy to push aside the bit of lacy silk that lay between his fingers and the soft triangle of curls hidden behind it. He trailed his thumb around the outline of her sex, then stroked her gently, caressing the spot he sensed had never been touched before.

Serena arched her back, gripped his shoulders, and lifted her hips off the seat, opening herself wider to his touch. He massaged her silky skin until she gasped, her voice a mixture of surprise and release. Then she collapsed against his chest, holding him tight.

Craig clenched his teeth to keep from crying out, too, cherishing this moment. Serena made him feel decent and honest, made him think about becoming the man he knew he ought to be. Serena could give him a reason to abandon the loveless routine he had fallen into with Diana. And he wanted out, very much.

Now, he held Serena tightly as she shuddered into quiet calm, stroking her hair until she raised her head from his chest and stared at him through half-closed eyes. He could see tears on her cheeks, a flush of relief, almost like gratitude, on her face, and excitement shining in her eyes. God, how he wanted to strip away her clothing, ease her down on the soft gray leather and take her fully, losing himself in her naked warmth. But his satisfaction would have to wait. This was neither the place nor the time to think about his needs. Backing off was what mattered now. He had pleased Serena, had gained her trust, and had made her see how much he wanted her.

Holding her close, he willed his arousal into submission, fighting the urge to touch her again.

Chapter Twenty

J oyce Ann felt a sudden jolt of satisfaction when she saw the credit card on the ground beside the trashcan near the door of the Tom Thumb grocery store. Barely breaking her stride, she calmly scooped it up and stuck it into the pocket on her shirt before the automatic door flipped open. Inside, she went to the wall of coolers at the back of the store and took out a six pack of Bud Light, a liter of Coke, and a quart of milk. Hidden from view behind the tall shelves, she quickly glanced at the name on the credit card. T. R. Knowles. Initials only. That was good, and the expiration date was a year away. Hopefully, the owner had just dropped it and had not missed it yet or reported it stolen. After grabbing a box of cookies and a carton of doughnuts off of a rack festooned with smiling Santas and jolly elves, she went to the Fast Check line, plunked down her groceries, and handed the credit card to the clerk.

While waiting for credit approval, she nonchalantly looked at the holiday cards hanging on a nearby rack, thinking that Christmas was only three days away and once again, she'd be alone. The familiar ache that always started deep in her stomach and worked its way into her chest when she thought about Christmas began, pulling her mind back to those unhappy Christmas mornings when she had sat on her grandmother's porch for hours, watching the street, expecting her mother to show up with gifts. Of course, it never happened, and even after the confirmation of her mother's death, Joyce Ann still felt that awful stab of disappointment whenever the holidays approached.

"Sign here," the clerk said, interrupting her reverie.

She scribbled an illegible T. R. Knowles, crushed the receipt he handed her into her pocket, then left.

That was easy, Joyce Ann thought, repocketing the card, hoping to use it for gas and food at least a few more times before tossing it in a trash bin along the road. Uncertain about when or where she'd be able to stop, she had to keep going, even though she had made it as far as Abilene without trouble.

She had been driving steadily for two days, heading west without any plan other than to get out of Texas. The last road sign she had passed said El Paso, four hundred fifty miles. Texas was huge, and it seemed as if she'd have to drive forever just to get out of the state.

The only thing she had eaten since her escape were the two Hershey bars she'd found inside the truck, and two doughnuts she lifted from a sample tray in the bakery section of a Kroger's. After running out of gas a half hour ago, she had ditched the stolen prison van on a trash-filled lot two streets over, and walked to the Tom Thumb, dizzy with hunger, determined to steal something to eat if she had to.

Now her mission was to find another car and keep running. Finding the credit card had been a stroke of luck that bolstered her confidence, but she'd have to be careful not to leave a paper trail that the police could use to trace her.

Walking through the parking lot, she began checking cars to find one with the keys in the ignition. When she came up to a yellow Toyota with the windows down and music blaring from inside, she eased to the side and watched the teenager, who was jamming to the music while sitting behind the wheel. This was much better than she had hoped, and it was going to be easy.

She went up to the driver's side window and stopped, giving the boy a hard stare when he interrupted his jerky movements and looked over at her.

"Whatcha want?" he snapped. "I ain't got no spare quarter, so don't even ask."

"Get out," Joyce Ann ordered.

"Who you think you talkin' to, bitch? Get out, my ass. You better get ottta here."

Joyce Ann reached through the window and grabbed the boy by the front of his tee shirt. "Don't fight me and I won't hurt you." She twisted the neck of his dirty tee shirt hard, cutting off his air.

The boy's mouth flew open. He tried to pry Joyce Ann's hard grip off his shirt, but when he realized how strong she was, gave up, nodding frantically, his head bobbing up and down like one of those wooden Mexican puppets Joyce Ann had seen for sale by the side of the road. She yanked open the door and when he stumbled out, she let go. The frightened boy took off across the asphalt, his sneakers slapping the ground like clapping hands as he raced between parked cars.

Peeling rubber, Joyce Ann fled, hoping no one had seen what went down. In her rearview mirror she saw the boy still running, then he hopped a fence at the edge of the lot and disappeared into the maze of apartments next to the grocery store. No one had paid him any attention.

Strange he didn't run back into the store to call the police, she thought, wondering what was up with him. Leaning over, she kept one eye on the road as she popped the door to the glove compartment, and just as she thought, a gun dropped out. She scooped up the Colt .45 and stuck it under her seat. "Guess he's got reasons not to call the police," she said under her breath, exhaling in a long sigh of satisfaction. This pit stop at the Tom Thumb in Abilene had been worth the walk.

As soon as she was up on the freeway and headed out of town, she switched stations on the radio, ripped open the carton of milk, took a long gulp, then opened the pack of Newports she had bought and stuck a cigarette in her mouth. When the lighter popped out, she pressed the red-hot tip to the cigarette and inhaled deeply. The smoke wafting up before her eyes unexpectedly jolted her back five years. The Dairy Queen. Marcella Jacobs. Joyce Ann slowly emptied her lungs, thinking about that night when she and Sara Jane had defied Marcella by smoking in her store. She flipped the ashes out of the open window and thought back over the past five years. Five long years, and it had all begun with a damn cigarette. Well, she was free now, and could smoke or drink or do whatever she damn well pleased. One thing was certain: She was not going back to prison.

Joyce Ann continued heading west, changing cars twice. On Christmas Eve she pressed her luck with the credit card once more and got a turkey dinner at Luby's, a change of clothes at Wal-Mart and a full tank of gas. Then she tossed the card into a ditch by the side of the road and kept driving.

An hour later, too exhausted to go on, she pulled up to a Dumpster behind a deserted mall and stopped, having learned that shopping mall Dumpsters were far safer sources for diving than those in residential neighborhoods where dogs sniffed around, and nosey neighbors might see her and call the police. And if she moved quickly and quietly, the mall security guards usually left her alone.

Getting out, she began to rummage around and came upon a hooded windbreaker lined with flannel, still in its plastic package, which she promptly took out and pulled over her Gatesview prison tee shirt. It would be safer to keep the tee shirt on than throw it away and leave evidence behind that the cops might use to find her. Though the weather was mild during the day, the nights could be cold, especially while sleeping inside a car.

The next morning, just as daylight began to break, footsteps outside the car woke her up, and she eased her head off the front seat and peeked out, curious who was there. A shadow of a man slipped past, then disappeared into the Dumpster. Joyce Ann sat up and watched the bin, waiting, until the man re-emerged holding what looked like a pair of shoes and a backpack. When he saw her inside the car, he froze and stared back at her, as if she were trespassing on his turf.

Joyce Ann rolled down the window and called out. He climbed down, came over, and boldly asked Joyce Ann for a cigarette.

"Sure, I got a smoke," she tossed back, sizing him up. The thin white boy had dirty blonde hair that looked as if it had neither been washed nor cut for months. His jeans were threadbare at the knees and the heavy black jacket he was wearing was held together in the front with a belt around his waist. He had obviously been on the streets for some time. Popping open the door, she got out and shook the pack at him, then took one herself.

"Who are you? What you doing here?" he asked, rolling the unlit cigarette between two smudged fingers.

Joyce Ann shrugged. "Sleepin'. Trying to stay out of the cold. Why do you care? This your territory or somethin'?"

"You could say that," he replied, moving toward a concrete stump by the curb. " I come here all the time and never seen you around before."

Pulling back her shoulders, Joyce Ann studied him. "Passin' through."

"Yeah? Where you headed?"

"Dunno yet."

"Humph," he grunted, then impatiently held up the cigarette that Joyce Ann had given him, squinting one pale blue eye nearly closed. "Hey, you got a match, too?"

Digging into the pocket of her jeans, Joyce Ann took out a crushed pack of matches and threw it at him. "Here. Help yourself," she said.

He caught it neatly in one hand, lit up, then sat down on the curb that curved around the parking lot. He blew smoke over his head as he watched Joyce Ann extricate the backpack from its plastic covering.

"You want that?" he asked.

After examining it, then securing it over her shoulders, she replied. "Sure, if you don't." Then she flopped down beside the man and lit up, too.

"I'm Joyce," she told him, omitting her last name.

"I'm Tonk. Where you from?" he asked.

Joyce Ann shrugged off the question and took another long drag.

"I live over there," he went on, hunching over his knees as he pointed to a dark space between the chain-link fence and another Dumpster.

Joyce Ann glanced over, saw his shopping cart filled with clothing, papers and plastic bags, then looked away.

Tonk got up and went over to his makeshift home, reached into his stash and took out a wine bottle. Returning to where Joyce Ann was sitting, he unscrewed the cap and passed it to her.

Joyce Ann waved the bottle away. "No thanks." She watched Tonk carefully, taking note of his long, dirty blonde hair. His tee shirt that peeked out from beneath his heavy coat. His skin was clear, his teeth were fairly white, but he had a bright red scar that ran from the right side of his upper lip to his nose that marred his once-good looks. His hands, slender and free of cuts and bruises, didn't look like those of a man who regularly engaged in manual labor. His tone and demeanor were nonthreatening, not those of a hardened street bum, or a gang member, but like a rich white college boy who'd gotten caught up in a situation beyond his control. She gauged him to be in his late twenties, maybe thirty at the most, probably handsome before drugs, or alcohol or whatever had forced him to the street got a hold on him.

He doesn't look so bad, but he sure could use a bath, she thought, hating that body smell that reminded her of Gatesview.

Tonk took a long gulp, then a drag on the cigarette, then sat back in a surprisingly relaxed way. He looked at the ground, hands dangling between his knees, as if preparing to answer the questions Joyce Ann had not asked. "Been out here too long," he stated. "Started out in New Orleans and got this far before my car died and my money ran out."

"Where you headed?" she asked.

"Vegas."

"Why Vegas?"

"It's a place where I know I can really get over. Start fresh, you know?"

"Doin' what?"

Tonk's lips fell into a straight line and he pressed them together as he set the wine bottle down on the ground between his legs, then clasped both hands into fists. "Whatever it takes to get a hold of some real money. There's lots of it out there."

Joyce Ann nodded, but knew better than to press him. He had secrets and needed money. Well, she did, too, so the less said the better.

Vegas, she thought. *A good place to lay low, mix in with the tourists and gam-blers. Lots of transient types in the casinos and on the strip.* Her impression of Vegas, gained from television and what inmates who'd been there told her, was of a town where high class, low class, and no class were lev-eled by the lure of a jackpot at a slot machine and truck drivers walked side by side with celebrities through any hotel lobby or restaurant.

She liked Tonk's easy manner. He'd accepted the fact that she was in a situation similar to his, but it did not matter what it was. He was not going to ask a lot of questions or pry. She wanted to trust him, and her instincts told her she could benefit from an alliance with him, so why not find out how?

"Wanna ride to Vegas?" she impulsively offered.

Tonk drained the last of the wine, then calmly assessed Joyce Ann. After taking a long breath, he said, "Sure. Why not? I got nothing bet-ter to do."

"Okay," she said, then added bluntly, "Go over to that K-Mart and wash up in the men's room. If you're riding with me, you gotta clean up."

"No problem," Tonk replied, tossing the empty wine bottle into the Dumpster.

Joyce Ann watched him amble across the road, no hint of hurry in his step, hoping she'd made the right decision. Tonk didn't talk much, and that was fine. His company on the road would be good. A white boy who didn't ask questions, care who she was, or want anything from her other than a ride might just come in handy. Joyce Ann took a long drag on her cigarette and looked up into the sky, wondering what Vegas would be like.

Chapter Twenty-one

It was dusk when the limo pulled up to the scrolled iron gates that protected Diana Devreux's Las Vegas home from the reporters, fans, and curious onlookers who were calling out for her to roll down the window so they could catch a glimpse of their idol. Serena was shocked to see people sitting on folding chairs, cameras in their hands, screaming for Diana. Some were flashing posters of the *One and Only* cover, photos of Diana, and CDs, begging for autographs. Others waved signs to tell Diana, who was watching them from behind the dark windows, a satisfied look on her face, where they were from and how much they loved her latest release.

"We love you, Diana! Roll down the window, so we can see you, Diana!" several people in the excited crowd shouted. But of course, Diana ignored their requests, ordering Craig not to stop the car.

"What a crowd! This is unbelievable!" Serena remarked as Craig continued to inch toward the anxious guard who was standing behind the entry gates waiting for the signal to open them.

"Oh, this is nothing," Diana remarked dismissively. "You should have been around five years ago when *Midnight Lover* came out. That was my biggest triumph. Absolute pandemonium for months. I had to hire six extra security guards to patrol the grounds night and day, and I can't tell you how many bouquets of flowers, photos of babies, and pieces of men's underwear they picked up and carried away." She laughed, shaking her head. "At least I know the publicity is working. Think how horrible it would be if I had returned home today to an empty driveway? No fans waiting to greet me? Now, that would be a disaster, Serena."

"Are people always hanging around outside your house like this?" Serena wanted to know.

Tilting back her head, Diana swept her fingers through her fluffy curls, considering Serena's question. "No, not always," she replied. "It's usually crazy like this at the end of a tour. You know, after I've been out on the road making appearances, pumping up the album. Give it a few weeks . . . things will begin to settle down . . . then I'll get back in the studio, start on my next release."

Serena watched the crowd in fascination, amazed by the mix of people: well-dressed middle-aged women, rumpled street people, young handsome men in jeans and tee shirts, demanding reporters, and quite a few teenage girls wearing tiny shorts and sunglasses. There were even two senior citizens in wheelchairs who must have arrived via the special bus for handicapped people that was parked on the side of the road.

Now that Serena had seen up close what it meant to be so unconditionally loved, praised, idolized, and pampered, she was enthralled. The crowd standing outside of Diana's house idolized the star, not only because of her music, but also because she was rich, famous, and stunningly beautiful. Diana's musical interpretation of a particular song could sweep them away from their ordinary lives, transport them into her world, if only in their imaginations, and for a very short time.

Serena had never considered the consequences of amassing such a huge, loyal following, and it was clear that fame meant giving up privacy, living under pressure, and dealing with the demands of the public, the industry, and those who depended on a star for their livelihood. But fame also brought power, which translated into control, and it was clear to Serena that Diana thrived on both.

Craig spoke to the security guard on his car phone, giving the man the okay to open the gates. As soon as they parted, he slid inside, then slowed down to watch the guard fight back the crowd that had rushed up behind the limo and tried to slip through behind him. When the gates swung closed again, the fans yelled in protest, then slowly began to scatter.

Blooming prickly cactus, thick hedges of red hibiscus, and soaring top-heavy palms lined the winding driveway. The limo stopped in front of a one-story, glass and steel house that was sleek, modern, and low. It hugged the rugged landscape like a flat polished stone that had been broken into puzzle pieces, then rearranged to fit into the arid desert scene. A wide, red door flanked by tall windows faced the circular drive, and two irregular wings extended from the sides of the house, angling back toward the desert. The compound, secluded, secure, and quiet was a stark contrast to the frenzied, fast-paced environment they had just left behind in New York. The peaceful setting was clearly a calm oasis where Diana could wind down and rejuvenate her exhausted soul.

"Hallelujah," Diana said, leaning forward in her seat. She hurriedly stuffed the contract she had been reading into her black DKNY tote, and whipped off her oversized sunglasses. "God, it's good to be here," she sighed, glancing over at Serena. "I bought this land fifteen years ago when it was nothing but a field of sand and rocks. Had this house built with the royalty checks from *Keep on Lovin'*. Best investment I ever made. Today, I'd never be able to find a piece of land like this, for any price. Twenty acres. Close to the strip. Pool. Tennis court. Studio and two guests houses. My own little piece of the world over which I have total control. It's wonderful."

"It's fantastic," Serena agreed, gathering up the brochures, cosmetic samples, and color charts she and Diana had been discussing during the ride from the Vegas airport. She shoved the papers into her leather tote and waited until Diana had stepped out before exiting the limo.

Craig touched Serena lightly on the arm, indicating she should wait at the car until Diana had gone inside.

"Give her a minute or two," he said, in a knowing way. "She likes to walk around, be alone in the house for a while. Kind of a ritual with her. She really loves this place and after being on the road, needs time to get reacclimated."

Craig's observation, as well as the soft tone in his voice touched Serena. It was evident that he cared deeply about Diana, and was much more than a routine driver and part-time bodyguard.

"Sure. I understand," Serena replied. "She's got to be totally worn out, and I'm so glad we stayed an extra day in New York to rest up . . . but I'm still trying to recover from the shopping, the concert, the after-party, and my whirlwind visit. Does Diana have servants living here with her?"

"Only Danny Li, her housekeeper," Craig answered, slamming the limo door. "He lives in during the week and goes home on the weekends, if she is not entertaining. He's a great cook, but a fanatic about keeping everything real neat and in its place. A warning . . . don't leave towels on the floor, dishes on the countertops, or anything dirty around. Put everything where it belongs, or you'll have to endure his yakety-yak all day."

Serena laughed. "Only a housekeeper? I thought Diana would have a much bigger staff."

"No, out here she's pretty independent and likes to be left alone.

Off the road, it's not her style to be surrounded by a lot of people." He walked to the back of the limo and opened the trunk.

Serena followed Craig, wanting to ask more questions about Diana, Vegas, what to expect, but instead, she ventured into the subject that had been on her mind since they left New York that morning. Awkwardly, she glanced toward the house, then moved closer to Craig. "You didn't say anything to Diana about . . ."

"Our night out on the town?"

"Yes," Serena replied, hoping she and Craig could somehow manage to keep their personal relationship separate from their professional commitments to Diana.

"No, I didn't. And I won't. We went out, had a good time, so what? We're grown. We don't have to report to her." Craig set Diana's square makeup case on the ground and leveled a serious look at Serena. "And please, never discuss me with Diana. Okay?"

"Sure," she whispered, watching him closely.

"I like you, Serena. A lot. And I'd like to spend more time with you, but right now you've got to focus on your job, on Diana's New Year's Eve bash at the MGM. You are going to be very busy and under Diana's thumb. You need to concentrate on your work, so I may not see you for a while."

"Will you be back, tonight?" Serena asked, hoping he might want to be with her. After all, it was Christmas Eve.

"Nope," he tossed back, taking another suitcase and two bags from the trunk, which he stacked by the red front door. "I stay at a hotel downtown, out of your . . . and Diana's way."

She should have known this night would not be much different from any other for Craig. His world was not a normal world, and neither was hers anymore. Now, it seemed her days and nights had been reversed, and her time zones had changed over the span of several days. And here she was, about to settle down in another strange place, no idea what to expect. The idea of a romantic, preholiday evening was absurd. She, Craig, and Diana were exhausted from the intensity of the past few days and needed time to regroup.

But he was right. She had to focus on her work, and with Craig under the same roof it would have been difficult. And still, she wondered about Diana. Since the moment they left New York until the plane touched down in Vegas, Serena had carefully observed how Craig and Diana interacted with each other, trying to define their relationship. They were friendly and very comfortable with each other, and were clearly accustomed to traveling together, but did not appear to be romantically attracted. Their conversations, in public at least, were friendly and not very personal, and in the limo and on the plane they rarely interacted, other than to discuss logistics and schedules. But Serena had noticed that when Diana had been out among her fans, Craig stuck close by, his cool professional demeanor evolving into an intimate, protective mode. No one else existed when he was with Diana in a crowd.

But that's his job, isn't it? Serena rationalized, wishing she hadn't felt twinges of jealousy when she saw him hover so close to Diana. *He has to watch out for her, give her his undivided attention, even if I am around.*

"So, you don't drive for Diana while she's here?" Serena prompted, trying to get a better fix on how and when she might see Craig again. He couldn't simply disappear.

"I'm only a phone call away if she needs me. She has four cars in the garage and likes to drive her Jeep, especially out into the desert. When she wants to go fancy, she calls me. Hey, I need my space, too," Craig stated, thumping a big Louis Vuitton bag to the ground. "I've been on the road right along with Diana, remember?"

Serena ducked her head, then looked up, her eyes flickering anxiously over his face. "Right. But I wondered . . ."

Catching the hesitance in her voice, Craig walked over to Serena, meeting her anxiety with a steady gaze. "Don't worry," he said softly. "I won't be that far away."

Serena forced a smile, then nodded. "I know. I'd like to hear from you now and then."

"You will," Craig assured her, placing a finger under her chin to tilt her face to his. He ran his thumb along the swell of her cheek. "Don't ever worry about that. Besides, you are not going to have much free time." He winked. "But call me if you get a break."

"Where?" Serena asked as Craig headed back to the limo.

"The Wind Way Arms. It's in the book," he called over to her. "Go on in. Danny will probably put you in the Blue House."

"The Blue House?" Serena repeated.

"Yeah, it's the guest house decorated totally in blue. Right next to the pool. You're gonna love it."

As soon as Craig pulled off, the front door opened and an attractive Asian man dressed in black slacks and a white short-sleeved shirt came out. He was beautifully tanned with the physique of a bodybuilder and movie star good looks. Only the streaks of gray at his temples, which enhanced his attractiveness, told Serena he was not as young as he looked. It struck her again, how much importance the people in this new world she had entered placed on appearance and illusion.

"You may come in now, Miss St. James," he said retrieving the luggage that Craig had placed by the door.

Surprised to hear him call her by name, Serena squared her shoulders, then immediately replied, "Thank you, Danny."

Danny smiled back at her, a conspiratorial gleam of welcome as he stepped aside to allow Serena to enter Diana Devreux's luxurious Las Vegas home.

But once inside, he did not take Serena through the house or even to meet with Diana, as she had assumed he might. He led her through the main house, which was a gleaming series of rooms hung with twinkling white Christmas lights, chrome, glass, and sparkling crystal chandeliers draped with greenery and red ribbon. They exited through a set of French doors and stepped onto the huge patio at the rear of the house. The garden was a rainbow of colorful blooming plants sprouting from big clay pots set among multicolored deck furniture. They wound their way around the aquamarine pool, down a short stretch of terraced walkway set with shallow pieces of stone, to a path that led to a low bungalow with a Christmas wreath on the door, which faced away from Diana's house. Danny opened the door and placed Serena's bags in the entry, then bowed slightly and left.

Serena remained outside for a moment, surveying the craggy landscape, struck by the beauty of the desert. The purple mountains in the distance were rapidly fading into the curtain of night that was creeping over the land. She stared after Danny until he disappeared inside Diana's house, then she turned and went inside her new home.

The Blue House contained a living area, a bedroom, a small bathroom, and a compact kitchen, but it was more than just a guest house. It was an elegant suite of rooms that created an azure cocoon of crisp linen, sheer imported lace, fringed satin throws, and quilted damask in every imaginable shade of blue. The gray stone floor in the entryway gave way to a richly carpeted living area that resembled a cerulean field upon which had been placed a pale blue leather loveseat and matching oversized ottoman. Plump floor pillows, richly tasseled and corded, were scattered around the room creating an opulent, yet comfortable atmosphere.

Serena turned on both of the matching Chinese porcelain lamps on the marble-topped tables flanking the sofa, then went to the impressionistic painting of an arrangement of hyacinths and lilies that dominated the wall above the fireplace. She could smell the rich scent of lush flowers placed around the room as she studied the piece of art.

Craig's parting words came back into her mind: *You're gonna love it,* he had said, inferring that he had stayed here, too. Had Craig stood in the very same room, sat on the sofa, and slept in the bed where she was about to sleep? Jealously, she wondered about the circumstances and frequency of his visits; had he stayed in the guest house alone or with another woman? She shook off the thought as she approached the open bedroom door.

Serena flipped on the light switch and threw light on the exquisite canopy bed that took up most of the small bedroom. It was draped in sheer blue tulle, laden with velvet pillows, and a lazy ceiling fan whirred overhead, gently stirring the sheer veiling that cascaded from the top of each finial and puddled on the floor.

In an alcove, Diana had placed a laptop computer, a printer, and a fax machine in a area set up like an office. Serena flipped the computer on. A welcome message popped up, giving her an access code to the Internet for her use. She smiled. Guests of Diana Devreux wanted for nothing.

The floor and walls of the adjacent bathroom, which included a shower big enough for two and a sauna, were lined with blue-veined marble. All of the faucets and fittings were shiny brass and the ceiling had been painted sky blue with rosy cherubs, hearts and flowers nestled among white clouds. Serena sat down at the vanity, the heat radiating from the huge round bulbs warming her face as she stared into the mirror and let the vast improvement of her circumstances sink in. Finally, she was separated from the life she had wanted so desperately to escape, but instead of feeling happy, she felt small and somewhat afraid.

Everything was beautiful, but nothing seemed real. The house, the opportunity to work for Diana, even Craig seemed magical and slippery. Could it last? she wondered. Here she was in the city of illusion where gambling, glamour, and good times ruled. A place where image meant everything. A city built on the hopes and dreams of people like her, where gigantic facades of enticement had been created to lure visitors into their dreams. In Vegas people could live out their fantasies, travel to worlds where they hoped to find the riches, attention, and all the elusive treasures they believed would make them happy. It was the perfect place for Serena St. James to come into her own. She hoped she was up to the challenges that awaited her and that Craig would be around to help her navigate this exotic world.

Leaving the bathroom, she went to the pile of luggage Danny had placed at the entry and picked up a brown cardboard box addressed to her. She examined the return address and realized it was from Nina Richards at Havensway. Tearing it open she found the personal items she had left behind. Diana had kept her word. Tossing underwear and grooming articles, shoes and blouses aside, she searched for her mother's book of sketches. Finding it, she tenderly leafed through the pages, filled with a sense of peace.

"Can you believe what has happened to me, Momma?" she whispered, holding the book with both hands. "I'm finally happy . . . and free." She felt her mother's spirit with her then, when a slight stirring of the air in the room brushed her cheek. No longer under her father's rigid control, or the watchful eyes of inmates and prison guards, she was eager to begin this exciting adventure.

She sat back on her heels on the blue carpet, thinking. The bungalow was a stark contrast to the childhood home where she had grown up, not to mention her accommodations at the Cave and at Havensway. From where she sat, she could see into the dark place beneath the kitchen table, where the table legs disappeared into the shadows. Serena's heart began to race and she instinctively made her hand into a fist, clenching it tight as old memories rushed to the surface and flashed into her mind: hiding beneath the kitchen table while her father cursed and drank himself into a fury; sitting in her dark cell, counting the days until her release; curling into a ball, praying for the pain of loneliness to go away. The unexpected fear that came over Serena threatened to make her sick.

Rising, she yanked open the front door, and hurried outside, striding away from the house. She walked far out into the desert, where she stopped beneath a palm tree and looked back at the muted lights in the bungalow windows. They beckoned her return, promised her peace and safety, the two things she wanted most, but she could not move.

Tilting her head back against the rough surface of the tree trunk, she waited for her fears to drain away. The desert landscape, stretching deep into darkness smelled of baked earth, blooming cactus, and hibiscus, while the night air was cool and calming, exactly what Serena needed to pull her emotions back under control.

Why did I let those awful memories get to me? she worried, surprised at her reaction. It had been a long time since she'd felt the pain of her past so sharply.

I've got to do better, she thought. *I've got to be vigilant, and never allow those old feelings to catch me off guard again.*

Squinting into the inky black sky, Serena searched for the brightest star in the heavens, and closing eyes made a wish. She did not wish for money, fame, or even Craig Alexander's love: She wished for Sara Jane Talbot to remain dead and buried so Serena St. James could live.

Chapter Twenty-two

Precious sang along with Diana Devreux as she logged onto her Internet connection, clicked her way through a series of annoying Internet ads and promotional banners, then arrived at the website she wanted: *Dishing with Diana Devreux*. The cover of the diva's CD, *One and Only*, which had been her Christmas present to herself and was playing now in Precious' room, filled the screen. The airbrushed image of Diana in a sexy black lace peignoir lying on a bed of red rose petals was, in Precious Trent's opinion, the best of Diana's many covers. And Precious should know. She had every one of Diana's recordings, even the early ones when Diana had been one of the Spirit Sisters, long before her runaway success and the release of the eighteen records, which had gone platinum and won three Grammys over the years. Precious was a devoted fan.

The fact that Precious was busy at work at her computer on Christmas evening and was humming a tune was due to the news she had received from her physical therapist yesterday: After returning to her grueling exercise regimen and sticking with it for over a year, the dedication had begun to pay off. Feeling was returning to her legs. Finally, she could think about a future of independence, of moving out of her parent's home and into an assisted-living apartment where she could be on her own, at last. Not only was her physical condition improving, her emotional state was, too. Her freelance work as a website tracker for *Celebrity Today* magazine was interesting, satisfying, and kept her mind off her impatience to improve. It also provided Precious a decent paycheck, which she deposited into her savings account, in preparation for her move.

Precious' interest in web-page design and construction had sprung from her volunteer work for the Mallard Baptist Church when the gospel choir director had asked her to create a web page to promote their fund-raising concert in Waco. Precious had never dreamed anyone other than the members of the church would ever log onto the church's site and view it, but Tony Reina, the editor of a new magazine in Dallas called *Celebrity Today*, had stumbled across her creation, and been impressed. He had e-mailed her and asked her to consider working for him as a freelance writer. Her job: to search celebrity Internet sites and provide him with updates on what was new and happening with musicians, actors, and entertainers. He wanted to incorporate this information into his regular magazine column, "A Peek at the Stars."

Precious had jumped at the offer, and now spent her days and quite a few nights settled in front of her computer gleaning gossip, news, and insight from the cyberlives of famous people.

Now, she clicked on the page entitled "Out on the Town with Diana Devreux" and prayed she'd find something Tony could use. She visited this section of Diana's website regularly and usually found something worth reporting.

Today, a photo of Diana dominated the page. It was from the Radio City concert in New York on December 22, during the final leg of her *One and Only* tour. Precious was still shocked at how different Diana appeared; her skin and hair seemed to shine, she looked as young and vibrant as when she first started out, and after this concert, Precious had noted, Diana's face and music had begun popping up on every television music channel.

Precious scrolled through the photos of the after-party at Trump International Hotel, her eyes flickering over the recognizable faces and standard party poses. She needed something hot, rare, and sensational for Tony, not the party-as-usual fare. While scanning the pages, a face in one of the photos stopped her, and after clicking to enlarge the image, Precious stared at the woman who was sitting next to Diana. The woman was leaning close to the star, as if speaking in confidence, while Diana, one hand thrust into her famous hair, was paying close attention. The caption identified the woman as Serena St. James, Diana Devreux's new up-and-coming stylist who had joined the singer in midtour.

God, she reminds me of Sara Jane Talbot, Precious thought, putting her face closer to the monitor. The resemblance was eerie, though the woman's hair was a lighter brown and longer than Sara Jane's had been the last time Precious saw her, and it was streaked with golden highlights that made her bright, flawless complexion shine. Her eyes were heavily made up, large and exotic, and her smile was wide, with white perfect teeth. And the way the woman was sitting, so poised and relaxed while chatting with Diana, demonstrated her comfort and familiarity in the heady world of money, music, and power that was swirling around Diana Devreux. Precious knew the woman in the photo could not possibly be her childhood friend and unwilling partner in crime, Sara Jane Talbot.

Shaken by the unexpected image and her thoughts of Sara Jane, Precious reached into the middle drawer of her desk and pulled out the letter that the postman had stuck in her mailbox yesterday with the scribbled note: Addressee Unknown. Opening it, she read it again:

> *December 20, 1998*
> *Dear Sara Jane:*
>
> *I hope this letter catches up with you and you are well. I've thought about you a lot since you stopped by to say good-bye and I just know you have started over and are not looking back. But I have some news you ought to know about. Your father died in a fire last night. It destroyed your house, too. Sheriff Goens thinks your father fell asleep while he was smoking. The place was gone in a matter of minutes. I know you didn't get along with him, but I promised Sheriff Goens I'd do what I could to find you and let you know what happened. The church took care of the burial. Put him in the Mallard cemetery next to your momma. Write me please, even if you don't want to come back. I promise not to tell a soul where you are.*
>
> *Love, Precious*

Precious examined the envelope, addressed to Sara Jane Talbot at Havensway House in Dallas, Texas, puzzled by the red stamped notation: "Dec. 22, 1998. Return to sender. Addressee unknown."

"Where are you, Sara Jane?" Precious whispered, returning to the computer screen to search the face of the beautiful, sophisticated woman sitting beside Diana Devreux. "I miss you, girl." Precious slumped back in her wheelchair and gripped its big rubber tires, bracing herself against the bone-weary loneliness she always struggled to keep at bay during her self-imposed isolation. She hated the feelings of abandonment that suddenly arose, though she knew there was no reason to feel jealous, angry, or resentful because Sara Jane Talbot had gone on with her life, leaving Precious behind just like everyone else had done.

Precious flipped off the computer, wheeled to the window, and looked out at the snowflakes that had begun to fall and create tiny white spots on the empty street. The world had not stopped the day she was injured. Life was going on outside her tiny room, and she had to stay strong or she'd miss out. Biting back her tears, she reminded herself that things were getting better, and by focusing on her therapy, her work, and on making enough progress to regain her independence, she could move on, too.

Chapter Twenty-three

Serena squinted at the neon-green face of the clock on the bedside table and lay still, waiting for the fuzz of sleep to clear from her brain, glad to see it was only six o'clock. She could relax in bed for a few more minutes.

After a week in Vegas, she still was not used to her new surroundings and often awoke in the night confused about where she was. The past week had flown by in a flurry of shopping, styling, makeup sessions, and color choices, all in preparation for Diana's New Year's Eve concert at the MGM Grand tonight.

Serena lay quiet, thinking, not about the impending concert, but the exciting discovery she had made on the computer last night. After finishing her work with Diana, Serena had taken a hot shower, wrapped up in her soft terry-cloth robe, and logged onto the Internet, resuming her search for information about natural cosmetics, sources for ingredients, and tips on how to launch her own natural cosmetics company. Serena had already given her dream a name: Beautopia, and wanted more than pretty bottles and jars filled with sweet-smelling creams and gels. She wanted to create a salon, a fantasy place where makeup, hairstyle, and a dash of illusion would come together to create a new image, balanced among the physical, the spiritual, and the dreams of the mind.

The research on her project was relaxing, and it took her mind off of Diana and her all-consuming needs. It was also very secret, a project that remained beyond the control of Diana Devreux, who Serena realized, was beginning to consume her, just as Craig had warned.

It was fun, but not so easy. There was much to learn about locating and combining ingredients, FDA regulations, and the manufacturing process required to satisfy regulations to create the line of cosmetics she envisioned: eye creams, lip balms, facial masks, shampoos, and lotions all derived from Spanish bayonet.

The plant, she now knew, was a wild tuber indigenous to the Southwest, a species of the familiar yucca, with roots that grew so deep into the earth that the Indians had used long iron spears to bring it to the surface. Because it was rich in saponin, the component that provided its sudsy characteristic, the Indians used Spanish bayonet for all types of washing purposes.

To make a basic soap, Indians broke the tough black rootstock into small pieces, washed it free of dirt and grit, smashed it with stones, then dropped it into vessels of water where it stayed until it got soft and mushy. Vigorous rubbing created the abundant lather, and the long-haired Southwestern Indian women used the shampoo before participating in religious ceremonies.

However, Serena wanted to improve it, add other natural ingredients such as honey, aloe vera, almond, and avocado to boost the softening effect of the basic soap. She learned that adding ginkgo biloba would aid in tissue regeneration for the treatment of cellulite, and adding various vitamins could provide much needed anti-inflammatory and antibacterial agents that would nourish and clean the skin.

Last night, she had come upon a web page listing line after line of sources for various natural plants that possessed medicinal and cosmetic purposes. After scrolling through most of it, she came to the words, Spanish bayonet, followed by the name, Raul Torres, and an address in Indian Springs, Nevada. Serena had quickly checked the Yahoo! map and discovered that the place was forty-six miles northwest of Las Vegas, in the middle of the desert. As soon as things slowed down, she'd make the trip and see what she could find out.

Now, throwing off the covers, she slid her feet into the gold Daniel Green's, which Diana had bought for her in New York, ready to jumpstart her day. From the moment she had arrived in Vegas, Serena's days had been a series of nonstop marathons focused on creating the perfect image to showcase Diana tonight. They brainstormed, discussed color, fabric textures, hairstyles, and arrangements, communicating openly and honestly about how to overhaul Diana's image. Serena enjoyed working with Diana, who was smart and knowledgeable, but very opinionated and direct. Serena often had to bite her tongue to keep from saying something she might regret, especially when Diana began micromanaging the details of Serena's area of expertise.

But when the curtain went up, Serena would see the results of her hard work. With six costume changes and four different hairstyles to keep up with, Serena was going to need every bit of energy and patience she could muster. Today, she planned to consult with Diana over some last minute changes that had come in too late to discuss yesterday.

The phone rang, breaking into her thoughts. Serena grabbed it, hoping it would be Craig, whom she had seen only once since her arrival in Vegas, on Christmas Day while Diana was out having dinner with her agent, Vincent Ruby, and his wife. Craig had called to wish Serena a Merry Christmas, then offered to take her for a drive and show her around Las Vegas. They had explored the city, eaten a steak dinner at the Beef Baron at the Flamingo, then come back to the guest house, where he had kissed Serena good night and promised to stay out of her way until after the concert. She had not been happy to watch him go, or to know that he was making himself scarce, but knew he was right. He knew how much pressure Serena was under and how focused she needed to be until the big event was over.

"Hello," she said, speaking softly, expecting to hear Craig's voice, but it was Danny, Diana's housekeeper, instead.

"Miss St. James? This is Danny."

"Oh, yes," Serena said, covering her disappointment. "Hello, Danny."

"Sorry to call so early, but Miss Devreux said to tell you she does not need to meet with you this morning, but to come to her office at two this afternoon."

"Oh?" Serena said, surprised, though glad for a break in their regular schedule, which had been starting at seven A.M. sharp and running until very late. "Fine. I'll be there at two."

After hanging up, Serena lay back on her pillow, thinking about how much she appreciated this tiny break in their routine, though she was curious about why Diana made this change. They had so many things to take care of.

At one minute to two Serena stepped through the French doors facing the pool and met Danny in the living room. As usual, he greeted Serena, then led her past the huge stone fireplace where a fire was blazing behind an ornate brass screen. The mantle was covered with evergreens, holly, and gilded fruit, which had been hung for the holiday season. Matching garlands were strung above the massive entry door and pots of red, white, and yellow poinsettias graced low tables, as well as the base of the tall fir tree that had been decorated with lacey silver stars, tiny white lights, and hundreds of crystal teardrop prisms. The spiraling steel and glass staircase that led to the upper portion of the house had also been hung with the fragrant greenery.

Along the corridor leading to Diana's office, framed pictures of her with many famous people were artfully coordinated and arranged on the wall. As Serena hurried along behind Danny, she recognized a few: Michael Jackson, Sting, Sinbad, Quincy Jones, Nancy Wilson, and Patti LaBelle.

At the end of the hallway a set of double doors opened onto a small library with a cozy sitting area. After crossing the library, Danny pushed the gold handle on a single door and stepped into the wing of the house where Diana's studio, office, professional salon, and fitness room were housed. This was the hub of her world.

Diana covered the mouthpiece of the phone with one hand and motioned for Serena to come in and sit down, never interrupting her conversation. Serena sank down into one of four beige leather chairs arranged in a semicircle in front of Diana's sleek, Plexiglas and steel desk, then smiled hesitantly at the three men who were already there. One of them she recognized: Vincent Ruby, Diana's manager, looking just as rumpled and distracted as always. Of the two strangers, one was an elderly white man with thinning hair, and beside him sat a younger black man who had propped one foot on his knee. When Serena glanced at him, he quickly scooted erect in his seat, putting both feet on the floor.

"Serena," Diana stated in a very brisk tone as soon as she hung up the phone. "Sleep well?"

"Fine," Serena replied, taking in Diana's perfectly made-up face and striking zebra print caftan. She looked radiant, rested, and at ease in the luxurious working environment she had created. "Ready to get the show on the road. I can't wait to see you on stage tonight."

"It's going to go great," Diana affirmed, before turning her attention from Serena to face the younger black man who sat farthest to her right. "Serena, I want you to meet a man who is very crucial to my career. You will get to know him very well, I'm sure." She lifted a hand, pointing with a finger ringed with a slender silver band set with chunky turquoise stones. "This is Dean Banks, my financial advisor."

"Welcome to Vegas," Dean said, his wide smile directed at Serena.

"Thank you," Serena nodded back, studying his smile, which to her, seemed genuine and warm. He had a dark tan complexion and black hair that was trimmed very close with a razor-cut part on the side. The small, crisply barbered goatee beneath his full bottom lip created a perfect anchor for the twin sideburns that extended down the sides of his face and across his strong jaw. His eyes, steady and deliberate, were leveled on Serena, who quickly averted hers to take in his clothing: an attractive blue and gray pinstripe suit, a red-and-blue-striped silk tie and a soft white shirt with the initials DB mono-grammed on French cuffs—the trappings of a professional who could be trusted to manage other people's money.

"And Marvin Erwin, my attorney," Diana continued, indicating the white man next to Dean.

He was very solemn and pale, and Serena wondered where he lived. Certainly not in sun-scorched Vegas, or if he did, he must never go outside. She'd never seen such a chalky white complexion on a white person; even the veins on the backs of his hands stood out like purple cords. "Hello," Serena said, inclining her head toward him.

"Hello. Good to meet you." Marvin Erwin returned her greeting with a tight, forced smile.

"And you remember Vincent Ruby, my agent and road manager?" Diana added.

"Yes, of course," Serena said, reaching for the hand he offered, thinking he was wearing the same wrinkled jacket and slacks he had been wearing on their bumpy plane ride to New York. Perspiration made his deep brown forehead shine, and his heavy lips were still oc-cupied with his ever-present stump of unlit cigar protruding from the side of his mouth.

"Hello, again," he mumbled over the cigar, briefly touching Serena's fingertips.

"Now that everyone is here, we can get on with the business at hand," Diana began.

Serena shifted nervously in her chair, settling down, wondering just what kind of business they were about to discuss. When Diana had bid her good night last evening, she had not mentioned a meeting with her financial manager, agent, and attorney today; three very im-portant men in Diana's world.

"While we were waiting for you, Serena, I filled the gentlemen in on how we met, the fantastic, last-minute job you did for me in Dallas and New York, and my plans to bring you on board full time as my image consultant, replacing Kahi."

"I see," was all Serena could think of to say, taken back by the offi-cial clip in Diana's words. This was serious business.

Dean Banks cleared his throat, tilted his bearded jaw down, and fo-cused on Serena. "Welcome, Miss St. James. You must know that join-ing the staff of a star like Diana Devreux is no different than going to work for a major corporation. There are contracts, financial arrange-ments, legal instruments involved, and we want to go over some of those areas with you today."

Serena tensed, then cautioned herself to be patient, to listen to what everyone had to say and learn everything she could. After all, Diana already knew about her past, had sworn her secrecy, and would not have brought Serena to Vegas if she'd have thought her advisors would not have respected her judgment.

"And by the way, Diana's never looked better," Dean continued, easing forward in his seat so that he could make eye contact with Vincent Ruby while he spoke. "I saw the video of the Radio City concert, and I am impressed. Seems Diana made a good choice." Then Dean shifted his attention to Serena. "You've got the vision and talent we need on our team, Miss St. James. I understand from Diana that you've worked with high-profile clients before?" he paused, his stare unflinching, his implication clear.

Serena blinked, then adopted a coy a hint of a smile and lifted the corner of her mouth. "Yes, at Upscale. Giani Pilugi's salon had quite a celebrity clientele." *Do not lie,* she silently cautioned herself, hoping Dean would not press for more details, initiating a full-fledged discussion of her past. She glanced at Diana for support, but Diana averted her eyes and kept fiddling with her slender gold pen.

"So," Dean continued, "you understand how image translates into dollars in this business?"

"Absolutely, I certainly do," Serena agreed, her voice stronger.

"As Diana's financial manager, that's where I come in . . . on the bottom line. In this industry, youth sells, and Diana believes you have the talent to keep her image current and help her remain a viable, financially sound investment. I don't know a thing about color pallets, hairdos, or makeup, or what dresses Diana should wear, but I do know her hair is her trademark and her appearance is a major component of what has made her a legend. Her image sells, and it must be preserved, with only enough modification to keep her at the cutting edge, ensure high turnout at her concerts."

"I totally agree," Serena injected. "And that's exactly my mission for Miz Devreux."

Dean sat back and reshifted his focus to Vincent Ruby, who now spoke to Serena.

"This is a tremendous talent sitting before you, Miss St. James. Diana's recording company, business associates, musicians, and behind-the-scenes personnel depend on her for their livelihoods. If you are coming on board as her image consultant and stylist, it is your responsibility to create and maintain Diana Devreux's public persona. It must be youthful and vibrant, reminding the public that she is a performer who will deliver more than a great song and a great performance, but a look the public clamors to see. I was in New York. I saw what you did for her. I saw the way the crowd reacted, and I believe Diana has made a good choice."

"Thank you," Serena said, pleased that Vincent Ruby was on her side. She looked at Diana, who was calmly listening to the discussion, giving no indication of her reaction to what either man had said.

Dean Banks picked up the discussion where Vincent Ruby left off. "But you seem very young, Miss St. James. No matter who you've worked for or what kind of references you have, you cannot have had very much experience."

Now, Diana spoke up. "And that's good. I am shaping Serena myself, giving her the only experience she needs. I am glad I don't have to undo old habits, you know?"

Dean smiled, nodding, then shrugged his shoulders at Serena. "Diana believes in you. Ruby thinks you have what it takes to keep the money rolling in." He lifted both hands in a dismissive gesture. "That's good. But I doubt you understand the enormity of responsibility you've accepted by coming on board here."

Serena locked eyes with Dean Banks, nervous, but ready to accept his challenge. He was clearly testing her, trying to see if she had the confidence and spirit to hang in for the long haul. She had to speak up, or he might go behind Diana's back and begin snooping, checking her out. Serena believed Diana's promise not to divulge her criminal background or who she really was, but that didn't mean Dean Banks would be satisfied with what Diana told him. Serena licked her lips, assessing the strong set of Dean's jaw, the impatient way he was tapping his index fingers together, the expectant tilt of his body toward her. She was perfect for this job and not about to crumble under the weight of Dean's inquiry. If that was what he was waiting for, he was talking to the wrong person.

Without smiling, Serena jumped right in, ready to take him on. "I beg to differ, Mr. Banks. I most certainly do understand the responsibility I am accepting, as well as what Diana needs and how to deliver it. The trial run we pulled off in New York was simply that . . . a test, where we worked under less than professional circumstances. As Mr. Ruby said, what we accomplished in a matter of forty-eight hours was nearly a miracle; he's admitted it was a success. With the resources available to me now, I can do so much more . . . with Diana's assistance, of course."

Dean Banks relaxed, sat back, and folded his hands on his knee.

Marvin Erwin, Diana's attorney now turned his somber expression on Serena, ready to speak his mind. "Diana trusts you. I trust Diana. But let's get one thing clear. The better Diana looks and performs, the more her competitors envy her. Even hate her. That is the nature of this business. And once word leaks out about you . . . that you are the talent behind this wonderful rejuvenation, others will try to woo you away. You'll be tempted by offers too fabulous to deny. That is why you must sign this." He reached over and took a document off Diana's desk.

"What is it?" Serena asked.

"It's your contract, an agreement all employees who work for Diana Devreux, Inc. must sign. The term is for five years, renewable upon discussions, and your compensation will start at two thousand dollars a week, increased at Miss Devreux's discretion. She will cover travel expenses whenever you are on the road with her. You are on call twenty-four hours, seven days a week, because of the nature of this business. Your close relationship with Miss Devreux will inspire reporters to try to get to you. If you divulge any personal information about my client, or talk about the services related to her makeup, hair, clothes, or image to anyone, you could be held liable." He handed the document to Serena along with a silver pen. "This contract also includes a noncompete clause, indicating that you cannot work in the beauty industry for a performer within the states of Nevada or California for one year after your employment is terminated."

Serena glanced at Diana, who nodded.

"That is not unusual, Serena," Diana added. "If, for any reason we part before the contract ends, it keeps you from setting up shop within my range of work, going over to the enemy, so to speak."

It sounded reasonable to Serena, who accepted the legal paper Erwin handed to her and sat back to read. It was six pages of finely printed wording, stapled to a blue back-sheet, and contained phrases Serena had difficulty comprehending. Her breath was shallow as she concentrated.

"It's a standard contract and confidentiality agreement, Serena. Believe me," Diana said, a hint of impatience in her words. "Most high profile people require them nowadays. Too many tell-all books out there, and too many scam artists ready to profit from an entertainer's private life. Kahi was under the same kind of contract, and gag order, and it had just run out the day before she left. I'd bet money Kitty Easton lured her away." Diana shrugged. "Whatever. It's worked out better for me. Now, I have you. Go ahead and sign it, Serena. These kinds of contracts are entered into everyday."

"I'm sure it's fine," Serena said hesitantly, flipping through the pages as she skimmed over the cold, formal clauses. She wished she had someone to help her decipher the what-if's and wherefores. But with whom could she discuss it, even if she had the time? Craig? No. She did not want him entangled in her personal affairs. Not yet, anyway. Their relationship was still too new, and her past was still too close. Her father did not care where she was or what happened to her, and she'd had to abandon her only friend, Precious, when she changed her life. There was no one she could turn to, so she might as well trust Diana and her lawyers, sign her name and move on.

Serena placed the document on the corner of Diana's desk. *This is a normal part of doing business,* she reminded herself, signing the document where the red Xs indicated she should write her name, then returning it to Marvin Erwin.

"Thank you," he said, snapping open his briefcase. He slipped the document inside, then took out two white envelopes. "Your Nevada State Cosmetology License," he said, handing her the first one. "And don't ask any questions, Miss St. James. It is perfectly legal. Here in Nevada we have a way of cutting through red tape." Then he handed Serena the second envelope. "Your first paycheck, Miss St. James. Two weeks, plus a bonus for coming on board."

Serena eased the unsealed envelope open and took out a pale blue check. Five thousand dollars. Her hand shook as she stared at the zeros on the dotted line. "But . . ." she began, unable to believe what she was holding, the reality of her new status quickly sinking in. She had never seen that much money printed on a check before and the sight flooded her with happiness.

"You came on board December nineteenth, almost two weeks ago," Diana said. "The extra thousand is my way of letting you know how much I value your skill and talent." Diana swept the flowing sleeves of her zebra-print caftan back, then pulled open the center drawer of her desk and took out a set of keys. "Here," she tossed them at Serena. "You need transportation out here in the desert. Use the RAV4 in the garage whenever you need it. It's just sitting around catching dust."

Serena caught the keys and closed them in her fist, beaming. "This is so good of you, Diana." She shook her head, as if to make sure this was happening. "When you waylaid me in your limo and asked me to go with you to New York, I was scared to death. I had never been anywhere, seen anything important, and now here I am in the middle of my wildest dream. You've given me more than I hoped for, Diana. How can I ever thank you?"

Diana winked. "Keep me beautiful, young, and rich." Then she laughed and the three men joined in with a few low chuckles.

Marvin closed his briefcase and stood. "Got to get back to the office, Diana."

"Will I see you after the show tonight?" Diana asked, turning from Serena. "I'm having the after-party here at the house. Nothing like the bash in New York, though, just a few friends." She glanced at Serena. "The perfect setting to introduce you to a lot of people we will be working with." She gave Marvin, who was already heading to the door, a pleading look.

"Can't make it, sorry," he reiterated. "Margaret and I leave for Aspen at six tonight. Spending the entire month of January skiing with her sister. But call my office if you need to. Mary will be in charge while I'm gone and she can get a message to me wherever I might be, even on the slopes." He nodded to Dean and Vincent, then at Serena. "I'll get a copy of this agreement over to you after the New Year." Then he opened the door and left.

Vincent left next, promising to call Diana about an offer for her to tape a commercial for a line of luxury leather goods, apologizing for missing her New Year's Eve concert because of a previous engagement in New York.

Dean got up as soon as the door closed behind Vincent. Diana, obviously annoyed, set down the pen she had been holding and asked, "You'll be at the concert, at least, won't you?"

"Wouldn't miss it, dear. And I'll be solo," he added, openly assessing Serena. "Perhaps Miss St. James would like to keep me company? Give her a chance to view her work from the audience's perspective."

"Good point," Diana replied, smiling. "Want to, Serena?"

"After the last costume change, perhaps," she hedged.

Diana nodded in agreement. "Right. You are going to be very, very busy backstage."

"Great," Dean broke in. "It'll give us a chance to get to know each other better. I'll guard your seat like a pit bull."

Serena met Dean's eyes, seeing much more than she wanted to see. He was still cautious about her, and curious, and probably the kind of man who could grill her in a subtle way, by simply chatting about everyday things, then analyze every word until he gleaned information about her past. His job was to protect Diana's financial interests, and naturally he would be on guard where new staff were concerned. She'd have to be careful, yet not appear as if she had anything to hide.

"It would be my pleasure to sit with you during the final set," Serena casually told him, feeling put on the spot. Standing, she shook his hand in a businesslike gesture, trying to make it clear that she was just as much a part of Diana's entourage as he, and was not intimidated by his invitation.

"Good. I'll see you there," Dean replied, slipping out of Diana's office.

When the three men had left, Diana began to gather her things. "Serena. You held your own, and that's an important part of surviving in this industry. Dean can be somewhat of a prick, but he's harmless. He, Vincent, and Marvin are looking out for my best interest, so don't let them rattle you. I don't know what I'd do without them."

"It's fine," Serena said. "They love you . . . want the best for you, and seem to be very competent men. You are lucky to be surrounded by people who are so caring, so professional." But as she spoke, she wondered if they would have been as accepting if they had known about her criminal record.

"Enough business," Diana said, tossing the strap of her black straw bag across her shoulder. "I'm off to the hotel for a final sound check and see about the flowers. I asked for live camellias and plenty of them. See you there about five?"

"Sure," Serena replied, her stomach a bundle of nerves. "Five."

"Later!" Diana called out, dashing out of the office, her caftan flowing behind her.

On her way back to the guest house, Serena nearly floated over the paved brick walkway, the check and the car keys squeezed in her fist. She was officially connected to this wonderful, magical, world of show business, illusion, and glamour, and was earning a great deal of money! Serena shook her head. Life as Serena St. James was absolutely perfect. The reality of her situation put a big smile on her face. She had a fabulous job, a beautiful place to live, and access to her own car! The only thing that could make it better would be to have Craig Alexander at her side.

Chapter Twenty-four

Diana Devreux's New Year's Eve performance at the MGM Grand was a smashing success. The packed house, teeming with police and hotel security, crackled with excitement from the moment people began to arrive until her final song. During the performance, the fans shouted, applauded, waved their hands over their heads, and swayed and stomped and rocked to the rhythm of every one of Diana's songs. And she reciprocated, giving them everything she had, moving like a tiny weightless star illuminated on the cavernous black stage, her presence shining as brightly as her voice. She joked and laughed with the audience, riding the high their love provided, gazing into their adoring faces, shouting her appreciation between sets.

The musicians followed Diana's lead, never missing a cue. The lighting men kept up with her sexy dance moves, and her backup singers rocked along to whatever tempo she set, embracing the frenzied pace in exuberant celebration that resembled an old-fashioned church revival.

Serena was completely enthralled, not only by the way Diana commanded the stage, but also by the wondrous image of vitality she had managed to pull off. Even Dean Banks, who sat in quiet attention throughout the concert, turned to Serena after Diana's final bow, grabbed her by her shoulders, and shouted above the clamor, "Do you realize what you have done?" Impulsively, he hugged Serena, then seeming surprised at his own validation of her skill, held her at arm's length and gushed on, dollar signs in his eyes. "Breeze Records' stock just shot up ten points!"

Serena giggled nervously and held onto Dean's arm as they pushed through the exiting crowd to make their way backstage.

* * *

Diana's small after-party for close friends turned out to be more like a freewheeling fiesta than the intimate, invitation-only gathering Serena had expected it to be. Close to one hundred guests roamed the house and the grounds, which had been lit with thousands of tiny white lights and festooned with camellias and shiny green holly. Platters of eye-catching finger foods, fancy hors d'oeuvres, delicate desserts, and a myriad of vegetables and fruits in every imaginable shape had been set out in the formal dining room, atop the huge island in the kitchen, and on long-skirted tables around the pool, where a four-piece band played music by request.

Diana shone like the star she was. Dressed completely in white velvet, her auburn curls bouncing, she bubbled over with enthusiasm as she personally escorted Serena through the throng, making sure her new stylist met everyone of importance.

Serena made small talk, answering probing questions about her background with great care, her story down pat, embellishing her experience with Giani Pilugi to make it sound as if he had personally chosen her to be his protégée. She sipped champagne, nibbled canapés, and circulated among the crowd, avoiding Dean Banks, keeping one eye on the door for Craig who did not show up until late in the evening.

When Craig approached her and broke into the conversation she was having with Sammi an attractive female impersonator in a blonde wig and blue spandex dress. Serena squeezed past the buxom performer and stood beside Craig, one hand on his arm.

"Well, Craig Alexander," Sammi started right in. "I was wondering when you'd show up." Sammi touched Craig on the shoulder, then let his hand rest there lightly as he spoke. "You are looking good."

"Thanks, Sammi," Craig replied, shaking his head as he deliberately removed Sammi's hand. "See you've met Serena."

"Oh, yes. The wonder girl of the evening." Fluttering his false eyelashes, he gave Craig a toothy smile. "I am jealous. I want her to come over to my dressing room and see what she can do with a dreadful auburn wig I paid a fortune for." He sighed loudly, then waved his fingers in exasperation. "Just think what she could do for me!" Laughing, he touched his shoulder-length hair.

"Well, Sammi, to tell you the truth, I'd rather not think about that," Craig said.

"You should," Sammi teased. "I'd love the attention." He jokingly edged closer to Craig, who laughed, then backed away.

"Don't waste your time courting me, Sammi," Craig tossed back. "Save the cutesy stuff for someone who cares."

"By all means," Sammi replied, flouncing off. Then, smiling, he turned around and winked at Serena, "And Serena darling," he called out, "you must come visit me at the Mirage."

"I promise I will," Serena called back, impressed with Sammi's outrageous style and flirtatiousness. He was certainly one of a kind. Laughing, she watched his dramatic exit with amusement, until he disappeared into the crowd of people gathered outside the French doors.

"He's a mess," Serena said to Craig. "He had me cracking up, talking about his act. I really want to go see him on stage. It's got to be a riot."

"It is, believe me," Craig said. "But this town is full of Sammis, and his act is really rather tame, compared to what else is out there."

"I'm sure you're right," Serena replied, inching closer to Craig. "I've never met anyone like him. He's fun. Devoted to Diana, isn't he?"

"Yeah, they go way back. He doesn't take himself so seriously, and according to Diana, really has a pretty good eye for fashion."

"If you say so," Serena laughed, moving toward the patio with Craig.

"Tired?" he asked.

"Um-hum," she murmured.

"Let's get some fresh air. It's a gorgeous night."

"Sure," Serena said, following him outside. It had been so long since they had been alone. He looked rested and relaxed while she felt edgy and uptight, but at least he wasn't working tonight and would not have Diana's needs uppermost in his mind.

"Now that Diana's big night has come and gone, I feel like a great weight has been lifted off my shoulders," she said, massaging her neck.

"I would think so," Craig replied, stepping down a short flight of stone steps at the edge of the patio, leading to the pool. "You did a fabulous job, Serena. The show was great. Diana looked wonderful, and it was her best performance in a long time. She told me she's been asked to cut a new version of her *One and Only* video, exclusively for BET. It will incorporate footage from the tour."

"Yeah, I know," Serena said. "She's flying to D.C. in the morning to get started. We spent quite a bit of time yesterday deciding what she should take, but she's all packed and ready to go. God, I don't see how she keeps up the pace."

"You're not going, are you?" Craig asked.

"No. Not this time."

"Good. You need the rest, because pretty soon, now that she is on a roll, companies will be calling for her to endorse their products and it will get pretty crazy. A real comeback kind of night, isn't it?"

"Yes. Dean Banks felt it, too. Of course he watched the concert with dollar signs in his eyes," she said, chuckling.

"What else?" Craig agreed, nodding. "Well, good for Diana. She deserves this."

"Exactly," Serena said. "I didn't know what to expect, but what happened on stage this evening was beyond fantastic. It was a real happening. Exhausting. I can't imagine what each performance must take out of her, but now I understand why entertainers collapse under the pressure and drop out of the business. It's brutal, at times."

"True, but Diana loves it, even though she complains all the time. There is nothing she'd rather do than work herself into a state of exhaustion, pull off a great gig, then get ready for the next one. It's a cycle she knows too well, " Craig remarked. "Look at her over there. She's the center of the universe again."

Serena studied Diana, who was talking to a woman in a stunning black-sequined dress, pleased with what she saw. When Diana linked arms with the woman and accompanied her back inside the house, Serena turned toward Craig, whose dark profile was illuminated by the twinkling lights strung overhead. Impulsively, she extended her hand. He took it in his, sending a warm surge of pleasure through her.

"She'll be in D.C. for at least four days," Craig said softly. "Maybe five."

"And?" Serena prompted, sensing what he wanted to say, anxious to hear him express it.

"Now you'll have time to spend with me," he murmured.

Precisely what I was thinking, Serena mused as she let Craig take her by the arm and lead her to a quiet table on the far edge of the pool. Hundreds of white camellias floated on the water's surface, giving off a heady perfume, and clusters of guests were standing together talking, sipping champagne, and nibbling exotic canapés. Serena sat down at one of the small round tables. Craig pulled a chair up next to hers.

"Are you telling me you'd like to spend tomorrow together?" she hinted, twirling the straw in her drink, keeping her eyes downcast, though the shadows from the palm trees camouflaged her anticipation.

"You read my mind," he admitted, bending his head closer to hers. "If not tomorrow . . . perhaps tonight."

Serena closed her eyes, feeling the buzz of desire race through her veins as she imagined what it would be like to lie in Craig's arms. She lifted her face to his and whispered, "Tonight? Is it possible?" Serena sucked in a short breath, stunned by the boldness of her own words, unsure if she should have said them.

"It's very possible."

"Then let's go," she murmured, casting a glance over her shoulder, as if looking for Diana.

"Relax," Craig said, reading her mind. "This party will last all night, just like the one in New York, then she'll be off to D.C. in the morning. She won't even miss you."

"Are you taking her to the airport?" Serena asked.

"No, Dean Banks is picking her up. Wants to talk to her about some business matters, on the way."

"So, we're both free?" Serena said, gathering the courage to leave. Diana was packed and ready to go to D.C. and didn't need Serena, which was fine with her. She needed time alone, to be with Craig, explore their attraction at last. So much had happened so quickly. The job, the move to Vegas, the concert, and now she had a bit of downtime and she wanted to spend it with Craig. But as easy as it would be to leave the party to be with him, something was holding her back.

She was nearly twenty-two, old enough to spend the night with a man if she wanted to, but still a twinge of worry set in.

Craig put a cautionary hand on Serena's arm. "Serena, I don't want you to do anything that makes you uncomfortable. If you want to stay . . ."

"No," Serena murmured, feeling foolish. "I want to be with you." All she wanted was to wake up and find Craig lying next to her.

"Fine." Craig motioned for Serena to come with him, and she took his hand to head down a path that led into a walled cactus garden near the driveway. Inside the garden, a lighted fountain bubbled over a ledge of flat rocks, and a narrow iron gate opened off the area directly into the driveway in front of the house.

Serena paused in the shadows and leaned against the cool stone wall, closing her eyes, pleased to have some privacy after a night of being surrounded with people. Craig placed both hands flat against the wall on either side of Serena's face, enclosing her in an intimate embrace. Trembling, Serena lifted her face to Craig's.

He kissed her softly at first, paused, then pressed his lips hard against hers in an insistent, yet tentative search until she opened her lips to his passionate search and allowed him to feel her response. When he pulled back, he gazed at her from beneath his dark brows, breathing hard as he studied her. "You are beautiful, you know that? I've wanted to hold you like this since we got here, since I realized how much I want to be with you. It's been hard for me to keep my distance, but soon, things are going to be very different."

Serena wasn't sure what he meant, and had no voice to ask, so she inclined her head in a quick affirmative gesture and surrendered her lips to his, once again, kissing him on the lips, the side of his neck, his ear, and in the soft place above his right temple.

"Yes," she finally whispered. "Things are going to change." Then she raised her arms to fit her body closer to his, and flattened her heart against the pounding in his chest. Shifting softly within his embrace, they held onto each other without speaking, drawing comfort from the dark, warm, secret place where they were finally alone.

When laughter on the patio stirred them, Craig took Serena by the hand, and together they exited the walled garden, leaving through the iron gate that led out to the driveway.

Once inside Craig's sleek black Lincoln Town Car, Serena kissed Craig again, then settled back, trying to control the sudden nervousness that overtook her.

What have I gotten myself into? she worried, as Craig released her and started the engine. Her hands were damp with sweat and her mouth had gone dry. Here she was, in a remote part of the Nevada desert, about to go to bed with a man she hardly knew. Yet, she did know him, and deep inside, she knew her fears were not about Craig. They were about herself: She was a virgin and had no idea what he expected of her, or what she should expect from him. She was not who he believed her to be, and what would he think if he knew the truth? Serena stared out the windshield as the long car swept down the drive. When he placed his arm around her shoulders and pulled her closer, she lay her head against his neck, trusting that nothing could possibly spoil an evening as magical as this.

Serena felt her way through the dark bedroom toward the soft glow of light coming through the crack in the door, not about to turn on a light. Stepping into the living room, she left the bedroom door partially open, pausing to make sure Craig was still asleep. She walked to the big window overlooking the brightly lit street, tugged the drapes open, and sat down on the sofa. She stared out into blaze of signs, marquees, and billboards that rose high above the traffic and pedestrians in the street below, hugging her arms around her waist as she recalled the wondrous experience of making love to Craig, unable to believe how easy it had been to give herself completely to him.

She pulled the soft tee shirt Craig had given her to sleep in down over her knees, tucked her bare feet under her bottom, and curled into a ball. She placed her chin on her knees, a hand to her mouth, wishing she could scream with joy. She had known her passion for Craig ran deep and true, but never in her wildest dreams could she have conjured up such a perfect experience. It had come as no surprise that Craig had been gentle, cautious, tender, and sincere. But she had surprised herself in being free, relaxed, and excited about the experience, eager to dispel her fears over losing her virginity. Her heart swelled to recall how it had felt to be a part of him, fused to him, their skin slick with perspiration and desire. With their arms and legs and lips locked together, they had risen to such heights of passion, she'd nearly burst with joy to be filled with warmth and happiness.

From his first kiss on the tip of her nose to the soft nuzzle of his lips as they trailed the length of her body, she had been able to toss aside her insecurities and accept him with complete abandon because he had shown her how special she was. Without pressure or subtle demands he had allowed Serena to come to him on her terms, not his, moving his hands with care, testing, then continuing, making sure she felt safe.

He must have known it was my first time, she thought, pleased to have survived their initial joining without embarrassing herself. She had feared she would freeze, cry, feel pain. But he had gently entered her and had not said a word about the stain on the sheet after the first time they made love. The second time was easier, and the third was pure heaven, binding them in a rare sense of need laced with trust. When they had finally exhausted themselves and were about to doze off, he had asked her to get him a glass of wine, and when she returned with it, the sheets had been changed and he had opened his arms to hold her close. Not a word about why she was a twenty-one year-old virgin. No unnecessary discussion or stress. Craig had simply said, "I have waited for you for so long," then gently pulled her to his chest when she whispered simply, "Me, too."

In the quiet of the room, Serena could hear Craig's slumbering breathing come in steady soft sighs from the bedroom. She wanted to go back in and run her hands over his shoulders, across his hard buttocks, along the heavy shaft of his manhood, yearning to feel him inside her once more, to experience the completeness of joining with him again. Was it possible to love the first man to come into her life? she wondered, certain she wanted no other. Craig Alexander was everything, and more.

Chapter Twenty-five

L as Vegas was the perfect place for Serena St. James to fall in love. The city was magical, with its brash neon signs, gigantic replicas of geographic wonders, and nonstop partying that kept thousands of people in the streets, casinos, and hotel lobbies twenty-four hours a day. Everything about Vegas fascinated Serena: the wealthy high rollers dressed in tuxedos and diamonds, the beautiful showgirls in elaborate costumes, the die-hard gamblers who blended in with the tourists who sat on stools in front of slot machines, their eyes glazed over in hope. There was a gay, but desperate edge to the city, a place where everyone expected to win big, score a hit, or impress someone for some reason. She felt at home among this odd assortment of characters who were busy trying to beat the odds. In Vegas, Serena felt lucky.

Diana's absence provided Serena and Craig their long-awaited opportunity to explore their feelings and spend uninterrupted time together. When Craig asked her not to return to the guest house after their magical night together, she agreed. And for the next four days they existed in a cocoon of kisses, caresses, lovemaking, and laughter. They swam in his hotel pool in the mornings, indulged in extravagant buffet lunches at the casinos in the afternoons, attended lavish shows at night, taking in Sammi's act at the Mirage two nights in a row. They drank bottles of champagne, watched old movies on TV, then made love until the sun painted the desert and the mountains pink. Their excesses should have exhausted them, but instead they glowed with a happiness that announced their contentment, derived from the joy that comes from knowing one has fallen in love.

Serena, who had no way to compare what was happening to her with any other experience, submerged herself totally in the emotional discovery of wanting, needing, and receiving the loving attention she had never been given before. To her, Craig represented the healing balm she yearned for, a soothing anesthetic to erase the painful memories of her past and allow her to step fully into her new future. She poured herself into the relationship, withholding nothing . . . nothing except the truth about who she really was.

Craig found in Serena, a reason to commit. To him, she was an odd mix of innocence and passion who never pressed him for information, probed into his affairs, or put heavy demands for material things on him. Her needs were simple, and her easygoing manner showed respect for his personal space, both physically and emotionally. She was perfectly content to listen to music, read a book, and entertain herself while he watched the tennis matches on television or read the paper, which he did every day from front to back. Serena did not want a lot of people around, and that suited him just fine, though at times he wondered why she turned down every invitation to lunch or a fashion show or a shopping spree extended by women she had met through Diana.

Craig liked the feeling of being needed, without being smothered, as he had begun to feel with his crazy arrangement with Diana. Their sporadic, freewheeling trysts were over, and as soon as Diana returned from Washington he was going to tell her so. The relationship had no future. What they had had was a series of stopgap measures to get by. Now, he had to make it clear: He would no longer be there for her when she knocked on his door in the middle of the night. He had found the woman he wanted, and it was Serena. The idea of ending his guilt-ridden episodes with Diana filled Craig with a sense of relief, yet he worried about how she would take the news.

At six A.M. on the morning Diana was scheduled to return from D.C., the phone in Craig's hotel room rang. He groaned, reached over Serena's sleeping form and picked up the receiver.

"Hello." He shifted back onto his side of the bed and curled one arm around Serena, who had been awakened by the call. She snuggled her head against his side and entwined her fingers through his.

"Craig? This is Danny."

"Hello, Danny."

"Miss Devreux called. She'd like you to pick her up at the airport at seven-fifteen tonight."

"Got it," Craig replied, grabbing a notepad off his bedside table. He began to scribble as he talked. "Which airline?"

"Continental. Flight six-twenty-one."

"I'll be there, Danny."

"Oh, Craig, one more thing. Two men are returning on the flight with Miss Devreux, a producer who is going to work on her new video, and a Mr. Hoss, of the PR firm, Hunter and Hoss. They'll be staying at the Flamingo, so drop them off first. Miss Devreux said to tell you she will need you for the duration of their stay."

"No problem," Craig replied, hanging up the phone, not surprised to hear that Diana had hired a new PR guy. Obviously, she was going to keep him very busy once she returned.

Five years ago, when he signed on as Diana's permanent driver, she had told him up front that he would be paid by the shift and the work could be sporadic, with heavy driving and traveling when she was on tour, but less need for him when she was at home in Vegas. That had been fine with Craig, then, because Diana paid him more than enough to weather short periods when he was not working, but he hated having too much time on his hands. If it were not for the exclusive-service clause in his contract, he would have been able to work for other limo services in Vegas, not only to stay busy, but to make connections he could use in the future when he started his own limo service. But the clause prevented him from driving for anyone other than Diana and her associates, in Las Vegas, New York, or Los Angeles, for a twelve-month period after his contract ended. For now, he belonged to her.

Working for a celebrity like Diana Devreux was exactly the job Craig had hoped to snag so he could learn the ins and outs of the limo service business, planning to eventually strike out on his own. He had worked hard over the past five years, building a reputation as a dependable driver with a solid understanding of what it takes to accommodate a celebrity client, and had been approached by several well-known limo services in Vegas to come on board with them. But he had refused the offers, his hands tied by his contract with Diana. Craig planned to go back to Los Angeles and start his own company in a city where personal service was always in high demand and he could finally be his own boss.

Now, Craig stroked Serena's bare shoulder, thinking about Diana's return. He had to be patient, careful and not do anything rash. Telling Diana about Serena had to be done right away, but approaching her about breaking his contract had to be put on hold.

The phone rang again. This second intrusion annoyed Craig, who quickly picked up the receiver and said, "Yes?"

"Sorry to bother you again, Craig, but I forgot to ask . . ."

"What is it?" Craig cut him off.

"Do you know where I can find Miss St. James?"

"Uh . . . Miss St. James?" Craig covered the mouthpiece with his fingers and cocked his head toward Serena, his mind racing over what he ought to say. "Is something wrong?"

"Oh, no. Not at all, but I haven't seen or heard from her since the night of the party. I don't believe she knows many people in Vegas and I hope nothing has happened to her."

Craig sighed and leaned back on his pillow, increasing his grip on Serena's hand. "Well, Danny. I'm the culprit. Serena told me she was dying to stay at a real Vegas hotel, so I arranged for her to have a suite at the Luxor for a few days. A real Vegas-style experience, you know? She's been working so hard since she got here, and never did get to see much of the town."

"Certainly," Danny replied rather tersely. "When she didn't answer her phone and I didn't see her around the guest house, I got worried. She's perfectly free to come and go as she pleases, but next time please tell her to let me know if she's going to be away."

"Sure. I'll call over to the Luxor and tell her to get back to you right away."

"Thank you," Danny said, clearly relieved.

Serena sat up, laughing, as soon as Craig hung up the phone. "What was that about?"

"Oh, Danny. He's such a fussy prick. He's just scared Diana will be all over him if she comes home and finds you gone. He's terrified of upsetting her."

"I should have called him," Serena murmured, turning serious. "I didn't mean to cause problems." She rubbed her cheek against Craig's upper arm. "But you cast some kind of a spell on me! Made me lose all my good sense! I can't believe we've been together for four nights."

Craig cuddled her closer, dismissing her concerns. "Forget it. You're grown. You can do as you please."

"I guess so. But why didn't you tell Danny I was here with you?"

"Whoa," Craig said, holding up both hands. "That's a different matter. You don't want it to get back to Diana that you and I are *this close*, do you? She knows I've shown you around town and taken you to dinner, helped you get settled here, and so on, but I doubt she'd be thrilled to know we spent four days together while she was gone. Leave this to me, okay?"

"Why?" Serena asked bluntly, pushing back from Craig. She shifted onto her knees, bringing her face level with his, her jaw tight and her mouth set in a firm line. "What difference does it make to Diana what I . . . or you . . . do with our personal lives? She doesn't own us . . . at least not me."

"And . . . what are you implying?" His tone was cool, suspicious.

"Sorry, I'm not implying anything . . . but . . . I guess I'd like for you to tell me. What *is* your relationship with Diana and why are you so cautious about her finding out we are attracted to each other?"

Craig noticed that Serena spoke with quiet insistence, as if trying not to express what was really on her mind.

"Because we both work for her," Craig said calmly, earnestly. "And she doesn't like her staff involved in personal relationships. I'd hate to get you fired . . . or even on her bad side. I could lose my job, too, so let's take it slow, you know?"

"Slow?" Serena threw back. "And . . . what does that mean?"

Craig flinched to see Serena lose her fragile hold on her emotions. "It means we've got to stay calm," Craig cautioned, reaching over to grasp Serena's shoulder. "Right now, Diana needs both of us very much . . . and, face it, we need her. Don't worry, it will work out." He held her still, giving her time to collect her thoughts and focus on what he had said.

"Work out on *her terms*, I suppose," Serena shot back. "Seems like you care more about her feelings than mine."

"Please, don't go there, Serena," he said seriously.

"Then explain to me what your feelings are for Diana, because they certainly seem to be more than professional."

"I know it seems that way, but I have to protect Diana, and maybe because we've been together so long, it looks like more than it is. Even when I'm off duty I have to stick close enough to get to her if she needs me. You know that. Serena, believe me. My concern for Diana is strictly professional. Nothing more."

"That's the truth?" Her voice fell, as did her shoulders. "You've never been romantically involved with her?"

"Never. That's the truth," Craig replied, and after a few seconds of silence, went on. "I care deeply for you, Serena, and I don't want us to self-destruct because of an impulsive act."

"Sure," Serena murmured, lowering her lashes.

Craig felt her anguish as well as a stab of guilt that spurred him to try and ease the tension between them. "Smile," he coaxed. "Please?" This was not the way he wanted to end their romantic episode, and felt terrible about Serena's disappointment. Yet, he knew Diana well enough to believe that their relationship might cost Serena her job and he could not let that happen.

Serena managed a weak smile, then slipped into Craig arms and lay against him, her feet curled under her hips.

He held her close, stroking her hair.

She raised her eyes to meet his. "I guess you think I'm being child-ish, but I had to ask. Sorry."

"Don't be," Craig said, running his hand along her bare, cool arm, thinking about what he had just said, knowing he had stretched the truth. "Diana tends to be very possessive," he explained. "But you've already seen that side of her, I'm sure. So it's best to keep what you and I have to ourselves for now. These four wonderful days belong to us, and we'll have many more, but I don't want them to cause you any trouble. Trust me. I'll handle it at the right time."

Serena drew the sheet over her shoulder, remaining quiet. When she spoke, she tilted up her chin to force his attention to her. "But I hate acting as if we are doing something illegal, something we should be ashamed of. I hate the secrecy."

"So do I," Craig agreed, kissing the frown on Serena's brow, then running his thumb along her cheek. "Leave it to me, okay?"

"Fine," Serena sighed.

"Good. Now you'd better get dressed."

Serena nodded, swung back the sheets, went into the bathroom and turned on the shower.

Craig sat in bed listening to the water in the shower running, imag-ining how it was slipping over Serena's sleek brown skin, glistening on her hard nipples, wetting her long smooth legs. He swallowed hard, remembering the way she had felt under him, how her fingers had made his blood surge through his veins and fill him with desire. He was tempted to call out, bring her out of the shower, back into his bed, but knew he could not do it. She was so trusting, fragile, and easy to love, that he knew in that moment that he would do everything possible to make her happy and protect her from Diana's fury when she found out he planned to marry Serena. His mind was made up. He'd pick the right time, tell Diana it was over between them, and hope Serena never learned the truth.

Chapter Twenty-six

Joyce Ann inserted the key into the lock of unit number seven, cursing as she pushed against the uneven door to get it to open. For the past thirty days, since the day she checked into the Roadway Inn, she had complained about it and the manager kept promising to take care of the problem, but obviously he was just stalling. After kicking the door shut behind her, Joyce Ann scowled into the dim, shabby motel room, a heavy plastic grocery bag clutched in one hand, a paper bag of McDonald's coffee in the other. She saw that Tonk was still snoring like a wounded bull, the television screen was still filled with images of Bugs Bunny and Daffy Duck, and the mess she had asked him to clean up while she went for coffee and food had not been touched. A heap of empty pizza boxes, beer cans, fast food sacks, and ashtrays overflowing with cigarette butts filled the small round table at the foot of the bed.

With a swipe of one hand Joyce Ann sent everything on the table crashing to the floor, then slammed down the groceries and the bag of coffee. She stomped to the side of the bed and glared down at Tonk, itching to slap him awake.

There was nothing pretty about Tonk, especially while sleeping off a night of too much company with Jack Daniels. His mouth was open, his teeth bared. His greasy blonde hair was slicked to his forehead, and the scar on his upper lip was standing out like a mark made with a red felt-tip pen.

He could be such a pig! He had cleaned himself up when they hooked up in El Paso, but during the three months they had been together he had slowly reverted back to his slovenly self. She tried to keep the shabby room they had rented clean, but her pleading and begging for him to shower, pick up after himself, and throw garbage in the trash can instead of on the floor had failed. Joyce Ann had given up. She should have known better than try to reform a twenty-six-year-old man who had lived on the streets. Besides, he had told her he liked things as they were.

Tonk was a slob, a user, and a loner, who made no bones about being a die-hard vagrant. But he was also a very clever vagrant who had begun to teach Joyce Ann many of his useful tricks that had helped him survive on the streets. Teaming up with Tonk had been a good thing, she reminded herself, and definitely added a measure of protection from the police, who were looking for a black female, most likely on the run alone. No one paid much attention to her as long as she was hanging with this white boy drifter. People averted their eyes from the road-weary white boy and the big, strapping black girl, perhaps afraid that staring at them might make them mad, give them a reason to lash out. Joyce Ann had been surprised that Tonk's theory was actually working, in restaurants, elevators, grocery stores, and even banks.

For two and a half months they'd been making their way west, finding credit card slips in dumpsters, drivers' licenses in glove compartments of parked cars, and even a computer in a Radio Shack delivery truck left unattended. But now, Joyce Ann wanted to scream at Tonk, make him get up, take a shower, and pull himself together so they could leave this dingy room in the desert of New Mexico. She was tired of the heat of Socorro, which was blistering hot though it was only mid-March. The pickings were slim, now, and she was getting nervous. They had been in one spot too long, made too many visits to the local Wal-Mart, and had eaten too many meals from white paper bags. She worried that their luck was running out, but Tonk insisted they stay put. At the pace they were moving, they wouldn't reach Las Vegas until July.

Joyce Ann went over to the television and zapped the remote, darkening the screen and the room. She started to open the drapes, then stopped.

Better let him sleep it off, she decided, not ready to deal with his pissed off attitude when he woke up with a big head. So, she turned on the lamp on the dresser, took a cup of coffee from the McDonald's bag, and sat down on the floor at the computer.

Tonk, who had been a computer technician and website developer before his drug habit took over his life, knew quite a lot about hacking into systems, identifying websites to attack, and how to create and launch viruses that could wipe out hard drives and entire programs. He also knew how to find almost any information that was floating out in cyberspace.

Joyce Ann plugged the connector into the phone jack, logged on with the password he had told her to use, a password that could not be traced, then typed in the words "Gatesview Prison" deciding to see if news of her escape had been posted online. Was her picture on the Internet? she wondered, grinning. What had old Warden Andrews posted on the web about her? And what else might she learn about the inmates of Gatesview, she wondered, clicking her way to the site.

"No, I told you back in December, I haven't heard from Joyce Ann Keller and I don't know where she might be hiding. Her family lives here, but she'd never come back to Mallard," Precious told Kyla Sharp, the policewoman who was questioning her for the second time. Precious wheeled her chair into the living room, exasperated by the inference that she would know Joyce Ann's whereabouts.

"What about Sara Jane Talbot?" the tall, slimly built policewoman asked in a fast clip of words. Her tone was insistent, driving home her need to get a lead on Joyce Ann's location, get a break in a case that had dragged on too long. She walked quickly into the next room, entering before Precious arrived, still talking. "She and Joyce Ann were friends. We can't locate her either. Do you think the two of them could be together?" Kyla tucked a springy coil of black hair back behind one ear, moved aside a fringed pillow, settled her narrow body on the center cushion of the sofa, then opened her spiral notebook and began to review her notes, anxious for any information Precious could provide.

"Together? Absolutely not," Precious replied, remembering her final conversation with Sara Jane. "No, Sara Jane would turn Joyce Ann over to authorities in a heartbeat, I'm sure."

"Has Sara Jane Talbot contacted you?"

"The letter I sent to her at Havensway came back. That was in December, right before Christmas. I don't know where she went, but maybe the director or one of the women living at the halfway house knows something."

Kyla shook her head, frowning. "Havensway is closed. I found out the director, a woman named Nina Richards, remarried her wealthy husband and the two of them moved to Switzerland to live. The house in Dallas is deserted and no one knows what happened to the records. I did track down a few former residents, but they were no help. A real dead end, that was."

The information saddened Precious, who would have liked to find

Sara Jane, but if the police had lost track of her, Precious knew Sara Jane must have deliberately made it difficult to find her. Shrugging, she told the policewoman, "Well, I haven't spoken to Sara Jane since the day she came by here with a suitcase in one hand and a duffel bag in the other, on her way to Dallas."

"But for some reason, she's vanished," Kyla stated flatly. "Seems rather strange. Both Joyce Ann Keller and Sara Jane Talbot disappearing at about the same time. Could be a connection there."

A flicker of doubt crossed Precious' features and she shook her head slowly, considering the possibility. "I don't think so. Just the opposite, it seems. With Joyce Ann on the loose, Sara Jane could be in danger because they fell out during the 'incident.' Joyce Ann blamed Sara Jane for us getting caught and for not taking the fall by holding the money. It was all so long ago, so confusing, but I've always believed that if given the chance, Joyce Ann would try to make Sara Jane pay for not following her orders that night. Yes, I think she could be a real problem."

"Possibly," Kyla reluctantly agreed scribbling what Precious had said in her notebook. "So, you think if we find Sara Jane, Joyce Ann might be close by?"

"Who knows? Maybe," Precious replied, unsure of what to think.

"Well, if you hear from either, please give me a call. You're still on probation, remember?"

Precious' silence indicated her understanding of the implication.

"Don't jeopardize your freedom by withholding information. Call the authorities immediately if you get any leads that could help us capture Joyce Ann Keller," Kyla said, standing. "She's been on the run for three months, but she'll slip up sooner or later. They always do. The police found the prison van she escaped in stripped and burned out on a back street in El Paso. Could be she's hiding out someplace in Mexico, but I don't think so. I've read her case file, a sad story there."

Precious nodded, recalling the wild Keller family's reputation, the way Joyce Ann tried to act as if her relatives were normal.

"She craves attention," Kyla went on. "Women like her want to be known as gutsy and clever. Power, revenge, and notoriety are their handles. Hiding out in Mexico wouldn't serve Joyce Ann's interest. She'll head to a place where she can make a big scene, to hurt someone she knows or dislikes. She may think she's gotten away clean, but we'll find her. It's just a matter of time."

Chapter Twenty-seven

After returning from Washington D.C., Diana Devreux dedicated herself to making certain this new wave of success would last as long as possible. She spent hours in meetings with Jerry Hoss, her new PR agent, whose job it was to control and shape this resurgence in Diana's career. By mid-March, the rapidly rising sales of *One and Only* had propelled Diana into a second tour with appearances in Denver, Seattle, San Diego, Albuquerque, Salt Lake, Tucson, and Kansas City, cities she had not visited the first time out. She hired additional crew members to manage the gigantic new set she had constructed, and chartered a bus for them.

This time out she aggressively worked the talk-show circuit, her zealous dedication equal to her dazzling new image, which never failed to evolve into a topic of discussion, much like Tina Turner's fabulous legs. Mature women approached her in boutiques and on the streets, begging for autographs, telling her how fabulous she looked.

Serena accompanied Diana on every leg of the trip, working long hours to keep up with her boss's skyrocketing comeback. Caught up in the excitement of the whirlwind travel and their frantic styling sessions, she submerged herself in Diana's hectic schedule, exactly what she needed to keep her mind off of Craig, who was consumed with logistics and details related to security. With work keeping them apart during the day and late concerts and after-parties taking over their evenings, their relationship was put on hold.

They moved from city to city on chartered jets that carried Diana, Vincent Ruby, the backup singers, Serena, and Craig, usually arriving in each city the day of the concert, giving Serena just enough time to work on Diana's makeup, hair, and line up her costumes in preparation for the six changes she made during each performance. And in addition to Serena's work backstage, there were run-throughs at the performance halls, impromptu meetings with local charities that Diana supported, and photo ops for the media that had to be squeezed into the overloaded schedule that required Serena's attention.

After each concert, almost as soon as Diana sang her last note, the stagehands and grips would begin disassembling her multilevel set, Craig would pull the limo around, and Serena would hurriedly pack Diana's dressing room so they could pull out in the middle of the night.

As Diana Devreux's stylist, Serena soon became nearly as well-known as her boss, and when fans spotted her with Diana, they often asked Serena for her autograph as well. The vicarious spotlight thrilled Serena, who enjoyed the attention that came her way simply because of her connection to Diana Devreux, whose friends and associates began begging for permission for Serena to work her miracles on them. But Diana quickly denied their requests, blocking access to her skilled illusionist. Under Diana's demanding, observant, and calculating guidance, Serena's knowledge of the business, as well as her reputation in it exploded, making her a newsworthy shadow that was never very far from her boss.

When the tour finally ended in early June, Diana returned to Las Vegas, shed her fancy clothes, put away her heavy stage makeup and went into seclusion to begin work on a new album, ordering Serena to have some fun and get some rest while she huddled in her studio with her trusted associates Vincent Ruby, Marvin Erwin, Dean Banks, and musical advisors who were consulting on her next release.

At last, Serena was able to devote herself to Beautopia, and hopefully, spend time alone with Craig.

Two days after their return, Serena called Craig at the Wind Way Arms with the intention of inviting him to ride with her to Indian Springs, where she wanted to locate the source for Spanish bayonet that she'd discovered on the Internet. But when he did not answer his phone, she decided to make the trip alone and catch up with him when she returned.

It was a beautiful day and the traffic was light on US 95 as she made her way north into the desert. She felt so happy and relieved. Free. The hard work she had done for Diana during the tour had bolstered her self-confidence and brought a deep sense of satisfaction. As she thought back over the past two and a half months, silently analyzing the fabulous crowds, the adoring fans, the blitz of media attention Diana had received, she could not help but smile. The schedule had been tough, Diana had often been edgy, and Craig had deliberately kept his distance. Yet, despite the hectic pace, the glitches and the tension, the tour had been a success: for her, for Diana, and for the fans. Serena could visualize her future unfolding as she had hoped. The only part of it that was missing was Craig, and she had plans to remedy that as soon as she returned.

At the road sign indicating the turnoff for Indian Springs, Serena exited the highway and entered a stretch of two-lane road that was desolate, dry, and rugged. She checked the printout from the web page and read the address again. RR #3, Indian Springs. Raul Torres. At a fork in the road she turned right onto RR #3 and drove until she came to a house that was little more than an adobe cabin with a wood-shingle roof. Slowing down, she read the name on the black metal mailbox in front of the house, which was hidden from view by a tangle of brush, tall prickly cactus, and blooming vines: R. TORRES. She stopped and assessed the place: a flat expanse of land dotted with weather-worn crosshatch trellises over which blooming vines trailed. The property resembled a junkman's paradise, with gardening tools, bird-baths, fountains, and huge clay pots filled with colorful flowers set between uneven rows of huge, scraggly plants that surrounded the house and blanketed the land.

After parking on the side of the road, she got out, struck by the quietness of the desert location as well as the isolation. She went up to the door, worried that perhaps she should have waited for Craig and not come alone. But after a few seconds of hesitation, she shrugged off her apprehension, deciding to at least find out if this Torres man might be a source for Spanish bayonet.

At the heavy wooden door, she knocked, her presence immediately initiating the loud bark of a dog that continued until a diminutive dark-haired man with a thin moustache and a welcoming expression on his face pulled open the door. He was wearing a clean blue shirt, faded jeans that were held up with woven leather suspenders, and scuffed boots with long pointed toes. He looked at Serena through the screen, then bent down to quiet the brown and white cocker spaniel barking at his side.

"Hello," he remarked, greeting Serena with a quick lift of one hand.

"Hello. Are you Raul Torres?"

"I sure am. What can I do for you? Lost?"

"No. I'm not lost. I'm Serena St. James and I drove up from Las Vegas to find you. Do you grow or sell a plant called Spanish bayonet?"

Raul broke into a broad smile, unlatched the screen door, and stepped outside. "Yes, I do," he answered, smoothing his fingers over his moustache.

Serena sighed, relieved not only that the long drive was going to be worth the effort, but that Raul Torres seemed pleased to have a visitor. "I'm very interested in seeing it, learning more about it, and purchasing some."

"Oh? And how did you find out I grow it?"

"Your name and address were listed on a website on the Internet. A website that contains information on edible, useful plants and their sources."

"That so?" he murmured, unimpressed. "Could be. I do sell Spanish bayonet to a few people, but I had no idea my name was out there in cyberspace."

Serena tensed, hoping he was not upset that she had come. "I don't know how it got there, but if you don't mind . . . if you have the time, could you show me what you have? I want some to make soap."

Hitching up the strap of one of his suspenders, he stepped out of the shade of the overhang protecting his porch from the hot desert sun, and followed by his dog, headed out into his garden, motioning for her to come along.

"You say you're gonna make soap?" Raul Torres asked Serena as he stopped at a patch of sharp pointed plants, took up a shovel propped nearby against a trellis and pried a plant loose. He grabbed it by its pointed leaf, and tossed it to the side, dug another one and added it to the pile.

"Yes," Serena replied. "I found an old recipe that my mother had written down, finally located a tiny bit of the root and tried it out. The soap turned out wonderful. I use it all the time and think it has greatly improved my skin and hair."

"Been used for hundreds of years. Now it's special, huh?" He laughed, then dug up another plant, which Serena cautiously examined.

"The leaves are so sharp," she commented, eyeing the leaves that looked exactly like the drawing in her mother's sketchbook.

"Your mother had a recipe for making soap with this?" he asked, then added, "She Indian?" He plunged his shovel back into the ground at the base of another stubborn plant.

Serena tilted her head to one side and studied the bent, tiny man, considering his question. She really didn't know much about her mother, but had never considered that she might have been an Indian. Her father would have mentioned it, wouldn't he? "Well, that, I don't know," Serena answered. "She died when I was very young."

"Oh," Raul remarked. "I just don't find too many folks, white or black, who know about Spanish bayonet. Just wondering." With a grunt he pried another root from the soil and added it to the fast grow-ing pile at Serena's feet.

She picked up one of the plants to examine it closer, never having seen it in its natural state. The leaves were long, pointed, and sharp, resembling the blades of bayonets. She ran her finger along the razor-like edges, thinking of her mother, realizing how much she did not know, how much she wanted to learn. How *had* Violet Talbot come to know about this plant? Where had she seen it growing? And did the mysterious sketchbook have more significance than Serena thought? A subtle ripple of excitement went through Serena as the questions tumbled through her mind.

"You have so much of it. Does it grow wild?" she wanted to know.

"Pretty much, once it takes hold. Can be a nuisance if I don't keep it under control. Got a root cellar over there full of Spanish bayonet, dry-ing out." Raul jerked his head in the direction of an overgrown plot of land near the driveway, on the other side of the garden, not far from where Serena's car was parked. "There's a man who comes up here from Mexico twice a year," Raul went on. "Buys all I can give him as long as its bone dry. He makes some kind of medicine, I think."

"Could I see the root cellar?" Serena asked, anxious to see and learn everything possible about the plant on which she was going to stake her future.

"Sure." Raul shouldered his shovel and led Serena to a patch of tan-gled vines and ground cover. Using his shovel, he cleared the bushes to reveal a wooden trapdoor with a big metal hinge in the center. There was no padlock, but the door was securely shut. With a grunt, Raul pried the door open and let it fall flat to the ground, then stepped closer. "Look down there," he said, moving aside so Serena could get to the edge of the hole in the ground.

Looking into the pit, Serena shuddered. The Spanish bayonet leaves, sharp and sinister, poked up at her like a thousand deadly knives. Bone dry and hard, many were as long as two feet and as wide as the span of her hand. She squatted down to get a better look.

"Be careful," Raul warned. "If you fall in there, you're done for, young lady. Like falling into a bed of daggers. The Indians used the leaves like hunting knives before they had steel blades."

"This is amazing," Serena murmured, inhaling the musty odor that wafted out.

"Tough as nails they are," Raul replied, bending down to grab the heavy door. He slammed the trapdoor closed, then stepped on it to pound it down level with the earth before replacing the vines and ground cover over the entrance.

They headed back into the garden, where Raul placed the plants for Serena into a wide woven basket. "That'll be ten dollars," he said, accepting the bill Serena offered. "And good luck with your soap."

"Thanks," Serena replied, following Raul to her car, where she popped open the hatchback so he could slide the basket inside.

"Come out anytime you want, young lady," Raul said once the plants had been stowed. "I got no phone, so don't try to call. Just come on out. If I'm not here, I'm probably over to my cousin Joe's, down the road. If you want, you can dig what you need and leave the money in my mailbox. Don't get much trade out here." He wiped his sweaty brow with a handkerchief. "Don't get much company either. How'd you like a cool drink before you get on the road?"

"That would be nice," Serena accepted, glad to have found not only a source for Spanish bayonet, but a friendly person to deal with.

He led her to a table under a stand of date palm trees that shaded the side of his house, then brought out a yellow ceramic pitcher of lemonade and two ceramic glasses.

"New to these parts?" he asked, filling, then handing her a glass.

"Yes, very."

"You like it? It can get pretty hot. Where you from?"

"Texas."

"Oh, then you're used to the heat," he smiled.

Serena nodded. "Yes, I am, and Las Vegas is fine, but I'd like it better if I had my own place. Outside the city, maybe, but not this far," she laughed. "Right now I'm living with a . . . a friend."

"What kind of place you looking for?"

"Something nice. Quiet. Away from the tourists and the strip. I've been too busy working to look around."

Raul bent down and snapped the wilted bloom from a pink geranium, then straightened up and watched Serena closely. "I got a piece of property on Spring Mountain Road. You'd like it. Not too far from town and real quiet. Only thing is, the house ain't finished. I was building the place for my son, but he got killed in a carjacking in Vegas. Terrible place. I knew he wasn't going to make it in that devil of a town. I can't bring myself to finish it. It's just sitting there. Empty." He blinked, then raised his eyes to the horizon, as if thinking about his son.

"Spring Mountain Road. That'd be perfect." Serena removed a pen and a piece of paper from her purse. "What's the address? I'd like to drive by and check it out on my way back home."

That evening, after dinner at Cafe Michelle, a charming European eatery in Mission Center, Serena and Craig were finally together, sitting in a dim booth at the back of the restaurant sipping wine, listening to the woman at the piano bar, reliving the tour, laughing about some of the mix-ups and problems that had stressed them out on the road. Serena enjoyed talking to Craig because he understood exactly what she had had to put up with to please the great diva, Diana. But Serena also now better understood why Diana demanded and took such control over everything. There had been so many details, situations, and pressures that Diana had to cope with, no wonder she had locked herself away at her house as soon as she came off the road. Even Serena had found it difficult to return to a normal pace after the incredible high she'd experienced for the past two and a half months. And now that she understood what working for Diana was truly like, she knew some things had to change. She had to move beyond the scope of Diana's world, create a space of her own over which she would have control.

"I'm planning on getting my own place," Serena told Craig, swirling the dark red wine in her glass. She had already told Craig about her visit to Raul Torres' farm and her plan to eventually develop the Spanish bayonet into a viable cosmetics formula. He had been encouraging. "I found the perfect place, too," she went on. "West of town, far from the crowds and the tourists. It's on a huge piece of land but the house is small, unfinished space downstairs with a loft apartment upstairs. The owner was building the house for his son, but he was killed in a carjacking two months ago. Since then, it's been sitting empty. Needs work, but the price is right and the space downstairs will be great."

Craig cocked his head to one side, studying her, but did not reply.

"I need more room . . . to work on my cosmetics. It's exactly what I had in mind. The owner is real nice. He's the man I got the Spanish bayonet from. I want to tell him I'll take it before someone else comes along and snatches it up."

"I doubt that will happen," Craig replied. "Who wants to be in the wilderness when they can live near the action?"

Serena slapped playfully at Craig. "It's not the wilderness. It's fifteen minutes from the Wind Way Arms. I timed it today. You, of all people, must understand that I need some peace and quiet to work on my cosmetics. I'm convinced Spanish bayonet is a viable ingredient to give women, especially black women, an alternative to the harsh chemicals they've been using . . . if I can get the formula right."

Craig sipped his wine, his brows pulled together. "Not to mention that it might make you rich."

"Maybe. That would be nice, but it's not the reason I am pursuing this. I'm fascinated with the process, the history, and the potential, and the fact that it came from my mother."

The questioning look Craig gave Serena, made her cautious as she continued. "My mother didn't have much to leave me, no jewelry or money . . . so, in a way, this is my inheritance from her."

"That's a nice way to think of it, Serena," Craig murmured, giving her a light kiss on the cheek. "I can see it is important."

"It is."

"I take it Diana doesn't know about this secret research of yours or the fact that you've already scouted out a place to live?"

"No. You're the only one I've told." Serena paused, then swallowed, gathering her thoughts. "I love my job, Craig, but I don't love living with Diana twenty-four-seven. It's too stressful and confining."

"I understand that, but it's cheap. Convenient."

"Maybe, but I can afford to support myself now. I've been living in her guest house too long and am beginning to feel like a . . ." Serena stopped before saying the word, "prisoner," though that was exactly what had been going through her mind. Diana rarely commented on Serena's comings and goings, and had never set foot in the guest house during the time Serena had been living there. But Serena felt Danny watched her every move, and the maid who came into Serena's rooms at will asked too many questions while cleaning, polishing, and restocking the refrigerator. Serena wanted a place of her own, to be surrounded by furnishings that belonged to her, to finally enjoy the privacy she had never had. She had gone directly from her father's unwavering surveillance to prison, to being watched by guards and living behind the iron bars. The gates of Diana's luxurious compound were not much different, intensifying Serena's desire to feel free.

"Living at Diana's makes you feel like what?" Craig prompted.

"Uh . . . like a child who needs supervision," Serena hedged.

"Okay, so, move out. I think it's a great idea, but I can tell you right now, Diana is not going to like it. She's paranoid that someone will lure you away. Do you realize how well-known you've become?"

Serena lowered her eyes, concentrating on the flame of the candle burning in the center of the table. "Yeah," she sighed. "Kinda scary. That piece in *People* was more about me than Diana. I don't understand why the reporter did that. I think Diana was upset."

"The reporter slanted the piece to feature you because you are an unknown. You're hot. You rejuvenated a fading star, and you came out of nowhere to do it. You are a mystery and the press feeds on discovery, mystery, the flavor-of-the-month mentality. You burst onto the entertainment scene while the pundits and gossipmongers weren't looking, and now they have to play catch-up."

"Sometimes, I feel the same way. Like I have to play catch-up. I've never had my own apartment, been responsible for myself, and I want to experience that kind of independence . . . and for us to be together whenever and wherever we want."

Craig shoved his wineglass to the side of the table and took one of Serena's hands in his. "I know, and I want even more, Serena. It was hell staying away from you during the tour, hiding my feelings, dodging Diana's questions."

"What happened? Did she say something about us?"

"Oh, she made some comments about me keeping my eyes on you too much. She tried to laugh it off, but I could tell she was jealous, testing me to see what I'd say."

Serena burst out laughing. "Really? And . . . what did you do?"

"I told her I had to be just as concerned about your safety as hers, because you are nearly a celebrity, too, now. She didn't like to hear that, of course and told me not to worry, protecting you was not part of my job."

"Did she get mad?"

"Who knows? But she didn't bring the subject up again, at least, not to me. But I realized, we can't go on this way, Serena. I want us to be together."

"Together? You mean live together?"

"Yes, and eventually, permanently," Craig finished.

Serena held her breath, hoping she had heard him right. Was he asking her to marry him? Move in with him? She sat quietly, giving him the opportunity to clarify his intentions.

Craig reached into the pocket of his coat and took out a blue velvet box. Opening it, he showed her an emerald cut diamond set on a thin platinum band, but did not take it out.

Serena gasped at the sight of the glittering stone nestled in the blue velvet box, but controlled her desire to reach for the ring.

"It's for you, Serena. At the right time."

"The right time . . . and when will that be?"

"After I tell Diana about our relationship. Then I'll put this ring on your finger," Craig stated, studying the ring. "If you'll have me," he added in a husky, low voice.

Serena leaned over and quietly kissed Craig on the lips, one hand caressing the side of his face. "Of course, I will, Craig. I couldn't imagine not having you in my life. Everything that happened is because of you. Getting run off the road during a rainstorm changed my life, brought you to me, and yes, I want to marry you."

Craig returned the kiss, taking hold of her hand. "I'll ask you again, in a more proper way as soon as this business with Diana is settled. She's got to know that you are not abandoning her, because one of us will have to leave her employ for this to work." He took a long breath. "And it can't be you. Diana needs you, you have a great job and a great future with her. I can easily move on."

"Are you sure you'll have to?"

"Yes. I know her . . . how she will react. She won't tolerate you and me together as a couple working for her. She runs DD, Inc., like a corporation, and I guess that's fine, but she's adamantly against serious involvement among her staff."

"But you're mean. Showing me this ring, then making me wait for it."

"I want you to know how serious I am, Serena. I bought this ring a while ago, when we were touring, and I've been thinking about when and how to tell you that I want to spend the rest of my life with you. I have plans, too."

Serena leaned across the table. "Tell me. What are they?"

"I have a good friend named Delbert Brooks who lives in Los Angeles. He's made me a proposition that is fantastic. He's got a line on six Lincoln limos that are coming up for auction." Craig stroked the back of Serena's hand. "He wants to bid on them. Wants me to go into business with him and start our own driving service. He's got the financing all arranged, a great business plan, and the contacts to make this work. All I need to do is tell him I'm available to start the ball rolling."

Serena reached up and cupped Craig's chin with her hand again. "I think that's wonderful, but you'd be in Los Angeles. Too far away."

"Just until we get established and work out the bugs, then I plan to move back here and open a second location in Vegas." He let Serena caress the underside of his jaw, watching for her reaction. "What do you think?"

"I think I'd better marry you before you strike it rich and some gold-digger gets her claws in you. And I don't plan to wait forever for that ring."

He chuckled, then thought for a moment, nodding. "That's settled. This weekend, on Saturday I'll tell Diana I'm quitting, and we're engaged."

Serena leaned back and scrutinized Craig's expression. "Saturday is four days away!"

"I know. But I've got to go out to L.A. tomorrow, meet with Delbert, settle the details of our partnership and nail everything down. Now is the best time for me to go, while Diana is involved with this new album and doesn't need me. I'll be back late Friday and on Saturday, Hunter & Hoss is throwing a reception for Diana's backers to preview her new album. Also, it's a surprise celebration for her forty-fourth birthday."

"God, Saturday is Diana's birthday?" Serena remarked. "I didn't know."

"Yep, June eighteenth. But don't worry, she doesn't like a lot of fuss, so don't rush out and buy her a gift. This reception will be a small affair in a private room at Caesar's. It will be classy and quiet, so she ought to be in a pretty good mood afterward. When I take her home, I'll break my news. It will go fine. You leave it to me, okay?"

"I guess," Serena hedged, sitting back, hoping Craig would be able to smooth the rough waters she feared might loom ahead.

Chapter Twenty-eight

"A six-pack of Coors Light and a small pepperoni pizza with extra cheese. Wind Way Arms, room 301," Craig said, ripping off his tie as he hung up the phone. He shoved the afternoon edition of the *Las Vegas Review* off the dining table and tossed his tuxedo jacket onto the sofa, anxious to eat. He'd been on the run all day and was starving.

He'd driven in from Los Angeles just in time to change into his tux, race over to Diana's, and pick her up for the reception at Caesar's and hadn't eaten since yesterday morning. Now he had a few hours before he had to pick her up, so he'd grab a bite and relax while he could.

The meetings with Delbert had gone smoothly, and everything was moving on schedule. Their bid on the six Lincoln limos had been accepted, they'd scouted out a great location, which Delbert was negotiating hard to acquire, and if the owner of the space came through, Craig would have to rush back to Los Angeles tomorrow and finalize the lease. Now, his main objective was to sever his ties with Diana Devreux, Inc., without a messy ending that would sour their parting. Would she understand? Agree that it was time for him to go? Diana had never loved him, he knew that much, and he had never told her that his feelings were anything other than respect and a deep sense of caring. Yet, he knew how her mind worked, how much she liked to be in control, and how insecure she had grown about her appearance. Having a young, handsome man in her bed from time to time had been as much about boosting her morale as having great sex, and when he dropped her, she was going to feel crushed, abandoned, and resentful. But it had to be done. They both knew their alliance of convenience had run its course and it was way past time to let go. But would she let go? he worried, dreading the fact that he had to tell her he was dropping her to put an engagement ring on Serena St. James' finger.

Craig thought about the ebullient mood Diana had been in when he left her at Caesar's, how excited she was about the new material and the support she was getting from her recording studio, knowing the news he was about to deliver was not going to go down well.

He went to the floor-to-ceiling window and pulled back the drapes, opened the door to his private balcony, and went out. He loved this tiny alcove above the world where he could get away to read, take in a little sun, engage in serious thought, or simply watch the people who frequented the Plaza, the Golden Gate, and the Las Vegas Club below. The Wind Way Arms, a midsized hotel at the corner of Freemont and Main, was sandwiched between a ten-story building and a small casino. He leaned over the wrought iron railing, trying to read the names of headliners at the clubs. The casinos downtown drew nice crowds but the real stars were over on the Strip: Gloria Estefan at the MGM Grand, Chris Rock was flashing on the marquee at Caesar's Palace tonight.

Those gigantic tourist traps on the strip did not appeal to him. The Wind Way Arms had full service beauty and barbershops, a grocery store, two video rental stations, and a business center with computers, faxes, copy machines and secretaries for hire by the hour. The glitzy world outside his balcony intrigued him and the price was right (Diana Devreux, Inc., picked up the tab as long as he was on call to drive), but tonight, the lively streets, happy tourists, limos, and busses annoyed him. Craig had always loved the outrageousness of the city: the giant neon letters and characters, the blazing marquees, the flashing signs inviting people to drink, dance, gamble and enjoy. But tonight he was feeling nonplussed. Maybe he was getting tired of hotel living. Maybe he wanted a real home.

Craig sank down into the chair beside the smoky glass table and let himself go limp, wishing he could get out of his tuxedo. But he had to pick Diana up in a few hours. His thoughts stayed on her. He admired her, yet felt sorry for her, having watched her fight to stay on top strengthen with each year, watch her deal with the pressure to stay youthful and competitive. Diana was forty-four years old today, and he knew she was having trouble accepting that fact. Though she had been lighthearted and expansive about getting one year older when he spoke with her earlier in the evening, Craig was worried. Serena's magic had definitely helped spark the kind of energy and confidence Diana needed to feel beautiful, alive, and confident, but even Serena could not get inside Diana's head or understand what made her tick.

His thoughts moved to Serena: lovely, curious, and extremely talented. Marrying her would be the best thing he ever did, and the timing was right. The idea of staying in one place, with one woman, was very appealing after five chaotic years on the road with a diva. His own fleet of limos, Serena as his wife, a real home, maybe a few kids. Why not? He smiled, proud of the dogged way Serena was working on her dream, making a name for herself and establishing a solid reputation as one of the best stylists in the business. Serena was going to experience her share of bumps and bruises as she moved farther away from Diana and deeper into the arena of producing and marketing her own cosmetics, and he planned to be there for her every step of the way. He just hoped Diana would play fair with Serena, and play fair with him, too.

The knock at the door broke his train of thought, and suddenly he was very hungry. No pizza, not even in New York, came close to what came out of the kitchen at the Wind Way Arms. He grabbed his wallet off the bedside table, and went to the door. When he opened it, Diana was standing there, a ruffle of black lace peeping out from the loosely closed opening of the cream satin evening coat she had been wearing when he dropped her off at the party. She was holding a bottle of champagne in one hand, a limp bouquet of red roses in the other.

Craig leaned against the doorjamb, annoyed, but not entirely surprised to see her like this. She had pulled this stunt before. He searched her face, struck by the desperation in Diana's eyes and the helpless way she was clutching the bruised roses to the front of her coat. The words he planned to say to her began rolling around in his mind.

She gave him a sly, knowing smile. He tensed, determined not to be a participant in her seductive game tonight, or any other night from now on. He had to tell her he no longer needed or wanted what she was offering, that he had found what he was looking for in Serena St. James.

"Happy Birthday, Diana," Craig said, breaking the awkward silence, surprised by the husky edge in his voice, terrified by the involuntary stir in his groin. He took a deep breath, stepped aside, and let her into his apartment.

Chapter Twenty-nine

Diana handed the roses to Craig, who brought them into the kitchen and took down a clear glass vase from atop the refrigerator. As he was filling the vase with water, Diana came up beside him and leaned against the sink, watching him with a sultry, expectant expression.

"Got two glasses?" she asked, hefting a bottle of champagne.

"Sure," Craig replied, sliding the vase of roses onto the counter before moving past Diana to get the glasses. "Have a seat," he motioned to the barstool at the counter, his back turned to her as he reached for two long-stemmed champagne flutes from the cabinet above the stove. "You should have called me to come pick you up, Diana. Did Caesar's limo drop you off?"

"Yes, I had to get out of there," she said, tossing off her satin coat as she settled on the stool.

"Not up for a long night, huh?" Craig asked, turning around, glasses in hand. "Well!" he said, surprised by what he saw. "This is certainly not the same woman I dropped at the party."

Diana, who was wearing the seductive black lace teddy she had worn for the cover shoot of *One and Only,* tossed back her head, shaking her unruly mane of famous auburn hair, ran her hands over her flat stomach, and laughed. "You got that right."

Craig's eyes flickered over her soft bare shoulders, her pointed breasts, which were rounded above the lacey edge of the sheer black lingerie, and the multithousand dollar diamond necklace settled on her chest. He swallowed hard, struck by her beauty, amused by her self-satisfied smile, and calmly walked around her to pick up her coat from the floor and place it over the back of her stool, forcing himself not to overreact.

"You should have warned me," Diana growled, crossing her legs, which were encased in sheer black stockings. She cocked one foot, admiring her four-inch black satin pumps, then stretched her arms out flat on the counter, placed her chin on top of them, then peeked up at Craig. "Why the hell did you let me go? You should have told me it was a birthday party! There's no fun in turning forty-four. None! And I sure as hell didn't want to eat ice cream and cake to celebrate this miserable day."

Craig was surprised to hear a slight slur in Diana's words. She liked to drink champagne, but always handled it well. During the five years he had worked for her he had never seen her actually intoxicated, maybe tipsy and giggly and out to have fun. Obviously she had consumed a bit more of Hunter & Hoss's imported bubbly than usual before leaving the party, igniting her insecurities, forcing her out of Caesar's Palace and into Craig's apartment dressed like this. *Here we go again,* he thought, feeling the tug in his guts.

"Aw, Diana, you told me you wanted to go to this affair. Thank Jerry Hoss and his backers for working so hard for your new release." Craig popped the cork on the champagne and poured some into the glasses, unsettled by the way Diana sounded.

"Yes, I went only to humor Jerry. You know, make an appearance, drink a glass of his imported champagne, and shake a few hands with the right people, then leave. I couldn't brush Jerry off after everything his firm has done to push my upcoming release, could I? But I never dreamed my birthday was going to be the highlight of the affair. What a drag."

"Guess you've got a point," Craig conceded, feeling her annoyance. Despite his uneasiness at Diana's unexpected visit, he was glad that she had come. It was going to be tough, telling her about Serena, but it might go over better if he told her here rather than in the limo as he had planned.

"I take it you weren't dressed like this when you left the party?" Craig teased as he twirled his glass of champagne, careful to keep his eyes averted from Diana's lovely, half-naked bosom. *She might be forty-four, but she's still got the body of a twenty-five-year-old,* he thought, realizing her maturity had softened her in the right places and made her lushly loveable.

Diana giggled. "No. A discreet inquiry, and a tip for the sister at the front desk, got me a private room that served my purpose." She lifted her glass, preparing to make a toast. Craig lifted his, too, smiling.

"To a great year," she proposed.

Craig nodded, tapping his glass against hers.

"It has been great, hasn't it, Craig?" she said, draining her glass in one swallow. She held out her glasss, and Craig poured her another drink. She took a sip, then set it aside and refocused on him. "Remember how we met, so long ago? The first time you went out on tour with me, all those wonderful nights in fabulous hotels?"

Craig simply nodded.

"Then, my career was so hot, I could hardly walk through a hotel lobby without getting mobbed, and remember when I dressed up like a hotel maid and sneaked into your room?"

"Oh, yes," Craig replied. "We had some crazy, but great times."

"Yeah, then it changed. Half-empty concert halls, fights with Vincent and Dean. All the tension when the money got funny, and Kahi skipped out. But we turned it around, didn't we?"

"You did," Craig corrected. "No one deserves this comeback more than you, Diana. You've got the tiger by the tail now. Enjoy the ride. You've earned it."

Her smile faded, and she frowned, biting down on her lower lip. "I should enjoy it," she murmured, tossing back the second glass of champagne, then abruptly getting off the barstool to approach Craig. She stopped inches from his chest. "I want to feel happy, but for some reason I don't."

"Why not? What's wrong, Diana?" He asked, surprised to see tears in her eyes, a despondent expression creeping over her face. She was obviously worried about something. "You were fine when I dropped you off at Caesar's. Now you're all upset."

Diana came nearer. Craig's first impulse was to take her in his arms and hold her, but he refused to move, as she expected him to. Their relationship had been like a dance, rehearsed until they knew the steps by heart, knew exactly what to expect and how to react. But now, Craig was deliberately out of step and he let his arms hang loosely at his sides, gazing into Diana's unhappy face.

"You want to know what happened?" she whispered, clearly surprised that he had not reached out to her, wanted to hold her. "I turned forty-four, that's what happened, and I'm not young anymore, Craig." She placed her cheek against his tuxedo shirt, remaining very still. "Even Serena's talent can't keep me looking young forever." Her voice was muffled and hoarse. "What can I do? Soon, makeup will no longer hide my wrinkles, and that mask Serena slathers on my face will no longer make the creepy lines go away. What then?" she worried.

"Diana." Craig tilted her face up to his, gave her a stern look, then eased her head down once more against his white shirt, not caring if she left smudges of lipstick and makeup on his shoulder. "Don't talk like that. You're blowing this birthday business out of proportion. The years roll on for all of us, not just for you. We just accept it." Craig stroked her hair, trying to soothe her, keep her calm, stifling his urge to wrap his arms around her shoulders and ease her despair. "Don't be so hung up on the way you look or how old you are. You're gorgeous. Your voice is strong, your fans love you. Ride it for all it's worth, and when the time comes to ease out of the spotlight, turn your talent in some other direction. Don't sell yourself so short."

Diana leaned back and stared hard at him. "It's not that easy, Craig. You're a man." She shrugged. "It is not the same with women, you know that . . . and it's not fair."

Craig remained silent as Diana assessed him, unable to respond. She was right, he knew. In her world, looks were everything, and the clock was her enemy. Her only ammunition was self-confidence and pride.

"Make love to me, Craig," Diana finally whispered, her voice breaking with need. "Make me feel young and beautiful, like you always do." She ran her hand along his belt, stopping at the buckle, which she began to unfasten. "We were always good together, Craig. No strings. No messy talk of love or commitment. Just comfort and understanding, and that's exactly what I need tonight. Being with you makes everything better."

When Craig eased his hand over hers, atop his belt, she tensed.

"That's right, Diana," he said. "Love was never a part of our deal, and I don't regret anything we ever did . . . or had. But . . ." He swallowed hard, aware that she was unbuckling his belt, untucking the tail of his shirt. Then her hands were on his bare back, massaging and kneading his skin.

Craig's blood raced through his body and settled between his legs. Diana's rumpled hair, the scent of her expensive perfume, and her nearness made him groan under his breath when he felt a stir of lust in his gut. But instead of giving in, he pulled away, determined to keep his promise to Serena. It was time to get real. Leave this fantasy that had consumed him too long.

"Diana, stop. Let's be honest. We can't continue like this." Then he stopped, waiting for her to respond.

She said nothing.

"As lovely as you are, and as much as I care about you, I can't make love to you, Diana. Not tonight . . . not again."

She immediately separated herself from Craig, pulling back abruptly to squint in question at his remark. "And why not?"

She seemed more surprised than hurt. Craig reached out to take her by the arm, but she moved away, walking to the windows where a blaze of blinking lights sparkled in the night. She kept her back to him.

"Listen to me, Diana. Please, listen."

"Why? What else is there to say?" she murmured, then turned. "Our cozy little arrangement has run its course and we're finished. I never loved you and you didn't love me. So let's leave it alone, okay?" She turned back to stare out the window, one hand on the arm of the sofa.

"I want to explain something." He stepped closer, then gently touched her soft, bare shoulder. "I do care for you very much," he began. "But it was loneliness that drew me to you, helped me push my troubles away. Sex was fun, a temporary fix for issues I had avoided too long."

"So? It worked," she replied, half smiling.

"For a while . . . but . . . I've found someone else, a woman I want to establish a permanent relationship with. I love her and want to build a future with her."

Now, Diana frowned, eyes narrowed in suspicion. "Really? Who might that be? Serena, perhaps?" Calmly, she went to the bar and poured more champagne into her glass. "I'm not blind, Craig. I know you say there's nothing going on between you, but I know better. People talk, you know."

"Who's talking about me and Serena?" Craig asked. The blinking marquee lights across the street were creating shadows on Diana's face, alternating light and dark, making it hard for him to read her expression. He thought about what he had planned to say, editing his thoughts as he sorted through the truth, feeling cheated by the way Diana had rushed him into confessing. He had wanted to take things slow and avoid a confrontation, not cause more problems that he'd have to deal with. But the truth was out now, he had to go all the way.

Leaving her glass on the counter, Diana approached Craig, the champagne bottle in one hand. She paused for a few seconds, then said in a quiet voice, "And I was foolish enough to bring my competition to you." She turned up the bottle and took a long swallow. "I made you happy. I have given you a pretty darned good life. And this is what I get?" Her laughter was laced with irony.

"We're in love," he blurted out. "And we plan to get married."

"Really?" She seemed genuinely surprised. "We've shared a lot Craig, talked about most everything. You never mentioned this desire to marry. I assumed the glitz and glamour and freedom of bachelorhood was what you'd grown accustomed to and wanted."

"That used to be the truth, but I've changed, Diana."

"So, who am I losing? You or Serena? You know both of you can't continue working for me."

The tension that had been building since the moment he opened the door to find Diana standing there suddenly left Craig, and his body relaxed. He was finally in control. "I'm leaving."

"Oh? To do what?"

"I'll still drive."

"Driving for a limo service or entering into an exclusive contract with an individual is in violation of your contract, Craig. Strictly, business, so don't push it, you'll lose."

He lifted one eyebrow, then said, "I won't be going to work for anyone. I'm starting my own limo service, and I had my attorney check everything out. You left me a loophole, Diana, whether you meant to or not, and I'm grateful. You see, I won't be violating my contract with you." Craig waited, anxious for her reaction.

"You've been planning this for some time, I see," Diana said.

"Yes," Craig replied.

Diana's lips turned down in a poignant smirk, and her chin began to tremble. "Fine, Craig. Have it your way. Leave. You could have waited until tomorrow to tell me this. We could have had one last night together. But no, you had to tell me you're leaving on my forty-fourth birthday." She put the bottle to her lips again, took a long swallow, then blinked. "Not what I needed to hear tonight."

Craig reached over, trying to take the bottle out of her hands. "You've had enough. Don't make yourself sick."

But Diana pulled away, keeping the bottle firmly in her hand. "'Oh, we're celebrating your good news. And it is my birthday, remember?" she gently rebuffed, taking another long swallow.

"Diana, please don't do this," Craig started.

But Diana cut him off. "Why? Does celebrating make you feel guilty?" She laughed. "Don't worry. I'm a big girl. I'll be fine." She sat down on the sofa, wrapped her arms around the half-empty bottle, and tucked her feet beneath her hips, her head tilted back, eyes closed.

Craig sat down beside her, filled with a strange sense of relief and, yes, guilt. He felt liberated from Diana's magnetic hold, yet he hated the fact that Diana was hurting, and he'd added to her loss of pride on this night . . . her birthday . . . a night that had not turned out as he had hoped. Here she was, struggling to stay afloat in a youth-oriented industry, juggling the demands of hundreds of people in what quite possibly was the most stressful point of her life, and he had added rejection to the heap. As he watched her shoulders rise and drop with each long breath she took, he grew more sympathetic.

Finally, she shook her tangled curls, tilted the bottle to her mouth once again, then surrendered it to Craig, giving him a weak, apologetic smile. "Enough. Drive me home. It's late." She tried to stand, but faltered and sat down quickly, one hand to her cheek. "Guess I did go over my limit, Craig." She curled her feet under her hips and rested her head on the sofa pillows. "Give me a minute. A glass of water, and I'll be fine. You know, I never drink this much."

Craig placed the bottle on the bar, glad she had voluntarily handed it over. "Relax, Diana. There's no need to rush off," he told her. "Stay here. Pull yourself together. I can drive you home in the morning."

Diana slumped back, as if too tired to argue, resigning herself to Craig's decision, and did not protest when he picked her up, carried her to his bed, and tucked her under the sheets. Craig turned out the lights, leaving Diana alone in the dark, hoping she'd fall asleep quickly.

The doorbell rang as soon as he pulled the bedroom door shut. It was room service, apologizing for being so late.

"The kitchen lost your order. I am so sorry. No charge, Mr. Alexander," the waiter said, wheeling in a cart that contained a rounded silver dome over a platter and a pitcher of water.

"No problem," Craig told him, absently handing the boy a twenty-dollar bill. "I lost track of time, anyway." He closed the door, went into the kitchen, scraped the pizza into the trash, opened a bottle of Coors and took a long, hard pull.

Serena paced back and forth in front of the empty fireplace in the guest house, trying to imagine the scene. By now Craig ought to be driving Diana back from the party, telling her about their relationship, clearing the way for them to finally bring their secret romance out into the open. The waiting was driving Serena crazy, and she kept one ear tuned for sounds of the limo coming up the driveway. Tomorrow, she'd tell Diana she was getting her own place. Surely Diana could see that once Serena was engaged to Craig, it would be best for her to move. She needed privacy. Space.

Serena sat on the sofa and watched the clock until two A.M., then dozed off, still dressed.

The sound of wheels on the gravel and brick driveway broke into her uneasy sleep, compelling her to sit up and listen. It must be Craig, she thought slipping off of the sofa to go to the window. Brushing her hair from her face, she peered out, startled that to see dawn was already breaking and light was easy over the horizon, pushing the desert night away. It was Craig's limo pulling up the drive.

Serena quickly shoved her feet into her sandals, attempted to smooth her badly crushed hairdo, then opened her front door and stepped out. Moving quickly across the damp grass, she passed through the walled cactus garden and went to the iron gate that led to the driveway, expecting to see Craig coming toward her.

But the limo had kept moving past the guest house, stopping at the front door of the main house. Puzzled, Serena remained just inside the gate, watching, until Craig emerged from the limo and opened the passenger door. Diana's slender arm appeared when she accepted Craig's extended hand. When she stood, her cream-colored satin coat swung open wide enough to reveal the black lace teddy and elaborate diamond necklace she was wearing.

Serena clasped a hand to her mouth. What was this about? Where had Diana been all night, and what had she done with the exquisite, and costly, cream satin sheath Serena had slipped over Diana's head the night before?

Stepping back into the shadows of the garden wall, Serena waited until Diana had gone inside, then started up the drive to speak to Craig. But after a few steps she realized he was not heading toward her, but had gotten back in the limo and was driving away. Serena stared after him in astonishment, more curious than ever about what had happened last night.

Chapter Thirty

A terrifying sense of rejection flooded Serena as she stood in the middle of the driveway and watched Craig drive away. He had not called her last night, as she'd expected, and now he was leaving without seeing her. What was this bizarre scene about? she wondered, crossing her arms at her waist.

Serena focused on the front door of Diana's house, frowning, a sudden, overpowering fear starting up. She was going to get some answers, now, and since Craig was obviously not anxious to speak to her, she'd start with the diva herself.

Hurrying up the short flight of terraced flagstone steps, Serena pressed her thumb to the shiny brass doorbell and held it down until Danny arrived and cracked it open. He blinked away the sleepiness on his face as he peered through the narrow opening.

"Miss St. James? Why, what are you doing here, at the front door? And at this hour?" He pulled the door fully open and checked his watch, as if assuring himself that it was really dawn, and entirely too early for anyone to be at the front door of Diana's house.

Ignoring Danny, Serena walked right in and went to stand in front of the massive fireplace in the den, unsure about what she was going to say to Diana, but certain that she was not going to leave until Diana gave her the answers she wanted.

"Are you all right?" Danny asked, slowly closing the door, cautiously eyeing Serena.

"No, Danny, I'm not all right. I need to speak to Diana."

"Oh, Miss Devereux's asleep."

"I don't think so. Go tell her I'm here. Please," Serena added, forcing a calmer tone, reminding herself that Danny had nothing to do with this situation, and had always been nice to her.

Again, Danny looked at his watch, frowned, then sighed. "I'm afraid I couldn't disturb Miss Devereux now. She's just . . ."

"Come home," Serena finished his sentence. "I know. I saw her come in only a few minutes ago."

"But . . ." Danny stuttered, then shrugged and left the room, leaving Serena to pace the cowhide rug in front of the fireplace as she gathered her thoughts and tried to make sense of the scene she had just witnessed in the driveway.

"Well, Serena," Diana sighed, entering the room, then leaning against the door frame for a moment, her heavy silk caftan puddling at her feet. "I had hoped we could chat, but not quite so early," She shrugged. "But since you're here . . ." Hesitating, she pulled her flowing gown closer to her body, then moved toward a deep brown leather chair beside the hearth and sat down, propping her feet on the matching ottoman. "Sit down, Serena. We do need to talk."

Alarmed by the calm, knowing tone Diana had adopted, Serena eased onto the matching leather sofa, never taking her eyes off Diana.

"I understand congratulations are in order," Diana began, tilting her chin low on her chest, threading her fingers into her auburn curls, clearly giving Serena her cue to reply.

Instinctively, Serena knew that Diana was not going to make this conversation easy, so she took a deep breath and plunged in. "So, Craig has told you about our plans?"

"Yes, indeed, he has. And I must admit that I am very unhappy. This is most disturbing, Serena. I could tell you were infatuated with Craig the moment I saw you two together in the same room, but love? No. He's been a very good friend to you. Helpful. Attentive. But marriage? Aren't you moving a bit fast?"

Offended by Diana's subtle putdown, Serena pulled back her shoulders, ready to make her case. "I don't think so. I love Craig very much. He's been a great friend, yes, but he's also been much more."

"Well, well." Diana shifted in her chair to better focus on Serena. "I see. I hate to hear that. And I hate that he's leaving my employ after five years, though I do understand his reasons for wanting to strike out on his own. But to marry you? He's being impulsive, and this is not a good move on your part, either, Serena."

"We're in love, Diana," Serena said, trying to muster a smile, hoping she could appeal to Diana, woman to woman, grasping for a sense of support that she desperately needed at this time. She had no mother, no close girlfriend. No one to whom she could turn for the concerned support she craved. But it was clear that Diana was not the one to fill that void. "We will be together, Diana. We will get married eventually, despite what you, or anyone, thinks."

"Do you think Craig Alexander really loves you, Serena?"

"Yes," Serena murmured, her earlier anxiety decreasing. She sucked back her fright, determined to keep control over her reaction to Diana's unsympathetic take on the news. "And I trust him completely," she added, her voice a little stronger, her emotions less confused. If there was one thing she was certain of it was Craig's love for her, and hers for him. From the first day she met him, he'd been nothing but kind, honest, and attentive. Never rushing her, never judging her, and never prying into her past. He accepted her as she was, didn't try to change her or mold her or influence her choices, always steady in his support of her work and her dreams. Craig Alexander was the man she planned to spend the rest of her life with no matter what anyone thought.

"Better be careful, Serena. You don't really know Craig very well, do you? How long have you known him? Six months, right?"

Serena nodded.

"Not very long. He probably does love you, I'll grant that, but he's not marriage material, and he is not what you need right now, Serena. You need room to grow, develop, create. If you marry him, you'll be stifled. He'll interfere with your career and undo all that I've helped you achieve. Don't let that happen. You can wait. You've got plenty of time. You'll meet many, many men during your lifetime, Serena. Don't settle for the first one who tells you he loves you."

"I am not settling. I love him, too, Diana."

"Love, love, love!" Diana threw back her head and laughed. "Honey, I could tell you so much about what love is . . . and what it ain't . . . but I doubt you'd listen, would you? It can be wonderful or horrible, take your pick. It can make you fly, or cry, and the ending is never pretty." She rose, clasped her hands together, then began pacing back and forth in front of the fireplace, her silk caftan sweeping the cowhide rug, creating a soft swishing sound in the quiet room.

Serena tensed, uneasy with the serious look on Diana's face.

"Craig is a nice enough guy," Diana continued. "He's handsome, polite, charming, a real gentleman, that's true. But . . . he's weak, Serena."

"What do you mean, weak?" Serena asked suspiciously.

"Craig is easily tempted. Ruled by his manhood, if you get my drift. Not a great candidate for marriage in my opinion."

"That's not fair, and it isn't a description of the Craig I know," Serena defended. "Since we've been together, he's been faithful, true, very open, and honest . . . the most understanding man I ever met."

"But how can you make any comparisons? You're very young, have little experience with men, you've said, and you don't really know Craig, not like I do. And he doesn't know you, either." Diana stopped her pacing and fixed Serena with a knowing stare. "He doesn't know about your past, does he?"

Serena's silence gave Diana her answer.

"I thought not," Diana said.

"Are you going to tell him about me?" Serena asked, tentatively.

"No, don't worry. It's not my place to tell him. It's yours." Diana went to the bar at the side of the room, put ice into a glass, opened a bottle of Perrier and poured herself a drink. "Want something?"

"No," Serena whispered, relieved that at least her secret past was safe.

"I am not ashamed to admit that I need you, Serena. Much more than I need Craig. I can get another chauffeur, another bodyguard. No problem. But you are irreplaceable and your future lies with me. Let me continue to guide you in this business, help you become a star in your own right, because once you marry Craig, everything will change. Men take up your time, your energy, and disturb your creative focus. It happened to Kahi; I watched it happen. And our relationship will deteriorate if you make Craig Alexander your priority. Perhaps it will have to end."

"I hope not. It doesn't have to be like that, Diana. Why do you think that way? I can still work for you and be married."

"Not to Craig Alexander, you can't," Diana abruptly replied, setting down her glass so abruptly she splashed her drink onto the counter. "Not to a man I have slept with too many times to count. Not to a man who has given me memories that I cannot erase. Having him hanging around, while he's married to you, would be most uncomfortable for me, you see."

"Slept with? You and Craig? That's not true!" Serena shot back, stunned. Fear crowded her chest, making it difficult to breathe, and she pressed a hand to the side of her mouth, staring in disbelief at Diana. "You're lying . . . admit it! You're saying these things to hold on to me, to control me, as you do with everything and everyone in your life. Stop it, Diana, it won't work. I asked Craig about you, and he assured me he had never been romantically involved with you." Serena pressed her lips together in a firm line, struggling to keep back the tears that were filling her eyes. "How can you be so self-involved and destructive that you would lie about Craig to keep me here?"

Diana chuckled, then calmly picked up her glass and sipped her Perrier. "I don't deny that I am extremely self-involved, and I don't apologize about it, either. But as for Craig and me, I'm not lying. Serena. We've shared many a bed on the road, all over the country, in the best hotels in the world. Ask him. Ask him about the champagne bath we took at the Ritz-Carlton in New York, the midnight skinny-dipping at the Fontainebleau, and how comfortable the carpet on the floor of the presidential suite is at the Mansion on Turtle Creek in Dallas."

"Dallas?" Serena whispered.

"Yes, Dallas. On the night before he met you, I think. Not so long ago." In a smug gesture, she lifted her glass, then set it down and went to sit beside Serena on the sofa, leaning close, then whispered in a conspiratorial manner. "And I was with him last night. All night. At his room at the Wind Way Arms."

The image of Diana emerging from the limo at dawn, dressed in a skimpy negligee, Craig in his dress shirt, popped into Serena's mind, making her stomach lurch. Craig and Diana . . . together all along . . . last night. How could she have been so stupid?

"Why are you doing this?"

"Because I care about you. Someone has to enlighten you about men. I want to protect you, and your career, Serena. Obviously, you need someone to guide you, teach you, keep you safe."

"Well, it sure as hell won't be you!" Serena shouted, having heard enough to know that now she and Diana could never work together, never rebuild the trust and confidence needed to move forward in a creative environment. Her relationship with Craig, as well as with Diana, had been a one-sided fantasy all along, Serena realized, understanding how blind she had been.

Serena stepped into the lobby of the Wind Way Arms and strode past the sister at the registration counter without a greeting, as she usually gave her, determined to get to Craig. On her way over she called him from the car several times, but got no answer. Her anger and disappointment in Craig had increased during the twenty minute ride into town, but she was determined to give him the opportunity to explain what Diana had implied. Had he been Diana's lover? Her boy-toy? A victim of her seductive beauty? And why hadn't he simply told Serena the truth at the beginning, sparing her this awful confrontation that had effectively ended her career with Diana?

Serena stepped into the elevator as soon as the doors opened, relieved that no one was inside. She looked at herself in the mirrored wall, not recognizing the distraught, pain-filled face that stared back at her. Trembling, she reached into her purse and took out her comb, ran it through her streaked blunt cut hair and tried to smooth it into place, and applied a swipe of lipstick. If she was going to have it out with Craig, she wanted him to see what he was tossing aside for a forty-four-year-old woman.

Nervously, she knocked on his door, half expecting him not to answer, but when he suddenly appeared at the door, now showered and dressed in jeans and a white open collar shirt, her knees went weak and her heart thumped with anxiety.

"Serena!" He stepped aside to let her in, smiling. "I just called the guest house and left you a message. I'm leaving for Los Angeles in a few minutes." He closed the door, then leaned over, as if to kiss Serena, but she backed away and went into the room.

"We need to talk," Serena started, wanting to clear the air right away. There was no need to play games anymore. She had to know what was going on.

Craig nodded. "I know you're upset because I didn't call last night, but . . ."

"But you were busy with Diana?" Serena finished, her words cool and distant, letting him know she was not only upset, but knew what had happened.

Craig grimaced, nodding. "Yes. Diana." He sighed, then moved toward Serena, reaching out to take her in his arms, but again, Serena shrugged him off and stepped away.

"Not now, Craig. I need to know what is going on between you and Diana."

"Going on?" He frowned. "Nothing. I told her about us, she got upset that I was quitting, but I calmed her down and that was it."

"Did she spend the night here?" Serena asked.

With a slow nod, Craig indicated, yes.

"And was it the first time she ever slept here? In this hotel room with you?" Serena pressed.

"Aw, come on, Serena. Where's this coming from?"

"Answer me, truthfully, Craig. That's all I want. Was last night the first time Diana slept here?"

"I prefer not to say."

"Why not?"

"Because you obviously have an ulterior motive in asking, and I want to know what is going on."

Serena silently counted to ten, determined not to lose her cool and start ranting and screaming, as she wished she could do. She had to hear him say it. Say that he and Diana had been lovers all along. That he had intentionally misled her. "Fair enough," she replied, focusing on Craig's bottom lip, which he had tucked between his teeth. He looked worried, tense, and afraid, just as she was feeling, she realized. Plunging on, she bluntly asked, "Have you ever had sex with Diana Devreux?"

With a droop of his shoulders, Craig turned from Serena and walked to the open drapes, looking out, his back to Serena.

But she came up to him, grabbed him by the shoulder, and forced him to turn around and look at her when he answered. "Well, have you!?"

"Yes," Craig replied, flinching when Serena thrust him away and glared at him, indicating her disappointment.

Serena was crushed. "And?" she pressed, wondering if Craig Alexander really thought she was going to let him toss her aside like an empty soda can without giving her an explanation. Serena silently raged as she strode to the counter, her eyes narrowed in offense.

"This is absolutely impossible, Serena. Sit down. Let me explain."

She pulled her shoulders back, assessing his expression. "Fine," she replied, moving to sit on a barstool. "Help me out, okay? I want to know if you and Diana . . ." she paused, watching Craig.

"Stop. Yes, Diana was here last night. With me."

Serena didn't budge. "Have you ever slept with her? In this hotel?" Her words were thick with disappointment.

"Yes. Many times," he confessed in a low voice. "I won't lie to you, Serena. It's true, I slept with her, but it wasn't love or even romance I felt for her. She was lonely. I was lonely. We used each other to survive on the road. It was wrong, perhaps, but we knew what we were doing and had no regrets afterward. Last night, on her birthday, I turned her down, told her I was in love with you. She was hurt. You see, Diana and I had used each other so long, we took each other for granted. Maybe it was selfish and stupid. But it happened. And I swear I never slept with her after I met you. And that is the truth. I can't say much more."

Serena tensed, her blood boiling. "What about last night? How did it happen that she stayed here? Why put yourself in such a position?"

"I was here, killing time until Diana called for me to pick her up, but she showed up in a coat over a lot less and didn't bother to hide what she wanted. I refused. We argued. She drank too much champagne. I put her to bed. This morning I took her home."

Serena slipped off the stool and went over to a deep club chair facing the door, sank down into it, weak with humiliation and shame. Craig had been lying to her all along about his relationship with

Diana. They'd spent many nights together! Here! Where she had lost her virginity. How could he have done this to her?

Serena bit down hard on her bottom lip, determined not to cry, thinking about the engagement ring he had shown her, the promise to call last night. She had paced the floor, waiting for the phone to ring, and all the while he had been sequestered in his room with a half-naked Diana, drinking champagne, enjoying himself.

"You bastard," Serena muttered. "You cowardly bastard. You didn't even have the courage to face me and tell me the truth. Well, I am certainly not going to let you ruin my life. Go back to Diana. I'm out of here, Craig, and out of your life. I've had enough of you . . . and Diana Devreux."

Getting up, she calmly opened the door, and without looking back hurried to the elevator down the hall from Craig's room, punching the button to go down, praying for the elevator to arrive quickly.

"Serena!" Craig was in the hall behind her. "Don't go. Wait."

She kept her back to him, refusing to turn around. She had to stay strong, not go back, not let him think he could smooth this over and go on as if nothing had happened.

When the elevator finally arrived, she saw that an elderly woman was already inside. Serena nodded to her, biting her lip to keep from crying, staring straight ahead during the short ride to the lobby.

But once she got into her car, she broke down, sobbing until she grew weak. Serena leaned forward, her head against the steering wheel, fighting mental images of Craig and Diana in bed, kissing, making love, laughing, sharing intimate moments that made Serena feel sick. How could he have thought she would never find out? How could he have thought that Diana wouldn't get a great deal of pleasure from boasting about her relationship with a younger man? Serena thought about the day, while they were lying in his bed when she'd asked him point blank if he'd been intimate with Diana. And he had lied. Flat out lied. Serena wanted to believe that if he had been truthful then, they would have been able to move past it, growing more secure in their love because of his ability to be completely honest with her. But no. He'd waited too long, and now everything was ruined. She was going to untangle herself from this disaster, fast. And that meant breaking away from Diana Devreux's control.

She wiped her eyes and started the car, knowing exactly what she had to do.

Raul Torres met Serena at the front door of his square adobe house, gave her a short wave of hello, then invited her inside. With his brown and white cocker spaniel at his side, he latched the screen, but left the front door open, then ushered her into his tidy living room.

"I expected I might see you again," he told Serena motioning for her to sit down in a brightly painted Mexican chair by the fireplace.

The morning was already warming up, but the tiny house was comfortable and a slight breeze moved the warm desert air through the room.

"You want the house, right?" he asked.

"Yes," Serena stated firmly, already taking her checkbook from her purse. "Seven hundred to move in?" she confirmed, leaning forward in her seat, hoping he was going to honor the figure he had first told her because that was all she could afford. With no living expenses to worry about, Serena had been able to save most of her salary and would be fine for a while. But she'd have to buy a car, furniture, clothes, pots and pans, groceries; everything to set up housekeeping, so she'd have to be very careful. She had made some good contacts while working for Diana, potential clients for whom she could work, if she was able to get out of her contract. She made a mental note to call Marvin Erwin to discuss the conditions under which she could work as an independent, freelance stylist.

"That's right, and six hundred a month after that," Raul Torres said. He sat down in a matching chair across from Serena and began scratching his dog behind the ears.

"Do you need me to fill out an application? References?" she asked, hoping this old man would not want to do a background check. She had no idea what might turn up if a credit agency punched in her social security number, and did not want to take the chance. She had no references: She'd walked out on Giani Pilugi, disappeared from Havensway without a word to Nina Richards, and asking for a recommendation from Diana Devreux was out of the question.

The less Raul Torres knows about me, the better, Serena thought, nervously toying with her pen.

"No application," Raul Torres said easily, shaking his head. "You look honest. Once you move in, I know where to find you, yes?"

"Yes," Serena replied, smiling. "So I can move in right away?"

"Today, if you want."

"Sounds good," Serena said, though she was worried about the logistics of getting herself and the few things she owned out of Diana's guest house and into her new place on Spring Mountain Road. "Do you know anyone who could help me move?" she asked.

Raul nodded, then pointed at the screen door. "Two miles down the road. Cross Terlingua Creek and go to the only house on the right. My cousin lives there. Ask for Joe. Tell him I sent you over. He's got a truck and too much time on his hands. He needs something to do besides play dominoes with his brother."

"That's great. Thanks," Serena said, her mind spinning. She'd get Joe to meet her at the front gate at Diana's late in the afternoon. That's all the time she would need to return the car, pack the few things she planned to take, and tell Diana good-bye. Leaving quickly, without a lot of fuss was the only way to do this. Their separation had to be clean and swift. There was no way Serena could spend one more night under Diana Devreux's roof.

"The place needs a lot of work, still, young lady," Raul reminded Serena, breaking into her thoughts. "Sorry I can't do more to make it nice, but when my son died I lost my interest, you know?"

Serena nodded as she scribbled her signature on the check.

"You have no husband? No boyfriend to help you?"

"No," Serena murmured, not raising her eyes, tensing as she thought about the diamond ring that Craig had shown her. She ripped out the check with a snap. "No," she repeated. "I have no one. I'll be living in the house alone."

"It's very isolated, young lady. Be careful," Raul warned. "Get yourself a guard dog, at least. Not good for a pretty girl like you to live out on Spring Mountain Road all alone. These are dangerous times. Look what happened to my boy." Raul Torres' eyes filled with tears. He wiped them away with his thumb, sniffling as she shuddered.

"Good advice," Serena agreed, feeling sad for Mr. Torres, who was clearly still grieving for his son. She thought of her own father, of the defiant expression on his face when she had told him she was leaving. Would he have shed tears if she had been killed in a carjacking in Las Vegas? she wondered. Had he given her whereabouts or well-being a second thought since she closed the door and walked out of his life? Serena's body made an involuntary shiver. Buster Talbot hadn't cried when his wife died, why should he cry over her?

Raul bent over and patted the top of his Cocker Spaniel's head, allowing his pet to lick his arm as he rubbed its ears.

"A dog might be nice," Serena admitted. "I've never had a pet."

"A good dog sticks close by. Be your best friend. Faithful to the end."

"More faithful than any man, I'd wager," Serena tossed back, handing the check to Mr. Torres.

Craig pulled his sunglasses over his eyes, which felt as if sand had been ground into them, blinking several times to ease the irritation. He took a deep breath, trying to put everything that had happened into perspective. He'd quit his job, terminated his relationship with Diana, and lost his fiancée, all in the space of twenty-four hours. Now, all he felt like doing was going to sleep; he had not slept all night after tucking Diana into his bed. He'd sat awake planning his future, which now seemed to be in chaos. He wanted to sleep, let his mind go foggy and dark, erase the memory of Serena's disappointed face, forget about the mess he was in. He stretched his neck to one side, then the other, feeling his taut muscles strain. He had to stay awake. There would be time enough to sleep once he got to L.A., though the 270-mile trip on the Old L.A. Highway was going to take four hours—if he didn't stop to rest.

Though physically and emotionally trashed, he was not about to give in to the pull of anxiety and fatigue weighing him down. Craig eyed the clock on the dashboard. Serena was probably back home, but what was she doing? Arguing with Diana? Crying? Cursing him? He wanted so much to call her, beg her forgiveness, try to set things straight, but knew he had to give her time to get over the hurt he'd caused. For now, he'd stick to his plan, keep his word to Delbert Brooks and get to L.A. today and sign the lease for their new venture. He'd call Serena later, after he had settled into his hotel and was finished with business matters.

The highway leading out of town was free of traffic and Craig made good time, but could not relax. When the jagged skyline of Las Vegas slid out of his rearview mirror and the tangle of shops, restaurants, gas stations, and billboards gave way to wide open stretches of desert, he sped up, his mind as blank as he could make it, though thoughts of Diana and Serena alternately shifted through his mind.

His five-year association with Diana was over, and the reality gave Craig a great sense of relief. He had wanted to concentrate on making Serena happy—loving her, protecting her, giving her everything she wanted. Now he had to start over, rebuilding her trust in him, convincing her to give him another chance.

Chapter Thirty-one

Adrenaline pumped through Serena as she raced around the guest house, trying to decide what to take and what to leave. It was nearly three o'clock. After leaving Raul's, she had arranged for Joe Torres to come by at three-thirty, had run some errands to pick up her dry cleaning, had purchased minimal supplies to set up housekeeping, and had gone to the bank to get some cash. She had even stopped by a used car lot and test-driven a few cars, but was still uncertain about which one she'd buy.

Now, she was packed and ready to go, determined not to take anything that Diana had bought for her, nothing to remind her of this disastrous situation. Unflinching, she passed over the expensive leather shoes, trendy purses, and stylish dresses that filled her closet, selecting only what she had purchased with her own wages. Luckily, she had bought a five-piece set of Hartman luggage before going out on the extended tour and had picked up enough casual outfits to get by until she could go shopping.

After clearing the bathroom cabinets of all of her personal items, she jammed the results of her Internet research into cardboard boxes, then looked around. The place looked no different than it had six months ago, when she had walked in on Christmas Eve and thought it was a dream of a place to live.

"A bad dream," she muttered, ashamed for having been so naive. She should never have accepted this job, never left Dallas, never believed she could become someone else. She was a small-town Texas girl who did not know how to maneuver the sophisticated landscape of casual sex, shallow relationships, and thoughtless self-indulgence that seemed to be normal in Craig Alexander and Diana Devreux's world. But Diana's offer had seemed so right, so much in line with

Serena's plans to erase her past and start over. But Las Vegas was light-years away from Mallard, Texas, and her life with a superstar could never have lasted. Her lack of sophistication had caught up with her and Serena had to admit she had gotten herself in over her head. Now she was really on her own.

Why had she been so dumb, believing that a man as mature, attractive, and worldly as Craig Alexander would have been content with a nobody liker her? He had toyed with her feelings, probably for the challenge, to see if he could woo her while keeping Diana on the side. He was nothing but a player who wanted a variety of playmates to keep him occupied, with Diana being his superstar playmate. Clearly, the two of them belonged together, in a world in which Serena would never fit.

Her body went cold as she thought, again, that he had made love to Diana in the same bed where she had lost her virginity. Serena looked at the phone on the desk, then quickly unplugged it, making it impossible for Craig to even leave her a message. She never wanted to hear his voice again.

After stacking her suitcases and boxes outside the front door, she punched the code into the intercom to speak to the security guard at the front gate.

"Hello, Leo. This is Serena. I'm expecting a man named Joe Torres in about half an hour. He'll be driving a blue van. Please let him in and direct him to the guest house. Thanks." She clicked off, took a deep breath, then started up the brick walk toward the main house, ready to confront Diana, groping for a way to convince her to let her out of her contract. If Diana refused, she'd still survive, but not doing the work she wanted to do. How ironic, Serena thought. *Since the day I left Gatesview, all I could think of was being on my own, being free to work in the beauty industry, living independently, creating my special vision of my future. And now Diana Devreux holds all the cards. Her decision today can determine my fate.* Serena swallowed a sob, wondering how she had let this happen, vowing never to allow anyone to have that much influence over her again.

Danny met Serena as soon as she stepped inside the French doors off the patio.

"Where have you been?" Danny asked, removing the kitchen towel he had draped over his shoulder. He calmly folded it in half, set it on the bar in the den, and placed one hand on his hip. He ran his eyes over Serena, as if inspecting her clothes for stains. "Miss Devreux was looking for you."

A hollow sensation filled Serena's stomach and her courage began to dissolve. "Why was Diana looking for me?" she asked, concentrating on Danny's reaction. The wrinkle on his forehead indicated discomfort about something, and it must have involved her. "Is something wrong?"

"Yes," Danny confessed, rather slowly. "Miss Deveruex was insistent that I find you this morning, but after calling the guest house, knocking on your door, and seeing the RAV4 was not in the garage, there was nothing I could do. I called Craig, and he said he didn't know where you were, either."

"Why were you looking for me?" Serena asked, drawing back her shoulders as she gripped the back of a barstool, feeling off balance. She struggled to put it all together. What was going on? "I had some important errands to run," she hedged, not about to let Danny rattle her. Joe Torres' van would be coming up the driveway any minute. She had to stay on track, move through this situation, and stick to her plan. "Well, tell Diana I'm back now, and I'd like to speak to her."

Danny sighed, clucking his tongue. "She's not here."

"Oh?" Serena said, a chill sweeping through her again. "Then where can I reach her? I really need to speak to her now," Serena went on, determined to sever this relationship before she lost her nerve.

"Miss Devreux left for Europe only minutes ago." Danny shrugged, then lowered his voice. "She was in an extremely agitated state, and disappointed not to be able to talk to you before she left."

"Disappointed? Why is she going to Europe?"

"For a rest, she said." Danny picked up the folded towel and ran his hand over it as he spoke. "She seemed despondent. I think it was that surprise birthday party. I was afraid it might set her back. Birthdays always have that effect on her, and I warned Jerry Hoss not to make a fuss, give her a party. But he would not listen. I don't think she had a good time."

From what I saw this morning, I think she and Craig had a blast, Serena thought, squinting at Danny. "Where in Europe?" she asked.

"Miss Devreux goes to the Regal Shore Resort . . . in the south of France once a year for a total rejuvenation. Usually, she goes in the fall, but maybe she decided it was time. She always comes back looking and feeling much better, in great spirits."

"How long does she stay?"

"At least a month. Maybe two."

Serena sighed in frustration. *Diana might be gone, but Serena was not going to alter her plans. She would contact Marvin Erwin to terminate the contract, then see where she stood.*

"I came to tell Diana I'm moving out today, Danny," Serena said, placing the keys to the car and the guest house on the glass-topped bar. "If Miss Devreux calls, tell her I'm sorry about the way things turned out, but this is best. I can't work for her or stay here any longer."

"But, I don't understand, Miss St. James. You're leaving?" Danny's mouth stayed open as he looked at Serena from beneath his straight black brows. "This is not good. Miss Devreux is going to be so disappointed!"

"I don't know about that," Serena replied. "But I've got to go. Today."

"Where can Miss Devereux reach you?" Danny asked, taking a pad of paper and a pen from the counter.

"I can't tell you now," Serena hedged, not wanting Danny to give Craig her address if he should call. "Tell Diana I'll be in contact with her attorney. She'll know what she has to do."

Craig let the phone ring ten times before hanging up. No answer. Not even a pickup on the answering machine so he could leave Serena a message. He had been calling the guest house every fifteen minutes for the past two hours without success, and now, as he sat on his bed in the Holiday Inn on La Cienega, he began to worry. What had Serena done after leaving him this morning? And why was her machine not picking up? He wished he had called her right away, had tried to make her see that he loved her, and was devastated that he'd hurt her by keeping his relationship with Diana a secret.

Next, Craig called the main house, and was not surprised to learn from Danny that Serena had moved out, but Danny didn't know where she had gone. All he knew was that a man in a blue van had carted Serena and her belongings away late in the afternoon, and Diana had left for Europe.

News that Diana had gone to Europe on the spur of the moment was not surprising, especially in light of their last evening together. She often ran off to a spa or some resort to pull herself together when she was upset or depressed, and though she swore she'd never had plastic surgery, Craig knew better. He had seen the faint scars behind Diana's ears, the evidence of stitches at the edges of her hairline, even the scar above the soft triangle of her pubic hair. She had been under the knife several times and most likely was going under again. Craig sighed. But where was Serena?

Hanging up the phone, Craig sat with his hands on his knees, thinking, his mind crowded with worry. Who would have helped her move? Impulsively, he called Sammi, who had grown close to Serena since New Year's Eve, but Sammi had not heard from Serena.

"Damn," Craig groaned, rubbing his chin. "Women. What a hassle." He probably should have shoved Diana into a taxi as soon as she showed up last night, then gone to Serena and told her the truth. But he let Diana stay, initiating this disaster, because he had felt he owed it to her. He'd hurt her deeply, refusing to have sex, telling her he was in love with Serena. His confession had added to her miserable insecurity, but he'd done the right thing and had no regrets about it. Why hadn't he handled Serena with the same brutal honesty a long time ago?

The sudden ring of the phone startled Craig, who grabbed it and held his breath, hoping Sammi was calling with news that he had tracked Serena down. But it was Delbert Brooks with a question about the contract they were taking with a uniform company. Putting the situation with Serena aside, he resigned himself to concentrating on his business, knowing he'd set things straight with Serena soon enough.

Chapter Thirty-two

Joyce Ann ignored the impatient honk of the car's horn as she studied the front page of the latest edition of the *National Enquirer*. Taking it from the convenience store rack, she read the headline: SONGSTRESS, DIANA DEVREUX, RECOVERS IN SECLUSION AT POSH RESORT IN THE SOUTH OF FRANCE. The story, given to the reporter by an employee at the Regal Shore Resort, included photos of Diana Devreux strolling the grounds, bandages on her face, and provided details of the recent facial plastic surgery and liposuction the star had undergone. The two-page exposé also included photos taken of Diana before her operation, during her New Year's Eve bash at the MGM Grand. In one of the pre-operation photos, Diana was chatting backstage with a young woman with brown, highlighted hair, dressed in black. Beneath this photo, Joyce Ann read the caption: "Backstage at the MGM Grand, Diana consults with her celebrated stylist, Serena St. James, who many say had a great deal to do with the recent upswing in Diana Devreux's career."

That woman sure as hell looks like Sara Jane Talbot, Joyce Ann thought, slipping the newspaper under her shirt, then pushing out the door.

"What the hell took so long?" Tonk snapped, taking the six-pack of beer from Joyce Ann. He popped the top of a can and took a long swallow. "You're the one who wanted to get to Vegas before dark. I'd just as soon we waited until tomorrow."

"Shut up, Tonk," Joyce Ann tossed back, buckling her seat belt. "I wasn't in there five minutes. We been trying to get to Vegas for months. A few minutes in a convenience store ain't gonna make any difference."

Tonk raised one shoulder nonchalantly, then started the car without responding.

"Drive," Joyce Ann said, tired of Tonk's whining.

Tonk stuck his beer between his legs, pulled out of the parking lot, then swung up onto the freeway, whizzing past the road sign that read, LAS VEGAS, 73 MILES.

Joyce Ann let out a long breath and stared down the highway. She could see the desert heat shimmering from the asphalt, feel the scorching July sun on her legs through her jeans. She couldn't wait to get to Vegas, check into a motel and take a long cool shower after being cooped up in a car with Tonk for so long. Actually, she was getting sick of him. His drinking, slovenly personal habits, and even his occasional use of pot, were tolerable, but now she suspected he was using hard drugs again, shooting up when she was out of the room or asleep.

Since teaming up, they had always managed to scrape together enough money to survive—using stolen credit cards, burglarizing parked cars, shoplifting in discount stores. But she wanted to score big, in a legitimate way at one of the casinos on the strip. Once they got to Vegas, she was going to take half of the money they had, sit down in front of a slot machine and not move until her money ran out or she hit the jackpot. For some reason she felt lucky.

She cut her eyes at Tonk, watching him as he drove, weary of their association, but thankful he had introduced her to the Internet and showed her all the ways she could use it to score. She could buy most anything she wanted with stolen credit card numbers online with very little chance of getting caught. She had accessed enough personal and financial information from strangers to create a fake ID card and a birth certificate, which she would need once she arrived in Vegas and settled down to making real money.

Joyce Ann also planned to make money ordering products online, then reselling them on the Internet, where her activities would be hard to trace, moving the merchandise simply through cyberspace. And she had begun tracking her prison escape on the Texas Department of Corrections website, relieved to learn that the authorities had no new leads posted about where she might be. But her attempt to find Sara Jane had stalled.

When she and Sara Jane had been in high school they had gone to the Mallard Post Office together to apply for their Social Security numbers. When their cards arrived, they had compared them, noting the similarities. Joyce Ann's number had differed from Sara Jane's by only one number: the last two digits on Sara Jane's card were five and six, while hers were five and four. The latest employment record Joyce Ann had found for Sara Jane had been at a beauty salon in Dallas, but her telephone inquiry had led to a dead end.

But Joyce Ann wasn't worried. *You'll be hearing from me soon, Sara Jane,* Joyce Ann silently mused, leaning back in her seat, the uncanny resemblance between the woman in the paper and her old buddy hanging in her mind.

By mid-July, after a month in Los Angeles, Craig had signed all of the contracts, refurbished his limos, started his advertising campaign, and hired six eager drivers to launch Prime Time Limos in Los Angeles. With the mountains of paperwork and long stressful days of putting the deal together behind him, he should have felt elated, but he didn't. What joy was there in reaching this goal when he still had not heard from Serena? Bringing Prime Time Limos into the market-place had helped take his mind off Serena during the day, but the nights were not easy to bear. He lay awake thinking about her, won-dering how she had managed to disappear so quickly, how he had managed to bungle his relationship with her so badly. Without Serena, the success of his business venture meant little.

Over the past month, Craig had spoken to Danny several times, questioned Dean Banks and Vincent Ruby, who had not been able to help him, and called Marvin Erwin. The attorney told Craig he had spoken with Serena on the phone on June 20, to explain the conse-quences of breaking her contract with Diana, but he did not know where she was living. Craig, remembering his conversation with Serena about the house she had wanted to rent from a man named Raul Torres, had tracked down and telephoned three men with that name in the Las Vegas area and called them. But none of them knew what he was talking about. Sammi telephoned often, checking in, hop-ing for news, worried that something may have happened to Serena. When he suggested hiring a private detective to track her down, Craig rebuffed the idea, knowing that Serena would feel threatened if he went that far. He had to respect her need to be alone, give her time to heal, but he was not about to give up on her completely.

The many candlelit dinners, lively conversations, carefree excur-sions, and intimate moments Serena had shared with Craig slipped into her thoughts at least once a day during the month it had taken for her to get settled into her new home and find a job. After moving out of Diana's compound, Serena was content to live quietly, normally, working as a hairstylist at the Heavenly Hair Salon in the Corona Hotel and Casino. It was a job, and it did not involve an exclusive arrangement with an individual client so she was not in violation of her contract with Diana.

The money was not great, but the tips were good, and the steady paycheck anchored her, fueling her commitment to make it on her own. The job had plunged her back into a reality she could understand and appreciate, because life with Diana had been too grand, too rich, too much larger than life. She never spoke to her fellow stylists about her stint with the famous Diana Devreux and enjoyed being anonymous, simply a beautician known as Sara who faithfully served her clientele, which included showgirls, tourists, waitresses, and entertainers, women, men, and quite a few who openly crossed those lines.

But on an evening in early August, her old friend Sammi walked in and called her by name.

"Well, Serena St. James," Sammi muttered, hurrying over to her cubicle, staring in disbelief.

Serena gasped, jumping up from her styling chair where she had been working on a hairpiece, terrified that her anonymity had been shattered. She glanced around, relieved to see that only one other stylist, three stations down from hers, was still in the shop.

Sammi stopped at her station and scolded her, wagging a finger. "Girl. I've been looking everywhere for you. Where have you been?" He spotted an empty chair, rolled it over to Serena's station, then sat down, scooting closer to Serena, who set aside the hairpiece and gave Sammi a quick hug.

"Hello, Sammi. Been right here for about three weeks," Serena replied uneasily, glad to see him, yet hoping her colleague, who was engrossed in conversation with his client, had not heard Sammi call out her name.

"Well, you must be doing okay. Beautiful as ever. Let me look at you! Wearing your hair a little shorter, a little blonder, I see?" he said.

"Not really, " Serena replied. Actually, her hair was longer and less highlighted than when she had been working for Diana, but that didn't matter. What mattered was the fact that Sammi was here; a connection to her life with Diana had finally surfaced. She had known it would happen sooner or later, and now she realized that it felt good to be recognized by someone who actually knew her.

"I was wondering if I'd ever see you again," he went on. "But Vegas is just a small town with a lot of people passing through, you know? It's difficult to get totally lost in this place. So, where in the world have you been hiding? Danny told me you simply walked out on Diana. Craig's a total wreck. I couldn't believe you would just up and leave Diana. Not a good move, girlfriend. You know she's the kind to hold a grudge."

"I don't doubt that," Serena nodded. "But it's a long a story, Sammi. Things got complicated, I had to get out. Let's leave it at that."

"Fine," he said, "but what about Craig? He's called me a thousand times in the past month. Going crazy trying to find you . . . and who would have thought you'd be here!" He rolled his eyes, taking in the salon, scrutinizing every corner. "This is my backup salon. When George, over at LaChere can't fit me in, I come over here to get my touch-ups." He put his slender fingers into the crown of his shoulder-length blonde hair and tugged it. "As you can see, I am in great need of your services."

Serena laughed, swiveling her chair. "All right, Sammi. I was planning on leaving after I finished this hairpiece, but come on over to the shampoo bowl. I'll fix you up."

"Where are you living these days?" Sammi asked after he was seated and draped.

Serena hesitated, not sure she wanted to tell Sammi about the sanctuary she had created for herself on Spring Mountain Road. The absence of visitors made it special, all hers, a place where no one came up the driveway leading to her house except the mailman and tourists who got lost and had to turn around. The isolation was soothing, helped her keep her perspective, and the quiet kept her calm. "I've rented a house on the outskirts of town," she said, letting it go at that.

"Okay, I get it. You want to be secretive. Fine, I won't pry. But what in the world are you doing *here?*"

"It's called working, Sammi," Serena replied. "And I would appreciate it if you did not tell Craig or Danny or Diana or anyone where I am. And call me Sara, please. I'm not ready to be recognized as Diana Devreux's former stylist."

"My lips are sealed." He put a finger to his mouth, smiling. "Well, at least I know you are alive and well."

"And back to normal," she added.

"Normal? After the madcap whirl of life with Diana Devreux, I can't image why you'd be content to be normal!"

"But I'm happy, Sammi." Serena tilted Sammi up and applied conditioner to his hair. "Enough about me. Look at you! Great color. What is this? Platinum? Blonde?" she asked. "This is not going to be easy to match. Help me out."

"Silver Snow," he told her, swinging around to see her. "Lovely, isn't it?"

Serena put Sammi under the dryer while she disappeared into the back room, then emerged a few minutes later, stirring a plastic container of color. She motioned for him to sit in her chair.

"Okay, tell me *everything* while you touch me up. *Everything,* you hear?"

"I don't know about that," Serena laughed, applying the color with a small brush to a section of Sammi's hair. How much did she dare reveal to the only person it seemed she might be able to trust? "However, I will admit that I miss Craig. Terribly. I wish things had turned out differently."

As she applied color to Sammi's dark roots, she explained what had happened, and that despite her disappointment with him, her feelings about Diana were torn. She was angry, yet she was thankful that Diana had given her a break and opened her eyes to the truth about Craig—a man Serena had thought she knew well enough to marry. As much as Serena wanted to hate Diana, she couldn't. None of this was really Diana's fault. He had been the one to insist they keep their relationship secret.

Serena confessed that she alternately cursed Craig, then craved him, holding back tears as she talked. She admitted that at a low point she had called the Wind Way Arms and asked for him, only to be told by the desk clerk that he no longer resided at the hotel and had left no forwarding address.

"So, where is he, Sammi?" she finally brought herself to ask, finished with the color job on Sammi's silver locks.

"Los Angeles, honey. Started his own business. Prime Time Limos. It's gonna go over big. First-class operation, he says."

"Prime Time Limos. Nice name. Good for him. It's what he wanted," Serena said, feeling a little jealous that Craig had moved so quickly on his dream, while hers still languished in unopened boxes and folders. The abrupt move, the separation from Craig, the time it was taking to get settled into her new routine had consumed her, forcing her to put Beautopia on hold. Maybe it was time to refocus.

"And what about you? Why are you wasting your talent like this, Serena?" Sammi asked. "You're too good, and too young, to toss away a fabulous career."

"Chalk my situation up to the noncompete clause in my contract with Diana. This is temporary, but okay for now. I have my reasons for keeping a low profile. I also have something great I'm working on." She thought briefly of telling Sammi about the line of cosmetics she wanted to develop, about her hope that one day they would be for sale at hotel salons and spas on the strip, but held back.

"And what is that?"

"Later, Sammi. Now is not the right time to let you in on my plan. But when it's set to go, you'll be the first to know."

Sammi tilted back his head as Serena blow-dried his damp hair, "Too bad about Diana, huh?" he said.

Serena paused, holding the dryer above Sammi's head, then asked, somewhat cautiously, "What about her?"

"I heard she's in a hospital in France, very sick. Got some kind of infection as a result of that surgery or liposuction she had in France. I ran into Marvin Erwin at Lucci's Deli the other day. He told me he flew over to see Diana, take her some legal papers that needed her signature. He said she looks like a skeleton. Not good."

"That's awful," Serena replied, genuinely sorry. "Why is she still over there, anyway? She's been gone almost two months. Might get better medical care here, or in Los Angeles or New York."

"That's exactly what Marvin told her, but she refused. Too much press, she says. If the legitimate press got wind of her condition, it might wreck future bookings, she thinks. But a tabloid already ran a story about her surgery. Some kitchen worker at the resort where she's staying took some photos of her walking around the grounds during her recovery, then sold the story. Didn't you see it?"

"No, I never read those things," Serena said, putting the finishing touches on Sammi's new 'do. "I've tried to distance myself from all of that, so this is news to me."

"Well, honey. Diana's a fighter. She'll beat this and come home. Back on top again."

"Right," Serena said, feeling sad for Diana, who had never done anything but try to help her. She remained quiet, thinking until she had finished styling Sammi's hair.

"Fabulous," he remarked, studying the results in the mirror. "I'm so glad I decided to pop in here today."

"Me, too," Serena admitted. "I needed to see a friendly face." She relaxed, nodding. "Let's stay in touch."

"Yes, let's." Sammi stood, opened his wallet and took a fifty and handed it to Serena. "Thanks, love. And a phone number, please?"

"Call me here, or on my cell phone, five, five, five, six, five, six, five."

"Honey write it down before I leave. You know I won't remember."

"No problem," Serena said, jotting down her number, before giving Sammi a hug, and walking him to the door.

During the drive home, Serena had a lot on her mind. Craig was in Los Angeles, launching his company. Diana was in Europe, very ill. The news about both had shaken her much more than she had thought it would, and forced her to admit how much those two people were still entwined in her life. She loved Craig. Still cared about Diana. But they had created a complicated situation that had been impossible to unravel. Getting out had been her best option.

Diana, she thought. They had become extremely close during the short time they had been together, and it had been stressful, but fun, working for her. The shopping sprees. The wild makeup sessions. The crazy hairdos and trendy clothes. Though the twenty-plus-year age difference had placed them in two different generations, they had often been more like sisters than employee and boss. And to think of Diana confined to a hospital in a foreign country was upsetting. Serena wondered who was with her, who cared enough to sit by her bedside and hold her hand. Not Craig Alexander, that's for sure. He was obviously too busy moving up in the world to break away and see about his old friend, Diana. His shallowness infuriated Serena, and made her glad, again, that she had not tried to find him.

Serena sped along the highway, her windows rolled down, enjoying the warm evening. The desert sky was deepening into blue, and a few stars were already peeking out in the vast expanse overhead. The scene reminded Serena of a night sky in Texas, sending her thoughts back home. She wondered how Precious was coping with her handicap. Had she had found work that made her feel useful and whole? What was going on with Nina Richards at Havensway? And Joyce Ann Keller? Was she still at the Cave, still angry at the world, or had she softened with time? Thinking of her old friends made Serena's pulse begin to race. It was unusual for her to allow her thoughts to wander to memories of Precious, Joyce Ann, or Havensway because such thoughts inevitably led her to thinking about Marcella Jacobs, bringing the horrible incident back into her head. And once she let it in, it was difficult to remove.

Nearly seven years had passed since that dreadful night, and still, the image of Joyce Ann shooting Marcella made her ill. Sometimes it would appear in her dreams, vivid and intense, waking her up, making her cry. Since moving into her own place, she had tried to keep busy—working at the salon while refusing to let loneliness catch up with her, but tonight it was striking her hard.

So many people were gone, leaving her isolated and lonely. Precious, Joyce Ann, Diana, and Craig—gone from her life. Now, there was only Sammi, a gregarious, friendly transvestite who understood Serena's mixed feelings about Diana and Craig, but who knew nothing about who she really was. But as sorry as Serena was feeling for herself tonight, she had brought this isolation on herself, and now wasn't sure she liked it.

When Serena entered the driveway leading to her house the

thought struck her that she ought to call Danny and find out how to get in touch with Diana. Their abrupt parting still bothered Serena, who had convinced herself that eventually the two of them would meet face to face and say a proper good-bye. But if they had to do it over the phone, so be it. Serena could not wait until Diana returned from Europe to straighten out that part of her life.

Serena got out of the car and headed to the house, which sat on ten acres of land among a stand of pines at the end of a gravel drive. The two-story bungalow had become her sanctuary, her retreat, a place where she felt safe. Safe from whom? she wondered. Craig? But deep in her heart she knew she yearned for him to come looking for her, catch her in a weak moment, and convince her to forgive him. She loved him, always would, but had not gone searching for him, hoping he'd seek her out. But now that she knew he was in Los Angeles and knew the name of his company, she could find him if she wanted. Serena put the idea out of her mind, afraid of making a fool of herself, of forgiving him for breaking her heart. She wondered if Sammi would keep his word and not tell Craig where she worked.

Inside the house, Serena took a bottle of water from the refrigerator and unscrewed the cap, then sat at the kitchen table, fighting the temptation to call information for Prime Time Limo.

"Leave it alone," she decided, taking a sip of water as she picked up the remote control and zapped the television.

The evening news was on, with video footage of a local bank robbery. Serena leafed through a magazine as she halfway listened to the description of the situation, her mind still on Craig. But when a special report came on, she turned her attention to the screen and Peter Jennings' face, which had replaced the local broadcaster.

"Legendary singer and entertainer, Diana Devreux, died this morning in a hospital in Paris," Jennings said. "Attending physicians report the cause of death as systemic poisoning, stemming from an infection she contracted after extensive plastic surgery three weeks ago. Diana Devreux shot to superstardom while a teenager, singing lead with the Spirit Sisters, then went on to carve out a successful solo career that lasted two decades. She won three Grammys, and a nomination for an Emmy for her role as Rachel in the TV docudrama, *Without Expectation*. Diana Devreux, dead on August fifth, at the age of forty-four."

A chill ran through Serena. She jolted forward in her chair, listening to the commercial that had come on after the Special Report announcement, feeling cold and empty. She wrapped her arms around her waist and stared hard at the group of people who were laughing and sipping Pepsi on the patio of a beach house, as if willing Peter Jennings to come back and tell the world he had made a mistake, and Diana Devreux was not dead. It was impossible to move, to process the fact that Diana Devreux, the woman who had believed in her, recognized her talent, rescued her from the drudgery of a life as a shampoo girl, and brought her into a world of illusion and glamour was dead.

"Why?" Serena whispered, wishing she had spoken to Diana, told her how much she hated what happened between them, and that Craig was to blame, not her. But that was impossible now. She'd never get the chance.

Serena began to cry, a soft sob that burned in her chest, and made her eyes water. The actors in the commercial evolved into a ghostly blur of heads and hands and moving mouths, a group of stammering people uttering words Serena could not hear. In a daze, she picked up the phone to call Marvin Erwin and tell him how to contact her. If any memorial service was planned, he'd know about it, and she had to be there, to tell Diana good-bye.

Chapter Thirty-three

Joyce Ann tossed the newspaper across the unmade bed and waited while Tonk read the article.

"You sure?" he asked, one eyebrow raised.

"Absolutely," Joyce Ann replied, rapidly tapping keys on her laptop computer as she spoke.

"Maybe it's a cousin, or something," Tonk hedged. "Been a long time since you seen her."

"Nope," Joyce Ann shot back. "Sara Jane Talbot and Serena St. James are one and the same. See, I know her social security number, and I've been doing some checking. They have the same number, and with it, I accessed records that show cosmetology licenses for both of them: one in Texas, another in Nevada. Same number."

Tonk slowly folded the paper, then tossed it back at Joyce Ann, who let it fall at her feet, not breaking her concentration on the computer screen.

She remained silent, typing, yet thinking about what she had discovered. Now that she and Tonk were in Vegas, she was ready to get serious about finding Sara Jane Talbot, maybe hitting her up for some major bucks to keep her little secret. She'd heard on the news that Diana Devreux had died, and that a memorial service was going to be held in Las Vegas at some big church. If she kept her eyes open and lay low, she just might learn what her old friend was up to. Who knew what might happen then?

After arriving in Vegas, Joyce Ann and Tonk had hit the casinos and played the slots, managing to win enough money to rent an apartment in a rent-by-the-week complex. She liked Las Vegas, a place where she blended in and no one paid any attention to her, where she could hang out for quite a long time, at least until some better options came along. Maybe Serena St. James would be it.

"What are you going to do?" Tonk asked, breaking into Joyce Ann's thoughts.

"Right now, nothin'," she replied. "I'm in no hurry to let Sara Jane Talbot know where I am. That's the last person I'd want to know that I'm in Vegas. Can't trust her to keep her mouth shut. I know from experience. For now, I plan to stay in the shadows and keep tabs on her. I got time. If I wait long enough, I'll find out what she's got going on, then move when the time is right. Oh, she's gonna hear from me, all right. But I'll be the one to say when." Joyce Ann reached down and picked up the newspaper and stuck it under her computer. "Let's get out of here. I feel lucky. Let's hit the strip and see what happens."

The management of the MGM Grand had placed an ornately framed life-sized photo of Diana Devreux in the hotel lobby as a tribute to the legendary diva. During the seven days between the announcement of Diana's death and the private memorial, which was scheduled to take place at Paradise Baptist Church, the area turned into a shrine. Fans, tourists, and curiosity seekers flocked to the hotel lobby, jammed the sidewalks, and cruised the street anxious to see who came and went, placing flowers or mementos of remembrance in front of the striking image.

As Serena dressed for the private memorial service, she watched the frenzy on TV, forcing back tears, as she had during the numerous tributes, in-depth biographies, and retrospectives of Diana's career that seemed to be on every television and radio station. And Serena had been shocked at how often her name had been mentioned, with Serena St. James being credited very often in the news reports for orchestrating the cutting-edge look that had boosted Diana's profile and helped boost her popularity during the past six months. Now, it all seemed like a dream. A wonderful, terrifying, exciting experience that had happened to someone else.

Serena pulled on her black linen jacket, picked up her car keys, and lowered her sunglasses over her eyes, anxious about facing the crush of reporters that would surely be stationed outside the church. Her phone had been ringing nonstop for days, and the amount of money the press was offering her for an interview was staggering. But her lips were sealed. As soon as the announcement of Diana's death hit the air, she reread the contract, aware that her confidentiality clause prevented her from writing about, selling, or discussing with the media, anything related to her experiences as an employee of Diana Devreux, Inc., for one year after terminating her employment. Serena had no problem adhering to the terms. All she wanted to do was to get through the service without breaking down and without an unpleasant encounter with Craig, whom Marvin had told her would be in town for the memorial. Serena wondered how long Craig intended to stay in Vegas.

The crowd was huge, but subdued, outside the church. Serena ascended the steep flight of steps leading to the front door of the church, her feet moving slowly, her heart sinking fast. At the entrance, a matronly woman dressed in white greeted her and gave her a pale blue program, then handed her over to an usher, who escorted Serena down the center aisle. In front of the altar an oversized oil painting of Diana stood on a gilded easel, banked by exquisite white orchids, pink roses, and sprays of delicate baby's breath. The organist was playing as a soloist sang. The setting was classic Diana: sophisticated and elegant, satisfying and stirring the soul, as her music had done.

Serena stood and gazed at Diana's image, taking in her beauty, her youthful appearance, her vitality, wondering why in the world she had gone to France to undergo unnecessary plastic surgery. What had pushed her insecurities to the point that she had taken such a drastic step? Was it the music industry that had pressed her to this breaking point, or had Craig's rejection had anything to do with her death? Serena shuddered at the thought of Diana being so desperate to remain competitive that she had felt the need to try to hold her own against the threat of the young talent coming onto the scene by going under the knife. To Serena, Diana had seemed perfect. Why hadn't she been able to see it? Serena pressed her handkerchief to her nose, shaking her head.

When she turned, prepared to take a seat, she glanced down the aisle and saw Craig entering the church. He caught her watching him, but made no gesture of recognition, so she lowered her eyes and started down the aisle to her seat. He came toward her, paused, as if uncertain about what to do, but did not speak. She walked straight past him and sat down. Craig leveled a questioning look at Serena, then continued up to the altar, leaving her to study the line of his back, the way he bent his head, the cut of his suit across his shoulders, and struggle to calm her rapidly pounding heart.

Outside the church, Joyce Ann leaned against a telephone pole and watched the crowd build. The reporters, fans, tourists, and locals who had come to watch the parade of celebrities paying their respects to Diana Devreux jostled each other, trying to get close to the velvet ropes that blocked them from the entry. But Joyce Ann remained on the fringes of the crowd, satisfied to have caught a glimpse of Serena St. James as she entered the church. Excited and pensive, Joyce Ann made up her mind to keep a close eye on her old friend and see what might develop.

Precious clicked through Diana Devreux's website with a heavy heart, reading the comments of condolence and sympathy posted on the fans' message board. The entries were coming in from all over the world, each one lamenting the loss of such a great talent. Throughout the site there were photos of Diana when she was young and starting out, of her two husbands, and of her accepting a Grammy Award. There were photos of Diana on stage in New York, Los Angeles, and Las Vegas, along with coverage of the crowds standing before the huge floral blanket that had sprung up outside the MGM Grand. The collage of memories was a stunning tribute to an enormous talent, but there was nothing new that Precious could use for *Celebrity Today*. The photos on the website had already been playing on television for days.

Precious clicked onto the tab titled, *Yesterday's Private Memorial for Diana*. The first image to come up made Precious catch her breath. The ceremony had been limited to fifty people who had been close to Diana, and their names were listed beneath their pictures as they came out of the church. First, Serena St. James, Diana's famous stylist, stepped out, followed by Marvin Erwin, Diana's long-time lawyer; Vincent Ruby, her agent and manager; Dean Banks, her financial advisor; and Craig Alexander, her bodyguard and chauffeur. The pain on each face was evident, and Craig was holding a handkerchief to his eyes. But it was the young woman's face that mesmerized Precious, and once again she felt the chill of recognition that had hit her the first time she had seen it, an overwhelming sense of familiarity. She had tried checking out Serena St. James several times, but always hit a dead end. The beautiful stylist had no website, no celebrity client history, and no address other than Diana Devreux, Inc. In fact, she had no past.

"It's Sara Jane Talbot," Precious murmured. "It must be her. No two people could look that much alike." She slumped back in her wheelchair, stunned, knowing she would not rest until she found out who that woman was. But how? Precious rubbed her thumb and index finger together, thinking. The best avenue to the truth might be though

Diana's attorney, Marvin Erwin, whose address was posted on his website. A letter to him would be delivered to Serena St. James, wouldn't it? Precious pulled up a blank screen on her word processing program and began to write, not certain about what was she going to say, only certain that she was going to find out if Serena St. James and Sara Jane Talbot were one and the same.

Chapter Thirty-four

The rush of desire that Serena felt when Craig entered the room was quickly replaced with anger. During the five days since she had seen him at the memorial service he had not called or tired to find her. He could have found her if he'd been as anxious to talk to her as Sammi had indicated. Obviously, he wasn't that interested. Now, his curt nod and his casual manner ignited a spark of resentment. Serena watched silently as Craig greeted Dean; Marvin; and Thomas Young, the attorney in Marvin's office who had overseen the changes in Diana's will.

After everyone had been seated around the boardroom conference table, Serena shifted her chair and twisted her body, presenting her profile to Craig. At least she'd had the good sense not to speak to him at the memorial service, she thought, remembering how excited she had felt when he came into the church. The short ceremony had been a beautiful musical tribute to Diana, with Vincent Ruby and the head of Breeze Records giving brief, but glowing tributes to her life and her talent. Afterward, reporters had formed a solid wall around Serena, hounding her for a comment, but she had escaped to her car and driven off, watching in her rearview mirror as Craig had done the same. Serena had thought he had gone back to Los Angeles. Now she saw that he had not.

Diana had no surviving blood relatives, as her immediate family had passed away long ago, and looking around the room full of business associates, Serena better understood why Diana had pushed herself to stay on top: her career had been her life. With no children, nieces, aunts, or uncles with whom to share her blessings, she had devoted herself to her fans, the people who had given her the love and attention she craved.

Diana had been alone in the world, just like me, Serena thought, realizing how much in common they had shared, despite the vast differences in their situations. *Diana protected my secret and gave me a reason to hope, pulling me into her fabulous life. She treated me much better than I treated her at the end,* Serena thought, hating the fact that Diana had died without knowing how sorry Serena was about having to walk out.

"I'll get right to the point," Marvin started, interrupting Serena's thoughts. He turned to Craig, then Serena, opening a folder that lay flat on the table. "Diana Devreux left no heirs. She earned vast amounts of money during her career, but she also was a world-class shopper. She had expensive tastes and purchased thousands of valuable items, many of which she stashed in storage lockers and safe deposit boxes that we are still discovering. Her debts were few, so the estate will wind up being quite large after everything is settled. With no immediate surviving next of kin, she directed a large portion of her estate to go to the Independent Recording Artists Fund."

"What is that?" Serena asked, curious.

Craig leaned toward her, forcing her to turn and look at him. "It's a nonprofit organization that awards scholarships to recording artists who want to go back to school and earn their high school diplomas or undergraduate degrees. Diana always regretted that she dropped out of high school. This is her way of helping others get an education."

"I see," Serena replied, locking eyes with Craig, hating the way her stomach flipped over, loving the way he looked. He had changed, she realized. Not so much in the way he looked, but in the way he carried himself. His impeccable suit, his tasteful gold jewelry, his soft, leather briefcase all screamed success. Obviously his business was doing well. But it was more than the outer trappings that impressed Serena. Craig seemed more calm, less arrogant and edgy than she remembered. She swallowed her joy at seeing him again, hoping he had suffered as much as she had since they separated, then lowered her lashes and turned back to face Marvin, who was concentrating on separating a bundle of papers.

"Now. The reason I wanted you two to come in," he began, clearing his throat as he glanced at the papers. "Diana made a very explicit bequest involving both of you. She requested that all royalties, past and future, from her album, *One and Only* be split fifty-fifty between Serena St. James and Craig Alexander."

Serena sucked in a gulp of air, shocked.

Craig whistled softly, then cocked his head to one side and gave Marvin a dubious look. "All royalties?" he clarified.

"That's right," Marvin said.

Serena jerked around and caught Craig's attention, her mouth open in surprise. "Why?" she asked, stunned. "I don't understand." When Marvin had asked her to come to his office, she had thought he needed to clear up some loose ends related to her employment with Diana, perhaps to sign another confidentiality agreement to prevent her from profiting from Diana's death with a tell-all book or a paid interview. Never had she dreamed that Diana had included her in her will.

"Why?" Marvin repeated. He took a deep breath. "I flew to France to meet with Diana to draft a codicil to her will. She was very fragile. I think she knew she was dying. When I asked the same question, she said, 'Craig made me feel safe. I could always depend on him. Serena made me feel young and beautiful at a time in my life when I wasn't so sure I could ever feel that way again. *One and Only* belongs to them.'"

The words sent chills through Serena. *Craig had made Diana feel safe.* She held her breath, recalling the pain she had felt when she learned about their intimate relationship, realizing how much Diana had depended on Craig.

Dean Banks, the financial wizard, broke the silence. "I've calculated the gross earnings on *One and Only*: three million two hundred thousand so far, and you can be sure it will not level off because Diana is gone. If anything, sales will increase since it was her last recording." Dean smiled at Serena, tapping the spreadsheet in front of him. "Congratulations, Serena. You're a very wealthy woman." He shot a glance at Craig, not smiling. "And the same goes for you." Then he uncapped his Mont Blanc pen and studied a legal form. "I think I have all the information I need to process the royalty payments for you, Craig. But Serena," he paused. "I need your address." Pen poised to write, he waited.

What the hell? Serena thought, tired of hiding, tired of avoiding Craig, exhausted with insulating herself from the world. She might as well come clean. "Eight thousand three Spring Mountain Road," she said, staring directly at Craig, who smiled at her for the first time, seeming to be relieved that he had not had to ask her for the information.

Dean scribbled the address on the form, then shut his folder. "Drop by my office for copies of the financial details . . . and any advice you two might need about managing your newfound wealth." He nodded at Serena, Craig, then left.

"Well!" Craig said, shaking his head. "I never expected anything like this!"

Serena focused on Craig, expecting him to say something to her now, but he simply grinned, giving her that familiar look that melted her heart and made her want to kiss him. She swallowed her desire and broke contact, turning back to Marvin.

"You both deserve it," Marvin said, gathering his papers. "Diana was extremely grateful for your enthusiastic dedication to her career." At the door, he stopped and looked back at Craig and Serena. "You two can stay as long as you want. I'm sure you have things to talk over. Congratulations. That's a lot of money. Work with Dean on how to best invest it."

Serena nodded. "Definitely."

"I'm off to lunch," Marvin said. "With Johnny Cochran. In town for that Torleoni hearing. You can lock the door when you go out." Then Marvin paused and reached into the packet of papers in his arms. "Serena, this is for you." He handed her a small envelope, the size of a greeting card. "Came to my office day before yesterday addressed to you."

"Thanks," Serena said, accepting the envelope. She glanced at it briefly and saw no return address. "Another sympathy card from one of Diana's fans, I suppose," she said, sticking it into the side pocket of her purse. Marvin departed, shutting the door softly behind him.

Serena quickly pulled her chair around to face Craig, ready to clear the air. After learning from Sammi how desperate he had said he had been to find her, why hadn't he even spoken to her since his return? And she wanted some answers, no matter how hurtful they might be. It was the only way to let go of the past.

"This unexpected windfall does not mean that we are partners or that I want to have anything to do with you, Craig," she started, testing him. "I don't know what you think of me now, or what you ever expected of me, but I have to tell you that I never expected you to make a fool of me. Not with Diana Devreux."

"But you disappeared. I called and called from Los Angeles, trying to find you, to let you know how sorry I was, but couldn't find you. No one, not even Danny knew where you had gone."

"You lied to me. You ripped out my heart by not being truthful from the start. I never wanted to hear your voice or see you again. It was just too painful."

Craig rubbed his lips with his fingertips, nervous. "All I ever wanted was you . . . and I blew it. Maybe I should have stayed around, not gone to L.A. right away, but I had to close that deal on those limos or lose everything. I never thought that you'd disappear."

Craig reached out and took Serena's hand, holding it tightly. "I hurt you and I am sorry. Believe me, I am. Yes, I did sleep with Diana, but I never loved her. It was just sex. A crazy attempt to find the kind of love I was searching for, that I eventually found with you. That's all I can say, Serena."

"Why didn't you speak to me at the memorial service? Sammi told me you'd been calling him, looking for me. Why the cold shoulder?"

"Because I was nervous, frightened that you would reject me again. I had to let you make the first move, Serena. If you didn't want me . . ." his voice trailed off.

Serena leveled her face with Craig's, locking eyes with him. "I know. I understand it all now, but I was still hurting, unable to see things from your perspective."

"You don't hate me?" His voice fell.

"No," she whispered. "We both went about it all wrong. I blamed you for mistakes in the past, acting as if I were perfect. I've made mistakes, too, Craig. Horrible mistakes that you don't know about."

"And which do not matter now," he added softly.

Serena's face went still and her long-held anger dissolved. She pushed away from the table, went over to the wall of legal books, and quietly gazed at them, her heart filled with hope that they could repair the damage they had done.

The silence in the room was alarming, and the absence of ringing phones and office noise in the outer rooms seemed eerie, making Serena feel suspended and confused. She wanted so much to hear him say, "Come back to me. Let's try again," because she could not bring herself to ask.

Craig broke the silence, urgency in his tone. "I love you. I fell in love with you the first time I saw you." He got up and came to Serena. "Our relationship wasn't complicated, we were moving too fast, unable to sort out the present, the past, or the future. It all became a blur, and for me there had been too much loneliness, so I probably put too much pressure on you, too soon."

Serena turned so he could put his arms around her.

"I want you back, Serena." His face was inches from hers. "I'm asking you to let me prove how much I love you."

Though she wanted so much to start over, Serena knew she had to be cautious. "I love you, too, but you hurt me deeply, Craig."

"I know. And I hurt Diana, too. She was upset over her birthday, and when I told her I was in love with you, I should have known how awful it would make her feel. I've often wondered whether or not my rejection that night pushed her into making a rash decision, made her think about getting plastic surgery. Don't you see? I didn't wish her ill. Maybe if it hadn't been for me, she might still be alive. I feel terrible about what happened to her." Craig turned away, pulled out a chair, slumped into it, crossing his arms on the table. He cradled his head on his arms.

Serena went to him, stroked his back, and felt his pain, his confusion. She sat down next to him, unsure of what to say or how to let him know that she wanted to forgive him, start over, and renew their love. She continued stroking his shoulders, his neck, his head, remaining quiet, thinking of how close they had been, how much fun they had had, the dreams they had shared, and the pain of living without him. At that moment, she knew it would be up to her to set things straight.

"I do love you, Craig," she murmured. "I've hated and loved you at the same time since I walked out of your room at the Wind Way Arms. I wish you had trusted me enough to tell me the truth at the beginning; none of this would have happened."

Craig lifted his head, tears on his cheeks. "I was so scared of losing you. I didn't think you'd understand."

The fear in Craig's eyes stung Serena, and she could not help but think about her own secrets, secrets far more damaging than his. How could she ever tell Craig that she was an ex-con, had served time in prison, been involved in a murder, and that her real name was not Serena St. James? No, it was too late for that now, and her secrets had far more serious ramifications than his liaison with an insecure older woman. Besides, with Diana deceased now, no one knew about her past and it could stay that way forever.

She kissed away his tears, her hands around his neck, seeking unspoken forgiveness with her gestures. When he reached out to take her in his arms, she let herself go limp, resting her head on his shoulder.

"I'm sorry, Craig. It was silly of me to think that hiding from the world would solve anything."

He kissed her on the lips, softly, tentatively, contrite in his movements. "I never wanted to lose you, Serena. I've been going crazy since you left. You're all that matters. Marry me. We can start over now that Diana is out of our lives, and at peace, I hope. Yes, she was a controlling, selfish, insecure woman who deeply cared for both of us . . . but we were selfish, too."

Serena nodded. "I know. We took from her what served our needs in order to get what we wanted, but it's over . . . and you can't feel guilty over the way she died."

"And you can't shut yourself away, Serena."

Serena did not resist when Craig kissed her. She eased onto his lap and arched her back to get closer to him, accepting his touch, his kisses, his caresses, starved for the love she had missed too long. Burying her face against his neck, she cried out in happiness to feel the warmth of his flesh against hers once again.

Chapter Thirty-five

Craig blinked into the sunlight glinting off the bumper of the Rolls-Royce stretch limo, taking in the car's sleek lines and soft dove-gray color. Everything about the car signaled luxury and class, exactly as he had hoped it would. The driver of the limo pulled into an empty parking spot beneath the sign, VEGAS PRIME TIME LIMOS, stopped beside a shiny black Lincoln trimmed in gold-tone chrome, and turned off the engine. The soft shudder of the Rolls shutting down, combined with the compact thud of its door slamming shut sent a curl of satisfaction through Craig. He smiled, put on his sunglasses, pushed through the glass doors leading out onto the parking lot, and walked under the green and white canopy toward the man who was waiting to be paid. Finally, after four months of nonstop work, his Las Vegas branch of Prime Time Limos was complete.

The royalties he had inherited from Diana's *One and Only* song track had been put to use very quickly, speeding up his ability to upgrade his Los Angeles location and expand his limo service into Vegas. Now, on New Year's Eve he had sixty-seven limousines between the two locations and would not have to turn down any job.

"It's a beauty, Mr. Alexander," the driver said, shaking hands with Craig.

"Sure is, Jake," he agreed, circling the Rolls to inspect it. He stopped on the opposite side of the car and looked at the driver over the roof. "How'd that dual security sound system work?"

The young driver nodded vigorously. "Like I had on my own personal set of headphones. Sure makes communicating with the clients a lot easier."

"Good," Craig said, glad he had made the investment to install the unique system that guaranteed his clients complete privacy, while allowing them to communicate with the driver. Once the window between the chauffeur and the passenger was securely shut, there was absolutely no way the driver could listen in on a conversation in the back. This was a feature that set his cars apart from those of other driving services.

Craig signed the delivery invoice and handed the slip of paper back to the driver. "I've got clients booked for this one tonight and tomorrow," he said, reaching into the pocket of his slacks. He took out a crisp fifty-dollar bill and handed it to the driver. "Thanks, Jake, for bringing this baby in on such short notice."

"No problem," Jake replied, shaking Craig's hand as he pocketed the money.

"You have a Happy New Year," Craig said, watching the driver leave.

Before going inside his office to finish up his work for the day, Craig took a few minutes to walk around his lot, greeting a curious couple who had stopped to admire his fleet, which gleamed like jewels in the bright winter sunshine. Among the super-stretch Lincolns and Cadillacs were several ten- to fifteen-passenger Lexus', Mercedes-Benz S-Class Sedans, four vintage Daimlers, three Bentleys, and a ten-passenger Jaguar that stayed booked. Most of his exotic cars came equipped with TVs, VCRs, fully stocked bars, and complimentary chocolates. He took pride in providing the kind of luxury that high rollers, celebrities, foreign dignitaries, and the superrich took for granted, and if a client requested a specific car he did not have on his lot, Craig had sources to locate it and have it available within four hours, guaranteed. Such service was expensive, of course, but that was no problem in a town like Vegas, where image, illusion, and luxury ruled, and dreams were meant to come true.

Craig opened the door to his favorite car, a 1958 Vintage Lincoln and slid behind the wheel. The smell of the leather, the gleam of the wood paneling, and the feel of the big wheel beneath his hands made him smile. In a few hours he would pick up Serena in the vintage limo and start off on what he hoped would be a magical evening of his own.

As he sat in the car, he could not help but feel happy. Over the past four months, they had been able to repair their relationship to the point where he believed Serena had forgiven him. Slowly, patiently, he was regaining her trust, by showing her how much he valued and respected her feelings, and letting her set the perimeters of the relationship. They had not made love since his return, but that was fine with him. His love for her was built on more than sex and he wanted Serena in his life forever—going too fast might have destroyed everything.

Craig began mentally clicking through the list of things he still had to do before he could leave the office: call Tile-Tex about that overdue order of chauffeur uniforms, call Channel 8 and confirm the date to tape his new commercial, get the payroll over to Dean Banks, who was handling his books, and send flowers to Betty, his assistant manager, whose father had recently passed away.

While thinking about the upcoming evening he had planned for Serena, his mind turned back one year, to last New Year's Eve, when after Diana's concert at the MGM Grand he had made love to Serena the first time. He sighed. So much had happened over the past twelve months, both good and bad, and from now on he was determined to make sure the good times outweighed the bad, and that included bringing Serena as close to him as possible.

Craig got out of the car and hurried back inside, thankful for the cool blast of air that greeted him, noting that it was going to be a very warm New Year's Eve. Throughout the showroom and in the conference cubicles, he saw that all of his sales staff were engrossed in conversations, helping clients make decisions, struggling to fulfill requests for last minute limos. The activity was not surprising, as every limo service in the city was probably booked solid, and after passing the desk of his assistant, Betty, who was explaining to a client why the car he had booked for next weekend would not be available tonight, Craig went into his office and shut the door.

Sitting in his rust-colored leather chair, he admired the decor, which Serena had helped him do in tones of brown, rust, beige, and black. The colors made a strong statement without creating a hard edge, providing an environment that signaled trust, security, and professionalism. He appreciated what Serena, to whom he had given carte blanche, had done to decorate the four rooms of his office. He had left all decisions up to her, setting no boundaries on what she could spend, and thoroughly enjoyed watching her spend it, with no worry about the bills.

With Serena's creative touches surrounding him, and a framed photograph of her on his desk, he always felt close to her, as if she were with him in the room. Now, he could hardly concentrate on the paperwork that needed to be completed before he left, his mind on tonight: dinner at Bally's Seasons, Eddie Murphy live at the Mirage, dancing at Club Rio, and after that, he crossed his fingers.

Craig opened his desk drawer, took out the square ring box he had held on to for months, and opened it. This time he was going to put the emerald cut diamond on Serena's finger, and if everything went as he planned, they'd be married by this time tomorrow night.

"Voilá," Serena said, spinning Sammi around so he could see himself in the mirror. "Is this what you wanted?" She presented him with a gilded hand mirror, then stepped back.

"Oh, my God," Sammi cried, bolting upright, staring at his reflection. "Oh, my God."

"Like it?"

"Yes!" He slumped back in the chair in disbelief, then shot forward again to take another look. "You really did it, girl. You made me into . . ."

"A bronzed Marilyn Monroe?" Serena prompted, unable to think of any other way to describe what she had done. He had come to her begging for a new look for his act, one that would set the audience up for a roaring evening of fun and leave them with an indelible impression. Sammi was a big man, but softly molded, and he walked with a swing in his step that could literally stop traffic on the strip. Now, the blonde wavy hair, pale makeup, false lashes and blue contact lenses that Serena had used to create his incredibly feminine illusion, had pulled together a fabulous and provocative image.

"Exactly what I wanted," Sammi breathed, examining every inch of his face and hair. "This is Marilyn, all right. Now all I need are my boobs."

"Which I see you left in your dressing room," Serena laughed, unsnapping the plastic cape from around Sammi's neck. She reached over to a shelf and took down a pink rose-shaped jar and handed it to Sammi. "As I promised. The newest addition to my line. The Beautopia Bayonet Mask. Use it three times a week, but no more, and it'll keep those hair bumps from coming back."

Sammi took the jar from Serena, balancing it in the palm of his hand, his eyes on her as he spoke. "You really got it together fast, girl," he said, running his thumb over one of the rose petals on the cap of the jar. He glanced around the salon, which was a buzzing cocoon of pink and white. "Didn't take you long to put Diana's money to use, did it? You've been working on this for a long time, huh?"

Serena sheepishly nodded. "My secret passion. This has been my dream . . . all my life, Sammi . . . to own a salon, to launch this line of products. They're based on an old formula of my mother's. All natural. Diana's gift allowed me to ditch the Corona, focus on this, and move forward."

"But why here? Brushton isn't the classiest part of town, you know?"

"Because this is where I need to be. There is not one beauty salon in a fifteen-block radius and I'm telling you, Sammi, I've been so busy . . . it's incredible. If I can stay one step ahead of the names on the books, I'm doing good. This section of Vegas had been written off as too dangerous, too isolated and rundown to support a business, but people are coming to my salon from all over. They don't seem to mind, and it's accessible to the strip without all the crowds and traffic. New businesses have opened during the past month, so good things are happening on the block."

"I guess you know what you're doing, girlfriend, but you're gonna have to get more phone lines, please, Serena. Your line was busy all afternoon, and I was frantic to get in."

"I've got two receptionists now," Serena assured him.

"Then get two more. And after I go on stage tonight, the word will be out! Beautopia will really be swamped!"

"Sammi, you're the best," Serena said, refusing to take the one-hundred-dollar bill he offered her. "Keep it. You are the best commercial I could ever have. I'll never take your money."

"I want a witness to that," Sammi said loudly, as he got out of the chair. "Serena says I never have to pay!"

Two stylists within earshot stopped what they were doing and laughed. "You got it," they called out at Sammi as he flicked his long fingernails at them.

"When I start showing up twice a week, y'all will start singing another tune," he joked

"Never," Serena tossed back.

Sammi winked playfully at Serena. "Honey, this salon is fabulous. I'm so proud of you. Your money sure talks."

"It wasn't easy, Sammi," Serena said. "Dean Banks was very helpful. Told me what I needed to do, and I followed his instructions. I walked the city, cruised in my car, and searched until I found this place. Then the hard stuff—paperwork, renovations, manufacturing the product line, hiring staff. I swear, in four months I went from doing hair at the Corona to ownership of Beautopia and I nearly lost my mind." Serena shook her head, as if she still could not believe how fast it had happened. "But I do have Craig around to keep me sane," she added slyly.

"Yes, you do," Sammi replied, leaning closer to Serena, lowering his voice. "So, how's it going? What's the latest?"

"We are fine, Sammi. He's got Prime Time Limos, I've got Beautopia. We stay so busy we have to make appointments to see each other. But I don't mind."

"And tonight?" Sammi asked.

"It's a secret. All I know is that I'd better get you out of here. I have to be ready at eight."

"I want details tomorrow," he called out.

"I'll think about it," Serena joked, grinning as Sammi sashayed out the door.

After he had left, she cleared her station, one eye on the clock above the entrance to the massage room. Seven-thirty. She had less than thirty minutes to get dressed and touch up her makeup. Thank God she had brought her evening clothes to the salon to get dressed, then meet Craig at the restaurant. She walked through the styling area, where ten stylists were busy curling, brushing, spraying, perming, and coloring clients, trying to get everyone out in time for whatever they planned to do to bring in the New Year.

Sammi wasn't the only one to question her decision to open Beautopia in Brushton, a predominantly black section of the city near downtown. Craig had been the first to caution her, expressing his concern for her safety in an area that had pockets of crime and could be rough at times. Shortly after opening the salon, burglars broke in and stole a TV, two hair dryers and her computer. But Serena persisted, installing a better security system and hiring a part-time guard, who arrived late in the afternoon and stayed until closing, which could be as late as eleven o'clock on a very busy Saturday.

Serena had replaced the stolen items and dug in, determined to stay. Her research and experience in the industry had shown she did not need to set herself up in competition with the hotel salons or the trendy, expensive white salons off the Strip. Here in Brushton, she had no competition and could provide her unique services to women who had never believed they could afford the luxuries Beautopia offered. Serena had no trouble keeping her appointment books full and waiting lists long. Women had begun to come to Beautopia from as far away as Lake Tahoe, now that the news had traveled beyond Vegas that she could provide makeovers, touch-ups, and unique rejuvenation experiences that only Beautopia could offer. She had learned a valuable lesson from Giani Pilugi: Find your niche and work it!

She hurried past the personal grooming salon where a half dozen or so women were sitting with their hands encased in paraffin wax, their feet propped on pedicure stools, faces covered with Beautopia mud masks.

In the midst of her assessment of her achievement, a sense of guilt hung over Serena. The salon was full, and in order to get everyone out, the staff would have to work far past the regular closing time, and she was tempted to call Craig and cancel so she could stay and help get everybody out at a decent hour. But she remembered Craig's warning: "I know you're the boss, but tonight we are bringing in the New Year together. Don't you dare get caught at work and cancel on me."

She had been working fifteen hours a day for weeks hiring staff, ordering equipment, shelving supplies, putting the final touches on the Beautopia Salon and Day Spa. The business had been successfully launched and she had staff she could trust to run the place in her absence. There was no reason to be late.

Serena retreated to her spacious office on the second floor above the salon, sat down on the pink and white print sofa, and put her feet up on the matching ottoman. She let her head fall back, closing her eyes, forcing the ache of the hectic day to drain from her body. Sammi was right. She needed more help, especially now that her website was up and she had begun selling products online. But there had been complaints about the turnaround time from initial order to product delivery, and three orders had fallen through the cracks. Her current distributor did not seem to understand how retail and e-commerce worked, and she needed someone to examine the system, overhaul her process, increase her reliability related to online sales. Internet revenue could be very lucrative if the product was accurately positioned and the right person was in charge. Serena sighed, her mind too full to take that on. She'd work on the problem tomorrow, when the salon was closed and she would be at home, hopefully with Craig, whose business advice she welcomed.

Sitting up, Serena opened her eyes and glanced over at the black-sequined dress hanging on the door that led to her private bathroom. The dress had cost twelve hundred dollars. More money than she had ever spent on an outfit, but tonight was special and she wanted to look fabulous for Craig. Serena wondered if he remembered what had happened between them a year ago tonight, and how drastically it had affected her.

"If I'm wearing that dress, I'd better dig out that black-sequined purse," she muttered, pushing herself off the sofa.

Serena still lived in the house on Spring Mountain Road, but had practically created another living space in the extra rooms above the salon because she was always bringing in changes of clothes, extra shoes, and purses to match. She kept her accessories in a pretty wicker three-drawer cabinet along with other personal items that had accumulated in the office over time. The bottom drawer was for shoes, the middle for underwear and panty hose; the top drawer held a variety of purses, scarves, and jewelry for quick changes when she and Craig went out directly from work.

Craig wanted her to move out of the house on Spring Mountain Road and into his spacious new condo that he'd bought soon after his return to Vegas, but she refused. The peace and quiet of her tiny retreat was too precious to give up, and if she ever moved in with Craig, it would be into a house built especially for them and she'd have a wedding band on her finger. Until then, their current arrangement suited her fine.

Serena opened the top drawer and rummaged around until she found the small black purse. Before closing the drawer, she noticed the edge of a card sticking out of her brown lizard bag, a bag she had not carried in months. Frowning, she removed the card and studied it, puzzled, then recalled that Marvin Erwin had given it to her the day of the reading of Diana's will. Her distraction with Craig had made her forget it, and she hadn't used the bag since.

Serena examined the envelope, a cream colored square, thinking it must have been a sympathy card a fan had sent after Diana's death. Then she read the postmark: Mallard, Texas, and a chill of foreboding raced through her. She tore off one end of the envelope, removed a folded sheet of paper that looked as if it had been printed from a computer and opened it. She immediately glanced at the bottom of the page, then gasped when Precious Trent's signature leaped out at her. Serena's hands shook as she began to read:

> *August 13, 1999*
> *Dear Miss St. James:*
> *Please do not think I'm some nutcase or a kooky fan of Diana Devreux's when you read this letter. I need some information and I hope you can help me.*
> *I'm looking for a friend named Sara Jane Talbot who used to live in Mallard, Texas. I have seen your photo on Diana Devreux's website several times and am struck by your resemblance to my friend. Do you know a Sara Jane Talbot? Are you related to her, perhaps? Or are you indeed her? If that is the case, please don't worry. Sara Jane—contact me—your father is dead. He died in a fire when your house burned down. It was a terrible accident. I know you didn't get along with him, but I am sure you'd want to know what happened. Father gave him a decent funeral, a nice service, and he is buried next to your mother. Other news—Joyce Ann Keller escaped from Gatesview this past December. Killed a*

prison driver and stole his van. The police have questioned me four times and they think you two may be together. I told them no way. Miss St. James, if none of this makes sense, simply disregard this letter. But if this is you, Sara Jane Talbot, call me. I miss you. I won't tell a soul where you are.

Your friend always,
Precious Trent

P.S. I have a great job as a website monitor for Celebrity Today *and have become quite an expert on the Internet.*

Serena felt as if she had been kicked in the stomach. Groping her way to the sofa, she sank down on it and crushed a throw pillow to her chest, feeling the ghosts of her past closing in. Her father was dead. The house she had grown up in had burned to the ground. Serena felt cold, unable to bring an image of either to her mind. Her eyes were dry and hard as she stared across the room and her body felt empty and numb, yet a tiny spark of hope stirred in the back of her mind: her final tie to Mallard was gone and there was no reason for her to ever return.

And Joyce Ann was a fugitive! Not surprising, Serena thought. The day of her sentencing, Joyce Ann had erupted in court, cursing the judge, vowing not to do the time she'd been given. Now she'd killed a guard to escape. Serena groaned, uneasy at having her past brought back so sharply, so close.

"What a mess Joyce Ann made of her life," Serena whispered, more eager than ever to protect what she had been able to create. "And Precious," she murmured, the sound of her old friend's name in the quiet room spiriting away her fatigue. "I miss her, too. She wouldn't believe what's happened to me since I left Mallard." The clarity of her isolation and lack of ties to her past seeped into Serena's thoughts like water dripping onto a sponge. She didn't want them in her mind, yet could not stop thinking of the girl she had been, and how lucky she was to have reinvented herself. Pressing her face to the pillow, she refused to let Precious' letter get to her, and rising, she went into the bathroom, tore up the letter and flushed it down the toilet, then turned on the shower and stripped off her clothes.

Standing under the hot water as it pounded her skin, Serena prayed for Precious to forget about her and never write again.

Serena arrived at Bally's at nine and met Craig in the bar of the restaurant. At their table, Serena was gorgeous in black sequins; Craig was elegant in his designer tux. They dined on lobster and caviar, three kinds of wines, delicate greens with slivered almonds, and a flaming raspberry crepe with fresh cream for dessert. And throughout the gourmet meal, Serena struggled to put Precious' letter out of her thoughts. There was nothing she could do about the news she had received, and if she never wrote back, what could Precious do? Nothing. Absolutely nothing. Her father was dead; her house was gone, finished. Joyce Ann had probably lost herself in a crowded city like New York or Los Angeles. Serena's life was light-years away from everything Precious had mentioned.

Shrugging off the ghostly memories, Serena danced and laughed, table hopping in the festive restaurant as she greeted business associates and dedicated clients who patronized both Prime Time Limos and Beautopia. When a reporter from the Star approached her for an interview to discuss the opening of her new salon, she put him off, more keenly aware than ever of her need to keep a low profile.

At one minute before midnight, Craig poured two glasses of champagne and circling the table, pulled his chair next to hers. At the stoke of midnight, he kissed her deeply, then together they tilted their glasses.

"Craig!" Serena cried out. "There's a ring in my champagne!"

"So there is," he said, smiling as she let him fish it out. He set down his glass, took Serena's left hand, and held it while the diners in the restaurant continued singing, clapping, and making noise with the silver horns Bally's had put on each table. When the streamers fell from the ceiling and confetti clouded the air, he asked, "Will you wear it now?"

"Yes!" she shouted above the noise, gazing at the brilliant stone. She kissed him again, then shouted once more, "Yes, Craig I will marry you."

Craig slipped the ring on her finger. "Tonight?" he urged.

"What? Tonight?" Had she heard him right? she wondered, her pulse racing. She looked at the ring, which was sparkling in the faceted lights crisscrossing the room, then pinned Craig with a serious expression. "Where? How?"

"At the Little White Wedding Chapel. I booked it for us tonight. All you have to do is say yes."

Serena leaned into Craig's embrace, wrapping her arms around his shoulders, holding him very close, loving the solid, secure feeling that came over her. Wasn't this what she had dreamed of, yearned for, and thought about every day since they reconciled in Marvin Erwin's office months ago?

Serena closed her eyes and ears against the distraction of the revelry and tried to focus on making the right decision, certain this was her path to true happiness. Owning Beautopia and launching the cosmetics line was very rewarding, but becoming Mrs. Craig Alexander was everything.

But hadn't they both vowed to be open and honest with each other? No more secrets or half-truths? Craig knew nothing of her criminal past, the past that had surfaced only hours ago in her office. She shuddered to think about Precious recognizing her, finding her, putting the pieces of her mirrored life together. But Craig would never know what Precious had discovered, if she played it right. Hadn't he told her not to worry about the stupid things they had done before they met? That everyone made mistakes and it did no good to dwell on them? Well, Sara Jane Talbot had been wiped from the face of the earth and Serena St. James was going to marry Craig Alexander. Nothing was going to stop her.

"Yes, Craig. I'll marry you tonight," she said, leaning back to admire her ring, a wide, but unsteady smile on her face.

Chapter Thirty-six

The information was incredible. Joyce Ann clicked through the pages of Serena St. James' financial portfolio that she had accessed on the Whitney & Whitney website. "Well, Sara Jane's sure come up in the world since Gatesview," she told Tonk, her voice almost reverent. "And now she's married to that guy, Craig Alexander, rich, too." The satisfaction that shot through Joyce Ann was encouraging. She had been right! Being patient and watchful for months had paid off, and now Sara Jane Talbot's net worth was staggering. It was finally time to let her old friend see that happiness was not guaranteed, that living a lie was not a good thing, and that sooner or later old debts had to be paid.

"And I'll bet that limo king she snagged doesn't know he married an ex-con, either," Joyce Ann snidely added, raising an eyebrow at Tonk as another website filled her computer screen. "Here it is! Beautopia." She began reading the home page aloud. "The newest full-service salon and spa in the Vegas area that provides its clients a natural experience. Let Serena St. James change your image and your life with her unique hair-care products and cosmetics made from a secret family formula." Joyce Ann threw back her head and guffawed. "Shit! This is a bunch of bullshit. A secret family formula, my ass. Her daddy was a drunk and her momma died when she was seven years old. I was there. Wasn't nothing handed down to her from nobody. What a crock."

Tonk propped his feet on the side of the bed. "Whatcha wanna do, Joyce Ann? Hit her up for a couple of thousand to keep her dirty little secret safe?"

"Hell no. That bitch owes me big time. If she hadn't punked out and stopped the car that night, I never would've gone to prison. She owes me more than a few thousand. She owes me a lot, and I know exactly how I'm gonna get it."

Tonk grinned as he got up and came around to the other side of the bed, where Joyce Ann was sitting on the floor with the computer. "This might be fun," he said, crouching down next to Joyce Ann. "What you got?"

"See this?" She tapped the screen with her index finer. "Beautopia is looking for a website manager." She squinted up at Tonk, her eyes pulled into narrow slits, thinking. They had been in Vegas for six months, and after Joyce Ann bluntly told him on their arrival that they had to go their separate ways unless he dumped the drugs, Tonk had promised to stay clean, afraid to go it alone in a city that was rife with temptation. He had said he wanted Joyce Ann to stick with him, help him stay clean, and she had agreed, considering Tonk an asset since he was a genius with the computer. Now he could help her put Serena St. James in her place.

He'll get a cut, she thought, *but he has to come through big time. I've waited a long time, but now we've got to move fast.* "You're qualified," she told him. "I want you to apply for that job at Beautopia."

The moon cut a silver path across the dark water. Serena took another sip of her Mai Tai, walked to the edge of the spacious lanai, and leaned over the railing, her face pressed into the tropical night breeze. The palm trees lining the road to Kaanapali Beach looked like lacey sentinels waving their fronds in salute, honoring the couples strolling past hand in hand.

The night before, she and Craig had been down there, walking along the shoreline, laughing as they skirted the waves that crashed and foamed and soaked their legs. The evening had been one to treasure, along with the mystical sunrise at Haleakala Crater and the thrill of exploring underwater lava caves.

Their honeymoon had been magical. Craig's love and devotion was so raw it made her shiver to think of how close she had come to missing out on being loved like this. Serena could still feel his arms around her when he'd pulled her beneath a coconut tree to tell her, with tears in his eyes, how much he needed her in his life and that she had finally banished the loneliness and confusion that had plagued him for years. He'd put his arms around her, vowing to be true, to protect her, and never give her reason to regret becoming his wife.

Savoring her final evening in paradise, Serena tilted her chin toward the moon, a flat, round silver disk hanging over the water. She could not resist a smile, recalling their spur-of-the moment wedding where the preacher's wife and son had stood as witnesses and his daughter had handed Serena a nosegay of silk violets to keep as a memento of the occasion. Soft organ music had drifted from a CD player someplace in the small chapel and the ceremony had been over in fifteen minutes. It had not been the kind of wedding she had thought she'd have, but it had been quick, convenient, and legal. Serena had only one regret: she had been married in her black-sequined dress—an unlucky color for a bride, she thought. But her worry had quickly dissolved when, back in the limo after the ceremony, Craig had sprung the second phase of his surprise on her.

They had gone directly from the Little White Wedding Chapel to the airport, boarding the private jet Craig had hired to fly to Maui. When she'd stepped from the plane, four and a half hours later, the first signs of daylight had been easing over the lush emerald hillside, illuminating the sky with a red-orange glow in a haze of violet light. The sight had caught Serena by surprise, stopping her in the doorway of the jet, her heart pounding in excitement.

Years ago, in prison, she had seen pictures of Maui in a *National Geographic* magazine, but had never believed she'd actually visit such a place. Then, her world had been confined to an area bound by bars and gates and guards, all she thought she deserved to see. Even her father, who had never left Bonham County, Texas, had not encouraged his daughter to believe that she could see more of the world than what lay within a fifty-mile range of her hometown.

Arriving in Maui had allowed the reality of Serena's good luck and good fortune to unfold in her mind like a blooming tropical flower: She was wealthy. She was free. She was married to the man she loved, and had come too far from Mallard, Texas, to ever think of going back.

From the lush courtyard below, Serena could hear laughter, cheers, and a ukulele playing jaunty Hawaiian music in the tiki room, where another hula contest was in full swing. On the second night of their honeymoon, she and Craig had been barefoot, dressed in grass skirts and fragrant orchid leis, swinging their hips and waving their hands, making fools of themselves. She had never laughed so hard in her life.

Their six days in paradise had flown by in blur of laughter, dancing, dining al fresco, and spectacular drives along curiously curved roads that meandered past pools, lush foliage, and breathtaking waterfalls. And long nights of making love.

Tomorrow morning they'd fly back to Las Vegas and back to the real world, where she'd be buried under paperwork, appointments, clients, and advertisers once more, but at least she did not have to face the world alone. Serena twisted her diamond wedding ring around her finger, letting it catch the moonlight and sparkle back at her. The sense of calm that came over her was alarming: Never had Serena felt so secure and so happy. Was it a dream? Would this feeling of safety and joy dissolve when she got on the plane and returned to the rat race? Serena arched her back and stared at the stars, holding on to the moment. Leaving Maui did not mean she'd have to leave paradise behind. As long as she had Craig, paradise would always be with her.

She let her eyes wander over the great expanse of silver water, the banks of red hibiscus and pink bougainvillea growing profusely along the road, the twinkling lights of cruise ships in the harbor, imprinting the view into her mind. Turning around, she eased the sliding glass door open and stepped inside, but did not shut it behind her. She wanted to listen to the waves pounding the beach and smell the salt breeze when she awakened in the morning.

Slipping off her green silk muumuu, she eased beneath the cool white sheets and curved her naked body against Craig, who reached over and took her in his arms. He was soft and warm from sleep, and smelled like the coconut bath oil she had lathered over his body during their shower together. Cuddling her head against his neck, she laid her arm across his chest and closed her eyes. If paradise existed, this was it.

"That's your real name?" Joyce Ann asked, stopping her typing to glance up at Tonk.

"Yep. Timothy Kline," Tonk said, pacing the floor as Joyce Ann entered the name on the online application form.

"Guess we'll have to use it. Who'd hire somebody named Tonk to create a website, no matter what kind of credentials he had? You have created and managed some important websites, haven't you?"

"Sure, but it was a long time ago."

"It'll work."

"I think they want way too much information, Joyce Ann. It's been three years since I had a real job, and I'm not sure what kind of references those guys back in Detroit will give me. I created their websites, but only one is still up and running. Maybe this is not such a good idea."

"Stop worrying," Joyce Ann snapped. "One current website with your name on it is all you need." She paused, thinking. "You've never been arrested, have you?"

"No, only detained for questioning a few times."

"All right, then," she went on, "it's best to tell the truth, don't give 'em any reason to go digging around. On paper you look great. You've got the real stuff going on. They won't suspect a thing. You're gonna get this job. No problem." Hunkering over the computer, she continued reading the form. "Says they'll fly the final candidate into Las Vegas for an interview. Hum . . . let's give you an address as far away from Vegas as possible. New York? How about Florida?"

Tonk frowned in question at Joyce Ann.

"Hey, why not? Once Beautopia e-mails the confirmation number for your ticket, you go to the airport, show your I.D., cash in the ticket and walk the damn five blocks over to Beautopia for the interview. Duh! That's not so hard to figure out."

Tonk nodded. "Sure. Sure. Sounds good."

"That's it." Joyce Ann checked the entries on the form, then clicked, "Submit" and grinned. "Relax. I've got this under control. All you gotta do is clean up and get your ass over there when they set the interview date. On time!"

Six days later, Tonk was sitting in Dean Bank's office describing how he would streamline the e-commerce portion of Beautopia's website to boost sales and better serve the customers. Referring to the detailed plan he had created, he outlined, step-by-step, where the current system had failed to live up to Serena's expectations and why. When he finished his presentation, Dean vigorously shook his hand, welcomed him on board and promised to give him the access codes he'd need to get started as soon as his references were checked.

Within forty-eight hours, the online management of Beautopia's business belonged to Timothy "Tonk" Kline.

When the news came through, Tonk and Joyce Ann celebrated his good luck. They ate steak at the Pegasus Room in Alexis Park, caught Steve Harvey at the Aladdin, and then blew the rest of the three thousand dollars Tonk had been refunded for his unused airplane ticket on chips at the blackjack table at Circus Circus.

Chapter Thirty-seven

The outburst of applause both surprised and embarrassed Serena. Rising, she made her way through the crowded room, squeezing between the round tables decorated with gilded topiaries, one hand holding the skirt of her fashionably styled red chiffon gown. As she passed each table, the men in tuxedos and the well-coiffed women dripping with jewels beamed up at her and nodded. Hurrying to the podium, Serena flashed a dark, but playful frown at Sammi, who was on his feet, smiling and clapping, obviously pleased that his nominee had won.

Sammi had entered her name into nomination for the Desert Flower Community Service Award to honor her commitment to the community. After opening Beautopia, Serena had launched a program of personal grooming classes for seventh-grade girls at Lincoln Avenue Middle School in Brushton. Sammi had decided, without consulting Serena, that her volunteer work, coupled with her gutsy decision to place Beautopia in an economically disadvantaged area of town merited recognition. The award, presented by the African-American Beauty Industry Professionals of Las Vegas, annually honored one individual for best using his or her talent and skill to enhance the lives of others.

Serena mounted the three steps that led to the stage, careful not to trip on her gown. A beaming smile was on her face, but her throat was dry and tight. Public appearances were not easy for Serena, who had little desire to be the center of attention. For that reason, she had told few people about the work she was doing with the middle school girls. After discovering Precious' letter, Serena had begun declining social invitations that might put the spotlight on her, preferring to stay in the background. Six weeks had passed since she'd read the letter, and no more had arrived. But still, she wanted to be cautious. The letter had served as a wake-up call: She had to be careful about being photographed, giving interviews, and making charitable donations that created too much interest. She had accepted Sammi's invitation to accompany him to the charity event tonight because Craig was out of town and Sammi had been very insistent that she attend as his guest. Because of the many new clients Sammi was referring to Beautopia, she had found it hard to refuse him, and now here she was center stage.

The houselights went down and the stage lights found Serena. She faced Ron Jeffers, a local radio personality and the master of ceremonies, who was holding the award.

"Serena St. James is an unsung hero," Ron Jeffers began. "She is a newcomer to our community, but for many weeks now, she has quietly been working her magic in Brushton. Her first good deed was establishing her salon and spa, Beautopia, in Brushton, giving the neighborhood an economic shot in the arm. And since her business opened, five new retail stores have come in. Secondly, the many hours Miss St. James is dedicating to disadvantaged young people at Lincoln Middle School must be applauded. This upstanding role model and talented businesswoman is an asset we cannot take for granted. For this reason, Miss St. James, we honor you tonight." The audience broke into applause, Mr. Jeffers paused, then went on. "I am sure most of you know the story of Miss St. James' unexpected windfall from her former employer, the legendary Diana Devreux. Miss St. James could have left Las Vegas and gone to Los Angeles or New York to launch her business, but, no. She took honesty to a new level, by choosing, not only to stay here, but also to sink her money into a much-needed establishment in an area of town where she is most valued. Not on the Strip. Not Downtown. But in Brushton, creating a hub of positive activity in an area that has been written off by the local politicians for a decade. The young people, and all residents of Brushton, will continue to benefit from Miss St. James' vision and her dedication to the betterment of this city. For this reason she is awarded the Desert Bloom Community Service Award this evening."

Serena sucked in a long breath, overcome by a mix of pride and surprise to hear such grand accolades attributed to her: role model, upstanding, honest. With trembling hands she took the award from the master of ceremonies and faced the microphone.

"Thank you so much for this honor," she began, after looking at the wooden plaque Ron had handed her. It had her name, Serena St. James, elegantly engraved on a brass plate beneath a blooming cactus.

"This is a complete surprise, and I must say that I never expected to be honored for doing what I feel is simply the right thing. The community of Brushton needs my services. I saw the potential for growth the first time I came through Brushton, as well as an opportunity to reach women who would not come to a salon on the Strip or inside a major downtown hotel. And after participating in career day at Lincoln Middle School, and learning from the counselor that the majority of the girls at her school were from single-parent homes, living in foster care or in transitional situations, I saw a void that needed to be filled. Those girls have been starved for the kind of information I provided that day, and I decided to take on the task of helping them deal with their adolescent concerns related to skin, hair, hygiene, image, and to let them know that they are beautiful. All they need is someone to show them how to enhance their natural beauty and look their best. These days, even the most well-intentioned parents, overworked and stressed out trying to make ends meet, may not be able to give their children the boost in self-esteem they crave, and need, to make it in this world."

A burst of applause interrupted Serena. She laughed to see Sammi waving at her.

"I can relate to the girls of Lincoln Middle School," Serena continued. "I was once a very confused, overweight, angry young lady without a mother to turn to. Instead, I fell under the spell of a girl I thought was my friend. But sadly, I found out too late that I had turned to the wrong person. And I paid dearly for that mistake. When . . ." Serena stopped, swallowing hard as she realized how close she had come to divulging damaging details about her past. Nervously she glanced around the room and saw the eager eyes of strangers gazing up at her, hanging on her every word, waiting to hear more. "I, I don't know what else to say, other than thank you," she quickly finished, clenching her jaw tightly as she returned to her seat.

"Touching," Sammi whispered, leaning closer to Serena. He raked his eyes over her slim body, feigning jealousy. "Overweight? Angry? You? I don't believe it. You are the calmest, most elegant woman I know."

"Oh, it's true," Serena whispered back, smiling sweetly. "I used to be a very different person."

The Desert Flower Community Service Award brought attention, not only to Serena, but also to Beautopia. As the salon's popularity grew, Serena worked long hours, desperate to keep up with her fast-growing business. The popularity of the salon, as well as her line of natural cosmetics gave Serena a great deal of satisfaction, and she began thinking of expanding into Washington, D.C., or Atlanta, where the African-American communities were large enough to embrace what she was offering. And the best part for Serena was that she had Craig with whom she could share her success.

In early March, she and Craig bought Raul Torres' ten acres of land on Spring Mountain Road and began planning their house, to be built on a rise that overlooked the road. The house was to be a multilevel stone and timber structure designed in a unique Southwestern style with Tudor touches. The architect they had selected had been instructed to blend Serena's desire for a solid, Old World look with Craig's request for lots of light and outside balconies, resulting in a striking four-thousand-square-foot structure that would sit atop a ridge overlooking Spring Mountain Road. Serena was working with interior decorators, determined to turn the place into a home that she and Craig would love and enjoy for many years, and was planning a trip to New York at the end of the month to buy furnishings that would be unique. The cottage, where they were living while the house was being built, would remain on the property as a studio retreat where Serena could work on new projects.

Life was hectic, but sweet for Serena, who moved through her days in a blur of smiles and bright color, touching thousands of women in her salon, in the community, and most of all on her website.

Serena was extremely pleased with the improvements her newest employee, Timothy Kline, had been able to make in her online presence. He had known exactly what was needed to make the site effective, attractive, and productive. She was grateful to Dean Banks for hiring the young man who had totally revamped Beautopia's website. With Timothy now managing the site, product sales had tripled and the feedback from satisfied customers was overwhelming. She'd been forced to hire two additional staff members exclusively to answer her e-mail. And when Beautopia's website was nominated for an award as one of the most successful e-commerce start-ups by Web Watch E-Zine, she sent a bonus check for $5,000 to Timothy, along with a personal note of thanks for a job well done.

Joyce Ann waved the check under Tonk's nose, grinning. "This is it. Precisely what we've been waiting for."

"Five thousand dollars?" Tonk replied skeptically, tossing his empty soda can into the trash. He went into the bathroom, leaving the door open, and turned on the cold water. After wetting his hands, he ran them through his hair, slicking it back from his face. Frowning into the mirror as he combed it down, he listened to Joyce Ann's explanation.

"No, not five measly thousand dollars," she said. "That's chicken-shit compared to what we're gonna get from Serena St. James." She fingered the check, then fanned her face with it, thinking. She had worked it right, taking her time, staying away from Sara Jane to let things come to this point. While Tonk was busy with his legitimate job for Beautopia, she spent most of her time on the Internet, locating websites, surfing for information that would help her lay her plans. In a large notebook, she had compiled information about how to use financial and personal histories to take over identities, surprised at how much information was available and the details that were provided. Now that Sara Jane Talbot was a wealthy, respected woman, Joyce Ann knew how vulnerable she was, and this weakness intrigued Joyce Ann, whose plans were quickly falling into place. But she needed the password and codes that only Tonk had been able to gather during his association with Beautopia.

"This check represents Miss St. James' trust in you. Her satisfaction . . . confidence. That woman is sold on you, Tonk, so it's time to make our move." Joyce Ann flopped, belly down, across the bed and watched Tonk splash aftershave over his face, knowing where he was headed—to Guy's, the bar downtown where he'd started hanging out way too much.

The legitimate paycheck that Dean Banks was mailing to Tonk's P.O. Box every two weeks kept Joyce Ann out of trouble, after months of living out of stolen cars and dingy motel rooms. Now, she and Tonk were living in a nondescript, yellow brick, lease-by-the-week apartment building where she had a two-room studio three doors down from his. Though living in separate quarters, they spent a lot of time together, and Joyce Ann often left clothes, magazines, and computer disks at Tonk's place, where she might crash if they worked on the computer late into the night.

Their partnership continued, and Joyce Ann, whose fugitive status was still posted on the Internet, knew she could not get lazy and let down her guard. When she ventured out to the casinos, shopping or to a movie, she often wore glasses, some kind of hat or cap, and even a long black wig. She no longer enjoyed hanging out in the casinos or running the streets as Tonk still loved to do, preferring to spend her time on her computer, focusing on a much bigger prize than any slot machine or blackjack table could offer: Sara Jane Talbot's growing wealth.

During the week, Tonk tried to stay straight: no booze, no drugs, no pills, working in his apartment on his own computer, diligently maintaining Beautopia's website. He spent hours on the Internet searching, learning, comparing, studying, and interpreting what Serena's competition was up to, staying on top of their Internet commerce. A major aspect of his contract with Beautopia was to seek out and compare other successful sites to theirs and continually update Serena's.

"So, when are you going to give up the passwords I need to get busy?" Joyce Ann asked. "It's time, you know." So far, Tonk had not passed along the specific passwords she would need to actually access Sara Jane's money, and Joyce Ann was getting impatient.

Tonk turned from the mirror and stood in the doorway of the bathroom, studying Joyce Ann. "I dunno."

"What's that mean? I dunno?" Joyce Ann snapped. "The only reason you took that job was so we could score big-time. What's up?"

Tonk returned to grooming his hair in the mirror, ignoring Joyce Ann, who jumped up from the bed and stood in the doorway. "Don't act like you can't hear me!" she shouted. "What's up with you?"

"I hear you all right, " Tonk said, now glaring at her. "Nothing's up with me. I just ain't sure I wanna go that route now. This gig is pretty nice. I'm working. I'm making good money. I'm clean. If we get greedy and blow it, I'll wind up in jail, and I ain't ready for that."

"What the hell are you talkin' about? You think you're clean? Have you forgotten the credit card numbers we got out of Dumpsters and used to finance this trip? Or the cars we hot-wired to get here? Not to mention those ATMs we busted up in Santa Fe." Joyce Ann gave him a curt laugh, then walked to the window, where she pulled back the flimsy drapes and looked down into the parking lot. The same blonde he'd spent last weekend with was sitting in her red sportscar waiting for Tonk. Joyce Ann's eyes narrowed into slits as she stared at the woman.

"So what? We didn't get caught, did we?" Tonk tossed back, picking up his wallet. He stuffed it into the back pocket of his jeans, then lit a cigarette. "That was surviving on the street. Necessary stuff. The cars can be recovered. We didn't trash 'em, and it's not like we ripped off thousands of dollars on those cards."

"Where're you going with this?" Joyce Ann asked, spinning around, her anger beginning to rise. "The cops don't give a rat's ass about any of that. Break the law, pay the price. That's the way it goes."

"You can't turn me in without getting caught, too, so forget it," Tonk challenged.

Joyce Ann jerked her chin high, assessing Tonk. She had thought he was with her on this and wanted to rip off Beautopia, help her get revenge on Sara Jane. Now it was clear: He had used her to get to Las Vegas, and now that he was clean and working, he didn't need her anymore. Joyce Ann grunted under her breath. Tonk had small dreams, she had big ones, and she was not about to let him play games with her. "Be careful," she warned. "Don't go acting crazy on me."

"I ain't actin' crazy. But I been thinking. Maybe gettin' back at your friend's not such a great idea. She's got big money. She'd hire a hotshot investigator and the cops wouldn't have a hard time tracing anything fishy back to me since I'm the one with all the passwords and shit."

Joyce Ann flinched, noticing how nice Tonk looked. He'd certainly begun paying more attention to his personal grooming since he met that blonde. "You worry too damn much, Tonk. Leave it to me. I can work it so you're not in the picture. Give me the codes."

"Naw. I got a bad feeling. Let's wait a little while longer." He picked up his sunglasses, slid them over his eyes, then opened the door, waiting for Joyce Ann to leave first.

"Sure," she said, walking past him, out onto the second-floor walkway. "We can wait a while, but not forever. We'll talk tomorrow."

At her apartment door, she looked back and watched as Tonk got into the red convertible and kissed the pretty blonde who was driving. Joyce Ann tensed. When they first met she had worried about Tonk, fussed over him, made sure he ate, bathed, and stayed off the hard stuff. Now he didn't need her, and he was getting too damn bossy.

"This shit has to stop," she muttered, the heat of envy flaring inside her as she watched the red car zoom away. Tears threatened to well up in her eyes, but she blinked them back, taking a deep breath. There had never been a physical attraction between Joyce Ann and Tonk, but the sight of him driving off with that blonde bothered her. Yes, she was jealous, a little lonely, and even frightened. She had grown to depend on Tonk to keep her company, make her laugh, make her feel needed. And his presence had made her feel a lot less vulnerable, too. But now that he was working for Beautopia, he was changing. Abandoning her. Trying to call the shots.

"He's messin' over the wrong woman," she muttered, hurrying back along the walkway to Tonk's apartment. She slipped a credit card into the lock and went inside, going directly to the corner of his bedroom where he had set up his workstation. She stared at the expensive laptop computer that Beautopia had given Tonk to use. She flipped the computer on, leaving it in standby mode. Then she straightened out a paperclip and inserted it into the back of the portable Zip disk drive. The disk, containing the passwords that would allow Joyce Ann access to Tonk's hard drive, popped out and she put another in, watching the screen, her heart pounding, her ears tuned to the street. She hoped Tonk was sitting in a bar by now, deep into his drinking.

When a screen prompt came up, she chose "remove protection" and entered a new password to give her access to valuable information on Tonk's hard drive that had previously been blocked. Now she could access everything she wanted.

Entering a new password she created a new file she named, "SJT" for Sara Jane Talbot, then downloaded the columns of nonsensical passwords made up of upper- and lowercase letters, numbers, and symbols that contained encrypted information, microscopic diagrams of every detail of Beautopia and Serena St. James's life. Using the passwords, she pulled together an astonishing amount of information, including Serena's overseas and domestic bank accounts, access to her online stock portfolios as well as the transaction codes, personal and business insurance policies, credit card account information, passport and frequent flier numbers, and even her suppliers' invoice records as well as balances on lines of credit.

Back in her own apartment, Joyce Ann sat down at her laptop with everything she needed to create the life she deserved, and she didn't need Tonk's permission to do it. After all, she was the one who had recognized Serena St. James as Sara Jane Talbot and had encouraged Tonk to apply for the job. She was the one who had pulled him out of a Dumpster and set him straight. Now she was lying low while he was out with a blonde, drinking and having big fun. She was broke and dependent on him for everything while he got a hefty paycheck from her old friend, Sara Jane, twice a month. "Something is definitely wrong with this picture," Joyce Ann grumbled, knowing things were about to change.

The once-crowded furniture store was nearly empty by the time Serena made her final selection: a quartet of deep rosewood chairs that were a perfect match to the oval table she had bought two days earlier in New York. Now she was in London where the shops were a bonanza of treasures, providing her with those hard-to-find pieces of furniture and unusual accessories that had eluded her until now. Back home, she had shopped many furniture retailers, wholesalers, and importers in New York with little luck, and rather than settle for something that was not exactly what she was looking for, she had flown from New York to London.

Craig had stayed behind, awaiting the delivery of a new superstretch limo. At first she had been disappointed, but now, as much as she missed him, she had to admit she was glad he had not tagged along. Making decisions had been easier and she had been able to move quickly from shop to shop, without the temptation to examine every possibility, as she and Craig liked to do while shopping together. She had been a woman on a mission, and now that it was complete, she wanted to go home.

For three days Serena had prowled the shops on Oxford and Baker Streets, which were brimming with armoires, bookcases, lamps, and pictures. Now she was in Wilton's and had found exactly what she wanted for her new house.

"Miss St. James," the sales representative gushed. "I am so pleased you decided to visit Wilton's today. I recognized you the moment you entered the door."

Serena lifted a brow in surprise. In London? How?

"Oh, yes," the woman went on. "Your photo was in all the papers when Diana Devreux died. She was such a talent. Saw her three times at the Palladium. Can't believe she is gone. Such a talent, such a beauty." She shook her head in regret.

"Yes, it was a tragedy. But," Serena began, anxious to turn the woman's thoughts away from the past, "after seeing what was in your window, I knew I would find what I was looking for in here." She pulled her checkbook from her purse, more relieved than the oversolicitous salesclerk could possibly imagine.

She had been away from home for ten days, and was anxious to get back, uneasy about leaving her new assistant manager, DeDe Wilkes, in charge. DeDe was efficient, industrious, and a licensed cosmetologist, but with only two years of salon management experience, she still had a lot to learn. Dean had hired her from a pool of candidates recruited and screened by a reputable employment service, so she would probably work out fine, though Serena struggled with delegating too much of her hard-won authority.

But Timothy Kline, her website wizard who exercised complete control over the e-commerce side of her business, had surpassed her expectations. The quarterly profits from sales of cosmetics on Beautopia's website were increasing, due to Timothy's aggressive marketing, freewheeling imagination, and detailed supervision of every transaction. She had to admit, it was nice having someone she could trust overseeing that part of her company.

"How soon can everything be crated and shipped to Las Vegas?" she asked the clerk.

"We'll put the order in right now, and we guarantee delivery to your door within two weeks."

"Great," Serena replied, happy to hear she would not have to wait six months for her furniture, glad to be finished and ready to go home. If the traffic cooperated, she could get back to the hotel, pack, and be on the midnight flight out of Heathrow to New York. She missed Craig terribly, though they spoke on the phone once or twice a day, a phone call couldn't make up for being with him. This was the longest separation since they married, and Serena didn't like it a bit. She glanced at the bill of sale the representative had given her.

"Not bad," Serena commented after examining the figures. Though the salon and website were doing well and royalties from *One and Only* still rolled in, she tried to be conscientious about her money. Dean placed her royalties into long-term investments, which she could not touch, and launching Beautopia had put her a quarter of a million dollars in debt, creating a real liability. "Sixty-five hundred? For the chairs, the two chests, and the lamps?" she remarked.

"A special price for you, Miss St. James. We hope you'll come back to see us again."

"I certainly will," Serena replied as she wrote out the check, shook the woman's hand, then left.

During the taxi ride to the hotel, she thought about the buying trip, which had evolved into a whirlwind of trekking through enormous warehouses, squeezing among crates in tiny furniture boutiques, matching fabric swatches by color and texture, and measuring and examining countless tables, chairs, chests, and lamps, all with an eye to their possible placement in her new home. It was just about complete, and she could focus on her plans to open a Beautopia salon in D.C.

Hurrying across the crowded lobby of the Mayfair Millennium Hotel, she entered the lift, making a mental note to leave a better than usual tip for the maid. The service during her stay had been beyond reproach, and Serena liked to reward hard workers for a job well done.

With her bags packed, she waited for the bellhop, standing at the hotel window looking down into Grosvenor Square. London was beautiful, fast-paced, and just as bustling as New York, she thought, hoping her schedule would allow her to come back with Craig. He had accompanied Diana here on her tour of Europe, but it was all new to Serena. They had the money to do it, all they needed was time.

"Who knows when that will be," she sighed, turning around. The telephone rang at the same time that the bellhop knocked on her door. Serena grabbed the phone first.

"Hello?"

"Hello, Miss St. James, please."

"This is she. Could you hold on a minute?" Serena ran to the door, let the bellhop in and showed him her bags. While he loaded them onto his cart, she went back to the phone.

"Yes. Sorry. This is Serena St James. Who's calling?"

"Mr. Lighton at Wilton's Furniture."

"Oh, hello," Serena said. "I was about to check out. What can I do for you?"

The man cleared his throat, then said in a hesitant voice, "I'm sorry to interrupt your departure but we have a small problem."

"A problem?"

"Yes, it seems our bank cannot honor the check you left with us today." The line went silent for a moment. "Perhaps you'd like to arrange another method of payment."

Serena's jaw dropped in surprise. "What are you talking about, the bank not honoring my check? There must be some mistake. I wrote a check on that account four days ago in New York."

"Uh . . . perhaps. But, I was informed that there are not sufficient funds in your account to cover the check. So, if you still want the furniture . . ."

"Of course, I want it," Serena snapped.

"A credit card, perhaps, . . . or cash."

"Fine," Serena replied, snatching her purse off the bed. She took out her American Express card, rattled off the numbers to Mr. Lighton, and then waited until he had electronically verified the charge before hanging up.

Following the bellhop down the hotel corridor toward the lift, she silently fumed. What in the world was going on at Bank Nevada? No one had access to her personal account but Dean, and he encouraged her to keep the balance above twenty thousand, earning eight-percent compound interest every month. Maybe she had screwed up the balance, forgotten to make an entry. With so much spending connected to the business, the new house, and her spur of the moment travel, she must have dropped the ball. She'd call Dean as soon as she got home and straighten it out. He'd probably already found her mistake.

Chapter Thirty-eight

Joyce Ann wiggled her toes in the warm sudsy water, then flexed her foot, rotating her ankle to release the tension in her leg.

"First time here?" the Asian pedicurist asked, lifting Joyce Ann's right foot from the bubbling warm water, then submerging the other one. She began massaging the ball of Joyce Ann's foot, then pulled firmly on her toes.

"First time," Joyce Ann replied, relaxing, looking around. She was impressed by the operation Sara Jane had established, as well as the efficient staff in white smocks, names embroidered on their front pockets, who were busy giving their clients manicures, pedicures, waxing, or facials at private stations throughout the salon. Joyce Ann, who had never had a pedicure, was enjoying the experience of being pampered, though having her feet massaged and her toenails clipped and polished was not the only reason she had come to Beautopia.

This morning, she had boldly called Beautopia, informing the receptionist that she was calling from Bank Nevada and had to speak to Serena St. James right away, trying to find out how accessible her beauty mogul friend really was. A woman named DeDe Wilkes immediately came on the line and informed Joyce Ann that Miss St. James was out of the country and not expected back until late that afternoon. Was there anything she could do?

Pleased with this fortunate turn of events, Joyce Ann had said, no, hung up, but called right back and spoke to the receptionist, booking a pedicure for this morning. Now she was inside her old friend's salon of beauty and illusion and was anxious to scout it out while Serena was not there.

The Asian attendant put a final brush of topcoat on Joyce Ann's newly painted toenails, then placed a small fan at her feet to air-dry the polish.

"Want something to drink?" the pedicurist asked, pausing at the curtained door.

"A diet Coke?" Joyce Ann replied, sitting back in her chair to enjoy the experience of being waited upon, of feeling special, and understanding why women paid dearly for Beautopia's services.

"Sure, be right back."

The atmosphere, the calm elegance, the entire facility was much more luxurious than Joyce Ann had imagined, and she had to give her girlfriend credit: Sara Jane Talbot had known exactly what she was doing when she opened her salon in Brushton. These women were shelling out hundreds of dollars a visit, sometimes twice a week, to look beautiful and feel good about themselves. No wonder Serena St. James' bank accounts and stock portfolios were so flush.

The pedicurist returned and placed Joyce Ann's Coke on the small table. As soon as the woman left to attend another client, Joyce Ann got up and peeked out the curtain. The corridor was empty. Moving quickly, but quietly, she walked toward a stairwell at the back of the building. The wall along the stairwell was hung with framed photos and newspaper clippings, awards and proclamations, each one with Serena St. James' name or photo on it. Joyce Ann walked up the stairs, assuming they led to Serena's private office, which she had learned from the pedicurist, was on the second floor. If anyone stopped her she'd say she was looking for a water cooler. It had worked in public places many times before.

Luckily, no one saw her enter the upstairs corridor, and Joyce Ann continued down the carpeted hall, easing past an office with a frosted glass door where she could hear a woman inside talking on the phone. She hurried toward a set of wooden double doors at the end of the hallway with a small placard with the name Serena St. James mounted on it. She listened for a moment, heard nothing, and then tried the shiny brass knob. It rotated smoothly in her palm. Joyce Ann slipped inside and closed the door, leaning against it as her eyes adjusted to the dim interior light.

The contrast in decor between the luxurious public rooms downstairs and Serena's private suite was stark. The only personal touches in the businesslike setting were the silver-framed photos of Serena and Craig scattered around the room, several bowls of potpourri arranged with three aromatic candles set in heavy silver holders on her desk. The pungent smell of peaches hung in the air.

Joyce Ann swept the simply furnished room in a glance, zeroing in on the stacks of folders on Serena's desk, color-coded and neatly arranged. At the desk, she rifled tabs on the folders, unsure about what she wanted, hoping to find some material or information that Sara Jane Talbot valued more than money, more than success and fame.

Joyce Ann wanted to show Sara Jane Talbot that she did not deserve all of this wealth, adoration, and love, especially from a man who knew nothing about her past. Joyce Ann had nothing, no one, while Sara Jane had too much.

Joyce Ann clenched her jaw as she opened the top drawer of a lateral file cabinet and took out a thick red binder bulging with papers. The wide rubber band that had been placed around it to keep the contents from spilling out slipped off easily, and Joyce Ann carried the file to the desk, where she quickly scanned the contents. She recognized sketches of the pink rose logo that was on every Beautopia product, along with several sheets of handwritten notes and a computer-generated list of sources for ingredients and supplies. There were pages that looked like formulas for items based on the Spanish bayonet plant, which Joyce Ann had learned from the Beautopia website, was the mainstay of all the cosmetics and products Serena had developed.

"Research," Joyce Ann murmured, continuing to page through the folder. There were letters from florists, chemists, government agencies, and local nurseries, as well as photos of plants in their natural habitat. At the back of the file she found a small booklet of paper that was brittle and yellow. The paper had faded with age, and the sketches appeared to have been hand drawn many years ago.

"Violet Talbot," she murmured, reading the name that had been signed at the bottom of every sketch in the book. *Sara Jane's mother,* she thought, recalling the item in the newspaper that said Beautopia had been founded on an old family recipe. *Must be true,* she decided, *and this book may be the heart of Beautopia.* Joyce Ann continued turning the pages, studying the sketches, understanding how valuable this material must be to Serena St. James.

Quickly, she wrapped the rubber band around the notebook full of papers, including the sketchbook and stuffed the bundle under her loose-fitting shirt, then took out her cigarette lighter, flicked it open, and lit the shortest of the peach-scented candles on Serena's desk. After placing the candle next to a stack of folders, she eased to the door, and listened for a moment. No one was in the corridor. Joyce Ann walked out, descended the stairs, and left Beautopia through the rear door that led to the employee parking lot.

* * *

Craig met Serena at the arrival gate, hurrying over to her as soon as she stepped into the terminal. He wanted to get to her before she came across a television in the airport and heard the news. He wanted to protect her from overzealous reporters who might be waiting for her, camera crews in tow, to get her reaction to the devastating fire that had destroyed Beautopia. All afternoon, radio and television reports had detailed the disaster, reporting that Serena St James was out of the country and not available for comment on her devastating loss.

Craig placed an arm around Serena's shoulder as soon as she de-planed, and quickly guided her through the busy airport to the exit, where a limo was waiting. After instructing the driver to come back for Serena's luggage, they took off. During the ride, Craig told her what had happened.

"What do you mean, it's gone?"

"The fire was unstoppable. Nothing is left."

"But when? How? Was anyone hurt?" Serena sat up straight, her eyes wide.

Craig held her by the arm. "No one was hurt. DeDe had been work-ing in the color room upstairs when she smelled smoke. She ran to your office, saw the flames, then got everybody out of the building be-fore calling the fire department. It took four hours to put it out, and the fire marshal suspects arson."

"Arson? At Beautopia? Surely, not. Why would anyone do this to me?"

Craig shrugged. "I don't know. But the marshal traced the fire to your office, to a silver candleholder and thinks someone left a candle burning on your desk. DeDe was adamant. No candles had been lit in your office during your absence, and definitely none on your desk, ever. If DeDe was the only staff member authorized to enter your of-fice, who else could have been in there?"

She sat back in the limo and squeezed her eyes shut, a tear rolling down her cheek. "I can't imagine. Everything is lost?"

"Yes, everything," Craig answered softly. "The building next door to Beautopia burned, too." He placed his hand beneath her chin and lifted her face, making her look at him. "Don't cry, Serena. This is awful, but the salon was insured. We can rebuild, start over, even im-prove the place and make it grander than before. Remember, no one was seriously burned or killed. We've got to be thankful for that."

Serena nodded, unable to think about rebuilding Beautopia. Brick and stone and wood meant nothing. It was the months of hard work and hope for the future that had vanished in the flames, along with her research, formulas, her mother's sketchbook—the heart and soul of Beautopia that had been stored in her file cabinet and on the hard drive of her computer. It was all gone. Serena shivered to think that her most valuable connection to her past was now dust, that her mother's simple, yet powerful, legacy had been taken from her. She wiped her eyes with the handkerchief Craig handed her, unable to fully comprehend what had happened.

"If it was arson, who did this? Who could hate me so much, be so cruel?" she asked Craig.

"I don't know," Craig said, "but you can be sure we're going to find out."

Tom Reilly, the investigating officer assigned to Serena's case, asked her the same question two hours later, but in a more indirect manner. "Are you aware of any disgruntled employees on your staff? Any recently fired?" He looked at Serena over the top of his small round glasses, eyebrows raised. He had worked the arson division of the Las Vegas Police Department for nine years and knew that many arson cases could be traced back to someone close to the victim. Rarely did a complete stranger set a fire, unless it was a vagrant living in an unoccupied building.

"No," Serena answered. "To my knowledge, everyone working at Beautopia was happy, and I've never fired anyone. I know my staff extremely well. We work closely together. I think I'd know if anyone were angry or upset with me."

"Use any outside contractors?" Reilly asked.

Serena thought for a moment, then nodded. "Only my financial manager, Dean Banks, but I've known him for quite some time. Totally trustworthy." She paused, then added, "My website manager is new. He works off site."

"What's his name?" Reilly held his pen over the pad of paper on his desk, ready to write down the name.

"Timothy Kline," Serena answered.

"What's he look like?"

"To be honest, I've never met him." She turned to Craig, a hint of alarm on her face. "Do you think . . . ?"

Craig's reaction was swift. "No. Dean checked him out. Said he had excellent references, and he's doing a great job for us. Why would Kline turn against the company that is paying his salary?"

"Never know," Reilly replied. "References are easy to manufacture." He wrote a few lines in his notebook, then asked, "This man Timothy Kline? Where can I reach him?"

"Call Dean Banks, my financial manager," Serena replied. "He screens potential employees, negotiates their contracts, and would have the kind of personal information you need." Serena rattled off Dean's phone number, then bit her lip, thinking. "Dean is so cautious. If he had thought there might be a problem with Timothy Kline, he would have discussed it with me. I can't imagine there is any connection between the fire and Mr. Kline."

"I'll get in touch with Mr. Banks and take it from there. I'll need to interview each of your employees, Miss St. James," Reilly concluded, shutting his notebook. He shook Serena's hand, then sighed aloud. "I know this is distressing, Miss St. James, but no one was hurt. Be thankful for that. I'll be in touch as soon as I have any information."

On the way home, Craig drove to the site where Beautopia once stood. Serena asked Craig to wait in the car while she got out to look around, needing time alone. It was dark now, and the sun had disappeared, leaving the pile of rubble dark and sinister where her beautiful salon had once been.

Slowly, she approached what used to be the front door, one hand over her mouth, trying to stifle the pain over seeing what was left. An acrid smell wafted to her from the rubble. A few curiosity seekers were hanging around, pointing, whispering, and speculating about what had happened. A teenage boy slipped under the yellow police ribbon and began poking at the ruins with a stick, forcing curls of smoke from the mound of twisted steel and charred furniture that had once been the culmination of Serena's dream.

Bending down, Serena picked up a hand mirror that had, somehow, escaped the inferno intact, brushed away the film of soot and held it to her face.

Why now? Just when everything was going so well? Am I marked for unhappiness and disaster? she wondered, studying her image in the smoky glass. Her mother's death, her father's emotional abuse, Marcella Jacobs' murder. Prison, shame, Diana Devreux's untimely death. Now this. Who could have done it? Why?

Serena sucked back her tears, fear rising in her chest. She wasn't naive. She was wealthy, successful, and married to a handsome man, a sister with reason to watch her back. But she had so few people who were close to her, and had never had a serious disagreement with anyone since coming to Las Vegas. "I will rebuild Beautopia and start over," she concluded, determined to hold on to the mirrored life that she had created in order to survive.

Pulling back her shoulders, she strode to the car, got inside, then went limp. Her world had seemed so solid and secure only a few days ago. Now it was shifting, changing, drifting away from her like the wisps of gray smoke that were rising from the ruins of Beautopia and breezing off into the desert night.

Joyce Ann watched Serena from across the street, enjoying the rush of satisfaction she got from seeing her old friend in pain. She arched her back and stretched. After crouching at the front window of the vacant office across the street from Beautopia, she was stiff. She had been there since the blaze erupted, and had watched in fascination as the other shopkeepers on the street had rushed out to assist and comfort the Beautopia staff and customers who had spilled out of the salon, plastic capes flying behind them, screaming for help. Some still had had rollers in their hair, others had come out with dark mud masks on their faces, and all of them had been frantic to get as far away from the burning building as possible.

Joyce Ann swayed back and forth, mesmerized at seeing Sara Jane Talbot again. Flashes of adolescent memories flickered through her mind: the red blood on Marcella Jacob's white uniform, the sound of screeching tires, the way her body had slammed into the dashboard when Sara Jane had wrecked the car, the police officer's expression when he had told them they were under arrest. Anger pricked Joyce Ann's brain. If she had been driving, they never would have gotten caught. She slipped her hand under her shirt and into the waistband of her jeans, pulling out the gun she had found in the glove compartment of the first car she had stolen after her escape. The memory of the fright on that teenager's face came back. She caressed the gun, enjoying the way it felt in her hand. "You can't run away from who you are and what you did forever, Sara Jane. You owe me, and you're gonna beg to be my friend again, when you realize that being Serena St. James ain't the fun you thought it would be."

Joyce Ann stepped onto the sidewalk and watched the taillights of the limo carrying Serena move down the street, itching to bolt after it, stop it, and confront her old friend. But she could wait. Slowly, she put the gun back under her shirt, turned and headed down the dark street.

Chapter Thirty-nine

"I'll be in meetings most of the day, and I have that dinner with Abe Burton in Boulder City at six. I'd cancel it, but Vegas Transport is after his contract, too, so I'd better hustle over and make my pitch." Craig leaned over and kissed Serena on the cheek.

"Go on, I'll be fine," Serena said, stifling a yawn.

"I want you to stay in bed and get some rest, " Craig ordered, taking his suit jacket off the valet, folding it over his arm. "You didn't sleep very well last night, did you?"

Serena shook her head. "Too much on my mind." She pushed herself up on the pile of pillows against the headboard and pulled her knees to her chest. "I've got to call the insurance company, and DeDe. She salvaged the appointment book and we'll have to get on the phone and cancel all our bookings. And the bank . . ." She stopped abruptly, the incident in London popping into her mind. Had it only happened the day before yesterday? It seemed eons ago. The flight home had been long, exhausting and mind numbing. She'd flown overnight from London to New York, then raced to make her connection to Vegas, only to arrive and learn that Beautopia had burned down. Amidst the fear and confusion, she had put the overdraft out of her mind. She'd call Dean and tell him what happened. He'd straighten it out. "And I've got to go up to Indian Springs and pick up that order of Spanish bayonet that Raul put together for me. I really need to do that today," she added.

"Don't try to settle everything today," Craig advised, taking his briefcase from the overstuffed chair beside the television. At the doorway he paused. "I wish you wouldn't drive to Indian Springs. You're under a lot of pressure, and this loss is going to take some time to settle in, Serena."

"I know," Serena replied. "But I'm fine, really. With arson suspected, the insurance company will take its time paying up, and I'd better keep production on the Beautopia line going. The trip to Raul's will be good. Give me time to clear my mind. Do you think we should rebuild at the original location or move? The area had been coming back, making a real turn around, and if I leave, others may follow. I think it's best to stay."

Craig frowned at Serena, uneasy. "There's lots of time to discuss that. For now, why don't we concentrate on finishing *our* house? Things need to get moving with that contractor. I love this little house of yours, but I'm tired of fighting you for closet space." He grinned at Serena, who had pulled the covers up to her chin and was staring out the window. "Serena?"

She jerked around, putting the overdraft, the fire, the Spanish bayonet that she had to pick up today out of her mind. "Right. The contractor. I'll get on that, too. Go on," she told him, waving. "Get out of here. I have a million things to do."

When Craig had left, Serena flipped on her laptop to check her e-mail and the status of product orders on the website. At least she could keep the online aspect of her business running until she rebuilt the salon. Sales on the website had been coming in nonstop ever since the e-commerce site was launched. The profits from Internet sales would keep things going and help fund construction of the new salon. Even with insurance, she knew it was going to take a hefty amount to rebuild and start over.

The phone line buzzed and crackled and hissed as it searched for the right connection, and when she eventually connected to her website, a series of blue and white lines came up, then the screen filled with unintelligible jargon instead of her trademark pink rose logo. Serena cursed softly, wondering what was going on. Something with the server probably, but she'd never had a problem before. She waited a few seconds, and when it didn't clear up, entered the URL for another site and was surprised to see it pop right in. So, the problem was with her website, not her computer or the server, she realized, returning to Beautopia's to study the strange-looking encrypted symbols and numbers on the screen. Her mind raced. Was this the result of overload from too many hits? A crash? A virus? A deliberate scuttling of her website? But she had internal protective devices on her computer that Dean had assured her would protect her from viruses and hackers and con artists who might want to invade her site. Immediately, she called Dean Banks.

"Dean. The website's down and I can't figure out what's going on."

"I know. I tried to log on this morning and got the same gibberish."

"Did you talk to Timothy Kline?"

"No."

"No?" Serena didn't like the sound of his reply. "What's wrong, Dean? I can hear it in your voice."

"The arson inspector asked me for Timothy's phone number, address. I gave them to him, of course. But Detective Reilly just called this morning and told me that Timothy Kline's phone number has been disconnected and he's disappeared. Seems his apartment is empty, except for what was there when he moved in, and there's no trace of him. The police confiscated the computer he had been using for Beautopia but the hard drive was compromised and all files stored on it were corrupt. They couldn't get any leads from it."

"Did they talk to the apartment manager?"

"Yeah. The information on his lease application was totally fabricated. Nothing checked out."

"How could that happen?" Serena snapped. "You said you checked him out and he was clean. Dean, do you realize how serious this is?"

The phone was silent for a moment, then Dean let out an audible sigh. "I did check his employment references, Serena. They were legit. But the former address and the person to contact in case of an emergency on his lease application don't exist. I called the company he used to work for; they were no help. He did work for them, and did a good job, but since he worked from his home, they didn't know him very well."

"That's just great," Serena tossed back, angry with Dean for allowing this con man to get to her. "I pay you damn good money to protect my financial investments and keep my business secure. You sure as hell haven't done a very good job of it."

"Serena, please," Dean began, but Serena cut him off.

"Don't Serena please, me. I'd advise you to get busy and find an expert who can undo this mess and get my website up and running. ASAP. Okay? Every minute it's down costs me money. And another thing . . . seems my personal account at Bank Nevada is overdrawn."

"Impossible."

"I thought so, too. But that's what I was told by a store in London who refused my check."

"How could that have happened?"

"I don't know, but get on it and straighten it out. Can you do that for me, Dean?" The confrontation left Serena flushed and jittery. She hated talking to Dean this way, but he had really let her down.

"Sure. Right away. Don't panic. It must be an accounting error on their part. I'll get to the bottom of it."

"Dean, where did Kline live?"

"Fourth Street. On the north side, in one of those lease-by-the-week units. Reilly said the place was a pigsty. Full of trash and garbage. Nothing there he could use to trace him."

"I'm going over there and see for myself."

"Leave it to the police, Serena. Kline could come back, might be watching the place. It's too dangerous."

"Well, I can promise I won't do anything stupid or dangerous. But I've got to go see for myself. Call me later, on my cell phone."

"Will do," Dean said, hanging up.

Serena zapped the remote control to turn the TV on, then stared uncomprehendingly at the television, unable to agree with Dean. If she could see where Timothy Kline had lived and worked, she might find a clue about who he was and whether or not he had done this to her.

The *Today Show* broke away for the local segment of the news. Video of the fire at Beautopia filled the screen as the announcer reported that the police were investigating the fire as a case of arson, but no suspects were in custody. Serena groaned. She had not seen this footage of the devastating fire, and flinched to see flames roiling from the top of the building, the smoke so dense the sky looked like midnight instead of midday.

Serena recalled her conversation with DeDe, who told Serena that no strangers, workmen, or deliverymen had been inside the salon that disastrous morning, and if an employee had been in Serena's office, DeDe would have known because she had been working upstairs most of the day, though she was in and out in the morning. She had not seen or heard anyone moving about on the second floor. So who could have gotten in, Serena wondered? A nosey customer? A customer! Serena punched speed dial for DeDe's phone number.

"Get the appointment book," Serena said in a rushed tone. With the salon's computer destroyed, it was the only record of her customers.

"Sure," DeDe answered. "I was getting ready to start calling everyone to cancel appointments. Most of them have probably heard the news about the fire, but a few clients live out of town."

"Right," Serena replied, barely listening to DeDe. "That's true. When you call, tell them we will have temporary quarters arranged within ten days, and Dean is working on getting the website back up. Encourage them to order product off the website until we get the temporary salon running. Even if I have to lease space for a year, I will.

This is just a setback, DeDe and you are still on the payroll. I'll need your help to put this business back together and get it up and running again as quickly as possible."

"No problem, Ms. St. James. I'll do what I can to help. This is so awful."

"Yes, it is." Serena took a deep breath, then asked DeDe to read the names of yesterday's appointments, before the fire broke out.

"Sure. Let me see."

Serena could hear the rattle of pages as DeDe searched the book for yesterday's bookings.

"Okay. We had mainly regulars. Mary Hightower, Betsy Fines, Coretta Thurber," she began, running down a list of names. "We only had one new customer, a call-in who made the appointment that morning."

"What was her name?" Serena asked.

"Sara Jane Talbot."

Serena went limp. This was a name she had hoped she'd never hear again. "Sara Jane Talbot?" she repeated weakly, her heart pounding. It couldn't be. "Was she white, black? What did she look like?"

"Big woman. African American. Kinda edgy. She must have left before the fire broke out because I didn't see her on the street once everyone got outside."

Serena nearly dropped the phone. Could Joyce Ann Keller be responsible for her problems? She suddenly felt overwhelmed, full of fear, as if her carefully crafted world was crumbling around her shoulders.

Trembling, she scooted to the edge of the bed and swung her feet down, staring at the floor as the name continued to fill her mind. For nearly three years she had been able to manage her emotions, maintaining the cool facade of someone in charge of her life. She had convinced Craig, Dean, Sammi, DeDe, her many business associates and social acquaintances that she was not the frightened, uncertain girl who had walked out of prison and turned her back on her true identity in order to create the life she wanted. Serena put her forehead into her hand, aware that her facade of poise, strength, and confidence was rapidly breaking apart.

"Anything wrong, Miss St. James?" DeDe prompted after the phone had been silent too long.

"Oh, no," Serena mumbled, forcing her mind back to the moment. "Did Sara Jane Talbot fill out one of our Beauty Index Profile cards?"

"No. And I don't see a phone number here, either. Nothing."

Serena nodded slowly. Why would Joyce Ann leave a number

when she could leave a fire behind as her calling card? Were she and Timothy Kline working together? Or was Serena being paranoid? It was very possible that another woman named Sara Jane Talbot existed somewhere in the world and her presence in the salon had been a strange coincidence.

Serena moved to the window and let her eyes roam over the tall pine trees and stately elms that surrounded the house. Her new Lexus was in the driveway. The heirloom roses the gardener had planted on the hillside along the winding drive that led to her unfinished house were in full bloom. She had always felt safe in this place, but not now. She suddenly had the feeling that someone might be watching her, waiting to deal her another blow. As she peered into the trees that shielded her house from the road she worried, but knew she had to be careful about who she talked to now. "Thanks, DeDe," Serena whispered. "I'll get back to you later."

The next phone call brought equally distressing news. Dean's conversation with an officer of Bank Nevada left her shaken. He told her the account in question had been closed only moments before Wilton's of London had presented their check. The bank officer assured Dean that everything had been done according to regulations, which had required verification of Serena's PIN and identifying information—her Social Security number and her mother's maiden name—before the money had been transferred to an account at American Savings in Las Vegas. Dean said the bank officer was extremely upset and was going over all of the details to find out how something like that could have happened since neither he nor Serena had authorized the transfer.

"Who would know your social security and PIN numbers and your mother's maiden name?" Dean asked shocked.

"I have no idea," Serena whispered, not ready to go any further.

"The bank is tracing this now. I'll get back to you when I hear back from them."

Serena hung up the phone, trembling. Joyce Ann Keller would remember her Social Security number because theirs had been identical except for one digit. She could almost hear Joyce Ann's laughter when they had compared their new cards, before setting off to K-Mart to buy matching red plastic wallets to hold them.

And her mother's maiden name? Joyce Ann could have easily gotten it from her granny, who had known Serena's mother for years and probably knew she had been born Violet Featherstone. If not Joyce Ann, then who else could have known this information?

Barely able to focus on the tiny buttons on the phone, she called information, then phoned American Savings, unable to wait until Dean called her back. But the bank would not divulge information beyond the amount deposited and the date of the transfer of funds into the new account.

Serena began to feel sick, aware that going into the bank to protest the transaction, meant divulging her connection to Joyce Ann Keller, and why Joyce Ann would have known Serena's Social Security number and her mother's maiden name. The truth about her past was about to come out, and what would that do to her relationship with Craig? To her upstanding reputation in the community? To the hard-won respect she had gained among her peers and professionals in the cosmetology industry, not to mention the field day the media would have with her criminal past.

Serena paced the floor, eyeing her nearly finished mansion atop the hill overlooking the cottage. Once Craig found out she'd been living a lie, he'd never forgive her, not after the hell she had put him through for hiding his relationship with Diana Devreux. He'd hate her for deceiving him. Would he leave her? Abandon their marriage? The thought was too horrible to contemplate.

I've got to tell him the truth, she decided. *Tonight, before he learns about me from some other source. It's the only chance I've got of salvaging our marriage.*

"Joyce Ann Keller, if you are behind this, you are going to be sorry," Serena vowed, snatching a pair of navy slacks from the closet. After pulling them on, she yanked on a white tee shirt and a red linen jacket, then grabbed her laptop and hurried to her car.

The manager of the apartment complex took the folded bills and shoved them into his pants pocket, then handed Serena the key to Timothy Kline's apartment.

"Stinks like hell in there, and I gotta foot the bill to clean the place up." He shook his head, stuck his cigar stub into his mouth, then tilted back in his swivel chair. "That's the problem running week-to-week leases. Too much trash rotates through here, and I ain't talking about garbage. The cops already been in there, so have at it if you want." He blew smoke into the air and squinted at Serena. "You're his sister, you say?"

"Hum, yes. Half-sister. We had different fathers," Serena tossed back, ducking out the door.

She hurried across the cracked asphalt parking lot and up the rusted stairwell to unit 204, where she stuck in the key and turned the knob. Bracing herself for whatever was inside, she pulled back her shoulders and took a deep breath.

The apartment was dim, smelly, and hot. Serena eased deeper into the living room, one hand on the wall as she felt for the light switch. She flipped it, but nothing happened, and realized the manager had already cut the electricity off. She felt her way along, not wanting to open the front drapes for fear that someone might see her through the window. The furnished apartment had a sofa, two chairs, a coffee table and a rickety television stand, where she could tell from the circle of dust that a unit had once sat. Newspapers, fast-food containers, plastic bags, and dirty paper plates were everywhere.

In the kitchen, on the counter were several empty cans covered with flies. When Serena poked at a crusty baked bean can, the insects flew up and buzzed her face. Swatting at them, she hurried into the bedroom, where a pile of dingy sheets had been heaped on the floor. She opened the dresser drawers and checked the closet. Nothing. She looked under the bed and behind the drapes. Only more dust and dirt. In the bathroom, she opened the cabinet door beneath the sink and saw a clump of soiled linen. Using a coat hanger, she picked through the pile of rags, separating them to see what was there. When she uncovered a white tee shirt, she gingerly pulled it out and held it away from her body, twisting it around so she could read what was on the front.

Serena let out a cry of surprise, then dropped the hanger, looking down at the shirt, one hand pressed to her mouth. The green letters, GCFW blazed at her feet. Gatesview Correctional Facility for Women. Her chest felt tight and it was suddenly hard to breathe. She was back in her cell, listening to the screams and grunts of inmates, holding her arms around her body, twisting her flimsy tee shirt into knots, counting the days until her release.

"Gatesview," Serena gasped, letting out her breath, listening to the sound of water running in the apartment next door. A new client named Sara Jane Talbot had been in her salon the day of the fire. Someone had used her Social Security number to transfer funds out of her checking account. And now a tee shirt from Gatesview was in the apartment of her former website manager. It all added up to one person: Joyce Ann Keller. But how was Joyce Ann connected to Timothy Kline? Serena had to find out, right away.

Stuffing the Gatesview tee shirt into a paper bag, she left the apartment, got into her car, and dialed Tom Reilly's office.

"Mr. Reilly? Serena St. James. I have a theory about who might know where Timothy Kline is, and this person might also know something about the fire at my salon."

Chapter Forty

Serena sped up US 95, leaving the skyline of Las Vegas glittering behind in the afternoon sun. Impatiently, she changed lanes, zipping past the slow-moving truck behind which she had been trapped too long. Maybe it was foolish of her to go on to Indian Springs after talking to Tom Reilly, but what good would it do to hang around her house worrying, when she had so much to do. She could not put her life on hold and hide in fear. If Joyce Ann was doing this, then sooner or later they'd meet. Reilly promised to call her on her cell phone if he turned up any information to corroborate her theory.

Serena had confessed everything about her past to Reilly, asking him not to divulge the information to her husband—she was going to do that tonight. She had told Reilly about her arrest, her childhood association with Joyce Ann Keller, and why she suspected her old friend might be in Vegas, doing this to her. And with Craig out of town and Joyce Ann Keller most likely roaming Las Vegas, Serena might as well go visit Raul, with whom she always felt safe and welcome. The drive gave her time to think, to plan and decide what to do.

The fifty-minute trip to Indian Springs was one she had made many times. Visiting Raul's farm always calmed her and brought her back to reality when her world was spinning too fast. Besides, she liked Raul, a charmingly simple man who was happy living in the middle of the desert surrounded by rattlesnakes, prickly pear cactus, wild geraniums, and sagebrush. Usually, the trip to Indian Springs was a pleasant adventure, but today it seemed more like an attempt to save her sanity. The sight of the GCFW tee shirt still registered in Serena's mind, forcing her to drive faster and faster, as if to get away from the evil the shirt represented.

She took her eyes from the road for a moment and glanced at the paper bag on the floor of the car, furious to think that Joyce Ann had invaded her new life so easily. Serena had convinced herself that nothing could harm her as long as Sara Jane Talbot stayed hidden away, but now she knew it wasn't so. Joyce Ann had stolen her old identity and was using it against her. Somehow she'd beat Joyce Ann at her own game. But how? Serena worried, taking a left turn onto a lonely stretch of unpaved road that wound its way west through the desert then turned north again, paralleling US 95 until it reached Indian Springs.

After driving for twenty more minutes, and not passing another car, Serena pulled off the dusty road and parked under a clump of pine trees but did not cut the engine. The temperature was close to one hundred degrees and she could see heat waves shimmering from the sandy soil, an iguana sunning on a rock. The cool air from the air-conditioner brushed her arms and dried the perspiration that had soaked the front of her shirt.

Nervously, she stared into her rearview mirror, grimacing at the desolate landscape, sensing someone was following her. Or was she being paranoid? Overreacting? Precious had written that Joyce Ann was a fugitive who had killed a man to break out of prison. She was dangerous, deranged, and cunning. She could easily make Serena disappear in order to run her game until Serena's funds ran out.

Pulling out her cell phone Serena made the first of three calls.

"Craig," she spoke into his answering machine. "Please cancel your meeting in Boulder City and come home tonight. It's urgent. I hate to ask you to do this, but I have to talk to you and it can't be done over the phone. I'm on my way to Indian Springs. Mr. Torres doesn't have a phone, so call me on my cell if you want. Don't worry, I'll be back before dark. Love you. Bye."

American Savings of Las Vegas was next.

"Hello, this is Sara Jane Talbot," Serena said, barely able to say the words through the fear that rose up and tightened her chest. "I'd like to check the balance on my new account." When the woman asked for the account number, her social security number and her mother's maiden name Serena rattled them off, and was told that the balance was now four hundred dollars and sixty-three cents. She clicked off without thanking the clerk.

Tears filled her eyes. Joyce Ann had emptied the account. With one finger poised over the keypad of the phone to make a final call, her thoughts spun off into the countless ways Joyce Ann could undermine her financial security. Unless the police found her and stopped her, Joyce Ann could take out loans, secure lines of credit, buy a car, or purchase anything on the Internet she wanted as long as Serena's funds and credit held up. Serena would have to move fast to protect herself, not wait on Tom Reilly or Dean or the bank to take action, and that meant calling the only person she could trust.

You will not take my life away again, Joyce Ann, Serena vowed, removing her Palm Pilot from her purse. In a special file, were the letters PT—and the only phone number that connected Serena to her past. When she had put it in, for sentimental reasons, she had not imagined she'd ever speak to Precious Trent again, but now, she had no choice.

She checked the number, punched it into her phone, then let out a sigh of exasperation. The line was busy. She'd try again when she got to Indian Springs.

Joyce Ann pulled off of Las Vegas Boulevard and parked her Chevy wide-bed truck on the Texaco gas station lot. It was a used truck, but new to her, and she had paid six thousand dollars cash for it. Now that she had wheels, she could finish with Sara Jane Talbot, bring her back down to where she belonged. But there were a few things she had to get out of her way. Tonk was first on her list.

She sat in her truck and watched the back door of Club Calico, where the blonde with whom Tonk was involved danced and waited tables. Joyce Ann knew she worked the lunch crowd and would arrive at any minute, hopefully with Tonk. Her hunch paid off ten minutes later when the red sports car pulled in, screeched to a stop, and the blonde got out and hurried inside.

Tonk, sitting in the driver's seat, lit a cigarette, backed out onto the street and sped away. Joyce Ann was right behind him.

She followed Tonk down the strip and through town to a gated entry that led to a condominium complex. Joyce Ann slipped in right before the gate swung closed, then hung back until he had parked and let himself into a corner unit where a basket of ivy was hanging outside the door.

Joyce Ann got out, went up to the door, and knocked. She hadn't seen Tonk since he went out on the town three nights ago, and from the cozy set-up he obviously had settled into with his girlfriend, she doubted he had ever planned to come back to his apartment.

When the door opened, Joyce Ann walked right in, pushing past Tonk without speaking. There was no time for small talk, and she didn't want his neighbors to see her standing at his door.

"Joyce Ann!" Tonk scratched his neck and squinted at her. "What you doin' here?"

"Came by for a visit, Tonk," she said wandering around the living room. The place was decorated entirely in red and white, with a vase of cheap red plastic roses on a table draped with gauzy white cloth. Even the white lampshades had been trimmed in layers of red ball fringe. She flopped down on a white fake fur ottoman and cut her eyes at Tonk. "Don't seem too glad to see me."

Tonk shrugged, closing the door, then scratched his arm while watching Joyce Ann, as if not quite sure what to say.

"What's her name?"

"Dorinda," he mumbled.

"Humm. Cute." Joyce Ann glanced around. "She sure as hell has bad taste."

Tonk crossed the living room and sat down at the table in the adjoining dining area.

Joyce Ann saw the mirror of white powder waiting for him there, and realized what she had interrupted. She shook her head. "You need to leave that shit alone."

"You need to mind your own business."

"Hey, your business is my business, or have your forgotten our plan."

Tonk rolled a dollar bill into a tube, pressed it to the mirror and inhaled, then sniffed loudly and wiped his nose. "You started that fire, didn't you?" he asked.

Stretching her legs, Joyce Ann studied her new leather boots. Real Western, with fancy stitching and slanted heels. Being Sara Jane Talbot was not so bad.

"So what?" she tossed at Tonk.

"So, the police are looking for *me*. You stole those access numbers and security codes for Beautopia from my hard drive, too." He sniffed, then scowled. "What'd I ever do to you? This police shit is messing everything up. Good thing Dorinda let me hide out here."

"You dragged your ass. I told you not to wait too long. I had to make a move."

"So, you burn down the woman's place of business? That was a bullshit thing to do, Joyce Ann. For the first time in my life I had a legitimate job, was earning decent money, then you go fuck it up."

"You never were going to hit Serena St. James for the big bucks, were you?" Joyce Ann pressed, suspicious. "You were just stringing me along, humoring me, treating me like a chump while you ran around town having fun with Dorinda." Jumping up, Joyce Ann went to stand beside Tonk, who was bent over the mirror, scraping it with a razor blade.

He looked up, blinked his red-rimmed eyes, a look of defiance coloring his face. "That's not true," he spat out. "I changed my mind. Dorinda and I are together now and I plan to stay legit. Enough of this shitty street action. I'm tired."

Joyce Ann grabbed Tonk by the back of his shirt and pushed his head down against the table. White powder flew onto the red carpet, sprinkling it like powdered sugar. "You're tired?" she screamed. "Who gives a fuck?" She tightened her grip until he managed to push her away and stand, glaring at her, fists clenched.

Joyce Ann did not back up, but moved swiftly to get right into his face. "You can't go legit, you sorry bastard. I've got too much on you: the cars, credit cards, and ATMs we busted into. I was there, remember?"

"Let it go, Joyce Ann. You won't call the cops on me and you know it, so shut up and go away. If you want to scam that friend of yours, go ahead, but leave me out. I'm sick to death of you and your obsession with that St. James woman. Get out of here. I don't care what you do; I ain't gonna tell no one." He held up a pale, shaky hand, as if pledging not to say a word. "Do what you want. My lips are sealed."

Joyce Ann reached under her shirt, eased out her gun, and jammed it into Tonk's belly. "I know they are," she hissed, teeth clenched. Then she pulled the trigger and jumped back to avoid the spray of blood that gushed out and colored the carpet a deeper shade of red.

Chapter Forty-one

Craig bowed his head in a friendly nod of agreement, then shook Mr. Yuosaki's hand. The negotiations had taken all morning, but the time spent with the electronics mogul had been worth it. Prime Time Limo was now the exclusive escort service for the International Convention of Electronic Engineers, set to open in Las Vegas in January. Mr. Yuosaki expected five thousand people to register for the meeting, held in the United States for the first time.

"We'll get the contracts to you within the week," Craig said to Mr. Yuosaki, walking him out of his office. "Thank you for choosing Prime Time."

"You are very welcome, Mr. Alexander. I'm counting on you to show the conventioneers the best of Las Vegas."

"Will do."

As soon as Mr. Yuosaki left, Betty, Craig's assistant came into his office, frowning. "Craig. I forgot to tell you when you arrived this morning, but John Tyler, the Mercedes-Benz rep wants to see you this afternoon. Will you have time to squeeze him in before you leave for Boulder City?"

Craig checked his watch. It was already after one and he had a luncheon appointment waiting for him at the Lanai Cafe in the Fremont Hotel. But he had missed John Tyler's calls for the past two days and needed to speak to him. "Call him back and see if he can drop by the Lanai about three. I'll be finished with my lunch meeting by then and can leave straight from the cafe to Boulder City. Beat the traffic on the I."

"Sure thing," Betty said, making a note on her pad.

Craig hurriedly gathered the papers he needed for his luncheon meeting, slipped them into his briefcase and snapped it shut. A photo of Serena on his desk caught his eye, and he paused for a moment to study it. He'd get over to Boulder City a little early, drop by the Turquoise Treasure Shop and pick up that necklace he had seen in the window the last time he had been there. Serena would love it: hand-crafted silver set with richly veined stones.

She's been through a lot in the past few days, Craig thought, hoping the gift might lift her spirits. Besides, he wanted to show her how much he loved and supported her during this difficult time.

Driving to the Lanai, he remembered that he had not checked for messages on his e-mail or cell phone all morning. "Later," he murmured, speeding up to make it through the intersection before the light changed. He'd have time to do that after he got to Boulder City.

Raul was not at home. His truck was not parked under the date palm tree beside the house where it usually was, and his cocker spaniel was not barking, either.

Must have gone to Joe's, Serena thought, heading toward the rear of the house where he would place the box of Spanish bayonet she wanted. Before loading it into her car, she sat on the swing in the shade and relaxed, assessing Raul's jumbled garden, where Spanish bayonet, cactus, vines, and plants she could not identify flourished under the harsh desert sun. It was hot, but the heat felt good. It seemed to help her focus, clear her mind, allow her to concentrate on pulling the pieces of this crazy puzzle together.

What was the connection between Joyce Ann and Timothy Kline? How had Joyce Ann found her in Las Vegas? And what was her next move? Precious had written that Joyce Ann had killed a man when she escaped from prison. She'd killed Marcella Jacobs, too.

Surely she isn't after me, Serena thought, horrified to think that not only her financial stability, but also her life might be in danger. The police had to find Joyce Ann and stop her. But could they before she did more damage?

Quickly, she punched in Tom Reilly's number, but got his voice mail, so she left a message requesting an update on his search for Joyce Ann, then punched in Precious' number again. This time she got an answer.

"Precious?" Serena whispered in a hiss, despite the fact that she was alone in an isolated spot in the desert.

"Yes, this is Precious Trent. Who's calling?"

"It's Sara Jane."

The line was quiet for a second, then Precious let out in a yelp of glee. "Oh, my God! I knew it! I knew that was you! Girl! Where are you? What is going on? You got the letter, didn't you?" Precious' excitement vibrated through the phone.

"Yes," Serena smiled despite her worry. It was so good to talk to Precious, the only person who could possibly understand what she was facing now.

"You fell off the face of the earth. I was shocked when I saw your face on Diana Devreux's website. How did you hook up with her?"

"Too much to talk about right now, Precious but I'm so glad you wrote to me." Serena wished circumstances were different and she could laugh and reminisce and fill Precious in on Craig, her business, and the crazy world she had fallen into when she left Dallas and became Diana Devreux's stylist, but there were more important things to discuss and time was short. "Precious, I'm scared."

"What is it?"

"I think Joyce Ann is stalking me, ripping me off. There was a fire . . ."

"I read about it," Precious interrupted. "Your salon in Vegas, right?"

"Yes. But that's not all. Money is missing from one of my accounts, and a virus invaded my website."

"Did you alert the authorities?"

"Yes, but you know how that goes. The investigator I am working with took all the information, but who knows what he'll find out before she hits me again?"

"Why do you think it's Joyce Ann?"

Serena filled Precious in on everything that had happened, the visit to her salon by a Sara Jane Talbot, the use of her Social Security number and her mother's maiden name, the Gatesview tee shirt she found in the apartment of the man who used to manage her website.

"He's disappeared," Serena said. "And the money that was illegally transferred from my account landed in an account under the name of Sara Jane Talbot. Who would use that name to get to me except Joyce Ann Keller?"

"Where are you now?" Precious asked.

"At a friend's house in Indian Springs. Rural Route number 3, off of US 95."

"Nevada?"

"Yes."

"Joyce Ann," Precious murmured. "Has to be her. I was worried that she might try to find you, but damn. She's out of control."

"Precious, what do you know about Internet fraud?"

"More than I'd like to. It's a big problem, but I've learned a great deal about how to deal with it since I started working for *Celebrity Today.*"

"Can you help me? What can I do? I can't wait for the police."

"I understand. Cyberhackers and con artists are hard to trace. They usually hit hard, then move on to the next victim. You may never get hit again."

"I can't take that chance. I've already stirred up my past, and I've got a lot on the line. Precious, I'm risking my marriage, my professional standing, and my personal reputation by allowing my true identity to finally surface, but there's nothing I can do about it. Right now I must protect the financial security that I have been able to achieve as Serena St. James."

"Let me do some checking. Kyla Sharp, the policewoman assigned to Joyce Ann's case, might be able to help. She may have already been contacted by the Vegas police, but we'll see. Maybe she will at least confirm that Joyce Ann is in the Las Vegas area. In the meantime, Sara Jane, get on the phone, or online, and check your credit report. See what's going on with that. Call your financial person and get him or her . . . to stop payments on all checks, drafts, wire transfers."

"Got it," Serena said.

"You must prevent any movement of your money until this is resolved. Alert all of your creditors, even your life insurance company that someone is impersonating you and using your personal identification to access your accounts. Find out what's going on and get to every financial institution as quickly as possible to let them know you've been compromised. Tell them not to process any applications, give out any information or transfer any money. Put a hold on everything and pray it's not too late."

"Oh, Precious, I miss you. I wish I'd stayed in touch, never tried to hide who I was. Look at the mess I'm in. Maybe I was wrong to hide my past . . ."

"No," Precious interrupted. "You did what you had to do in order to get out of Mallard and be somebody. You've created good life, even though you used a false identity to do it, and you deserve everything you've worked for, Sara Jane. And don't worry, it will work out. Can I get back to you via e-mail?"

Serena thought for a moment. "Yes, I have my laptop and can run it through my cell phone."

"Good. Give me your e-mail address and I'll give you mine. Stay put. I'll get right back to you. For all we know the police already have Joyce Ann in custody."

"I don't think so," Serena replied, scribbling Precious' e-mail into the notepad she pulled from her purse. "Reilly would have called and told me if that were the case."

After clicking off, Serena retrieved her laptop from the car, then looked around. The car was stifling hot and dark clouds had begun to roll in from the west, bringing the threat of a late afternoon rainstorm. She went around to the back door and tried it. Sure enough, it was open, and knowing Raul wouldn't mind if she waited inside until the storm passed, she entered, plugged in her computer, hooked it to her cell phone, and within seconds was online.

Quickly, she fired off a quick message to Precious, testing the connection.

> Precious: I'm online now and will start contacting everybody you suggested. Please get back to me soon. I'll be here for an hour or so, then I must head home. Raul Torres doesn't have a phone here in Indian Springs and I forgot to give you my cell phone number. If I log off and you need to call me it's 702-555-6565. It was great to hear your voice! S.

Serena kicked off her shoes and tucked her feet beneath her hips, determined not to move until she had alerted everyone that she was under attack.

"Please let Joyce Ann be behind bars and out of my life for good," she whispered, clicking her way to the first of many contacts.

When the Online Buddy symbol flashed onto the screen, Joyce Ann popped her fingers and grinned. "Yes! Sara Jane is talking to someone. Let's see who it is." She entered Serena's password and went straight to the Mail Sent file, then into Old Mail, not happy to see that Sara Jane and Precious Trent were talking about her. "The bitches," Joyce Ann muttered, clicking over to Yahoo! maps to see how far Indian Springs was from Las Vegas. Forty-six miles came up, along with the directions. "Not far," Joyce Ann said, determined to confront Serena St. James tonight, and once she was out of the way, Sara Jane Talbot could surface, at least in cyberspace, where no one knew or cared what she looked like—and anything Joyce Ann wanted would only be a click away.

Completing her list of contacts took longer than she had hoped, and after e-mailing Dean about what she had done, Serena was exhausted. Dean Banks had been to the bank and was full of questions about this person Sara Jane Talbot, but Serena put him off, promising to explain when she returned home. He had instructed the bank to put new security codes in place, and Serena felt relieved that most of her assets were now beyond Joyce Ann's reach. Next, Serena phoned Craig. No answer on his cell phone. Thinking he must have it turned off during his meeting, she checked her voice and e-mail messages. Nothing from Craig.

She was eager to talk to him—tonight—and tell him the truth about her past before he heard it from someone else. He deserved that much, but Serena still worried about how Craig was going to handle the truth.

As sunlight faded, a strong wind came up, rattling the trees against the house, sweeping through the cracks around the doors and windows. Raul's tiny, ancient house trembled with each gust, and Serena jumped at the sound of gravel and sand as it pounded the walls and the flat wooden roof.

She went to the window and looked out, thinking she ought to get on the road and head home since it seemed that Precious might take a while to get back to her. But the leaves on the trees were rubbing together like tiny hands clapping in the wind and birds were twittering and squawking, flying frantically across the yard, searching for a safe place to hide from the storm. The patchy dark clouds that had been scattered across the sky had drawn themselves together in an ominous clump that resembled a giant bear paw suspended over the house. Swirls of dust and sand rose up, blocking Serena's view of her car, and beyond the yard, she saw purple rain clouds hanging so low over the land, she knew she'd drive smack into a major storm if she tried to start back now.

She squinted in the direction of the road, hoping to see Raul's truck emerging from the dark, but saw nothing but swaying trees and shivering plants and lots of blowing sand. She had no choice but to stay put.

Once the rain began, it did not slack off. By six o'clock it was dark, and the rain had begun coming down so fast and hard it was tearing limbs from the trees, crushing Raul's clay pots as if they were ripe tomatoes, and cutting tiny rivers into the rock-hard ground. Flashes of lightening followed by sharp cracks of thunder sent Serena running from the window as the house plunged into darkness.

Chapter Forty-two

"The Torres place?" the man behind the bar repeated, continuing to pour beer into a frosted glass. He shoved the foamy drink to the lone man sitting in front of him, then picked up a towel and gazed down his nose at Joyce Ann. "Which one you looking for, you say? Joe or Raul?"

"Raul," Joyce Ann snapped, wiping rain from her face. Using the map she had printed off of Yahoo! she had managed to find Indian Springs, but had no idea where Raul Torres lived. "This spot in the desert can't be that big. You must know a guy named Raul Torres."

The bartender arched a brow, then nodded, folding his damp towel into a small square to begin wiping down the counter. "Sure. I can tell you how to get there, but I'd bet the road's washed out. Might not be a good idea to head out to the Torres' place tonight. Best to wait until morning."

Joyce Ann wanted to reach across the bar and shake the man, who was wasting precious time. She had to catch up with Sara Jane. Tonight.

"Listen, buddy," Joyce Ann tossed back. "Don't give me a weather report. Just tell me which road to take and what the Torres place looks like."

"Sure, but if you get stranded, you're on your own out there in the desert."

"My problem."

"Okay. Exit 95 at Encino Road. Go west until you come to the first crossroad. Turn right, if the road is still there 'cause it ain't nothin' but a dirt track. Go up about three miles and you'll run right into Raul Torres' yard."

Joyce Ann grabbed a newspaper off the stand by the door and held it over her head as she raced back to her truck. Inside, she stared into the sheet of black rain, determined to get to Sara Jane tonight, even if she had to turn around and go back to Las Vegas to find her. She turned the key in the ignition, backed out of the gravel parking lot, then sped north on 95, watching for Encino Road.

The crack of thunder sounded like the sharp bark of a dog that had discovered an intruder. Serena clenched her fists, her heart pounding with fright. The rain had not let up since the first drops had begun to fall and now there was no electricity. Determined not to panic, she groped around in Raul's kitchen until she found an old-fashioned oil lamp. After lighting it, she placed it on the table next to her computer, where it cast a yellow glow over the screen and created black shadows in the corners of the room.

Two more hours passed with no word from Precious, Craig, or Reilly. Serena worried that the battery of her cell phone was quickly running down. Without a phone or her computer she would be totally cut off, but the idea of getting out on the road and heading home in such a terrible storm was unthinkable. She'd better stay put. Pacing the room, Serena tried to remain calm, but after fifteen more minutes, she went back to her computer and sent Precious a message.

> *Precious. Do you have any information from that policewoman yet? Please get back to me. I'm really getting worried. S.*

Almost immediately, a response popped into the screen:

> *Sara Jane. You were right. Kyla Sharp got back to me. She has been in contact with Tom Reilly, the investigator on your case. He identified Joyce Ann, accompanied by a white male, in footage from a security camera of a Las Vegas casino. Joyce Ann is in the area. Be careful. I told the police where you are and someone will be out there soon. Stay put.*

Blood pumped through Serena's veins as she struggled to concentrate on hitting the right keys on the keyboard. Shaking, she frantically tapped out her response:

> *Do the police know where Timothy Kline is now?*
> *Dead. His body was discovered this afternoon at his girl-friend's apartment.*

Precious wrote.

Serena jerked her fingers off the keyboard, as if she had been scalded. Kline was dead!

How? she frantically typed.

Gunshot. Precious sent back.

Just as Serena was about to tap out another question, a bright beam of light splashed through window, interrupting her response. She swung around and gaped at the light, then relaxed. The police. Soon this nightmare would be over. She'd get in her car and head home—to Craig—to tell him the truth about the woman he had married. As much as she dreaded facing him and admitting she had been living a lie, she was ready to confess. The prospect of shedding this heavy burden filled her with a sense of relief, and she prayed Craig would forgive her for lying, and would understand why she had thought that creating a new identity had been the only way for her to survive.

Leaving her e-mail conversation with Precious in midsentence, Serena ran to the window and put her hands to the sides of her face. The rain had slacked to a misty drizzle, and it was too dark to see much more than shadows and headlights, but she could hear the vehicle's engine getting louder by the second.

He's driving close to the house so he can stop at the door and avoid a good soaking, Serena thought, watching the headlights grow brighter. But suddenly, Serena was frightened, and she began backing up. Something was wrong. The police car wasn't stopping! It was coming right at her!

As it grew closer, light bounced off of the house and illuminated the truck's interior. Serena quickly saw that Tom Reilly was not at the wheel of the truck that was coming toward the house. It was Joyce Ann Keller, smiling directly at her.

Frantically, Serena ran toward the back door, desperate to escape, but just as she grabbed the doorknob, the truck slammed into the front of Raul's adobe house. She felt debris raining down, the floor begin to vibrate, and the thrust of the truck as it barreled deeper into the house, tearing through it like a wrecking ball. The impact jolted Serena to her knees, and she gripped the leg of the kitchen table for support, staring in horror at the woman who got out of the truck.

Joyce Ann scanned the room, her eyes small and hard. "Sara Jane Talbot, you can't get away," she yelled, putting her hands on her hips, tilting back her head. "You ran all the way to Las Vegas, changed your name, spruced up your image, and still, I found you," Joyce Ann taunted. "Why do you think you can hide from me now? Come on out and tell your old friend hello."

Serena ducked down, holding her breath, thinking. Her laptop was on the table above her head, her connection to Precious' e-mail still running. Easing one hand up, Serena slid her fingers along the edge of the table's surface until she made contact with the computer, then shoved it over the edge and caught it. Quickly, she began to type: *Joyce Ann is here! She's here!* Then she pressed, SEND, praying that Precious would get to the police, tell them what was happening and to hurry.

The exhaust fumes from the truck, which was still running, were cutting off Serena's breath. She put a hand over her mouth to keep from coughing as she watched Joyce Ann's feet, clad in expensive-looking cowboy boots, clomping toward her. A sharp pain hit Serena in the stomach, jolting her back fourteen years, to the day her mother died. She had been under a table then, too. Terrified. Watching the shoes of the men from the church who had come to take her mother away. Serena felt the same sickening sense of helplessness, the same awful fright that something terrible was about to happen.

She remembered Joyce Ann crossing the street that day, anxious to be her friend. Serena's father had run the girl off, called her nasty names. Now, Serena understood why he had done it, and for the first time in her life wished she could tell him he'd been right. If only she had listened.

Suddenly, Joyce Ann squatted down, leveling her face with Serena's. The truck's headlights created an eerie backlight that silhouetted her image against the wreckage of the room.

"Well, hello, Sara Jane," Joyce Ann said, nodding. "Whatcha got there?" She reached for the computer, but Serena moved it out of Joyce Ann's reach, trying to disconnect her cell phone.

"Leave me alone," Serena shouted, one eye on Joyce Ann as she tugged at the connection cord.

"Hold up," Joyce Ann snapped, grabbing the computer, only to hurl it into the rubble that used to be Raul's living room. Then she pushed the table aside, sending the oil lamp to the floor. Flames shot across the wood floor and spiraled up the crumbling walls toward the low wood-shingle roof. Serena raced to the back door.

"Well, Sara Jane," Joyce Ann said, kicking away the debris at her feet. "Should I call you Serena? Or maybe Mrs. Alexander? It's hard to know what to call you these days."

Deciding it would do no good to run, Serena faced Joyce Ann, ready for the confrontation. "What do you want, Joyce Ann? Why are you after me?" Serena yelled, her voice rising above the rumble of the truck's still-running engine and the crackle of the fast moving fire. "Aren't you in enough trouble without coming here to threaten me? I know everything. You stole my money, started the fire that destroyed my salon, and you killed Timothy Kline, didn't you?"

"You have it all figured out, don't you, Sara Jane? You're right. I did all those things, and more."

"Why? What do you want? Money?"

"For a start, yes. You can spare it. You have more than you deserve, and you ought to share your good fortune with your old friend. Besides, you owe me big time, you cowardly bitch. You owe me for all the years I spent behind bars because you were too scared and too stupid to do what I told you to do. Maybe now you'll pay attention."

"Don't threaten me!" Serena yelled.

"I'm not threatening you," Joyce Ann replied. "I plan to get what I deserve." She stepped closer to Serena, forcing her back. "I came to settle a score with my old friend from Mallard, Texas. You fooled a lot of people into believing you were innocent and sweet, but I know better, don't I?"

Serena struggled to speak, aware that she was in real danger. Joyce Ann's menacing tone and her calm insistence were frightening. "I have nothing hide. You can't hurt me now. Go ahead, tell my husband, tell the world who I am. It doesn't matter anymore."

Joyce Ann pulled her gun from beneath her shirt and held it on Serena. "Are you sure? You're not very smart, Sara Jane. You should have done a better job of hiding, if you didn't want me to find you."

Serena, realizing how useless it would be to try and reason with Joyce Ann pressed her spine flat against the rough pine door, one hand behind her back, feeling for the knob. When her fingers curled around the cold metal ball, she tugged hard, then pulled the door open, and with a hard swing, slammed it into Joyce Ann's face, sending her old friend to the floor.

Serena raced outside and tore through the garden, stumbling over pots, tools, trellises, and the many broken containers Raul had scattered over the grounds. She had to get away, find help, but without her car keys, she wouldn't get far. Serena followed the crooked paths that criss-crossed Raul's land, the wet, sandy soil pulling her down. But she hurried deeper into the desert, snagging her arms on prickly cactus as she raced away from the house, confused and unsure of where to go.

In the middle of a tangled patch of waist-high brush, she remembered peering into the dungeonlike opening in the ground where Raul stored his razor-sharp plants. His words of caution came back to her: "Falling in there would be like falling onto a bed of knives," he had warned, and the sight was one Serena would never forget.

Where is it? she thought, dropping onto her hands and knees to feel for the slatted door among the wild vines and dense foliage that crowded the area. The soft earth oozed between her fingers and over her hands as she prodded the earth and scrambled up one crooked row and down the next, desperate to locate the hidden trapdoor. She tried to remember how far had it been from the back of the house, from the gravel drive, from the date palm tree on the side of the house.

"You can't get away, Sara Jane," Joyce Ann shouted.

A shot rang out.

Serena flattened her body flush to the ground and lay still, her eyes wide, her heart pounding, trying to get her bearings. Digging her elbows into the mud, she dragged her body forward, pushing shards of broken clay pots and wooden stakes out of her way. At last, she felt the hard wooden door beneath her chest, and frantically, began tearing away the vines that covered it, feeling for the curved metal hinge. Grabbing it, she swung the trapdoor open, then rose to her knees and intentionally allowed Joyce Ann to see where she was.

In the distance, flames had begun to rise from the house, making it easier for Joyce Ann to navigate the garden.

"You no longer exist, Serena St. James," Joyce Ann yelled, firing the gun again. "I've already wiped you out. Now, it's Sara Jane Talbot's turn to die."

The closer Joyce Ann came, the harder Serena bit down on her bottom lip. She flinched to feel the skin break and taste the blood on her tongue.

When Joyce Ann stopped no more than six feet away from Serena, she jumped up and ran. A gunshot ripped the air. Serena screamed and fell, taken down by the impact of the bullet hitting her in the back. She lay face down in a muddy swirl of water, conscious, listening to Joyce Ann's footsteps come closer, but wondering why she did not feel any pain.

"It's all over, Sara Jane. You really don't exist anymore," Serena heard Joyce Ann call out.

Serena held her breath, hoping her plan would work, then let it go in a whoosh when she heard Joyce Ann's high-pitched scream, followed by the thud of her body hitting the bottom of the jagged pit. Serena squeezed her eyes tightly shut, imagining the nest of deadly daggers claiming Joyce Ann Keller.

A sharp pain exploded at the base of Serena's spine. She began to cry, the image of Precious Trent sitting in her wheelchair in her kitchen in Mallard flashing into her mind. She raised her head, trying to get up, but slumped back to the ground. Then the world went black.

Chapter Forty-three

Craig felt uneasy and distracted during his drive home from Boulder City. The meeting had gone well and he was certain the Burton account was his, but he was worried about Serena, whom he had not been able to contact at home or on her cell phone for several hours. He'd gotten her message to come home instead of going to Boulder City, but had been running late and hadn't taken the time to call back and let her know he could not cancel the meeting, but would cut it short and hurry back as fast as he could. Before leaving Boulder City, he'd called, but her cell phone was down.

He had not wanted her to drive to Indian Springs, and he'd heard on the radio that a storm had blown through the area. Where was she? And what did she want to discuss with him? he wondered, uneasy with her tone. Too many strange things had happened lately and he was very worried.

Impulsively, Craig pulled off the highway, swung into the parking lot of a McDonald's, and took out his cell phone again. But this time, instead of calling home, he called Tom Reilly. He had a gut feeling something was going on that he needed to know about.

"Mr. Reilly? Craig Alexander here. Heard anything about Timothy Kline?"

"Trying to find next of kin to identify his body right now."

"His body?" Craig repeated.

"Yep. His girlfriend came home from her job at the Calico Club this afternoon and found him dead. She told us Kline was involved with a woman named Joyce Ann Keller. An escapee from a Texas prison. The authorities are looking for her, and according to your wife, she is a friend of hers."

"You spoke with Serena?"

"Yes, earlier today. She gave me quite a bit of information that is helping us get a lead on Keller. You need to know that Mrs. Alexander may be in danger, but I have the authorities on it. Do you know anything about this Keller woman?"

"No," Craig answered, slumping back in his seat, shocked. "I don't understand. Where is my wife?"

"In Indian Springs."

"What kind of danger?" Craig demanded.

"Apparently Keller has a grudge against your wife, and may be the one who set the fire. I'm working with the Clark County authorities up near Indian Springs right now, trying to zero in on her."

Craig ran a hand over his face, unsure about where to start. "Reilly. I've been out of town all day and haven't been in contact Serena. What should I do? How can I help?"

"Go home. Let us handle this. I'll get back to you as soon as I know more."

"Please do," Craig said, then clicked off. For the rest of the drive home, he could barely concentrate on the road, unable to stop thinking about Detective Reilly's news. Serena was in danger . . . stalked by a fugitive? Kline had been murdered. A woman named Joyce Ann Keller was a suspect . . . and a friend of Serena's. He'd never heard Serena mention that name. What in the world was the connection?

As soon as Craig entered the house, the telephone rang. He tossed his car keys on the kitchen counter and snatched the phone, hoping it might be Reilly, or Serena, but instead, a strange woman's voice asked for him by name.

"This is Craig Alexander. Who's calling?"

"My name is Precious Trent. An old friend of your wife's." A short pause followed, but Craig remained silent, mulling another name he'd never heard before. To his knowledge, Serena had no old friends, classmates, relatives, or even acquaintances who cared enough to track her down. She'd told him she'd been a loner in school, and while growing up in Dallas had never made many friends because her father had forbidden her to bring people into his house. At least, that's what he'd been led to believe. Obviously, that was not true.

"What do you want?" he asked.

"Your wife is in Indian Springs," the woman continued in a deliberate voice, as if making sure Craig understood the importance of each word.

Panic seized Craig. He pressed the phone tighter to his ear. "I know where she is! How do *you* know this and who are you?"

"There isn't time to explain, Mr. Alexander. I was the one who alerted Detective Reilly to call the Clark County sheriff's department. Sara . . . I mean Serena needs you. Hurry to her." Then the line went dead.

Craig stared at the phone, terrified. Reilly had told him to stay put. This mystery caller was telling him to go to Serena. What was going on? The woman had called Serena, Sara. Wouldn't she know his wife's name if they were such good friends? Had it been that Keller woman the police were looking for, or someone working with her? He checked the caller ID and saw that the phone call had come from an area code in Texas, then dialed the number to the police department and asked for Tom Reilly, to whom he relayed the bizarre message, hoping it had been a prank.

"Don't move. You sit tight," Reilly told Craig. "Hold on, I've got the Clark County sheriff on another line right now. Don't hang up. I'll get back to you."

The next three minutes were the longest of Craig's life. He walked from room to room with the phone pressed to his ear, terrified. Who were these people? Joyce Ann Keller? Precious Trent? Timothy Kline? Why were their lives intersecting with Serena's? He held his breath when Reilly came back on the line.

"The sheriff is on the scene. Don't know yet what went down, but they got your wife."

"How is she?"

"Alive."

Craig slid into a chair at the kitchen table and ground his teeth together, staring out the window at the dark hillside. Serena had to be okay. She just had to.

The pounding inside Serena's head sounded like a thousand drums thumping out a discordant tune. The wail of a police siren in the distance seemed too far away to be coming for her, but the sound of tires crunching the sodden gravel road motivated Serena to try to sit up. She raised her head and opened her mouth to call out for help. But no words came, and blackness claimed her again, sending her reeling back down into the mud.

Chapter Forty-four

Craig arrived at Nevada Memorial Hospital emergency room only minutes after the doctor on duty had wheeled Serena into surgery. A nurse showed him to the waiting room where Tom Reilly and two sheriff's deputies were huddled in conversation.

"Mr. Alexander," Reilly said, hurrying over, shaking Craig's hand. "Glad you made it so fast. Your wife is unconscious, but the medics think she'll pull through. She's lost a lot of blood, but the bullet missed her spine. These are the two deputies who got to her just in time."

Craig shook hands with both of the uniformed men. "Thanks for your quick response. How did this happen? Who was the assailant and why was she after my wife?"

One of the deputies stuck his hat under his arm, then nodded. "An anonymous tip came in to Detective Reilly, informing him that there was trouble up at the Torres place in Indian Springs. That a woman was under attack. I took the call to check it out, and sure enough, we found your wife face down with a bullet in her back and the assailant dead. Fell into a pit full of strange-looking sharp sticks. We had to call the fire department to bring in a ladder to get to the body. A real mess, let me tell you. Really bad."

Craig gasped, both surprised and relieved, then pumped the officer's hand again, weak with fear. "I can't believe what's happened."

Reilly walked over to the table at the back of the room, got a paper cup of coffee, then joined Craig and the deputies. "Working in Vegas brings all kinds of surprises, Mr. Alexander. I can assure you, I've seen stranger cases than this."

Over the next half hour, Reilly filled Craig in on what he knew, confirming that Joyce Ann Keller had murdered a man in her prison escape, shot Timothy Kline, then set out to kill Serena, quite possibly to assume Serena's identity and gain access to her financial assets. With Serena out of the way she planned to continue siphoning money from Serena's company and access bank accounts and charge cards in Serena's name.

"This kind of identity theft is very common nowadays," Reilly said. "You can't imagine how sophisticated and creative these criminals have become. Difficult to trace, but as in your wife's case, they are usually caught because someone knows something and informs us."

"What else do you know about Keller?" Craig asked.

"Joyce Ann Keller was sentenced to the Gatesview Correctional Facility for Women in Texas, along with two other women: Precious Trent and Sara Jane Talbot, for a murder and robbery committed in 1992. Authorities in Texas have questioned Precious Trent many times, with no results until tonight."

"And Talbot?"

Tom Reilly lifted an eyebrow and assessed Craig, then shook his head, as if he did not want to go on. "I hate to be the one to tell you, Mr. Alexander. Sara Jane Talbot is your wife." He placed a hand on Craig's arm. "Hey Buddy. I've worked in Las Vegas a long time. Come across too many strange scenarios to tell you about. Women who have changed their names is nothing out of the ordinary."

"For me it is," Craig replied grimly, stunned to learn that Serena had been connected to such people, had withheld her true identity, and lied to him about who she was. He felt ashamed for not having been more suspicious of her refusal to talk about her past, of her reluctance to talk about her childhood, her friends, and her disinterest in developing close acquaintances. He had trusted her, believed in her, loved her, and yet she had deceived him. Why? he worried, mentally groping for answers.

"My advice . . . take it slow, Mr. Alexander. When Ms. St. James is well enough, she'll give you the answers you need."

Leaving Reilly standing in the middle of the room, Craig went into the corridor and paced the hallway, fear and pain and shame in his heart. Serena had escaped with her life. She'd fought off her attacker and managed to survive, but barely. It had been a horrible experience for her, and now his nightmare had begun. How could she have allowed herself to become the target of a deranged fugitive and not confide in him? Where had he failed? Why hadn't she trusted him?

Craig sank down into a chair in an alcove waiting area and put his head into his hands. What a mess! He never should have left Serena alone today. She had seemed restless, nervous since the fire, and now, she was fighting for her life because he had not been there for her.

Maybe if he had pressed her, she would have told him what was really on her mind.

Two hours later, the nurse came out of a cubicle and called his name, interrupting his miserable thoughts. He jerked his head up and stared at her, wiping tears from his cheeks. Her expression was serious, but he tried not to read it, afraid of what he might find. She crooked her finger. Craig hurried over.

"Your wife is out of surgery and the doctor would like to speak to you." She led Craig down the hallway, stopping outside an open door. "Go right in. The doctor will be with you shortly."

"Sure," Craig said, sucking back his self-loathing, his disappointment in Serena, his uncertainty about their future. He entered the room and sat down.

From the doctor he learned that the assailant's bullet had ripped through Serena's back, tearing through her right kidney before exiting her body. The doctor had successfully removed the injured kidney and repaired damage to other internal organs. Serena was still unconscious, but her doctor felt certain she would recover completely and live a normal life with one kidney.

Four hours later, the doctor alerted Craig that Serena was awake, and took him into Serena's room, advising him not to stay long. Serena needed to rest. She was weak and shaken, barely able to remember what had happened, but she smiled at Craig, who entered her room, filled with sadness and trepidation.

"I'm so sorry, Craig, " she whispered, tears in her eyes.

Craig was unable to speak for a moment, then he murmured, "I'm sorry, too." He saw how pale and drawn she was, how fragile she seemed and did not have the heart to press her for the answers he wanted.

During the hours of waiting for Serena to come around, he had mentally run the gamut of scenarios and emotions: blaming her for destroying his trust, cursing her for making a fool of him, hating her for deceiving him, even considering walking out of their marriage all together. He needed answers. He had to hear her side of the story, but that would have to wait.

He took her hand, which was warm and soft, then said, "I don't understand what happened, Serena. Reilly filled me in on what you told him and I can't believe you hid so much from me. How . . ."

"Craig," Serena interrupted in a hoarse whisper. "I love you. I never meant to hurt or deceive you. I was stupid, selfish, and wrong. Sit down."

"No," he said. "You rest. We'll talk later." Then he turned and walked out of the room without kissing her good-bye, something he had never done since they married.

He spent a miserable, restless night on the couch at his house, unable to go into their bedroom. Who had he married? How had this happened? Would he be able to forgive her? The questions swirled, the answers escaped him. And when the tension of the past twenty-four hours finally caught up with him, he entered a deep heavy sleep with no dreams.

At daybreak, he awakened, showered, drank a cup of coffee, then returned to the hospital, arriving just as Serena was finishing her breakfast.

He sat in the chair by the window until the attendant removed the tray, and when Serena patted the space on the bed beside her, insisting he sit with her, he complied.

"Now," she began. "I want to explain."

Craig listened as Serena described her mother's death, her father's emotional abandonment, and how she had turned to Joyce Ann Keller for companionship and confidence. Craig sat very still, not interrupting, watching Serena's face as the bizarre puzzle finally came together. Serena told Craig about her rebellious years in Mallard, her friendships with Joyce Ann and Precious, the robbery and shooting, her years at Gatesview, and why she had felt compelled to hide her past.

Craig's face crumbled in shock and disbelief to hear the truth about the woman he had married, hating what hurt more than the truth: if she had really trusted him and loved him, she never would have done this! Not after all they'd gone through to get back together.

When Serena finished talking, Craig calmly got up and looked down at her.

"What do you want me to say?" His temper flared, then subsided, as he saw how worried and fragile she appeared. "You can't expect me to understand why you would allow a psychotic killer to intrude on our lives or why you never warned me what we were facing. That was wrong."

"Yes. It was wrong, I know it now. But I was so afraid of losing you."

"I would never have left you. Not as long as you were honest with me. Isn't that what we promised once before? How could I leave you over something that happened when you were a teenager? My love for you is not that shallow."

Serena averted her face to the wall, then said in a low, contrite tone,

"I wish I had handled my life differently, but I didn't." Looking back at him, she said, "After Diana hired me, and told me how she had changed her name, her image and had made it, I thought I could, too."

"But don't you see. I don't care about who you were. I love who you are . . . and I had the right to know that your past might put us in danger," Craig said, his words carefully chosen to convey his concern. He was disappointed, hurt, and in pain, but he would have wanted to protect her from a dangerous situation. "You had no right to shield me from a truth that nearly got you killed."

Serena didn't reply, and after a few seconds, Craig left the room, unable to trust his voice or his temper to continue with the conversation.

In the corridor, he leaned against the wall, stunned. What could he say to her now? How could he deal with this pain? He wanted to be alone to think about what he had just learned, to decide what to do. In the hallway he saw Tom Reilly coming toward him.

"She awake?" he asked

"Yes, Detective Reilly," Craig said. "Serena is awake, and I think she can give you the answers you want." Then Craig hurried down the hallway, a chaotic mix of emotions swirling inside, knowing he loved Serena too much to let her go. He had to find a way to repair this disastrous situation and go on, protecting the love they shared.

Chapter Forty-five

The next day Craig isolated himself in a miserable cocoon of self-pity, unable to face Serena, or the world. He loved her so much, yet resented what she had done, and found it hard to simply forgive her. He did not go to see her, but spoke to her on the phone, then took a long drive into the desert, where he walked in the sun and thought about Serena, their past, and their future.

Back home, he went up to the unfinished skeleton of their new house, realizing he was the only person Serena had in the world, that she needed him now more than ever, and he needed her. They could have a future, but she would have to conquer the terrible insecurities that had driven her to deny who she was.

Walking through their dream house, Craig continued his soul-searching, determined to find a way to help Serena. She had forgiven him once, when he had misled her, and though the circumstances were very different, their lack of trust and communication had brought the same results: separation and unhappiness. He owed her the chance to start over. Proud to be Sara Jane Talbot, and his wife.

Serena's two-week stay in the hospital finally came to an end, and she was anxious to go home. Joyce Ann was dead. Serena's financial resources were secure. The Beautopia website was back up and making money, and the contractor had informed Craig that his crew was working overtime to finish their new house. But what brought Serena the most peace of mind was Craig's renewal of trust in her and his determination to hold on to their marriage.

"Ready to split this joint," Craig teased, pushing through the door of Serena's hospital room.

"Too ready," she confirmed, smiling, anxious to go home and be alone with Craig. He may have forgiven her, but she knew he would need time to get over what she had done. Serena was ready to do everything in her power to keep their love from wavering. No more secrets, ever.

"For you," Craig said, handing her a box.

The package was so beautifully wrapped, Serena didn't want destroy it. She stroked the wide satin ribbon and touched the delicately embossed paper, reluctant to undo the dainty arrangement.

"What could possibly deserve such elegant wrapping?" she asked, smiling.

"A very special gift," he replied, pulling a chair closer to Serena's hospital bed.

Serena propped the package on her sheet-draped knees and let her head fall back on the pile of pillows behind her. "You're spoiling me," she taunted Craig, turning her attention to him, extending a hand.

"You deserve to be spoiled more often," he remarked, leaning over to kiss her.

Serena gently pulled Craig closer, enfolding him in her arms. "It's all behind us now. We can put our energy into our future and see where it takes us." Serena kissed Craig softly, then slipped her hands around his neck, leaning back to study his face, struck by the devotion she saw in his eyes. "I really don't deserve you."

"Oh, yes you do," he playfully replied, sitting back when she let him go. "And after two operations and two weeks in this hospital, you deserve to be spoiled," he insisted.

"This better not be a blender," she joked, pulling off the first layer of the delicate paper. While she had been bedridden, they had passed the time making lists of things they needed for the new house. A food processor had been on hers, a blender on his.

"Open it," Craig urged, reaching over to help her pull the top off the square box.

Serena reached inside and removed a flat package wrapped in tissue. Unfolding it, she gasped.

"Craig! Where did you find this?" She gently removed her mother's yellowed sketchbook from its nest of delicate wrapping and began gently leafing through the pages, tears in her eyes.

"The police recovered it from Joyce Ann's apartment. Luckily, you listed the book among the items you thought had been lost in the fire. When Reilly saw it among Joyce Ann's things, he called the insurance company, who confirmed it belonged to you. I got lucky when I asked him about it, and he said yes, it had been recovered." Craig hooked Serena with an earnest expression. "This book . . . this inspiration, represents a big part of who you are. This is your past, and I realized that we could never sort out our problems until you accepted who you truly are, and that means reconnecting with Sara Jane Talbot, no matter how difficult it may be. This is just a start."

Serena pressed the book to her chest, feeling a sense of peace. "Craig," she whispered. "I thought it was lost forever. This is the most wonderful gift. Thank you." Plucking a Kleenex from the box on her bedside table, she wiped away tears that had come to her eyes. "This means so much. It's my only connection to my past."

Craig removed the box and tissue from the bed, scooted closer, then placed the palm of his hand on Serena's cheek. "Maybe not," he whispered into her ear.

She moved back, holding him at arm's length. "What are you talking about?"

"Wait and see." Craig said, a gleam of mystery in his eye. "Now hurry and get dressed, we've got a stop to make before I take you home."

Suddenly, Serena realized how wrong she had been about Craig's ability to forgive, and even her own knowledge of herself. She never should have believed that running away from who she was would bring happiness or peace of mind.

"I want you to be proud of who you are, Sara Jane Talbot," Craig told her, "and believe that you have the right to exist in this world with a man who loves you just as you are."

Chapter Forty-six

"Why are we at the airport, Craig? I want to go home. I'm tired." Serena craned her neck to see out of the limo window, wondering what he was up to.

"I know and I'm sorry. But I will only be a minute. I have to pick something up."

He asked the limo driver to pull into the fifteen-minute parking space, then jumped out. Holding the door open, he leaned in and told Serena, "Relax. I'll be right back." Then he plunged into the crowd and disappeared inside the terminal.

After a few minutes he returned, one arm linked with Precious Trent's, grinning as he headed toward the car.

"My God! Precious!" Serena cried out when Craig opened the door.

"Hey girl," Precious laughed, slipping into the limo beside Serena.

"How can you be here? This is such a surprise." Serena wrapped her arms around Precious and pressed her face into her friend's shouder, drawing in the feel of her, filling the void that had been with her for so long. "Is your probation finished?"

"Yes, and Craig was very helpful in arranging for me to be here," Precious replied, leaning back. "Finally, it's finished."

Serena smiled, tears brimming in her eyes. She and Precious were together again, and they had traveled very difficult roads to come to this point in their lives.

"And you're walking!" Serena remarked.

"With a cane, but on my own feet at last."

Sitting back, Serena swept her eyes over Precious, who was back to her petite self again, very sophisticated in a leopard print pantsuit and matching low-heeled boots. Her hair was cut in a short, feathered style, with a fringe of bangs that touched tops of her softly arched brows. Her makeup was light, yet flawless, heightening her natural beauty. "And look at you! You are gorgeous" Serena said, wiping tears from her eyes.

Precious grimaced. "I may walk like somebody's granny with this cane, but I don't have to look like one."

Craig, who had remained to the side while the two women reunited, slipped inside the limo and put his arm around Serena's waist.

"How did you do this, Craig?" Serena asked.

"Oh, we've been having regular conversations on the phone," Precious laughed.

"This is wonderful," Serena said through tears of joy. "Seeing you again makes all those bad years seem as if they had never happened."

Craig broke into the reunion, turning to Precious. "Give me your baggage claim tickets and I'll get your luggage." He kissed Serena quickly, then got out and strode off.

"Girl, he's too fine," Precious remarked, moving to better watch Craig as he entered the terminal. "I see why you hid your past and didn't want to mess this up."

Serena giggled, then turned serious. "He's the best thing that ever happen to me . . ." She paused. "Besides your decision to come out here and see me. How long can you stay?"

"Well, Craig mentioned that you need someone to take over the management of Beautopia's website," Precious hedged.

"You mean you'd do it? Stay here?" Serena started, hoping it was true.

"What reason do I have to go back to Mallard? " Precious laughed.

"Precious! You can live in the cottage on our grounds for as long as you want. Our house is almost finished."

"Thanks, but I am perfectly capable of living alone."

"But you don't have to," Serena said softly.

"I know . . . and what do I call you now?"

"Sara Jane."

"Good. I'm so glad I came."

"Yes, and we'll be working together, lunching together, shopping . . ." Sara Jane paused and sighed. "I've missed the satisfaction that comes from having close friends in my life, Precious. I've missed you. And now it will be like . . ."

Precious held up a hand, stopping Sara Jane. "Please, don't say, 'like old times.' "

"No, not like 'old times,' at all," Sara Jane agreed, smiling as she gripped her girlfriend's hand.

MIRRORED LIFE

ANITA BUNKLEY

ABOUT THIS GUIDE

The suggested questions are intended to enhance your group's reading of Anita Bunkley's MIRRORED LIFE.

DISCUSSION QUESTIONS

1. What characteristics initially draw the characters Sara Jane, Joyce Ann and Precious together? Which of these characteristics remain constant as the story unfolds?

2. Would you ever do something that you knew was dangerous or illegal to help out your girlfriend/s? Why? Why not?

3. How do you think Sara Jane's term in prison impacted her future both positively and negatively?

4. Do you think both Craig Alexander and Diana Devreux benefited from their unorthodox relationship? How?

5. What do you think Joyce Ann was emotionally longing for while she was on the run? How did Tonk help fulfill in this need?

6. Do you think it could have been possible for Serena St. James and Diana Devreux to maintain a friendly relationship over a long period of time? If so, how? If not, why not?

7. Serena and Craig had very different backgrounds, yet they were compatible. What attitudes/outlook on life do you think they had in common that helped strengthen the relationship?

8. Which do you think was more important to Serena: to develop her cosmetic line in order to gain financial independence or to pay tribute to her mother?

9. If you had been Craig Alexander, how would you have felt about Serena hiding her true identity? Do you know anyone who has re-created her/himself?

10. Childhood friendships often crumble and fade over time. Why do you think Precious and Sara Jane's survived when it would have been easy for them to forget about each other and go on with their lives?